PRAISE FOR W

Summertime Guests

"At a glamourous hotel by the ocean, four people face up to truths that can no longer be hidden. *Summertime Guests* is compelling, surprising, and a wonderful summertime read . . . I devoured it."

—Nancy Thayer, bestselling author of *All the Days of Summer*

"Idyllic coastal settings, drama, dynamic characters . . . this story has it all."

—*Woman's World*

"Francis shines as a master storyteller. A must-read for anyone who could use an escape."

—Kristy Woodson Harvey, bestselling author of *The Summer of Songbirds*

"A smart, probing drama that skillfully unravels the complex emotional lives of an ensemble cast . . . a reflective, deeply engaging, and suspenseful story with many threads sure to ensnare the attention of rapt readers."

—Shelf Awareness

The Summer Sail

"A great summer read for fans of Jennifer Weiner and Emily Giffin."

—*Library Journal*

"What could be more fun than a summer cruise with old friends . . . A thoroughly entertaining summer read!

—Shelley Noble, bestselling author of *Whisper Beach*

The Summer of Good Intentions

"Wendy Francis's book thrilled me like a ride in a race car along the coast with the top down. It is everything a summer read should be."
—Elin Hilderbrand, bestselling author of *The Five-Star Weekend*

"A tender and vivid portrait of a family by the sea."
—Luanne Rice, bestselling author of *The Shadow Box*

Feels Like Summer

a novel

Feels Like Summer

a novel

wendy francis

LAKE UNION
PUBLISHING

Published by Lake Union Publishing, Seattle

www.apub.com

Amazon, the Amazon logo, and Lake Union Publishing are trademarks of Amazon.com, Inc., or its affiliates.

ISBN-13: 9781662520693 (paperback)
ISBN-13: 9781662520686 (digital)

Cover design by Shasti O'Leary Soudant
Cover image: © icemanphotos / Shutterstock; © Christopher Kimmel, © Elektrons 08 / Plainpicture

Printed in the United States of America

Tomorrow is a new day. You shall begin it serenely and with too high a spirit to be encumbered with your old nonsense.

—*Ralph Waldo Emerson*

Prologue

When Lieutenant Robin Shipman gets the call, she's been in the office for half an hour. It's seven thirty, but already she's running behind. That's because her 110-pound Bernese mountain dog, Hemingway, escaped through a hole in the backyard fence this morning while Robin showered. She scoured the neighborhood in her cruiser, wet hair dripping down the back of her uniform, until she found him eight doors down, digging through the Sullivans' trash. When she pulled up beside him, Hemingway lifted his head, egg carton in mouth, as if he was expecting her. The dog didn't even protest when she climbed out of the car to leash him. *Guilty as charged.* Tail between his legs, he trotted over to the cruiser. Now he's home in his crate, a wire box roughly the size of a small car, which fills a quarter of Robin's living room. She'll deal with him later, give him a stern talking-to—and absolutely no treats. The dog walker has already been texted this mandate.

All of which is to say, Robin is feeling slightly hassled, despite the fact that everything appears to be more or less in order at the office. Most of her cases are in good standing, save for a stolen car that was, in a stroke of good luck, recovered last night near Gunrock Beach and a rash of break-ins around the Alphabet streets. Not that their seaside town of Hull typically sees much crime, but summertime means visitors, and their presence can spark an uptick not only in restaurant and hotel sales but also robberies and late-night brawls.

She has a hunch that these recent break-ins are the doings of a particular group of high schoolers who've already amassed a spotty record for destruction of property on school grounds. They're not a gang, exactly—Hull doesn't have gangs—more like a group of bored teenagers looking for a distraction. It's the stuff that's gone missing that points her to this conclusion: costume jewelry, Xboxes, cell phones. Of course, there's also the possibility that the case is drug related—but she doubts it. This one doesn't smell like drugs to her; the stakes aren't high enough.

It's only a matter of time before a security camera captures one of the punks at a cellar door. Thus far, they've been lucky, heisting from only those houses that lack security systems or have turned off their cameras. Which is telling in and of itself: whoever the interlopers are, they've most likely already set foot in these homes, know how to gain access. Robin suspects they're familiar with the families they're robbing. Locals.

So when the early-morning call comes in on her cell, mild surprise ripples through her chest. She's just taken a sip of her coffee, scalding hot, and curses herself for never giving it the proper time to cool. Stopping off at Breadbasket before work has become as much a part of her daily routine as brushing her teeth. She's flipping through the Alphabet files, trying to discern a burglary pattern that might have eluded her earlier, when a name pops up on her cell. If it weren't Eric Landry, Boston's chief of police, she'd be inclined to let it skip directly to voicemail.

But it's exceedingly rare for Boston police to reach out to Hull's small—and some might say, amateur—department of men and women in blue. Aside from its seaside charm, Hull can feel as removed from Boston as Nova Scotia from Toronto. In the last fifteen years, the town has seen a total of three homicides. And so, when Robin picks up and says good morning, it's with an amalgam of interest and trepidation.

The chief's booming voice is characteristically upbeat. "How's my favorite lieutenant doing out in God's country?" He seems to relish giving her a hard time on the rare occasion when he does call, likes to tease her about reining in the seagull population on Nantasket Beach while he's out fighting bad guys in the seediest corners of the city. "Catch any scumbags today?"

"Not yet, but it's still early," she says, humoring him. Robin grew up in Hull; this is her home. And like so many other Hullonians, she has found it difficult to stay away for very long, the peninsula pulling her back time and again, like an old lover. While being a Boston cop surely provides more adrenaline rushes than presiding over her sleepy town, Robin prefers this landscape, or seascape, to the one in the city.

"Right. Give it time, Shipman." Most in the force would agree that the chief is a likable guy, so long as you stay on his good side, which she has somehow managed to do. Piss him off, so rumors go, and . . . you don't want to know. Robin has met him a few times, mostly at work functions. A beefy guy, easily two hundred pounds, with closely cropped red hair and lucid blue eyes, his presence fills a room. They've been seated next to each other at the occasional banquet, long enough to learn that they both grew up in rowdy, chaotic Irish families—eight kids in his, six in hers. The chief recently weathered a divorce, though he's never mentioned it to her. She knows this only from what she's gleaned along the "blue grapevine," which weaves a lengthy and twisted path through Boston and its outlying towns.

"Listen, I'm sorry to bother you, but I know your boss is on vacation this week and that he left you in charge."

"So to speak." He's correct that Hull's chief and his wife are, at the moment, touring Switzerland for their fortieth anniversary.

"Anyway, we've got a possible situation happening down in your neck of the woods."

"Is that right?" Robin hooks the phone between her cheek and shoulder, grabs a notebook, uncaps her pen. It's possible the chief is toying with her. It might be nothing more than a boat of interest that docked in Boston Harbor last night and is pointed their way. The Coast Guard is almost always involved when he calls. "Do tell."

He clears his throat. "There's a sailboat loose around Bumpkin. Doesn't appear to be anyone on board. Coast Guard got an alert on

Channel 16 from another boat that spotted it drifting. They're going out to investigate. Wanted to give you a heads-up." Robin's heart starts pounding a little faster. Bumpkin Island is one of several Boston Harbor islands, so theoretically, it falls under the chief's domain. Hull Harbor, however, lies squarely within her purview.

She sucks in her breath. "Any idea if it's local or from out of town?"

"We're working on it. Hoping maybe you can help."

In a town of roughly ten thousand people, Robin prides herself on knowing pretty much everyone. But the summer folks are different. Some of them rent for a month; those who own summer homes typically move in from Memorial Day to Labor Day, then shutter the windows for the grueling winter months. It could be a couple of foolhardy teenagers, hamming it up on an early-morning sail, or a pair of older guys, trying to outsail middle age. Right now, it's anyone's guess.

"Sorry, Chief. This is the first I'm hearing of it. Strange I haven't gotten a call from my harbormaster yet."

"Oh, you will, I'm sure."

Robin understands that pretty much any New England coastal town will see its fair share of visitors over the long weekend, setting out on their yachts or sailboats to watch the night sky. Some cast anchor and sleep on board. Problem is, the sailing often comes with copious amounts of drinking. Which can lead to unfortunate accidents.

"Well," she says, "fingers crossed it's no big deal. Maybe the boat broke free of its mooring." Even though they both understand how unlikely that is, given the calm waters last night. "I'm on my way to check it out."

"Thanks," the chief says. "Let me know what you find, would you?"

"Sure thing." Her other line rings. It's the harbormaster.

"And Robin?"

"Yeah?"

"Be careful. I gotta feeling about this one."

"Will do." She swallows hard before she picks up her other line. She doesn't need to ask the chief whether it's good or bad.

1

KATE

Kate Dowling could use a bit of summer. As in, right now. It's mid-May, and the remnants of spring poking through the dark earth—crocus blooms and buttery daffodils—have come and gone as quickly as they arrived. Her pale skin hungers for heat, for the sun licking her calves. She longs for sea breezes and sand between her toes, toes that have been manicured and polished, maybe in a ballet pink or sky blue. Little Chiclet toes, her husband, Trey, calls them. She wishes she could head home right now, pack their bags, and drive out to their house in Hull, a full week and a half ahead of when they typically make their annual pilgrimage. Wishes she could race into the Atlantic, where the ocean turns from wading pool to wild expanse in a number of steps, the bottom dropping out so swiftly beneath her feet it sometimes snatches her breath away.

That Kate is daydreaming about summer is probably related to the fact that she and her three-year-old daughter, Clara, have been wandering the dark, dank halls of the New England Aquarium for the last two hours. Along with about a hundred other parents and their sweaty, glassy-eyed children. Despite the air-conditioning, the air feels heavy, the pungent scent of penguin guano hanging in the cavernous space. Clara darts from one fish tank to another, a whirling tornado, while Kate trails behind, armed with antibacterial wipes. Her efforts to sanitize her daughter's hands, however, are laughable—Clara insists on jamming her middle two fingers into her mouth and sucking delightedly—no, *victoriously*—before Kate can grab her. Lately, it's become a battle of wills between them, a game that Clara insists on playing whenever she senses her mother's strength waning. A sly hyena teasing its prey.

And even though Kate hates to consider how many germs are smeared on those glass tanks, the gazillion other little hands that have pressed up against them, she tells herself that her toddler is building a first-rate immune system for the school years ahead. Counsels herself to *let this one go* if she has any hope of maintaining her sanity until she can push through her front door, plop Clara down in front of *Sesame Street*, and pour herself an enormous glass of rosé.

If Kate's mother, Susan, were here, she would tell her not to worry, that Kate and her sisters used to eat *dirt*, for goodness' sake, and they all turned out perfectly fine. But her mother can't tell her this because a decade of Septembers ago, a drunken twenty-two-year-old erased her parents from the world forever. In one heartless, obliterating swipe. They'd been celebrating their thirty-ninth wedding anniversary, heading home from the Scarlet Oak Tavern in Hingham, when a cardinal-red Mustang skidded across the wrong lane, colliding with their Toyota Prius. No one, not even the young driver, walked away from the accident. It took years before Kate was able to stop wondering what might have been if her parents had left the restaurant a few minutes earlier. A few minutes later. Now the memory is more like an infrequent visitor, popping up unbidden, a wave of sadness washing in over her, then out again.

"Mama, look! These fishies got funny tails." Clara is standing in front of a tank crowded with brightly colored seahorses, their bodies hooked like bold question marks in the water.

"You're right." Kate comes up behind her and loops a dark curl around her daughter's ear. Where Clara gets her curls from is anyone's guess. Kate's hair is straight, a murky dishwater blonde without highlights. Trey used to have light-brown hair, a slight wave cutting through it. Now it's cropped short, a smattering of salt and pepper throughout.

"Mama, you're not looking!" Clara's tone is suddenly accusatory, the voice she uses whenever she's on the verge of a meltdown.

"Sorry, honey." Kate leans in closer, so close that she can detect the faint scent of apple juice on her daughter's breath. "They *do* have funny tails, don't they? Those are called seahorses." And Clara bobs her head knowingly, as if she has suspected this all along.

When Kate straightens, there's an audible cracking sound along her lower spine. Surely she can't be the only parent here who's counting down the minutes until closing time? The first few times she and Clara visited the aquarium, Kate had marveled at the ethereal jellyfish, the velvety scales of the sleek stingrays in the touch tank, and Myrtle, the aquarium's five-hundred-pound sea turtle, who would slowly rise to the top of the giant ocean tank for feeding time. But the bloom has fallen off the sea anemone, so to speak. Today she can't wait to get out of here.

About two months ago, Clara swore off naps for good, and trying to fill those once blessedly quiet afternoons has become Kate's greatest challenge. Because all she really wants to do is crawl back into bed, as she used to do after she'd laid her daughter down for a nap. That toddlerhood suddenly demands Kate forgo her *own* afternoon siesta strikes her as one of the greater injustices of the terrible threes. Because that's what they are. Not the terrible twos, but the awful, soul-sapping terrible threes.

Two-year-old, chubby-cheeked Clara was an angel, toddling around, gurgling with endless appreciation for the world. But shortly after she turned three—actually, pretty much the very day she turned three—it was as if a switch flipped, and Clara transformed into a miniature, malevolent bully. She'd stick out her pointer finger, knitting her eyebrows together, and if Kate or Trey didn't fetch the desired item quickly enough, her high-pitched screams would pierce the air.

Some days, Kate worries that all their parental love, focused solely on this one child, has created a monster. A horribly spoiled monster. *It's only a stage,* Trey reassures her after she's stumbled back into bed after maybe the third or fourth tuck-in of the night. And Kate thinks, *Please, Lord, let it be true.*

She and Trey have talked about having more kids, maybe in a year or so. But honestly, she doesn't know if she has the stamina for a toddler *and* a baby. It sounds a bit like signing up for skydiving and scuba diving at the same time—two diametrically opposed sports, impossible to pull off together. Nor does her daughter strike her as the type who'd take kindly to stepping out of the spotlight. More like the sister who'd be tempted to sneak into her baby brother's room and pull his hair while he naps.

For another fifteen minutes, they meander through the aquarium— Kate wiping Clara's hands and Clara lurching away—until finally the gift shop materializes at the end of the hall. Soon enough, a plush gray dolphin is secured beneath her daughter's arm, Kate's shameless bribe to skip the meet and greet with the seals later this afternoon.

"Seals," she explains, "are overrated," and Clara nods agreeably, nuzzling her new stuffed animal against her cheek.

Back at the car, her daughter wriggles into her booster seat and waits to be buckled in. Her toddler bottom barely fits anymore, and Kate makes a mental note to go online later tonight to research when Clara will be old enough to switch to a bigger car seat. She's pretty sure it has something to do with a child's weight.

"Mommy, what do you think I should name him?" Clara asks, cradling the dolphin in her arms.

Is it odd, Kate wonders, that her daughter automatically knows the gender of every stuffed animal she owns? Are dolphins more masculine than, say, sea turtles? "I don't know, honey. Do you have any ideas?"

Clara appears to ponder this for a moment before exclaiming, "Dolphie!"

"Dolphie is an excellent name," Kate says enthusiastically, grateful to have a name decided upon so quickly, so definitively. Once it took three days for Clara to name a stuffed bear—George—and it had nearly driven Kate insane.

She circles the car, opens up the back hatch, tosses in the stroller (a complete waste of time since Clara refused to ride in it), and hits the "Close" button. She climbs into the front seat and starts the engine. The Land Rover, her fortieth-birthday present from Trey, was meant to ward off the "middle-age blues," as he put it. As if the car were some kind of talisman, even though technically, Kate doesn't think forty counts as middle-aged. Maybe forty-five, but definitely not forty.

Still, it's possible that she's grown to love this car slightly more than life itself. The gorgeous forest-green exterior, the lush tan leather interior that's remarkably resistant to sippy-cup spills, the soft green light emanating from the dashboard. Sometimes after an exhausting day with Clara, she'll climb behind the wheel when Trey gets home from work and cruise around the neighborhood, the radio blasting Van Morrison, her heart flush with freedom. It's enough to persuade her to pull back into the driveway and begin all over again the next morning.

Not that she's in a position to complain. In fact, being married to Trey Dowling, partner at Murray and Sloane, has afforded Kate privileges in her life that were, frankly, unexpected. Her roots stretch deeply into middle-class soil—her mom was a kindergarten teacher, and her dad a beloved Methodist minister in their town of Weymouth. She and her sisters, Shelby and Bree, spent their childhoods about fifteen miles south of Boston in a dilapidated duplex that abutted the church's backyard.

Although it made for an easy commute for Kate's dad, she'd hated how the neighbors' late-night arguments would inevitably drift through the open windows, the paper-thin walls. One day, she promised herself, she'd live in a house free of strangers' bickering. And with their well-appointed, five-bedroom Tudor in Boston's tony suburb of Wellesley, she and Trey have already fulfilled that dream and more.

The fact that her husband hails from a well-to-do family (part of a protein shake dynasty, a few cousins removed) has further made their young lives brim with possibilities that even Kate, a natural dreamer, would have been hard-pressed to imagine back in her teenage bedroom, its walls covered in lily-of-the-valley paper. Trey has ascended the ladder of Boston's young influencers with surprising swiftness, Kate gladly clasping his hand along the way. Already, they're members of the country club (an almost impossible "get" by any standard), where on a typical Saturday afternoon Trey can be found shooting a round of golf with his buddies while Kate and Clara lounge by the club pool. It's where Kate rubs elbows with the other moms, and more often than not, with the other children's nannies.

Kate tries not to feel guilty about leaving her consulting job at Bain & Company when Clara was born. But the more she talks to other moms at the club, the more she has come to understand that most of them don't work outside the home either—they've hired nannies simply because they can afford to and because, as one mother confided, "It just makes life so much easier." And although Kate has never been one to embrace the unspoken battle lines between mothers who work at home and those who don't, hiring a nanny when you're a full-time mom strikes her as, well, *excessive*. Her younger sister, Bree, couldn't agree more.

"I don't understand why you and Trey are buying into the whole rich-people world," Bree chided when Kate first mentioned that they'd joined the country club. "It's like he wants to turn you into someone you're not."

The comment made Kate bristle. Who was her baby sister to judge? Shouldn't Bree have been happy for her? It's easy for Bree to point a finger, though, because Bree's own lifestyle can only be described as ascetic. Monklike. Bare bones—and, to Kate's mind, slightly ridiculous.

Her baby sister lives in a one-bedroom apartment in Somerville, outfitted with a couch, a table, a pull-out futon for a bed, and a handful of mismatched lamps. Bree is an artist—or, more specifically, a lithographer who has met with limited success (meaning her work is recognizable among a small coterie of local artists but not widely enough known to generate a reliable income). Currently her job is working long hours as a barista at What's Brewing? in Porter Square until she gets a "real" job, maybe teaching at the Rhode Island School of Design (RISD), her alma mater. Or until she gets discovered, as artists are wont to do.

Kate has no doubt of her sister's natural talent, but sometimes she wishes Bree would slide her art into the hobby category instead of insisting it's her one true vocation. Kate has tried steering her sister toward art teacher openings in the Wellesley public school system, to which Bree turns up her perfectly pert nose.

"I'm not teaching finger painting to a bunch of rich people's kids," Bree said one Saturday morning not so long ago, and it was all Kate could do not to remark that someday one of those rich kids would be Bree's own niece. But "stubborn" defines Bree's nature. Years ago, in order to beat her sisters in a contest, Bree held her breath underwater for so long that a lifeguard had to drag her eight-year-old body from the pool and breathe life back into her lungs.

"Very few *good* artists are appreciated during their lifetime," Bree likes to remind Kate. Which only makes Kate think, *All the more reason to move on to something else.*

"We're not buying into it," Kate explained patiently, but the words rang false even to her ears. "Trey likes to play golf, and it's an important part of his job, schmoozing with potential clients. Besides, you and Shelby can hang out with us at the pool this summer."

On the other end of the phone, her sister made an exasperated sound. "Just please don't tell me what your monthly membership fees are—I don't want to know. Because they probably exceed my rent by a couple of thousand, easy."

No swift retort jumped to Kate's lips because they both knew it was true. "Whatever. I still hope you'll hang with us by the pool," she replied.

That conversation took place over a year ago, and Bree has yet to find her way to the club. Granted, her baby sister is always armed with a convenient excuse—a friend asked her to cover a shift, her car broke down—but Kate is determined to get both her sisters together at the club one day.

Even Shelby, who seldom has time for Kate these days between her real estate job and raising a teenage son, has managed to join them for a poolside cookout, an occasional dinner at the club. Shelby has no qualms whatsoever about luxuriating in the perks that come with being Trey Dowling's sister-in-law. She tells Kate to enjoy every minute away from the corporate world, to dispel any guilt about not sprinting back to the office.

And on the rare occasion when Kate *does* feel guilty, she reasons that she's working harder now than she ever did as a consultant. And it's true. It's also kind of wonderful to luxuriate at the club on weekends instead of poring over spreadsheets in the office, where they shut down the air-conditioning on Saturday afternoons.

After Trey joins them at the pool, they'll shower and make their way to the dining room overlooking the golf course, where a rustic koi pond sits adjacent to the ninth hole. Trey always takes a few minutes to exchange pleasantries with other guests before sitting down, Clara always looks adorable in her little dress, and Kate will smile kindly, knowing that soon enough she'll be throwing back one, maybe two, gin and tonics with an olive, never a lime.

Even though they've been members for more than a year and she's made a handful of friends, the sense that Kate is an outsider, looking in, still sweeps over her from time to time. Is it because Bree planted the seed in her head? Kate knows she blends in easily enough. That's to say, she looks the part: golden honey highlights, thick, straight hair that sweeps past her shoulders. And unlike her petite sisters, Kate has been blessed with their dad's tall stature, his lean legs. So yes, physically, she belongs among this burnished, attractive crowd, where all the men dress in handsome polo shirts and khakis and all the women in tasteful Lilly Pulitzer dresses.

If Kate cared to dig deeper, though, looking the part of the wife of a successful attorney probably sparked Trey's attraction to her in the first place, when they initially met for drinks at Trident on Newbury Street several years ago. A blind date set up by a mutual friend. He loves her, she knows this, but having her slide into his life as easily as a gleaming Rolex onto his wrist has its benefits, too. She notices Trey drinking in the admiring glances of other men whenever they walk into a fundraiser or work event, of which there is a never-ending parade. The pride in his voice when he introduces her as his wife, his hand resting firmly on her lower back, is hard to mistake. And Kate smiles willingly, playing her part to a T.

Whenever she mentions that her father was a minister and her mother a teacher to the other women at the club, the comment typically elicits a maternal pat on the forearm, as if to say, *And look at you now!* Or maybe not. It's possible she's imagining all this. Maybe the pats are sincere and nonjudgmental. But Kate doesn't think so. Once she inadvertently stepped into the ladies' room when Marjorie Winters and Steph McCallaster, the head of the school's booster club, were talking at the sinks, and Kate stopped in midstride as soon as she realized they were talking about her.

"You'd think she'd want to get together with us for girls' night." (Girls' night was a social event held every Tuesday at the club, when members played golf and sipped wine before dinner.) "She probably thinks she's too good for us. Didn't she go to Princeton?"

Kate held her breath, afraid to move. She'd graduated from Brown, but she supposed Providence (where Brown was situated) was easy enough to confuse with Princeton. The truth was, playing golf held zero interest for her, and becoming a member of the country club had done little to change that. Sure, she enjoys the pool and the treat of a meal she doesn't have to cook, but golf—and getting tipsy with wealthy women who'd been Botoxed and de-cellulited—is decidedly not her idea of a fun time.

When Marjorie and Steph exited the ladies' room, Kate was still standing in the adjoining powder room. "Oh! Kate, we didn't see you there," Marjorie exclaimed, her face flushing a bright crimson. "How's everything? Good, I hope?"

They pushed past her, not stopping to hear her response, although Kate piped up, "Great! Everything's great." She returned from the ladies' room in time to see Marjorie and Steph making a hasty exit from the dining room, their bewildered husbands on their arms.

Kate's memory of the unfortunate incident is interrupted by Clara's feet kicking the back of her seat. "Mommy, I need more juice!" For a brief moment, Kate panics. Her daughter already drained the two juice boxes she'd packed for the aquarium. But maybe there's an extra one, left over from another outing, hiding somewhere deep inside the muck that is her bag.

"Hold on a sec. Mommy needs to pay for parking first." She feeds the ticket into the slot and waits for the total to flash on the screen— *Forty bucks!* After the highway robbery of aquarium tickets, it seems parking should be free. Kate digs in her wallet for her debit card, slides it in. Meanwhile, Clara's kicks grow more insistent, sending tiny shock waves down Kate's spine.

"Stop that, Clara. It's not nice." While the machine whirs, her hand searches in her bag for a spare juice box.

"But Mommy, I *need* more!" The decibels in her daughter's voice have climbed an unfortunate ten notches since her last request. They've been trying to teach Clara the difference between *needing* and *wanting*, a difference that has conveniently slipped her daughter's mind today. Kate swears under her breath, freshly aware of the long line of cars snaking behind her in the parking garage. There's no juice.

When the screen flashes *Denied* and spits out her card, she yells, "Shit!" without thinking. The metallic-blue G-wagon behind them honks impatiently. It's probably just a fluke with the bank's electronic lines—her card has been acting wonky lately. She shoves in another and waits, prays.

"Mommy said *shit!*" Clara pipes up gleefully.

Kate can feel the sweat beading on the back of her neck and cranks the air conditioner to its highest setting. "That's because the silly computer won't take Mommy's card." She's striving for levity because aren't children supposed to follow their parents' lead?

"Bad 'puter," Clara scolds, her shorthand for computer.

Kate stretches her arm out the window, willing the machine to accept the new card. "Mommy! I thirsty!" *Kick, kick, kick.* There's no sense in arguing with Clara when she gets like this.

"Stop kicking Mommy's seat or no more juice!" At last, the monitor flashes *Thank you!* and her card pops out, the gate beginning to rise. "Where's your dolphin, sweetheart?" she asks, channeling her best placating mommy voice. Some days Kate worries that she is vaguely schizophrenic, swiveling from irate adult to cajoling mom in a matter of seconds.

But in response to her mollifying tone, her daughter's stuffed dolphin collides with the back of her head. "Clara!"

She puts her foot on the gas pedal and floors it. Not until they reach the next traffic light at the corner does she allow herself to breathe. Hands trembling, Kate grabs her bag off the passenger seat, desperately digging for any kind of token to distract Clara, who's now full-on screaming. At last, her fingertips land on a lollipop. She holds it aloft for her daughter to see. "Look, a lolly!" Incredibly, it's still wrapped.

"What favor?" Clara demands, skeptical.

"Cherry!" Kate has no idea if it's cherry or not, but it's Clara's favorite.

Clara claps her hands together. "Yay, I love cherry!" And as easily as that, the tantrum subsides, frantic ripples radiating and disappearing as swiftly as a stone tossed into a resting pond.

Kate takes a deep, soothing, cosmic breath. "Okay, now pay attention because we're driving past Daddy's building. Look up high and see if you can spot him in the window."

It's a game they play whenever they venture into the city. Trey's skyscraper office sits several blocks down from the aquarium. If he's not having too crazy of a day, he'll join them outside for lunch, maybe a picnic on the Greenway, the long stretch of grass that divides the city side from the buildings lining the Boston Harbor. But today's schedule was filled with back-to-back meetings, and Kate didn't press him because tonight they're going out for dinner, just the two of them. Amelia, their sitter, will be arriving at six o'clock sharp, which should give them plenty of time to make their six-thirty dinner reservation at the Farmhouse. Kate can almost taste the tiger shrimp tacos, the flourless chocolate cake, the expensive wine. She can't remember the last time they've gone out on a date.

"Do you see Daddy?" she asks in an attempt to keep the game going while she navigates the late-afternoon traffic.

"Nooo." Clara's voice rises at the end, playing along.

When a delivery truck tries to edge its way in front, Kate lays on the horn, sending it swerving back into its lane. (When she and Trey first dated, she'd picked him up in her Miata, slicing in and out of Boston traffic, prompting him to say, "Dang, girl. You can *drive*.") They're still a few streets away from Trey's office when Kate slows for a red light. And then there's a high-pitched squeal from the back seat.

"Mommy, I see Daddy!"

"You do?" Kate checks the light to make sure it's still red, then turns to follow her daughter's pointing finger. "Right there!"

Her first instinct is to assume that Clara has spotted a man who resembles her father, similarly tall, with salt-and-pepper hair, dressed in a suit like so many of the other businessmen in the Financial District. But as her gaze follows the short arrow of Clara's finger, just off to the side of the restaurant on the corner, she spies Trey, too.

Except it isn't the Trey she kissed goodbye this morning, his breath still sour from sleep, his snuggles still welcome. No, this man, who looks exactly like her husband, is holding another woman's hand, his head thrown back in laughter. A colleague? A friend? Her mind races with possibilities. And then she watches as he leans in toward the petite brunette . . . and presses his lips to hers. When the light shifts to green, Kate fails to notice. She can feel her jaw dropping, sees herself from afar, as if watching herself in a movie. Not until the car behind them honks aggressively does she remember to remove her foot from the brake pedal and step on the accelerator. The tires squeal as the car lurches forward, and Clara pounds the window with her tiny fists, trying in vain to get her daddy's attention.

2

SHELBY

Top down on her black Mercedes, Shelby winds along the main boulevard that hugs Nantasket Beach, an undulating ribbon of windswept pavement. It's chilly—probably too chilly—for the convertible, but she doesn't care. Because she just closed on the Vendler property, a historic Victorian perched atop Allerton Hill (pronounced Awhll-er-ton), one of the most coveted neighborhoods on Hull's six-mile peninsula. Allerton Hill boasts grand summer homes and breathtaking views of the Atlantic, where the colors shift from dark blue to azure depending on the season and the sun's positioning in the sky.

Despite the brisk sea breeze, a handful of people wander the beach today, their windbreakers and sweaters knit tightly around their bodies. The bright sun hints at a warm summer afternoon, but it's a mirage. They're not quite there yet—it's only mid-May. In a few more weeks, temperatures will climb into the eighties, and the beach will be scattered with throngs of people, mostly moms toting their young children from Quincy and Weymouth and the locals who venture out to remind themselves that *this* is why they tolerate New England winters along the shore, when the ocean can sweep in and swallow up a road whole, sometimes for days.

There's a toughness, a saltiness to the people here that Shelby admires—the Hullonians, as they refer to themselves. Walk into Jo's Nautical Bar out near Pemberton Point, and you'll be regaled with stories of the town's intrepid mariners who've survived storms worse than Hurricane Katrina (or so legends go). The walls of the Hull Lifesaving Museum, a quaint blue house set on Nantasket Avenue, are dotted with photos of sundry heroes like Joshua James, who rescued more than a thousand lost souls off Hull's coast during the 1800s. All this rugged history makes Shelby feel alive, as if she, too, has adventurers' blood coursing through her veins, as if she might dive into the water one day and swim the eight nautical miles to Boston on adrenaline alone.

Hull has been Shelby's home ever since she graduated from Boston University, twenty-four years ago on a Thursday morning in the pouring rain. It was the summer of her senior year, and she was in love with a boy she shouldn't have been (Ethan), who persuaded her to apply for a summer job waitressing at Hull's landmark restaurant, Jake's Seafood. A buddy of Ethan's who bused tables there told her she was more or less a shoo-in, which she was. All she had to do was fill out an application, answer a few questions, and before she knew it, the manager was pressing a uniform into her hands. Each day at noon, Shelby would arrive in her black pants and Jake's T-shirt and collect orders for lobster, mussels, clams—everything carried fresh off the boat that very morning.

It served as the perfect job because Ethan had already secured a gig teaching kids how to surf on Nantasket. Together they rented a shoebox apartment on D Street, a short skip from the water, and pretended they were married already. That summer had been the kind of postcollege idyll every girl dreams of, filled with brilliant sunshine and late nights at the Dry Dock (now Daddy's Beach Club), which also happened to sell generous pitchers of beer for two bucks. Five years later, they were married.

Not that she credits Ethan with introducing her to the charms of this coastal town. No, it didn't take much arm-twisting to persuade her to join him. Shelby already had fond childhood memories of the place:

when she and her sisters were young and school broke for summer, their mom would pack up the station wagon with a cooler; a basketful of shovels, buckets, and beach chairs; and whisk them off to Nantasket Beach. Occasionally, one of her mom's friends would tag along with her children, lending an aura of festivity to the day. Not until Shelby was twelve did it dawn on her that the adult drinks were kept in a separate cooler for a specific reason.

Nantasket Beach is where Shelby and her sisters spent hours building elaborate sandcastles, where she first learned how to bodysurf, and where she and her sisters scoured the tide pools for clams. It's also where she experienced her first kiss (too much tongue with Justin Fletcher, but still) and where she tasted her first New England lobster, so buttery and tender she couldn't believe she'd survived eight years of her life without it. Although technically Shelby is a "washashore" (not born and raised on the peninsula), Hull still feels like home. In fact, if she were pressed to describe the area to a friend, she would say that the town feels like a tangible part of her, like her kidney or heart, her big toe.

It's impossible to imagine living anywhere else, even though her life here has hardly turned out as imagined: she and Ethan parted ways three years ago when Noah was just shy of thirteen. After too many late-night arguments about seemingly nothing, they agreed to a swift divorce, and Ethan promptly moved out, along with his few prized possessions, including a guitar, his surfboards, and several boxes of clothing and books. That it took Shelby years to realize her husband had no intention of ever holding a "real" job still shocks her some days. How could she have been so obtuse? All his talk about becoming a professor, of earning his doctorate in marine biology, when all he ever did was dabble in graduate studies at Boston University. Seven years later, and there was still no doctorate degree to show for it. Never mind that she often paid for those courses with her own money!

She thinks back to how they used to daydream about traveling to far-flung archipelagoes, where Ethan would conduct research on threatened species, like the West Indian manatee. Their summers and vacations would be filled with nonstop adventure, and Noah's child-hood would be a veritable treasure trove to draw from when it came time to draft his college essay.

None of that happened, of course.

Ethan held some odd jobs over the years—a neighborly handyman, a local bartender at the Parrot, a surfing instructor, a section leader for a freshman class on coral reefs—but the biology books continued to pile up in their living room, teetering towers of wasted knowledge.

Where was the charmed life he'd promised her when they first moved into their D Street apartment so many years ago?

And then one Saturday morning, while she was sitting on the beach wall and gazing out at the blue surf, it dawned on her: Ethan was like a second child. She wasn't supporting her husband's career plans; to the contrary, she was *enabling* him to slack off, to take courses for fun while she struggled to build a client list in real estate. He was never going to get his dissertation written. They'd been living off her salary for years, and she was done with it.

Now her ex-husband lives in a shabby apartment in South Boston, tending bar in an even shabbier establishment. On the rare weekends that Noah reluctantly spends with his dad, he crashes on Ethan's sofa bed in the living room.

The fact that her ex-husband turned out to be such a dud seems to have had slight effect on Shelby's real estate career, however. If any-thing, it's improved her visibility, upped her cachet. When the news first broke, the locals felt sorry for her, this poor woman who was left to fend for herself and her young son. But Shelby took all that pity and rolled it into one big, fat cigar for business. Soon enough, the formerly junior agent at Hullistic Real Estate became one of the most sought-af-ter Realtors in town.

Shelby's current client list is as polished and enviable as her finesse for matching buyers with the right house (almost a second sense, she's been told). No house is too small, too bereft of character, too derelict for her consideration. Her gift is spotting potential where others might see only a financial black hole. She'll walk prospective clients through a home, highlighting its attributes like an adored one's best features until they're completely besotted.

Imagine what a fresh coat of paint will do, she might say. Or, *Don't you love the wainscoting in the dining room?* she'll ask, distracting a potential buyer's gaze away from the water stains on the ceiling. A spell caster, a wizard, a witch. Shelby has been called all sorts of names, but she doesn't mind. It adds a certain mystique to her reputation.

Of course, knowing that the man she thought she knew so well—with whom she crawled into bed every night and whose every freckle she could map—that this same man turned out to be a perpetual child, a Peter Pan, comes with an entire raft of emotions. But she prefers not to dwell on it. Not now. Someday in the future, perhaps, when she'll pay for expensive therapy sessions to sift through her myriad, complicated feelings. But not today. Not when there's still so much to do.

Because if she stops, there's a chance she might not get started again. If Shelby allows herself to think too much about how precisely her life has unraveled, the temptation to stay in bed for days, maybe weeks, could overwhelm her. And she won't do that—can't do that—to Noah.

Not when she's the only one in this family who's supporting her son. Thankfully, over the past few years, Shelby's commissions have soared—if not into the stratosphere, then at least into a place where she has nearly paid off the mortgage on their oceanfront property (which, while nice by Hull standards, is admittedly not half as swank as the captains' mansions to be found along Nantucket or the Vineyard). Soon she can stop worrying about Noah's college fund, wherever he decides to go, because his 529 plan has been faithfully augmented each year—a sizable nest egg awaiting him. Against all odds, Shelby has managed to secure her son's financial well-being, and she's damn proud of it.

The question remains, though: Has she secured his emotional well-being?

For a sixteen-year-old boy, Noah has already weathered so much more than any boy should have to. Only a few years ago, it seemed he told her everything (his first crushes, how he worried he wasn't good enough or smart enough). In recent months, though, Noah has slid into the dreaded, awkward stage known as "being a teenager." Their time together now is most often marked by protracted silences, leaving Shelby to wonder: Is he tired, angry, sad? Hungry? When she does press to find out more (usually while stirring a white sauce on the stove as nonchalantly as possible), he gives her the brush-off. "I'm *fine*, Mom. Can we please not talk about it?" And she thinks, *Duly noted.* Not because she doesn't care, but because they can't afford to screw up anything else between them.

For the past year, Noah has been dating Lindsay Graydon. Shelby likes Lindsay in that way that any mother who hopes her son's girlfriend will provide a sounding board, a life raft, for him does. Lindsay is grounded, a star lacrosse player at Hull High School, and has curly black hair that somehow manages to fall in luscious waves and not turn to frizz the way Shelby's hair always did at that age. Lindsay has become such a regular in the Lancaster house that she helps herself to a glass of water, an orange, and notices whenever a new item appears, like a doormat or a fresh bar of lemon soap in the downstairs bathroom. Changes that Noah would never remark on, even if Shelby were to illuminate them with flashing lights.

It's nice having another female around the house, and Shelby reminds herself of this whenever Lindsay and Noah are tucked behind his closed bedroom door, ostensibly doing homework. Shelby hopes against hope that if they do dare to have sex in her house, they'll at least be safe. For this very reason, a box of condoms, purchased and placed there herself, is tucked into Noah's top bureau drawer.

Still, there's an unfortunate blind spot in Shelby's field of vision that she can't quite bring herself to acknowledge.

And that blind spot is called Bo.

When Q Street comes into view, she points the car to the left. The houses lining this Alphabet street, as they're called in Hull, are quaint, some admittedly more charming than others. Most have been passed down from one generation to the next, which is what makes this particular listing so rare. The son and daughter of a ninety-year-old woman who recently passed away are listing it. Both kids live out in California and don't want the headache of upkeep. The son is a movie producer, and the sister does something Shelby can't quite recall—a script editor, maybe? She's not sure, but what Shelby *is* certain of is that she'll help them find the ideal buyer for their childhood home.

She pulls into the driveway and performs her initial assessment, as she does for any new listing: *What would a prospective buyer think?* There's a well-manicured lawn and an inviting front porch with two white rockers. The cheerful yellow siding screams starter home for a young couple with a dog, or perhaps a baby. Naturally, the property will need a proper walk-through to ensure that the water heater hasn't exploded or a squirrel hasn't launched itself down the chimney—or any of the other thousand unthinkable but entirely possible mishaps hasn't occurred since she accepted the listing last week.

The first open house is two weeks away; Shelby doesn't want any surprises. She hates surprises.

Before heading in, she makes a quick call to her baby sister. The answering machine picks up, asking her to leave a message. "Hey, Bree. It's me, Shelby. Just checking in to see how you're feeling. Give me a call when you get a chance."

Yesterday, Bree had her wisdom teeth pulled, and between the drugs and the gauze crowding her mouth, it was difficult to make out what she was saying when Shelby called last night. This morning, Shelby special-ordered a crate of peanut brittle from Nantasket Sweets to be delivered to her sister's doorstep. It's an old family joke that she hopes will make Bree smile. (When she and Kate had their wisdom teeth out in high school, her dad gave them peanut brittle as a gag.) Shelby will try her sister again later, after she's cracked a bottle of prosecco on the deck and toasted her most recent success. Her commission on the Vendler property alone will easily pay for an extravagant vacation (or two!), maybe to Turks and Caicos. She's always dreamed of visiting the turquoise waters off the Caribbean coast. Maybe she'll invite her sisters along. Or maybe, she thinks, she'll take Bo.

Bo.

He's the one person she really wants to talk to right now.

Bo, who for the last eight months, has been her on-again, off-again boyfriend. Bo, who has the softest gray-blue eyes and the most delicious wavy dark hair. Bo, whose real name is Brian but who's been known as Dr. Bo since anyone in town can remember and certainly since Shelby moved to Hull and brought her first pup, Teddy, in for his wellness checkup. Shelby has watched Dr. Bo grow up in his business as much as she has grown up in hers. First Teddy, and now Tuukka, their golden retriever (named after former Bruins' goalie Tuukka Rask), have been loyal patients of Dr. Bo's.

After they put Teddy down for intestinal cancer, Dr. Bo had shown a remarkable tenderness toward Noah, going so far as to press the number of a child therapist into Shelby's hands. "Just in case he needs to talk to someone. Like the old adage goes, losing a dog can be like losing a best friend for a kid." Tears had pricked the edges of her eyes. Especially when Noah's own dad had merely offered to buy him an ice-cream cone afterward, as if cherry chocolate chip could be a salve to a twelve-year-old boy who'd moments ago said goodbye to his beloved companion.

Bo has a soft, loving touch with animals, a skill that Shelby can attest is deftly applied to the people in his life as well. Whenever his hand sweeps across the back of her neck or when he tucks a stray piece of hair behind her ear, goose bumps race up her forearms. He has the sculpted calves of a guy who's accustomed to running half-marathons. And, as her friend Julia says, he's the kind of man it's easy to imagine yourself falling into bed with . . . and staying awhile.

Shelby understands that seeing Bo is wrong on so many levels. (Yes, she's been over it a thousand times!) There's no excuse for it. Most especially because of one exceptionally inconvenient fact: Bo Bannister is married.

To Cindy Bannister, whom Shelby knows in that casual way that everyone in Hull "knows" everyone else. They've bumped into each other at the Village Market on more than one occasion and once at the movies at the Shipyard in Hingham. Cindy Bannister is cute and spunky, sporting the same dark bob that so many women around town do. From what Shelby can gather, Cindy is a fabulous stay-at-home mom, wholly devoted to her girls, the kind who whips up brownies for fun. Shelby suspects that if Cindy were asked to identify Shelby, Cindy's response would be along the lines of, *Oh, didn't she get divorced recently?*

Although maybe not. Shelby does have a reputation as a top-notch Realtor, after all. It's not as if Cindy lives under a rock. However, what Cindy most decidedly does *not* know is that nearly every Thursday night for the past eight months (and the occasional Saturday), her husband, Bo, has been spending time with Shelby. Thursday is when Noah's sports teams—hockey in the fall and winter, track in the spring—practice late.

What Cindy Bannister also doesn't realize is that her husband has been unhappy in their marriage for a long time, that he's only staying for the kids' sake. The physical side of their marriage, according to Bo, fell away a long time ago.

Shelby has further been able to justify her subterfuge by telling herself that she deserves every good thing after surviving her divorce. Surely, being married to a man who failed to support her financially— and emotionally!—warrants some kind of karmic payback from the universe. She rationalizes her feelings for Bo by telling herself that she works incredibly hard to ensure her son has all that he needs, and if Thursday night is the one evening she looks forward to each week, so be it. She tells herself she's making Bo's life at least marginally better. She tells herself it's Bo who's committing adultery, not her. She tells herself she loves him.

But she knows it's all a pack of lies.

Except for the last part. She *does* love him. Or at the very least, she's *in love* with him. That one's true.

She thinks back to when she and Bo first struck up a conversation beyond their usual chitchat at the vet's office. It was a muggy August day, and she'd stopped off at the coffee shop on Atlantic Street, safely hidden away from the main drag of summer tourists. When the store's blast of air-conditioning hit her, it was as if a strong wind swept her up and spun her around. Bo was standing in the pickup queue, and when he turned and spotted her, his face cracked into a grin, his eyes crinkling at the sides. Her stomach leveled out somewhere around her knees.

"Hey, Shelby. Where's my best friend?"

Shelby's first instinct was to feel guilty that she'd left Tuukka at home. Sometimes she brought him into the office, where he'd lie at her feet and snooze away most of the afternoon. But that day she'd had two open houses, and juggling an occasionally hyper golden retriever and potential buyers was never a winning combination. Plus, it was late August, and Noah was home from school, enjoying the last languid days of summer. The very least he could do was watch the dog.

She ordered her regular—iced hazelnut with milk and two sugars— and Bo waited with her, sipping his own chai tea. That he was a tea drinker, not a coffee addict, surprised her.

"It's weird I've never seen you here before. You'd think after all this time we would have bumped into each other."

He grinned sheepishly. "Can't say this is my go-to spot. I'm usually at Breadbasket or Toast, but I was on my way to Gunrock."

"Ah."

She asked after his girls, both slightly younger than Noah, but neglected to inquire about Cindy. Was it because she'd somehow picked up on the radio waves of interest radiating off him?

"Care to join me at Gunrock, where you can enjoy your coffee in the sun?" he asked.

And with those fateful words, the door between them swung open ever so slightly . . . and Shelby stepped through, all the way through.

"Sure." She shrugged. "Why not? I've got a few minutes," she lied. There was a ton to do before her noon showing, but she followed him in her car to the beach anyway, and then down the wooden steps onto the sand, where she pulled off her sandals and slung them over two fingers. The crescent beach was mostly empty, aside from an older man cocooned in a blanket and reading a book. Bo led her to the boulders hugging the shoreline and offered her his hand so she could scramble up after him.

"Take it easy," he warned. "I don't want my favorite dog owner to break an ankle."

Was he hitting on her?

"This is where I like to go and take a break. Especially after surgeries." He explained that he'd just finished operating on a German shepherd with a broken hip, a surgery that had turned out to be more complicated than anticipated. They watched as two paddle boarders out on the water struggled to get traction, until one boy took a nosedive off his board.

"Ouch! That looks painful," she cried.

"It's harder than it seems," Bo offered. "Believe me, I've tried."

She laughed. "I'll bet. I wouldn't know, though. I've never been brave enough myself. I'd probably tear my ACL."

His warm eyes appraised her for a moment, setting off a clutch of butterflies in her stomach. "I bet you'd be great."

She shrugged off the compliment as gracefully as she could and steered the conversation back toward his work, to the tsunami of emotions that came with raising teenagers. He inquired after Ethan, which struck her as bold. Most people dodged the question as best they could; after three years, her divorce was practically considered old news. But Bo wanted to know how she was doing and how school was for Noah (were kids bullying him?), and in response to his simple concern, her emotions unspooled like a tightly wound ball of string.

Gently, he patted her forearm and asked if he could maybe be a friend, acknowledging that Hull could be a lonely town. And somewhere in that conversation, though she can't recall exactly at what point, he asked for her number. Was it on the beach? At her car? She'd never pegged him for a player, although the thought of sharing a lovely dinner with him did cross her mind. Bo's initial offer was more of the I'm-sorry-to-hear-what-you've-been-through variety, a maybe-I-can-check-in-and-see-how-you're-doing suggestion. She handed over her cell number gladly, maybe even eagerly.

Two days later, he called. They shared lobster rolls on the beach, settling on a remote spot several yards away from the other beachcombers, and shooed away the persnickety gulls vying for their dinner. He told her that Cindy and the kids had headed into Boston for Shakespeare on the Common and then proceeded to share anecdotes about some of the animals he'd tended to—parrots and lizards, even a Berkshire pig. And the next thing she knew, Bo's hand was sweeping her hair off her shoulder. "You're very pretty," he said, and confusion must have swept across her face. What was he doing? He was still married, wasn't he?

"Are you hitting on me?" she teased.

"What if I were?"

So many thoughts raced through her mind that day: she was nervous, excited, mortified that she was having this conversation with a married man. Had she secretly been hoping that the evening would unfold this way? Shelby hadn't been with another man in three years. After Ethan, she'd sworn off the male species for good, hadn't felt the slightest attraction to anyone else. Her life was focused solely on Noah and her job. But there was something about Bo Bannister that couldn't be so easily dismissed. That hair, those gray-blue eyes, his gentle tone. She didn't dare cross that line, did she? Her dad had been a minister, for Pete's sake! Shelby knew right from wrong.

"I think that would be very bad," she managed to say, jumping up and brushing the sand from the backs of her calves. "You're married."

"That I am," he said and sighed. "Happily married, though? That's another matter."

"Oh," she said. "I'm sorry to hear that. Marriage is so tough. Sometimes I wonder why anyone does it." She turned back to look at him. "For the kids, I suppose, right? Where would we be without our kids?" She was reluctant to discuss it more. They packed up their bags and headed to their cars. Another week passed, then another. Shelby suspected she'd never hear from him again and began researching new veterinarians.

But then he called, asked if he could take her to dinner in Boston. Against her better judgment, she agreed; she didn't tell Noah, obviously. She drove to the boardwalk, parked her car, and met Bo there, where she hopped in his Porsche, feeling like Julia Roberts being whisked away in *Pretty Woman*. On the deck overlooking the water, they shared plates of shrimp scampi and swordfish and two bottles of the most delicious pinot grigio. Afterward, when they pulled up beside her car on the boardwalk, he leaned across the seat and asked if it would be all right if he kissed her. She nodded yes, although her mind cried out, *Stop! Married!*

The next morning, she blamed the kiss on the wine—she'd had more than her customary two glasses. She blamed it on bad judgment, on a much-belated rebound after her divorce, on anything but the fact that she'd given in to temptation. Because Bo Bannister was undeniably handsome—who hadn't noticed him about town? He was confident, funny, warm. She hadn't been thinking at the time. How could she? *Poor Cindy!*

But then Bo called the next day and asked when he could see her again, and Shelby, her thinking crystal clear, said before she could stop herself, "How about next Thursday?"

It was obvious she was getting into trouble, but it couldn't be helped. At least that's what she told herself. And if Bo were unhappily married, who was she to deny him a relationship that he might actually enjoy? Shelby wasn't expecting to fall in love. At most, it would be a brief fling, a romance to reassure herself that she was truly over Ethan, that they'd made a clean break. A little dalliance to help her through the ugly realization that, but for her sisters and Noah, pretty much no one else on earth gave a hoot about her existence.

But somewhere in the last few months, her feelings for Bo have undeniably shifted, a plate tectonics of emotions. There's more to this relationship than a brief fling. Shelby has fallen, hard. For a married man.

To say that she has spent roughly eight months or 243 consecutive days thinking about him would be an understatement. Five thousand seven hundred and sixty hours. A gazillion minutes.

And each time, despite the fact that she keeps promising herself she'll cut it off, tells herself that the relationship can't possibly sustain itself, she falters. Because Bo makes her feel alive again, as if she *deserves* to be the object of someone's affection. The thought of him makes her want to crawl out of bed in the morning, which is no small thing. And whenever she decides *this* will be the last time, Bo inevitably appears at her back door armed with a bouquet of lovely orange-pink dahlias and a wicked grin to slay her misgivings, crumble her resolve.

Is it so awful that she's finally found someone whom she can talk to? Who makes her feel beautiful—and seen? Someone with whom she can let her guard down? Who brings her hazelnut iced coffee without her even asking?

No, she tells herself. It's not awful. To the contrary, it's actually quite wonderful.

She steps out of the car now and punches in Bo's private number, filed under "health club," should Noah ever check her phone. A few abandoned plastic bottles litter the front lawn at the new client's house. Out-of-towners get lazy when returning from a long day at the beach and tend to chuck their trash wherever they've parked. (Shelby has long been advocating for more public trash cans for this very reason.) There's a Sprite bottle, a few water bottles, an empty bag of Doritos. She tosses them all into the trunk of her car while she waits for Bo to pick up. It's early, only two fifteen—he's probably with a patient—but she can't help that he's the one person she wants to celebrate with. She imagines the special ringtone that plays on his phone whenever she calls ("Here Comes the Sun" by the Beatles because "it makes me think of you," he said) playing in his office.

"Hello?" Hearing his voice sends a pulse of excitement through her.

"Hi there, stranger. You busy?"

"Hang on a sec." She hears him excusing himself, probably from an exam room, then the sound of a door closing. "What's up?"

"I closed on the Vendler property today. Thought maybe you'd want to celebrate with me? I know it's Wednesday, but Noah's going over to Lindsay's after school for dinner and to study. He won't be home till eight at the earliest."

"Congratulations! That's terrific. I'd love to celebrate with you, but I've got a pretty full docket this afternoon."

She pictures Bo standing in his office, beyond the examining room, running his fingers through his hair. She doesn't want to seem unreasonable, but she *really* wants to see him. Somewhere in the background a dog barks. Persistence is one of Shelby's more dominant, if not noble, traits. "How about when you're done, then? We should still have some time."

"Hold on one sec; maybe I can figure something out." She hears him jostling the phone on the other end, maybe flipping through his calendar. She knows it will be the leather-bound agenda book that he carries with him everywhere and in which his assistant faithfully records all his appointments—he's old-fashioned that way. A few seconds later, he's back on. "I'm going to ask Derek to cover my last two cases of the day. Meet you at your place around five?"

Derek is Bo's assistant vet, whom Shelby knows Bo is grooming to one day take over the practice.

She bites her lip in victory and slides the house key into the lock, the door swinging open. Her trusty cleaning company scoured the house last week, but a faint musty smell lingers. She'll have to air out the downstairs, throw open some windows, maybe warm up some already-made cookies in the stove—an old Realtor trick. It will lend a homey feel to the new property. *It's okay,* she thinks. She has plenty of time.

"Perfect," she says. "I'll see you then."

"You know I can't wait."

3

BREE

Brianna, a.k.a. Bree, flips through the channels, searching for a daytime show that's remotely appealing. Months ago, she canceled her Hulu subscription, so what's left is a predictably mind-numbing lineup. Soap operas, cooking shows, the programs where doctors furnish their patients with a fresh nose or a brand-new set of double-Ds. But she's stuck in bed, surrounded by eight million pillows, so she might as well get used to it. At least until her mouth reaches the point where it no longer needs cotton stuffed into the gaping caverns that formerly held her wisdom teeth.

To Bree's surprise, it turns out that extracting your wisdom teeth is a lot like having your tonsils out or catching the chicken pox: it's better to get the whole thing over with when you're young and the body heals quickly. But Bree's wisdom teeth never bothered her until last week, when she experienced such mind-blowing pain that it kept her up all night, pacing the floor. The next day her typically conservative dentist prescribed antibiotics for a double infection and said, "Yep, we need to get those out, preferably as soon as possible."

Both her sisters, Kate and Shelby, had theirs extracted when they were seniors in high school, and by day two, they were wolfing down hamburgers. Bree, however, can't imagine ever craving a hamburger again. She will drink milkshakes for the rest of her life, if only it will make the throbbing in her mouth stop.

Nor does she have any desire to dip into the pile of books that Kate left on her bedside table yesterday after picking her up from the oral surgeon. There's *The Leftover Woman* by Jean Kwok and *Golden Girl* by Elin Hilderbrand. A biography of Ruth Bader Ginsburg. *Romantic Comedy* by Curtis Sittenfeld.

Although Bree doesn't need to read that last one since she's pretty sure she's been *living* a romantic comedy of late, where the joke, alas, has been on her. In the past year and a half, her heart has been entangled in a serious relationship, ripped to bits, and is only now beginning to reemerge for consideration. All because of one person.

Hannah.

Tall, thin, wearer of tortoiseshell glasses, Hannah was the curator at an upscale gallery on Newbury Street in Boston. She had a huge smile and a throaty laugh that was sexy as hell and that caught Bree's attention as soon as she stepped foot in the gallery. Bree had come to see an exhibit by an old RISD friend, Erin, and was feeling a tiny bit jealous that Erin was the first in their coterie of friends to have landed a major gallery showing. It was a coup, worthy of months, if not years, of envy.

When Bree arrived, art critics from the *Globe* and *Boston* magazine were already circling Erin, so Bree said a quick hello, then helped herself to a glass of chardonnay from a passing tray. She wandered alone down one corridor, then another, eventually landing in the room that featured a series of Erin's paintings. Her friend's work, while technically sound, had taken a decided turn toward the abstract—broad brushstrokes of paint resembling, well, not much. But maybe that was what galleries were looking for these days? Art that defied easy categorization? Bree didn't think the paintings were as strong as Erin's vibrant still lifes back in school, although it was entirely possible that her own judgment was clouded by jealousy.

When Hannah materialized by her side, Bree was interested but not entirely surprised—she'd spotted Hannah as soon as she'd arrived, and they'd exchanged that brief glance that passes between strangers taking note of each other. Hannah was older than Bree, probably by several years, and the deft way in which she floated from circle to circle at the party—inserting herself flawlessly and extricating herself just as gracefully—implied Hannah was in charge. Later, when Bree learned she was the gallery's curator, it made perfect sense. "Do curators typically make out in the supply closet during an exhibit's opening night?" Bree asked while Hannah worked to slip her blouse off, Bree's back pressed up against something scratchy, maybe paper towels. "Never," came Hannah's reply.

The next week, she invited Bree out with some friends to catch a band at the Cantab Lounge in Central Square. The band was new to Bree, but their sound reminded her of Fleetwood Mac. Most of Hannah's friends were older, and Bree watched, transfixed, observing Hannah in her natural habitat, squeezing this one's arm, whispering in that one's ear, making each person feel special. (Bree knew this precise feeling because she'd been on the receiving end of it at the gallery.) She wondered privately if such ease, such grace, came with maturity or if it was simply Hannah's way of being in the world.

How many of these friends, Bree wondered, *has Hannah already slept with? Three? Ten?* The thought launched an unexpected dart of jealousy through her. Later, back in bed, when she screwed up the courage to ask, Hannah blew her off. "Old friends, that's all they are. Sure, there might have been some fooling around back in the day, but I assure you none of them are ex-girlfriends. I'm *very* particular." Then she licked the outer rim of Bree's ear, snuffing out any possibility of further conversation.

A month later, Bree was storing a week's worth of clothing on the right side of Hannah's closet and spending nights at her apartment, an old warehouse studio, an outlier of Central Square. The Cambridge apartment boasted high ceilings, exposed redbrick walls. Waves of lambent light splashed through multipaned windows. It was the kind of place Bree always imagined herself living in one day if she could ever afford it. She packed up her Sonic toothbrush with its plug-in charger, her favorite fuzzy slippers, her laptop, and moved it all in like a mistress staking a claim to her lover's heart.

"Whoa, your Sonic?" Hannah teased. "I know how important good dental hygiene is to you, so this must be getting pretty serious." (She'd been using a cheap plastic toothbrush that Hannah had gifted her the first time she stayed over.)

Soon, Bree's days became split between her shifts at What's Brewing? and the co-op art studio where she rented space with a handful of other local artists. Nights unfolded back at Hannah's place, where they ordered takeout, maybe shared a bottle of wine. Her head resting in Hannah's lap, Bree would listen to her girlfriend's stories about the artists who behaved badly at the gallery that day. This one needed a particular kind of lighting for his paintings. That one wanted the walls behind her artwork painted a celery green to better accent her drawings. A million niggling requests that each artist claimed must be met if the "integrity" of their art was to be preserved. She and Hannah laughed at their deplorable, childish behavior, and Hannah made Bree promise that she'd never become one of *those artists*.

When Bree finally had the nerve to bring home a few lithographs of her own, Hannah was encouraging and dismissive at once. "They're really good. Especially this one." Gently, she removed a print of three robins from the portfolio, one of Bree's favorites. It was inked in separate fields of color—a vibrant red, a light blue, a yellow that bled a touch at the corner. "The colors, the simplicity is brilliant." Hannah's head tilted to the side, her eyes narrowing, as if trying to see more deeply. After combing through the remaining prints, she gave a tidy summation that bordered on praise but fell short of an actual offer to showcase Bree's work at the gallery. "Keep going. You're really talented, honey, but you're still finding your voice." At the time, the words stung. Hadn't Bree already devoted four years at RISD to *find her voice*? She resented the implication that she was the student, Hannah the teacher.

But eventually, she came around to understanding what Hannah had meant. When they walked through galleries together, her hand clasped in Hannah's, it was evident that the work lining the walls conveyed a certain sophistication that Bree's own prints lacked. Just because she'd chosen to pursue the centuries-old art form of lithography, transferring her drawings from stone to paper via a printing press, it didn't necessarily grant her pictures a timelessness. Hannah was right to postpone Bree's time in the spotlight. She wasn't ready. It should happen because she deserved it, not because of a lover's favor.

And then the phone call came. *The phone call that changed everything,* as Bree would later tag it, a bright-red flare in her mind. It was late December, a few days shy of Christmas. Outside Hannah's apartment, the snow fell in thick, leafy flakes. *Doctor Zhivago* played on the television. A classic movie, which (Bree thought) was showing its age—and not in a good way. Bree wasn't paying much attention to Omar Sharif or Julie Christie (although Christie *was* undeniably stunning) but instead wondering how to delicately broach the topic of giving up her apartment entirely so that she might move in full time with Hannah. They'd been dating for nearly a year; Bree was ready. She couldn't decide if Hannah felt the same way.

When the landline rang, Hannah paused the movie and got up to answer. The Getty Museum in Los Angeles, it turned out, was looking for a new curator for its old masters' wing; Hannah had come highly recommended by a few different people in the business. Would she be interested in flying out for an interview? After nodding her head several times and saying, "Yes, yes, I understand. That would be incredible. Thank you, thank you so much," Hannah set down the phone, her face beaming, and screamed, "I'm going to LA! The Getty!" Even then, her choice of "I" instead of "we" struck Bree as somehow telling, foreboding.

"Come with me," Hannah pleaded a few weeks later, after she'd accepted the job. Bree found this touching despite herself, because she couldn't possibly go—and Hannah knew it.

Packing up and abandoning the East Coast, her home of thirty-six years, wasn't something she was prepared to do without the guarantee of a job out west. And perhaps more important, the thought of uprooting her life when the object of her affection had yet to proclaim her ever-lasting love seemed unwise, imprudent even. What if she got out there and Hannah dumped her? Then where would she be?

"You could come for a few months, try it out," Hannah suggested. "See if you like it."

But the lilt of her voice insinuated that Bree would be the one taking a chance, the one with the most to lose. The Getty call was what Hannah had been waiting for—quite possibly her entire life. Bree imagined herself spending lonely days in their LA apartment, eating her way through bags of Doritos, missing Hannah and frustrated that she'd found no place to show her own work.

Every now and then Hannah will shoot her a text, ask how she's doing, maybe tell her about some fabulous new exhibit she's oversee-ing. The texts are flirty, suggestive, noncommittal. Their breakup, while mutual, was like most other breakups: one party suggesting it, the other hurrying to agree so as not to be upstaged. Or emotionally flattened. Hannah didn't "do" long-distance relationships. Bree tries to keep her texts upbeat, hoping the spaces between her words won't reveal how much it hurts to know that Hannah is still out there, untouchable. Sometimes she wakes up at night in a cold sweat, her ex-girlfriend's name on her lips, their lovemaking so real in her dreams that she could swear Hannah lies beside her.

Bree lets herself sink deeper into her pillows. For someone who graduated with grand intentions of becoming the next Frida Kahlo or Toulouse-Lautrec, both lithographers, Bree can only be described as a colossal underachiever. Instead of enabling her to create art full time, her degree has ensured that a hefty debt will follow her around for the rest of her life, her student loans compounding interest by the minute. Unlike her big sisters, who've somehow managed to figure out life, Bree always feels as if she's swimming behind, playing catch-up. She under-stands that she's the baby in the family (and so by default is the one everyone worries about), but it would be nice to reassure her sisters that they've nothing to worry about. Bree is thirty-six for goodness' sake. She should be fully capable of taking care of herself.

When her cell phone dings—Shelby's name flashes on the screen— Bree lets it go to voicemail. She lacks the necessary stamina to talk to her sister right now and instead listens to the message as the wind whips in and out of Shelby's words, asking how Bree is holding up. Although she appreciates her sister's concern, Bree also understands that this is Shelby's modus operandi, dutifully checking off the responsibility box. It's moments like this when she really misses her mom.

If her mother were still around, she'd be at Bree's side, ready to fluff her pillows or fetch a glass of water. They would laugh and cry into their tissues while they watched *When Harry Met Sally* for the hundredth time. But Bree stops herself from treading too far down this particular path—there's no sense in feeling sorry for herself, no sense in trying to wish her mom back into this world. Because it's never going to happen. And the realization, as obvious as it is, still stings, even a full decade later. The knowledge that she can't pick up the phone and ask her mom to come over and take care of her.

Still, Bree reminds herself to cut Shelby a little slack, if only because Shelby's own life is so bananas. The whole divorce with Ethan a few years ago would be enough to derail anyone, and Bree had felt truly sorry for her. And yet, there was a part of her that had also thought, *Finally!* Her big sister was getting her comeuppance.

Because frankly, Shelby has been getting away with murder ever since they were girls. Shelby was the sister who would sneak out late at night to meet her boyfriend, the one who smoked Pall Malls in the church parking lot, the one who got sick on peach schnapps after her graduation ceremony. The first to get inked, a tiny blue butterfly hovering above her navel. If anyone would drive their dad to drink, he used to say, it would be Shelby. And yet Shelby almost never got caught; it didn't hurt that Bree and Kate covered for her with their flimsy excuses. However mean-spirited it might sound, the fact that Shelby's marriage detonated into a thousand pieces, at the time, struck Bree as a reassuring example of the yin and yang of the universe.

Kate, on the other hand, has always acted like the firstborn, the annoyingly responsible sibling, even though she's solidly the middle child. Straight-A student, Phi Beta Kappa at Brown, a varsity field hockey player, a rising star at Bain & Company before she had Clara. And as if that weren't enough, she managed to snag one of Boston's most eligible bachelors, according to *Boston* magazine. Like Midas, pretty much everything Kate has ever touched turns to gold. Or, at a minimum, to silver.

No, with sisters like Kate and Shelby, Bree never stood a chance of standing out during her teenage years, except, she supposes, for the fact that she was queer. But even that announcement—over dinner at Chili's in Braintree her freshman year in college—came about more as a whimper than a bang. "We're so glad you told us," her dad said, relief threading his voice, as if he'd known it all along. "We're proud of you."

That was several years before Massachusetts even sanctioned gay marriage, her family light-years ahead of the rest of the country, the world. Each time Bree brought home a new girlfriend, her parents would welcome her with open arms—even crazy Irene, whom Bree dragged to Kate's graduation party and who proceeded to get so drunk that she fell into the hotel pool fully dressed.

Bree checks the clock. Another forty-five minutes before she can pop the next Percocet. From the back of her mouth, she gingerly pulls out the bloodied cotton gauze and deposits it into the metal bucket on her bedside table, which Kate thoughtfully placed there earlier. She swings her legs out of bed and lumbers down the hallway to the bathroom to gargle with salt water, per doctor's orders. When she spits, the water is rust colored and metallic-smelling, prompting a gag reflex, but she manages to push it down before peeing and pressing on to the kitchen. Ginger ale, she decides, is what she really needs. She pulls out a tumbler from the cupboard, grabs the soda from the fridge, and pours herself a generous glass. As soon as the icy tonic reaches her lips, there's instant relief. Sweet and bubbly, the soda explodes on her tongue, which feels as thick and dry as leather.

Eventually, she makes her way back to bed, clicks off the TV, and prays for sleep. When her landline rings, she thinks maybe it's her manager checking in or her coworker Jill calling to say that she's going nuts without her at the café. (Bree is one of the few people who still has a landline because she likes the privacy it affords.) But after Bree's familiar outgoing message plays, there's a beep followed by the sound of a man clearing his throat. "Hello, Miss Lancaster, um, this is Monty Gaines at the collection agency, calling to follow up on your overdue credit statement. Please call me at blah, blah, blah at your earliest convenience. I look forward to speaking with you."

She groans and throws a pillow over her face. First, she has to deal with her wisdom teeth, and now this? Somewhere in the back of her mind is the knowledge that she can always ask Kate, or even Shelby, for help. Kate's husband, Trey, seems to print money in his basement; they're forever buying expensive new cars and toys. To do so, however, would require swallowing what little pride Bree has left, an admission that her artist career, like so much else in her life, has been a total bust. The handful of lithographs sold this month, mostly seaside scenes at small galleries down on the Cape, won't even cover her rent. The only thing keeping her afloat right now is her barista job and the occasional freelance work she gets designing book jackets. Even the freelance work has been drying up lately.

She tries to distract herself by thinking about the approaching Memorial Day weekend, when she and her sisters will all be together again for a week's vacation in Hull, a family tradition that began a few years after Shelby moved there with Ethan. Bree will crash at Shelby's place on Beach Avenue (even though Kate and Trey invited her to stay with them in Allerton Hill) because at Shelby's, she can hang out with Noah, who also happens to be her godson. At Shelby's house, it will feel like old times again, and, as an added bonus, Trey (a pompous ass, in Bree's humble opinion) won't be around as much.

At Shelby's, they'll have easy access to the beach, the water only steps from the back deck. They can swim all day and then head over to Schooner's for their famous lobster rolls, which Bree thinks of as the official "taste of summer." Their cheeks will feel tight from the sun, and they'll finish off the night gathered around Shelby's farmhouse table for a game of Scrabble. Everyone will turn off their phones (their dad's rule) and argue about whether a word like *irrespective* is a word (it's not, no matter what the dictionary says).

With all its quirks and seafaring history, Hull might not be the tony spot that most people would choose for their summer getaway; the haute cuisine, the trendy shops, and the people-watching so coveted on Nantucket or the Vineyard are nowhere to be found. But for Bree, that's part of its ineffable charm. Being able to visit and disappear, to blend in with all the other families who've been returning there summer after summer, makes it easy to think of Hull as her second home. She shares the town's unspoken reverence for hard work and unvarnished truth, a reverence that permeates the summer air just as surely as the scent of cotton candy from the century-old carousel that all the kids adore or of the warm bagels from Weinberg's Bakery.

Outside, the daylight has dwindled when Bree finally wakes to her phone buzzing on the bedside table. Her cell flashes four thirty. Asleep for over two hours! It's Shelby, again.

"Hello?" Bree's voice sounds groggy even to herself when she answers. Maybe her sister is standing outside her front door, ready to unload a giant chocolate milkshake.

"Oh, Bree, I'm so glad you're there. Listen, I just hung up with Kate." Shelby pauses, takes a deep breath on the other end. "She's kind of a wreck." Bree's mind struggles to process what her sister is saying. Kate's a wreck? Doesn't she mean Bree? Bree saw Kate yesterday, and if there's anyone who's decidedly *not* a wreck, it's her impeccable middle sister.

"It's Trey," Shelby continues before Bree has a chance to voice her confusion. "Kate saw him kissing some random woman downtown."

Oh, Bree thinks, the words a prick on her hot skin. *Oh, that.* For some reason, it doesn't surprise her. And then she realizes why: downtown last week, she saw Trey with some woman but assumed it was a colleague. It was around lunchtime, and Bree was coming straight from the studio to pick up supplies from her favorite art store in the city. She was still wearing her yoga pants, a sweatshirt flecked with ink stains, and couldn't recall the last time she'd washed her hair. Not wanting to engage in an awkward meet and greet with her brother-in-law and his coworker, she hightailed it across the street.

But she forgot to mention it to Kate the other day. Now a part of her wonders: *Did she subconsciously choose not to?*

4

ROBIN

Memorial Day Weekend
Sunday, May 26

When Robin arrives on the scene, a small group of curious onlookers has gathered along the shore, a stone's throw from the marina and Robin's favorite restaurant, Local 02045. Nearby, there's an ambulance, Hull fire trucks and—this is a surprise—a couple of Boston police cruisers and state police. The presence of the city's and state's brass puts her on high alert. This is no run-of-the-mill drill, and Robin feels slightly blindsided that she's one of the last to arrive.

What's going on that warrants the top guns hauling themselves all the way out to Hull on a brisk Sunday morning? And on Memorial Day weekend, no less? There's got to be more to it than a runaway boat in Hull Bay. She parks near the cruisers, climbs out, and heads over to say hello. On the way from the station, she silenced her siren to avoid alerting any rubberneckers, but it's clear that the word is already out. The crackle of radios and the hushed voices of people talking near the water's edge pepper the air. The only saving grace is that no camera crews have arrived on the scene yet.

Robin's gaze follows that of the harbormaster's assistant, Bobby, who's pointing to the right of Bumpkin Island. About a quarter mile out, the harbormaster's boat and a handful of Coast Guard response crafts, their signature orange stripe visible, can be seen circling the vessel. It's a beauty: a sloop rig, if she's not mistaken, but it's hard to tell from this distance, even with binoculars. It's curious, to say the least, that it's drifting without its sail raised. Did it break free of its mooring? Was the owner too drunk to remember to hoist it before setting sail? Or has the sail been purposely dropped?

Then she sees the Boston police boats. *Whoa.* Something's not right if the city police are already on the water.

Robin walks farther out to the dock and introduces herself to the three officers, all men. There's a lot of throat-clearing, but eventually the youngest-looking of the bunch—Officer Stephen Rusco, according to his badge—provides a brief update. She listens quietly, nods her head. The last thing she wants is to turn this into a territorial pissing match; she knows how easily her male peers can dismiss a female lieutenant, not to mention a lieutenant from a small precinct like Hull.

It's still early, but the particulars of the incident—as Officer Rusco relates them, at least—are as follows: Turns out there's a male, in his midforties to early fifties, already aboard the rogue sailboat. He was passed out (likely alcohol-induced) when the patrol boarded, and they're in the process of trying to rouse him. She's about to ask the kid, as she's mentally dubbed him, why Boston's team is here in the first place. Sounds like a pretty straightforward case of a partygoer who forgot how to sail a boat after a few too many martinis. But she doesn't want to risk alienating the force before they even know whose boat they're dealing with. If it's an out-of-towner, she'll most likely have to step aside, anyway.

But then Rusco's radio buzzes to life, and there's a report that crackles in from the Coast Guard. Now alert, the guy on the sailboat is apparently "going out of his mind" because he claims to have had a companion with him—and his companion is missing. Says they motored out "around four o'clock that morning to wait for the sunrise," but that they both "fell asleep" on deck. This news usurps Robin's momentary annoyance over the Boston police having inserted themselves into her territory.

Because they now have a proper search-and-rescue mission on their hands. They'll need all the help they can get. A few minutes later, as if on command, two Boston police helicopters materialize overhead, their rotor blades buzzing loudly, and begin circling the water.

Robin can count on one hand the bodies lost at sea near their sleepy town in recent years. One was a woman who drove her pickup truck into the Hull Gut and kept driving until the truck was completely submerged. It had taken both city and state patrols and divers to locate the truck—and the deceased woman—some six hours later. Another body, belonging to a young man who was fleeing the police and tragically ran into the ocean to escape, washed ashore a few days later. Robin prays this doesn't turn into another instance of having to wait out a body that drifts ashore.

From her vantage point on the pier, she tries to gauge the distance from the sailboat's location over to Bumpkin Island. It's to the island's right, drifting farther out toward Hingham Bay. For someone who's in moderately good shape, the distance looks swimmable—maybe an eighth of a mile. But for someone who fell overboard and was most likely inebriated to begin with? That's when the odds in their favor start to diminish precipitously. Along with the fact that, according to the harbormaster, the water temperature hasn't even hit fifty-five degrees yet, which means that hypothermia would set in quickly. The very thought of it sends a chill straight through Robin's body. For someone who hates it when the pool temperature at the Y falls below a balmy seventy-five, it's tough to imagine treading water or swimming in that kind of cold for long without a life jacket.

Although, stranger things have happened. It's possible that the guy on board is hallucinating his companion, too drunk to discern dream from reality.

After a few more minutes, she excuses herself from the officers' huddle and heads back to her cruiser. It's evident that the state troopers and Boston police are coordinating the rescue effort, and it occurs to her that the chief requested her presence here mainly as reinforcement. Someone familiar with the area, to be consulted as needed. That's fine; she just wishes he would have filled her in on the chain of command sooner. And told her a bit more about what, precisely, is going on.

Back inside her cruiser, she cranks the heat, scans the water with her binoculars. She tries to signal the harbormaster, Tommy, on the radio; she wants live updates as soon as possible. What's happening out there? What else have they found? Is there any evidence of foul play?

She decides to call over to the medical center on George Washington Boulevard. Maybe someone was admitted earlier this morning, thanks to a Good Samaritan who brought them in on their boat. A person can hope, at least.

She props the radio up on the dashboard so she's sure not to miss any updates. If her usual partner for Memorial Day weekend, Sheila, were here, they'd toss around possible theories about what might have happened (on holiday weekends, the officers will often pair up for reinforcements). But Sheila is in Cabo, Mexico, enjoying her honeymoon. Which leaves Robin by herself. And even though she could have requested another partner for the long weekend, the thought of it was less than appealing. Why risk being paired with someone she couldn't stand (and there were a few too many of those on the force) when she could work more effectively alone?

Now, though, she regrets not requesting another officer. It would be nice to have a partner to talk through the facts with.

She dials up the medical center and waits for an answer while the phone rings in her ear. The Coast Guard boats continue to buzz around the bay, wherever the helicopters hover to open up circles on the water for a better look. It will be a long day of waiting, she thinks. *But there are worse things than waiting,* Robin reminds herself.

Like being at the bottom of the ocean.

5

KATE

Earlier
Wednesday, May 15

As soon as Clara is settled in front of the TV with a juice box and graham crackers, Kate races upstairs to start packing. Her eyes sweep the room: the bed still unmade, the white down comforter puddled at the bottom from their lovemaking earlier this morning. Her mind zigzags all over the place. She can't think of what she needs, so she starts throwing everything into her blue-and-white canvas tote bag. Toothpaste, toothbrush, makeup bag, favorite fisherman's sweater.

In Clara's room, she grabs Peppa Pig (Clara's must-have for bedtime), clothes, underwear, hairbrush. Clara's eczema cream. *What else?* Kate's hands are shaking. At the periphery of her mind hovers the question: *Where will we go? A hotel?* They can't sleep at Bree's place—it's a train wreck and not exactly toddler proof. Shelby's house presents the most obvious solution. It's about an hour's drive away. Shelby would take them in, and it will be an easy sell to Clara. *We're going to spend some time with Auntie Shelby and Noah. Won't that be fun?*

Whatever they do, Kate knows this: they can't stay here tonight.

Back in her room, she yanks a handful of T-shirts from the closet, her favorite pair of jeans from the bottom bureau drawer. She needs familiar territory, someplace to straighten her jumbled thoughts. Then it hits her: What's stopping her from opening up the summer house in Hull? They're only a week or so shy of Memorial Day weekend, the traditional start of summer. The key already dangles from her key chain, a plastic yellow cap encircling the top. *What's stopping her?* The answer zips across her mind almost as quickly as the question appears: *absolutely nothing.*

There's a part of her that desperately wants to call Trey and ask him what the hell he was doing with that woman. *Explain yourself in thirty seconds or else.* But that plan threatens to backfire; she doesn't have the presence of mind to engage in anything resembling a civil conversation at the moment. Besides, what, exactly, does she expect him to say? That her suspicions are correct and he's having an affair? Or that she's crazy and it was only a friendly kiss?

But that kiss!

Its significance has already registered in her gut. Even if Trey denied it, she wouldn't believe him. She witnessed it with her own eyes. No, nothing good can come of calling him right now.

Instead, from the privacy of her bedroom, she taps Shelby's number into her phone. The torrent of words that she's been holding back in the car spills out now, hysteria threading her voice.

"There must be some kind of explanation, don't you think?" her sister says calmly when Kate finally comes up for air.

"And what else could that be, other than that my husband is having an affair?" Kate does not want to be talked down off her cliff, does not want to hear any explanation beyond the obvious. In her eyes, Trey's kiss constitutes a betrayal, not some inconvenient, meaningless act.

"I think you need to at least give him a chance to explain himself."

"Why?" She pokes her head outside the bedroom door to make sure Clara is still glued to *Sesame Street* downstairs, where Ernie is singing about the letter *E.*

"Come on. This is Trey we're talking about. Your *husband*. The guy who loves you?" Shelby counters.

Kate pauses to consider this. "Yeah, well, love and sex are two very different things."

"Whoa. *Sex?* That's a pretty huge leap to make from a single kiss. You don't even know what it was about, Kate!"

"I think I have a pretty good idea. It was *not* some innocent kiss. I saw it."

Shelby sighs on the other end, and Kate can almost see her sister worrying her long auburn hair into a braid, her go-to habit whenever she's deep in thought.

"What did you tell Clara?"

"That she was a friend of Daddy's. She wanted to know why Daddy was kissing 'that lady.'"

"Ugh," says Shelby. "Listen, why don't you come out here? I'm done for the day. We can hash it all out over a big glass of wine. And you and Clara are welcome to stay at our place for a couple of days until this blows over. I'm sure it's a simple misunderstanding."

But that's the problem: Kate doesn't *want* to give Trey the benefit of the doubt. Not even a sliver of it. Because she's certain of what she saw. That woman had been *expecting* Trey to kiss her, inviting it. It's this feeling, above all else, that lingers. The familiarity of that kiss. A wave of nausea ripples through her.

"Listen, I've gotta go, Shel, but I'll call you later. I think I'm going to head out to the summer house with Clara."

"Wait, what? Why? Why don't you come to my place instead? You haven't even opened up the house yet." Kate's summer house is only a few short miles from Shelby's, but at the moment, that distance feels significant, necessary.

"I know. It'll be fine. I'm sorry, Shel. I just need to be alone right now. We'll catch up tomorrow."

After she hangs up, Kate steps into the bathroom to splash water on her face. She looks terrible. How long have those bags been under her eyes? Her hair has been up in a ponytail for days. *No wonder Trey is looking elsewhere,* she thinks. But *No!* She stops herself. She won't go down that particular path, the one where she's at fault for her husband's infidelity. Whatever is happening, *this is not on her.*

She slams off the light, grabs the canvas bag stuffed with clothes, and tromps downstairs, her flip-flops making sucking noises against the hardwood. "Come on, squirt. We're going for a sleepover at the summer house." Trey won't be home for another few hours, but she wants out of the house as soon as possible. What she might say, what she might do if forced to confront him tonight in front of their daughter, frightens her the most.

Reluctantly, Clara pulls her gaze away from the TV, her tiny brow furrowed in confusion. "What did you say, Mommy?" Her daughter's surprise is understandable; usually a visit to the summer house gets announced days in advance. This impromptu trip must seem strange and out of place, as if Kate has just announced that they're setting off on a rocket to the moon.

"The summer house, you know. You love it there!" Her voice trills upward on the last word, making her internally cringe. She's trying too hard.

"But what about Daddy?" Kate's heart cartwheels across her chest. How is it that her daughter possesses some kind of sixth sense when it comes to her parents?

"It's just you and me today, squirt," she reassures her. "Daddy's busy working." Clara's LeapFrog is sitting on the kitchen counter, and Kate sweeps it off the counter into her bag. "C'mon," she cajoles sweetly. "We'll have popcorn, and you can sleep in Mommy and Daddy's bed with me tonight."

"Yay!" Clara instantly leaps off the couch, any former hesitation vanishing.

The mention of popcorn reminds Kate: they'll need food. The cupboards in Hull are bound to be bare. At the end of each summer, they toss the perishables and tote the rest back to Wellesley. From the drawer next to the stove, she yanks out a Trader Joe's recyclable bag and proceeds to stuff it with microwave popcorn, peanut butter and jelly, half a loaf of bread, a few boxes of macaroni and cheese, juice boxes, a couple of bruised pears. A bottle of pinot noir and a bag of dark roast coffee for her. Whatever else they need can be purchased at the Village Market tomorrow.

She performs one last check of the lights, switches off the television, hands Clara her Peppa Pig, and grabs the keys. There's a moment of hesitation: Should she leave a note for Trey? If she were alone, she might not. But there's Clara to consider; she doesn't want to worry him unnecessarily. *Heading out to the Hull house with Clara. See you in a few days?* she scribbles on the notepad next to the phone.

That the note ends with a question mark seems fitting. Assuming she *wants* to see him in a few days. She takes her daughter's hand, and with a shudder, the heavy oak door closes behind them.

~

They make good time around the city; the commuter traffic is light so early in the afternoon. Kate leaves a message for the sitter, saying she and Trey need to postpone their dinner plans tonight. *So sorry for the late notice.* In the back seat, Clara's LeapFrog has slipped from her hands into her lap, and her eyelids flutter open and shut, open and shut, before finally closing for sleep. The rare nap provides a much-needed slice of quiet for Kate to think, to process last night.

Was Trey acting any differently?

She tries to remember. Home around eight, he wandered into the living room to give her a kiss before pouring his customary glass of scotch. She got up to fix him a dinner plate, leftover chicken-and-broccoli ziti. And even though he'd missed Clara's tuck-in time *again*, she decided to let it slide. She was familiar with how easily the delicate balance of a marriage could be upset, sent off-kilter by a poorly timed question. Especially on nights when Trey was working late, his patience already wire thin.

She inquired about his day, plopping down on the couch next to him. The *Nightly News* with Lester Holt, automatically recorded on weekdays, played on the television, reporting yet another wildfire raging across Northern California.

"Fine. Same as always." Trey's typical response, as if he were afraid that going into further detail would bore her or, perhaps, reveal client secrets. "Another day at the salt mines," he added wryly and shoveled in a bite of ziti.

"You and me both. Clara was a bear today."

"Really?" He turned his head, as if seeing her for the first time. "Huh. Guess she's at that age." He reached over to pat Kate's knee, almost avuncularly. "Sorry I missed tuck-in again tonight. I had to get a document out to a client for review."

Kate nodded, her mild irritation at his being late half assuaged by his apology. There was always something—a deposition to prepare for, a motion to file, a discovery process that was taking forever—to explain his absences. She thought she understood; she'd had similar work demands, logging insane hours at Bain & Company before Clara, and it was largely why she'd quit. But it didn't necessarily make Trey's absence any easier. Especially when she was ravenous for adult conversation, for any intel from the outside world beyond *Sesame Street* and *Paw Patrol* and the playground talk that constituted the majority of her days now.

Although familiar with only the vaguest details, she knew that the firm was caught up in a potentially high-profile case at the moment—a personal injury lawsuit involving a manufacturer of children's swing sets. Trey's firm was representing the manufacturer. Once she'd inquired if he'd had any misgivings about taking on this particular client (i.e., if a child *had* been injured, how could the firm defend the manufacturer?), but Trey had been quick to snap at her, saying she didn't know the facts. Which was true. She suspected it was this very case that had kept him late at work again.

Last night, she mentioned that she was taking Clara to the aquarium today and asked if he wanted to join them for lunch. She remembers his response all too well: *Sorry, honey, but I'm completely booked.* And she brushed it off: *No worries. We'll do it another time.*

And then this morning, he rolled over and wrapped his arms around her, his erection pushing against her back. When she turned toward him, he kissed her lightly, his hand reaching up under her pajama top to caress her breasts. They made love hurriedly before he climbed out of bed to shower. "Sorry, busy day," he called over his shoulder.

Perhaps, she thinks, he already knew then what he was apologizing for? Tears prick at her eyes, and she swipes them away. Has her husband been having an affair behind her back all this time? And what, exactly, is "all this time"? A few weeks? Months? A year?

She turns the car onto the causeway leading into Hull. To the right, the giant white turbine spins, and on either side of the isthmus, the narrow vein of the Weir River wends its way below. Kate flicks off the air conditioner, rolls down the window, and inhales, inviting the salty sea air in to cleanse her lungs of the deceptions of the last twenty-four hours. On her dashboard, her cell phone rings in its holder.

Trey. Impeccable timing.

Without thinking, she hits "Decline." She doesn't want to wake Clara, and she most certainly doesn't want to have this conversation while driving. No, she'd best have a glass of wine before signing up for that particular brand of hell. A few minutes later, the phone rings again. Kate hits "Decline" again. *Let him stew for a while,* she thinks. He can't possibly know that she saw him.

Soon enough, the sweep of a slate-blue ocean greets them, and a weight that Kate didn't even realize was present lifts from her chest. The car traces Nantasket Road onto Hull Shore Drive, passing all the familiar, favorite places of summer—the Parrot, Tipsy Tuna, Daddy's Beach Club. Places where she and Trey and her sisters have logged untold hours, downing cocktails, devouring buttery lobster, dancing on sandy floors. She wants it all back right now, in this instant. Wants to conjure up the people she loves most and have Trey explain how that silly little kiss was precisely that. A French greeting gone astray, a mistaken slip. She wants her husband's arms around her while they sway to Jimmy Buffet's "Margaritaville" and then make out later like teenagers on the beach.

Trey, how could you?

A seagull squawks noisily overhead, and soon the car is making the steep climb up into Allerton, the section of Hull where the houses grow larger and more ostentatious by the yard. Theirs is an old, restored cedar-shingled Colonial perched high on a cliff above the sea. Shelby knew Kate and Trey were looking for a summer home in Hull, and one day, roughly three years ago, she called to say "this mansion" was about to go on the market. An atypical event, to be sure; Hullonians preferred to pass their real estate on to the next generation. But this particular house needed work, too much work for the tastes of the nephew of the widow who'd lived there and who was, ostensibly, the estate's sole heir. If Kate and Trey wanted the home, Shelby advised, they needed to jump quickly. As in yesterday.

So they packed baby Clara into the back seat and drove over early that evening, the late-spring sun still perched high in the sky like an enormous peach. As soon as Kate laid eyes on the house, she knew she had to have it. Six bedrooms, three and a half baths. Good bones. Two large winding staircases of dark oak on either side of the first floor. A separate, charming maid's entrance that led up to its own private garret. The kitchen needed an overhaul, which they agreed to tackle before moving in. There was ample room for themselves along with, Kate liked to imagine, a handful of their friends and family members for summertime visits. In some ways, the Hull house, where she and Clara spend three months of the year now, is where she feels most at home.

"Oh, wow," she whispers when they pull into the driveway. A meadow appears to have sprouted up on their lawn since last September. Purple clover dots the tall grass in the front, and the shrubbery framing the house verges on wild. Pink roses hang off trellises like drunken frat boys, and the rhododendron bushes at the side of the house spiral out of control. She'll have to make a call to Charles, their landscaper, and demand an explanation. Is he ill? Has Trey forgotten to pay him?

In the back seat, Clara stirs, stretching awake.

"We there yet, Mommy?" she asks in a sleepy voice.

"Good timing, kiddo. We just arrived." Kate turns around to face her daughter and knows better than to ask if she had a nice nap; the answer will invariably be *no*. Instead, she coaxes, "C'mon now. Help Mommy with your things." She climbs out and goes around to release Clara, who scrambles down from her car seat and races to the front door, her little backpack bobbing.

"First one here!" she shouts and tags the front step, a game that she and Trey play whenever they arrive to open up the house for Memorial Day weekend.

"You won!" Kate exclaims, although the moment feels bittersweet without Trey. She wonders if Clara senses his absence, too. She grabs the remaining bags from the trunk and joins her daughter on the steps. When she yanks open the storm door, a sea of school board committee flyers and ads for the upcoming Memorial Day parade spill out. Kate gathers them up awkwardly before jiggling the master key into the lock.

Last summer, Trey researched alarm systems for the house, but like so many other well-intentioned projects, it fell through the cracks. Still, there's something about an old-fashioned key unlocking the entrance to their own private Narnia that strikes Kate as appropriate, fitting. The front door swings open, and inside, a damp, musty odor greets them.

"*Pee-yoo.*" Clara pinches her nose dramatically.

"Oh, c'mon. It's not that bad." She flings the mail on the entryway table and strides into the living room to pull back the floor-to-ceiling curtains, releasing dust tornadoes into the air. Despite the chill, she works to undo the window sashes and pushes them open, allowing in a fresh gust of sea air. In the distance, the profile of the lighthouse blinks out its familiar, reassuring beats. "There, that's better," she proclaims and turns to find Clara already absorbed in the Chinese Checkers game on the coffee table, arranging the smooth marbles by color.

Behind her, above the fireplace mantel, hangs the Lancaster family's trademark sign, THE RULES OF SUMMER, inscribed on a three-by-five slab of dark oak. Shelby, who'd been gifted the plaque by their parents years ago, gave it to Kate and Trey as a housewarming gift when they moved in. And what started out as a few scribbles on an easel board one rainy day when their mother was surely trying to keep the girls from killing each other is now a plaque that's as much a part of the house as the pipes running behind its walls.

Kate smiles to see the familiar rules:

IF CAUGHT IN THE RIPTIDE, SWIM PARALLEL TO SHORE.

BE KIND TO YOUR SISTERS.

NO WET BATHING SUITS (OR TOWELS) ON THE FLOOR!

LEAVE A NOTE IF YOU GO OUT.

THE MAID IS OFF DUTY; CLEAN UP AFTER YOURSELVES.

NO ARGUMENT SHOULD LAST LONGER THAN TEN MINUTES.

One by one, she begins liberating the sofas from last summer's protective sheets. The couches are white slipcover sofas from Crate & Barrel, relaxed, easygoing furniture that children can hop onto with damp swimsuits without getting scolded. Even though the slipcovers have yellowed a bit over the winter, they'll be good as new after a quick wash in Clorox. Upstairs, she throws open the bedroom windows for a blast of fresh air, then cranks the thermostat from sixty to seventy-two to cut the chill.

She and Clara decide to go for a short walk down on the beach, and by dusk, they've collected dozens of shells and devoured the pepperoni pizza they picked up from L Street Pizza (delicious as ever). Now Clara snores softly beside her on the sofa while the credits roll on *Paw Patrol: The Movie.* Ever so gently, Kate scoops up her pajamaed daughter and carries her upstairs to their king-size bed. The temperature upstairs is almost comfortable since the heat has been blasting for a few hours; nevertheless, she goes to the linen closet in search of an extra blanket and finds the blue-and-white quilt her mother stitched for her when she complained of the drafty dorm rooms in college. It makes Kate wonder: What would her mom advise, if she were here?

Would she insist that Kate pick up the phone and talk to Trey? Or would she counsel her to let Trey sleep on the error of his ways? Would she encourage Kate to look the other way? Gently, Kate spreads the patchwork quilt across her daughter, whose body is curled up like a tiny comma. In profile, she reminds Kate so much of Trey it almost hurts. The same sloped nose, eyes edged by thick, dark lashes. Lightly, she plants a kiss on the delicate curve of her daughter's cheek.

Back downstairs, she pours herself another glass of wine and unplugs her phone from the charger in the kitchen. Three voicemails and a text from Trey have piled up while she's been watching the movie with Clara in the other room. *Let him worry,* she thinks again. There are also two texts from Shelby; another from Bree. Momentary panic swoops over her. Has something awful happened?

But, no, it's *her* they're calling about. She listens to Trey's messages, his voice growing more urgent with each one. *Katie, hey, where are you? I thought we were having dinner tonight?* Next: *I just found your note. I guess you guys had a change of plans. That's cool. Wish I'd known sooner, though. I could have stayed at the office to get some work done.*

Ha! I bet! Kate thinks. And finally, *Call me back. I'm starting to get worried. Did you guys make it out to the house okay?*

Kate's thumb hovers above Trey's number. She should call, let him know that they're all right. But she's consumed more than half the bottle of pinot noir, and rather than extinguish her fury at her husband, the wine has only served to fuel it.

She decides to text him instead: Hi, we made it here fine. Clara's asleep and I'm wiped out. Going to bed. Talk to you tomorrow.

The text achieves its purpose, letting him know they're okay, but not much else. There are no emojis or hearts or I-love-yous. He must suspect she's pissed. She texts her sisters the same, saying she's going to bed and will catch up with them in the morning.

Upstairs, she brushes her teeth, then climbs into bed, the sheets already warm from Clara's body. Kate drapes a protective arm across her daughter and nestles in more closely. When she does so, her shoulder rubs up against something sharp, sending her fingers searching blindly for it in the dark. But the offending object turns out to be only a stray earring that she removed earlier. She sets it on the bedside table and prays for sleep to reach out and mercifully drag her under.

6

SHELBY

The kitchen table is tipping again. When Shelby puts her elbows down and leans on one end, the other side elevates like a flying saucer. Usually, it's a simple matter of tightening a screw, but she's been under the table several times already and there are no more screws to tighten. She'll have to put Noah on the case. Luckily, her son enjoys projects around the house and has assumed ownership of his dad's toolbox in the garage. Over the past few years, he's amassed an assortment of random screws and nails, epoxy, and wires of various lengths. He'll figure out what's throwing her table off balance.

For the time being, though, she's stuck a crumpled paper towel under one of the legs to hold it level. It'll have to do for now.

She supposes she could ask Bo to investigate once he gets here, but she has the sense that fixing things is not his forte. He's recounted a handful of stories featuring domestic mishaps—crooked picture hangings, flailing gutters, jammed garbage disposals in need of rescue. Plus, Shelby isn't sure that handyman tasks fall under the job description of being someone's lover. Although "lover" sounds so quaint and old-fashioned, almost Victorian. Then again, Bo's not quite her boyfriend, either, seeing as he's already married. Still, why get hung up on semantics when she's got a good thing going?

Bo. Where are you? Her fingers drum the crooked table.

For the last half hour, Tuukka's head has been resting on Shelby's bare feet while she impatiently awaits Bo's arrival. She's wearing a summery white maxi dress with delicate ribbon straps, and her auburn hair is pulled up in a loose bun. A bottle of prosecco sits in the middle of the table, two oversize champagne glasses beside it. The glass closest to her is already halfway drained because she couldn't bear to postpone a sip any longer after the day she's had. First the closing on the Vendler property, then talking Kate down off the ledge. After Kate's call, Shelby texted Bo, telling him not to come over (she was certain her sister would change her mind and show up on her doorstep with Clara in tow). But when Kate texted at seven thirty to say that she and Clara were crashing at the beach house, Shelby took it as a sign that her night was meant to include Bo after all. That and the fact that Noah is staying at Lindsay's until ten o'clock.

Any chance you can still come over?

His reply: Be right there.

But Shelby's definition of "right there" and Bo's definition appear to be off by a good twenty minutes. It's no more than a ten-minute drive from Bo's house down near Gunrock to her place up on Beach Avenue. Maybe Cindy needed him to load the dishwasher or run out to the corner market for milk? Shelby wonders what Cindy must think when Bo announces he's headed out for a few hours. In the past, he's used excuses like meeting up with his buddies at the Beer Garden or going into the office late to finish up paperwork. But does Cindy ever doubt him? If Shelby were she, a nagging suspicion would have crept into her mind months ago. For both their sakes, she hopes Cindy doesn't have a clue.

Because what Shelby has going here is most definitely a clandestine affair. On the evenings when they meet at her house, Bo parks a few blocks away. From there, he walks to her place and circles around back, where he lets himself in through the patio door. Other times, she'll meet him at his office where they'll make love after hours, or on his boat in the marina, or even on Telegraph Hill. And on the rare weekend when Noah stays with his dad, Bo will occasionally sleep over (she has no idea how Bo explains his overnight absences to Cindy, nor does she care to know).

Sometimes, when she's out with her girlfriends at the C Note, dancing to a live band, she can feel herself longing for a man who will wrap his arms around her, maybe even engage in a little PDA. Her friend Diana has a gorgeous thirtysomething boyfriend—long blond surfer hair, muscled upper torso, dimples the size of lagoons—who is *very* into public displays of affection, and Shelby will find herself twirling alone on the dance floor while Diana's and Colin's bodies writhe together rhythmically. Just once, it would be nice to enjoy a sunset at Local 02045, the charming restaurant perched over the bay on the west side of town, with Bo sitting beside her. She imagines them sipping super-potent margaritas while Bo secretly tries to snake his hand up her leg underneath the table. Every so often, she fantasizes about these dates while also understanding they're impossible.

At least until Bo leaves his wife.

And that is the ultimate, never-ending question, isn't it? Because as unhappy as he claims to be in his marriage, its pull on him is like nickel or cobalt, magnetic and binding. It's his two daughters, he says, who are keeping him there, and while Shelby admires this, considers it noble even, it's also exceptionally inconvenient. Bo's daughters are around Noah's age. Which means at least two or three more years until they're officially off to college and out of the house. Three long years before Bo could potentially be a free man. Can Shelby wait that long? She tells herself she can, but honestly, who knows?

So much can change in a month, let alone a year.

There's also a part of her that wonders: Once their relationship no longer requires sneaking around, will it lose its power, its allure? Is it possible that Bo Bannister is being cavalier with her heart? She shoos the question out of her mind. After all, he's told her that making love to her is the best he's ever had. That his feelings for her are so intense, they scare him.

Just then, there's a slight tapping at the back door. *Bo.* As soon as he lets himself in, Tuukka bounds across the living room floor.

"Tuukka, stop that!" Shelby demands, trying to pull his paws off Bo's chest, even though she kind of loves that her dog is as excited as she is.

"Whoa, there, buddy. How're you doing?" Bo says, laughing. If he weren't a vet, Shelby would be mortified by Tuukka's behavior, but Bo has come prepared. From his back pocket, he pulls out a treat and tosses it into the kitchen, sending the dog scrambling after it.

"Well, hello there," he says, turning toward her. "Maybe now I can give *you* a proper greeting." He folds her into his arms, and for a long, intoxicating minute, they kiss. Goose bumps race up and down her body while she inhales his scent, a mixture of fresh soap and spearmint gum.

"Sorry it took forever," he says when he pulls away.

"No need to apologize," she teases. "I like long kisses."

"I had to clean up a bit. Before heading over."

But the reason for the delay doesn't matter anymore. Bo could have been napping, for all she cares; he's here now. Before she can get the words "I've missed you" out, his hands are climbing up under her dress, along her thighs. He leans in to kiss her again and walks her backward, while she works hurriedly to unbutton, then unzip his jeans. She peels off his shirt, runs her hands over his tanned torso. When he begins to lower her onto the kitchen table, she cries out, "No!" and Bo shoots her a confused look. "I mean, not here," she explains. "The table's broken. I have to get it fixed."

"Couch?" he suggests agreeably.

Shelby nods, and he works to slide the straps of her sundress over her shoulders.

"It unzips in the back," she whispers.

"Damn zippers," he says, fiddling with it, and she can barely suppress a laugh.

Once unzipped, the dress slides off easily enough, and a passing thought—that they should move to the bedroom in case Noah returns—disappears as soon as her body connects with Bo's. On the couch, his tongue traces her skin, from her neck to her abdomen, where he tells her he loves her butterfly tattoo. Then he's back on top of her, inside her, and Shelby's mind travels to a faraway place where all her worries evaporate like iridescent bubbles popping in the air; there's no room for thoughts about house closings or Noah's salty attitude or her sisters' problems. Only colors, undulating swaths of warm blues and brilliant purples, until it's over, almost as quickly as it began.

Shelby lets herself linger in the moment, reluctant to open her eyes and allow reality to sneak back in.

"Soo . . ." Bo nuzzles his face into her neck. "That happened kind of fast." His five-o'clock shadow scratches against her skin. "Was it, um, okay?"

"Better than okay," she says softly. Reluctantly, she cracks one eye open, then the other, only to discover his gray-blue eyes mere inches away, staring directly into hers. For a moment, she wishes she could make herself minuscule—the size of an amoeba, maybe—and backstroke through his pupils so she could see herself, quite literally, through his eyes.

"You're so beautiful," he says now, gently running a thumb across her cheek and making her stomach do a happy, surprised flip. It's a word that Ethan never uttered to her, not once in twenty-some years. Did he think it was corny? Or was it possible he didn't consider her beautiful? Pretty or cute, sure. But beautiful? It was as if the adjective hadn't existed in her ex-husband's word bank.

"I've missed you," Bo says.

"Me too." Almost every time they're together, he offers this sentiment, and Shelby naturally agrees. But what can she say that will make him come over more often? That will make him *stay*? It's simpler to agree and move on. *Live in the moment,* she tells herself. *Enjoy what you have now. You're beautiful,* she reminds herself. Her fingers comb through his dark hair.

They lie this way for a few more minutes, Bo's arms cradled around her, his heart so close to hers that she can feel it beating through his skin. She allows herself to imagine what it might be like to do this every night, any morning they chose. Would it grow old, a gesture that they'd eventually take for granted? Or would it serve as the perfect bookend to the start and close of each day? Her mind tries to take purchase on the idea until there's a rustling noise at the front door. Tuukka starts barking and races to the entryway.

"Oh no," she says. *Noah!*

She catapults out from underneath Bo and drops to the floor, performing an awkward crab crawl to her dress. "No, no, no," she repeats and whips Bo's T-shirt and boxers in his direction, which land on the floor in a heap.

"What the—"

"Noah!" she whisper-screams and grabs her bra. All these months and now they've blown it—her son will know her secret, that she's been sleeping with Ashley and Caitlin's father. They've gotten too comfortable sneaking around; they've let their guard down. *Such idiots!*

She checks the wall clock. Noah is early, as in two hours before curfew! She shimmies into her dress, tucks her bra underneath a sofa cushion, and nods frantically toward the deck, signaling for Bo to sneak out the back. But as soon as he gets one leg into his jeans, Tuukka ceases barking and collapses on the braided mudroom rug, as content as a drunken slug.

Shelby holds her breath and tiptoes to the long rectangular window that runs parallel to the door. What will she say to her son if he's waiting on the other side? But after a peek, her lips part into a smile. "Come look," she says, practically giddy.

Bo tiptoes cautiously in her direction, glances through the window, and starts to laugh—a huge belly laugh. And then Shelby's laughing, too, and she can't stop. *It's such a relief!*

Because it's not Noah standing on her seagrass welcome mat but a medium-size Amazon box. The new coffee press she ordered two days ago.

"Want me to grab it?" he asks, once they've stopped.

"Um, absolutely not. We don't want the neighbors seeing you here."

"Ah, right. Manners—an old habit."

"Come on, let's have some prosecco."

He shakes his head, says, "Not sure I'm fully recovered from that little scare. What if Noah found me with one leg in my jeans going out the patio door?"

Shelby giggles, despite herself. "I honestly have no idea how we'd explain it. But I'm sure glad we don't have to."

She grabs the bottle, pouring him a fresh glass before refilling her own. Out on the deck, they settle into the Adirondack chairs facing the water. The happy result of a long-ago remodeling project, a sturdy, ten-foot-high fence encloses either side of the backyard to guard against any nosy neighbors. Here they can relax in total, blissful privacy.

Until Bo's phone rings.

He glances at it and holds up a finger. "Sorry, this will just take a sec." Shelby smiles and prays that it's not Cindy, calling him home. But then, after a minute, Bo says, "I wouldn't worry about it, Ms. Harding. I'm sure Archie will be fine. There's no need to pump his stomach if it was only a couple of cookies. I've known dogs to do much worse." He pauses, then laughs. "Not a problem at all. That's what I'm here for. Okay, then, I'll talk to you later."

When he clicks off, he apologizes again. "Sorry for the interruption. That was Maeve Harding. Worried because her schnauzer got into a bag of chocolate chip cookies."

"Ah." At the mention of Maeve's name, Shelby's displeasure must show on her face. "The downside of being an on-call vet. Everyone's got a crisis."

Bo laughs easily. "It's not so bad. Why do I get the sense that you two aren't best friends?"

Shelby shrugs. She doesn't feel like airing other people's dirty laundry at the moment. Not on this gorgeous almost-summer evening. Even though, if she wanted to, she could give Bo an earful about how Maeve has badmouthed just about all Shelby's girlfriends at one time or another.

"It's not important," she says now. "Maeve is who she is, you know?"

Bo tilts his head. "That's another reason I like you. You have a hard time being mean."

Shelby laughs. "Um, have you met me?"

"I have." He smirks. "And I like what I see. In fact, I'd like to make a toast." He hoists his glass in the air. "To wonderful you. You've managed to sell the one house in Hull that no one thought would ever sell."

Shelby clinks his glass and sips. "*Of course* it was going to sell. It was only a question of time and for how much."

"Your confidence is enviable." He hikes his bare feet onto the bottom railing. "You've gotta admit, though . . . that place needed a ton of work."

"True. But it's transformed. Really, you wouldn't recognize it now. *South Shore Magazine* is coming out to do a photo shoot next week. They're featuring the house in their 'Best of Summer' issue." She watches surprise register on his face.

"I'm impressed."

Shelby thinks back to the cobwebs running along the banisters. The stale smell permeating the stained carpets, the ancient kitchen appliances. But with a little ingenuity and the help of a few contractors, she was able to comb away the cobwebs, pull up the carpets to reveal gorgeous hardwood floors underneath, and replace all the appliances with top-of-the-line stainless steel. A fresh coat of cream paint for the dark wooden beams accenting the ceilings, and voilà! The Vendler property was transformed, every bit worth its asking price of $2.5 million. It *had* been much more work than she'd imagined, more of a house flip than a straightforward sale, but in her humble opinion, the Vendler house is one of her finest achievements.

Above them, the purpling sky is starting to darken, and the fading light dances across the water like a million tiny silverfish. A soft breeze sends her flag flapping in the salty air. After a quiet moment, Bo shifts in his seat and asks, "Hey, how's your sister doing? Everything okay?"

Shelby tilts her head over one shoulder, then the other, and ponders how best to respond. Honestly? Cavalierly?

"I think so," she says finally. "She's doing all right, considering." Earlier, when she had to cancel their date night, she explained, in murky terms via text, the reason for Kate's distress. Explained that her sister was freaking out over something stupid her husband had done and that she might be coming over tonight. Shelby failed to mention, however, that Kate's husband might be having an affair. Because the irony of the situation isn't lost on her. How can she judge Trey (if, in fact, that's what he's doing) while she's the biggest adulteress on their small peninsula?

"She's staying at her beach house with Clara. That's my niece," Shelby reminds him. "I'm going to talk to her tomorrow."

"Sounds good," he says. "I'm sure you guys will figure it out." The way the words tumble out of him, as if heartache, anyone's heartache, were so easily fixed, gives her a brief pinch of irritation, though she can't exactly say why.

Bo has never met Kate, so he has no idea of the complicated history the sisters share or that Shelby has been jealous of Kate pretty much her entire life—or, at least, as long as Kate has existed in the world, which is six years fewer than Shelby. Kate is everything that Shelby is not—stunning, whip smart, gregarious. A natural extrovert. Throughout their childhood, everyone naturally gravitated toward Kate. It was Kate who could recite the presidents in chronological order at dinner parties. Kate, who, at age ten, memorized Robert Frost's poem "The Road Not Taken." Kate played the role of the charming, precocious daughter, while Shelby was the child who awkwardly stood by in the shadows. Bree, the baby, was nothing but cuteness personified, easily loved and doted upon.

Add to that Shelby's paralyzing shyness as a young child and it was a cinch to forget her, overlook her. On the first day of kindergarten, she famously *ran away* during recess, back to her house a few blocks away (this was before every elementary school had electronically controlled doors and gates). Her mother spun her around and marched her straight back to the classroom. But Shelby made up for her childhood diffidence during her teenage years, rebelling every chance she got. Billy Joel's

"Only the Good Die Young" quickly became her mantra; even though she wasn't Catholic, she *was* a minister's daughter, and it felt as if the song's lyrics were singing directly to her soul. When Hank Reacher stole her virginity at age sixteen in the back of his Chevy, Shelby was only too happy to hand it over.

If the sisters were a set of dinner plates, Shelby thinks, Kate would be the most exquisite Tiffany fine china, whereas Shelby would be Crate & Barrel tableware—functional, attractive, but nothing fancy. Bree would be . . . Well, the jury was still out on that one. Monastic wooden bowls?

It's possible that somewhere buried deep inside her subconscious, Shelby has been trying to upstage her younger sister, not by beating her at what she does best but by being Kate's polar opposite. Shelby was grounded more times than should be humanly possible, whereas Kate and Bree were shackled to the house only a handful of times. But when Ethan came along, something in Shelby shifted. It was as if she could finally stop pretending that she was someone she wasn't. When Ethan presented himself at a football game junior year (he was the guy standing in front of her in the hot chocolate line; when he got an extra by mistake, he handed it over), it was as if her own personal measuring stick—Kate—fell to the wayside. All that mattered was that Ethan loved her, that Ethan thought she was enough.

Until, many years later, when she realized that Ethan wasn't enough for *her*.

Bo reaches his hand across the open space between them and winds his fingers through hers.

"I really missed you last week," he says again. His voice is softer, more serious. He leans toward her, and she can almost feel the heat rising from his skin. His gray-blue eyes search hers, and a flicker of emotion—vulnerability? love?—crosses it. For a second, Shelby thinks he might actually say it, articulate the one word she's been running over her tongue for the last few months. She cocks her head, waiting, encouraging.

"What?" she asks. "What's that look for?"

But then it passes, the flicker snuffed out as quickly as it arrived, making her wonder if it ever existed in the first place. "Oh, nothing." He settles back in his chair, his gaze returning to the ocean. "Just that I've missed you."

Shelby's heart dips down somewhere around her diaphragm. "So you said." There will be no grand declarations of love, apparently. At least, not tonight. Earlier, she'd been considering mentioning Turks and Caicos, thinking they might be ready to take the next leap—a vacation together. But in the descending twilight, the idea strikes her as ridiculous, foolhardy even. *No, Bo needs more time,* she decides. More time to realize how fabulous she is. Tomorrow, Shelby will remind her sister how lucky she is to have Trey and how being "back out there" is no fun. To not jeopardize her marriage with silly second-guessing. And although there might be a part of her that would secretly enjoy watching her sister fail at something as profound as her marriage—call it "sibling schadenfreude"—she suspects Kate is in the wrong here. Trey, despite his occasional bravado, strikes Shelby as a genuinely good guy. There's no way he would cheat on her sister.

It's then that she notices the wide grin on Bo's face. "You know what I'm thinking?"

"Nope."

"It's only ten minutes to nine," he says, glancing at his watch. "Noah won't be home for another hour." He nods toward the outdoor shower. Shelby has lost count of how many times she and Bo have made love under its warm spray, the milky night sky unraveling above them. "Feeling dirty?" he asks.

And Shelby, against her better judgment, says, "You know what? As a matter of fact, I am." She jumps up and pulls him from his chair.

Why not? she thinks as she leads him by the hand to the shower. *Why on earth not?*

7

KATE

Thursday, May 16

The next morning, Kate wakes slowly, last night's wine knocking at her temples, a thick web of confusion muddying her thoughts. Tylenol, coffee, beach. It's her self-prescribed cure-all for last night's mistakes. Clara stirs, and Kate gently nudges her awake before dressing her in a pair of sweats. It's too cold for bathing suits this morning. They head out to the garage, where she grabs an assortment of pails and shovels, her chair from last summer, a raggedy beach blanket. It all gets tossed in the car, and they make a quick stop at Weinberg's for coffee and bagels (she promised Clara last night) before heading to Nantasket.

With a good night's sleep (or a drunken stupor) behind her, Kate allows that she may have overreacted to the whole Trey incident yesterday. When she checked her phone this morning, he'd already called and left a voicemail. _Hey, babe, call me as soon as you guys are awake, okay? Missed you last night._ She'll call him once she gets Clara settled on the beach.

They pull into one of several free parking spaces near the bathhouse, a rarity in the height of summer. There's not another soul around. Eventually, they wind their way down to the beach, where the rocks give way to an inviting stretch of sand. A cool breeze nips at their cheeks, but otherwise, it's a gorgeous morning, the sun making its slow ascent in a cloudless blue sky.

Kate shakes out the beach blanket and dumps the water toys from the bucket, making Clara's pudgy hands clap in delight. "I dig, Mama!" she exclaims.

"You've got it, squirt."

While her daughter entertains herself, Kate settles into her chair and takes a moment to replay yesterday's events in her mind.

So: she witnessed her husband kissing another woman. The shock of it, the instant outrage has dulled to more of a slow burn in the last twenty-four hours. Or, she supposes, it's possible she's numb. She feels marginally embarrassed by her theatrics yesterday, calling Shelby and insisting Trey was having an affair, absconding with Clara as if he couldn't be trusted with his own daughter.

Was it really all necessary?

At the time, absolutely. But now, through the prism of time, she can see how her reaction might be construed as a colossal overreaction. It was only a kiss, for heaven's sake. There could be a million different explanations. Whatever she thought she saw or felt in her gut isn't necessarily the truth. Shelby is right: she needs to at least give Trey a chance to tell his side of the story.

On the first ring, he picks up. "Hey, babe. Where are you? Still out in Hull?"

"Yeah, Clara and I are sitting on the beach as we speak."

"Nice. I'm jealous. I missed you guys last night. What happened?"

Kate chews on a fingernail, uncertain where or whether to begin. She laughs nervously. "Um, I guess a lot has happened, actually." Her statement is initially met with silence.

"What's going on, Katie? It's not like you to take off like that."

She swallows—and begins. "So Clara and I saw you yesterday when we were in town. Remember, we went to the aquarium? And we were, um, driving home, through the Financial District, and Clara saw you."

She pauses, unsure whether or not to continue. "And you were kissing someone." The ugly, jagged words spill out of her.

On the other end, Trey inhales sharply. "What? What are you talking about?" She imagines him in his brown leather swivel chair at the office, his eyes trained on the city below, taking measure of his proverbial kingdom. A Starbucks caramel latte will sit at his left elbow. To his right will be a yellow legal pad enumerating a lengthy list of tasks to be completed by day's end. She wonders if "call Katie" appears anywhere on that list, and if, when he left her a message this morning, he drew a neat line through it and thought, *Task completed.*

She imagines his clear green eyes, the deep dimple in the middle of his chin, the salt-and-pepper hair that's in need of a trim. The way his forehead furrows whenever he's concerned. She wonders if he took the time to shave this morning, or if there's a midnight shadow peppering his jawline. The physical pang of missing him cuts through her body, despite the fact that she'd also like to give him a solid kick.

"Trey, I *saw* you with that woman."

"What woman?"

"Oh, come on. Please don't make this worse by trying to deny it." Yesterday's anger resurges in her chest. She thinks back to when Clara first spotted him on the street. Even Kate had been skeptical that it was Trey, but when he turned to look at that woman and she glimpsed his face, there was zero doubt in Kate's mind that she was staring at her husband. "You know, the petite woman with the long black hair?" She can't bring herself to spit out the word *attractive*. She won't give him the satisfaction.

"Oh, *her*," he says, as if he's known all along whom she's referring to, and makes an attempt at casual laughter. "Katie, it's not what you think. Not even close."

"And what am I thinking? Tell me, Trey. I'm really curious. Can you even begin to guess?" Clara's shovel stops in midair, and she gazes up at her mother, concerned. Kate blows her an air-kiss, as if to say, *Don't worry. Mama's not mad at* you.

"Well, you're pretty pissed at me. That much is clear. But that kiss was *nothing*. You're getting worked up for no reason. Come on, you know me, babe. Do you honestly think I would cheat on you?"

The question stops her. *Does she?* Does she believe that her husband, whom she loves, would cheat on her while he's away at the office? It's so predictable—woman quits job to stay at home with baby (and loses her sense of self-worth in the process) while husband goes cavorting around with a mistress, having the time of his life—that it's almost too ludicrous, too *prosaic*, to be true.

But, of course, it's still possible.

"So tell me what I saw, then. If I'm so clearly misreading the situation." Sarcasm coats her words, even though she's hoping that he'll offer up a credible explanation—anything, really, to prove that this is all a huge mistake. She's ready for it to be over. To move on, to climb out of the sandbox and dust off her hands, if only he'll say the right thing now, whatever that might be.

"Look, it's not what you think."

"Uh-huh, you've said that already. So tell me. What was it?" The fact that he's stalling is doing little to calm her nerves. Does he really need time to devise an excuse?

He lets out a long sigh. "Look. I'm gonna be honest."

"How refreshing," she snaps.

"Liz was in town yesterday for a business meeting. She called me at the last minute to see if I wanted to grab a bite for lunch."

Kate's mind spins until she feels dizzy. Liz? As in *Liz Macintosh*? Trey's old girlfriend from law school? A skewer of jealousy twists up through her chest, and she has to push up out of her chair to go lie prostrate on the blanket. Her left arm is bent upward, her wrist resting on her forehead. "I'm sorry. For a minute, I thought you said Liz. As in your ex-girlfriend?"

"Yeah. Katie, listen to me. It was no big deal. We were saying goodbye, and I guess I kind of leaned in to hug her and it turned into a quick kiss. Just a friendly kiss goodbye. Nothing more."

Kate struggles to process this. The woman she saw, petite with long, dark hair, did not at all resemble the woman she remembers Trey showing her pictures of when she asked to see some long ago. The few photos she's seen of Liz were all taken at the beach, when she was sunburned and had short, spiky brown hair. It's possible, she supposes, that Liz has lost some weight, grown her hair out, taken up Bikram yoga in the last ten years. Admittedly, Kate only got a glimpse of her from the car yesterday.

It's a risky move, she thinks, *dredging up his old girlfriend to skate past potential trouble.* Why bother, unless he knows Kate is onto him? Unless it's true?

"Kate, come on. You know Liz is married with two kids."

Does Kate know this? No, she does not, but whatever. Liz's marital status strikes her as entirely irrelevant at the moment.

"Anyway, you saw that one moment in time. The rest of the time, we were talking about our families. I told her all about you guys, how awesome you and Clara are."

The absurdity of this comment prompts an outburst from Kate. "Ha! I'll bet."

"She lives in Seattle. I'll probably never see her again."

Kate considers this. Is Trey lying? Her husband of five years? When she tries to speak, a small, incoherent squeak comes out.

"Katie, come on," he pleads. "It's me." How she wishes she could see his expression right now; it's so much easier to tell face-to-face when someone's lying. "Listen," he continues, "when I say it was nothing, it was *nothing.*"

There's an aggressiveness to this comment that makes her skin prickle, as if it's been decided, case closed. It's the same manner in which Trey will occasionally address her over the phone when he's at work—curt, so sure of himself. Exasperating. There's no room for doubt or equivocation of any kind. But something else is bugging her: If Trey is so innocent, why didn't he mention the lunch to her beforehand?

"Why didn't you tell me you were having lunch with Liz in the first place?" she presses.

"I explained that to you: she called at the last minute."

"When?"

"What do mean, when? I don't know. Sometime yesterday morning. Before lunch," he adds, moronically.

A hot shimmer skates across the back of her neck. "But you told me the night before that you were completely booked for the day. That you couldn't possibly meet me and Clara in town for lunch. Honestly, what gives, Trey?"

There's a weighty sigh. "Okay, look, you got me. Satisfied?" Kate pulls her body upright, wraps her arms around her knees, and digs her toes more deeply into the sand, bracing for the truth. "Liz emailed me a few days ago to say she'd be in town. I didn't mention it because I thought you'd get upset. Which clearly you are. Over nothing, I might add."

This knowledge somehow rattles Kate even more than the kiss itself. Trey *knew* Liz was coming to town, made plans with her, and never once mentioned it?

"I'm not crazy, Trey. I saw you guys holding hands, too." This, she realizes, is the other memory that's been fighting to bubble to the surface. Now that she's said it, however, the image surges fully into focus. Trey and Liz holding hands, their arms practically swinging as they stood on the curb and waited to cross.

"Christ, give it up, will you? I don't know what else to tell you, Katie. We're old friends. End of story." Trey muffles the phone with his hand while he tells a colleague, "Be right there." She hates this version of her husband, the one who's suddenly too busy, too important to talk to her. She imagines him rolling his eyes, mouthing the words, *It's my wife*, to whoever has stepped into his office. "Listen, we'll talk about it later, okay? I've gotta go. I'll drive out tonight after work."

It's a stunning retort, given the conversation they're having. There's so much more to unpack, such as: Does Trey still have feelings for Liz?

Is there unfinished business between the two of them that he's not sharing? Her husband can be dangerously convincing when he needs to be, his attorney skills impeccably honed, like a carving knife. He's great at thinking on his feet. Which makes arguing with him often futile—and hugely frustrating.

"Sure, whatever. I've got to go, too. Shelby's on the other line," she lies.

But Trey has already hung up. Kate flings the phone across the blanket, sending it skittering onto the sand like a startled crab. Clara looks up, surprised, then resumes digging.

Could she, Kate wonders, ever give an innocent kiss to an old boyfriend? She tries to imagine it, but . . . *No!* The thought makes her physically recoil. She knows she wouldn't—*couldn't*—do such a thing. She's *married*.

Deep in her bone marrow, Kate understands that straying isn't a possibility for her. It would be akin to leaving Clara behind at the park or burning down her own house. Unthinkable acts. It's true that the kisses exchanged with her husband of late have been underwhelming. But Kate's loyalty is steadfast, unwavering. If the circumstances were reversed, there's no way she would have leaned in for that kiss, nor would she have accepted it.

She sips her cooling coffee and tries to think if she's always been the jealous type. Probably not since George Thompson dumped her for Charlene Winthrop, senior year in high school. Kate had been devastated—she and George were voted homecoming king and queen. But then they got into a huge fight (Kate can't even recall about what now) and George blew her off and invited Charlene instead. Kate ended up going with her girlfriends, although she had to march into the gymnasium—transformed into a winter wonderland—on George's arm while she seethed.

All through college, there was a procession of young men in her life, boys to whom she never gave much thought. Dating as many guys as possible seemed the most promising route to figuring out what she wanted in a boyfriend, a husband. There was Joshua, then Matt and Shane and Harry. Most of them sporty, fraternity types—a parade of masculinity. But the one who came closest to stealing her heart was Rowan, part Irish poet, part artist. Junior year, they spent hours together, getting high on cheap weed in Rowan's off-campus apartment. While she soaked below the bubbles in his glorious cast-iron tub, he'd perch on the tub's edge and read Allen Ginsberg to her. It was, perhaps, the sexiest foreplay she's ever experienced.

When college ended, though, it quickly became evident that Rowan would forever be a writer/artist, both in spirit and in wallet. And Kate, quite simply, wanted more. More than what she grew up with. More than a shabby house and well-meaning parents for whom a "trip" meant a visit to the Boston Common on a Sunday afternoon. Kate dreamed of a life that included vacations in Paris and Rome, a rambling house filled with dinner parties and witty conversation. Somewhere along the way, she acquired a taste for the good life, and when she met Trey, it was as if the heavens handed her her very own tastemaker. Handsome, intelligent, funny, thoughtful, and a lawyer. But loyal? She never gave it a second thought. He loved her; naturally, he'd be loyal.

She and Trey will talk later tonight. This *thing*—whatever it is—is a mere hiccup, a speed bump. It will all get sorted out. It has to, for Clara's sake. Kate reaches for the bright-blue pail, the one with the broken handle, and asks, "Okay if I play, too, honey?"

Her daughter bobs her head in the affirmative. "Yes, Mama. You can dig over here." She points to an area beside her, and Kate goes to sit where directed.

"Maybe I'll build a sandcastle," she says absently, pulling up great heaps of sand with her hands.

At least now, she thinks, she knows the truth.

There's that.

Or does she?

8

Bree

On Thursday morning, Bree wakes up feeling almost human again. Her mouth is as dry as a martini, but the exquisite pain has subsided. And her cheeks, when she touches them, feel more like small plums than apples. She climbs out of bed to gargle with salt water, but once she's in the bathroom, the thought of standing under the shower's warm thrum is practically irresistible. She's been wearing her pajamas for the past two days; even she's starting to notice a ripe smell emanating from her body, and a quick glance in the mirror confirms that she looks like crap.

She turns on the spigot, waits for the water to warm. When the spray hits her body, a ridiculous sense of being reborn sweeps over her, as if regular life might be possible once again. Her head no longer feels detached from the rest of her body. Her stomach is still sour, but that's probably just the medicine's fault—and the fact that she hasn't eaten much in the last forty-eight hours. For the first time in days, she's hungry. As soon as she's dried off and changed, she'll make french toast.

When she tries phoning Kate later, her sister's cell instantly goes to voicemail. "Hi, it's me. Finally starting to feel a little bit better. Just wanted to say thanks again for picking me up the other day and for all the books. Um, I guess that's it. Call me." She refrains from mentioning Shelby's call last night. Better to let Kate fill her in herself.

Besides, chances are the whole thing has blown over by now. Even though Bree isn't surprised to hear that Trey was spotted with another woman (she witnessed it herself!), that doesn't mean he's having a full-fledged affair. The woman might still be a colleague or a friend—although the kissing part is harder to explain. Maybe, Bree considers, Kate *thought* she saw Trey kissing another woman, but it was actually a different guy. All those men in the Financial District look alike, anyway. It could have been an easy mix-up.

And yet.

And yet, there's a feeling in the pit of her stomach that this is serious. That this time differs from the other little tiffs that Kate has chronicled for her over the past few years, such as Trey forgetting about a dinner date or Trey signing up for a weekend golf tournament and neglecting to tell her, leaving Kate home alone with Clara.

She tries Shelby next, to thank her for the peanut brittle (*ha!*), but she's not picking up either. Then Bree remembers that it's Thursday, and Shelby—and the rest of the world—is probably at work. She could call into What's Brewing?, hear what she's missed, but does she really want them to know that she's feeling better? She planned on taking the rest of the week off.

No, she decides she'll get dressed and head into the studio, try to get some work done on a lithograph she's been preparing for weeks, the abstract bodies of two women bent toward each other, as if twirling in the air. A take on Matisse's famous painting *The Dance*, it's the best thing she's produced in weeks. She's been imagining it printed in vibrant, bold colors, like the ones Matisse used. Maybe a bright yellow and cerulean blue, a touch of indigo. For the moment, the working title is *Two Women in Passing*, although maybe that's too obvious. *Too quaint,* she thinks now, given her dating history. Before heading out, she throws some clothes and her toothbrush into her backpack along with her sketch pad. If she can get ahold of Shelby later, she'll ask if she can drive out and spend the night at her place, maybe stay the weekend.

Because as much as Bree hates to admit it, she doesn't like being alone. Especially when she's sick, or in this case, recovering. When Hannah was around, she'd bring Bree homemade Chicken Thukpa from the Tibetan restaurant down the street whenever she caught a cold. When Hannah was around, she'd fix her cups of ginger tea and massage the sore spot between Bree's shoulder blades, where the sickness inevitably seemed to settle.

When Hannah was around, life was, well, *better*.

And even though the past few months have been peppered with an occasional one-night stand, usually after barhopping with her friends downtown, the intimacy of those hookups doesn't compare to what she and Hannah shared. The passion, intense in the moment, flickers out shortly thereafter, sometimes so quickly that a random lover will leave Bree's apartment before daylight even breaks. And as much as she's loath to admit it, Bree's starting to feel her age among the younger women she meets at the clubs. A serious relationship seems like the furthest idea from their minds. Bree gets it; she remembers the insouciance of her twenties. But she misses the way Hannah's fingers would trail along her skin, sparking an almost electrical current through her veins. Misses the way Hannah could finish her sentences. Misses spying her girlfriend crossing Newbury Street to meet her for a post-work drink.

Since Hannah's departure, there's been no one to fill that void.

It's hard enough that every time Bree finishes a print, she's reminded of her ex-girlfriend. That her art, her very job, is tied up in her complicated emotions for her former lover. There's a piece of her, she knows, that yearns for Hannah's expert opinion. On this most recent drawing, for instance. Probably because it features two women dancing happily together—or are they? There's enough space between the figures that they could also be spinning away from each other. If she sends a photo of the finished print to Hannah, Bree wonders, will it remind her of their time together? Will it make her want to come back home?

If she cared to probe more deeply, there's also probably some weird psychological reason why Bree still hungers for Hannah's praise, her approval. Has Bree found "her voice," the one Hannah told her over a year ago that she needed to refine? Bree can sense a new maturity creeping into her most recent projects, a firmness in both her choice of subject matter and in its evocation. It's secretly thrilling, but she trusts only Hannah to confirm this, to tell her that she's ready.

The catch-22 aspect of her dilemma does not escape her. Hannah wants Bree to be more sophisticated—both in life and in her art—and yet Bree can't mature fully in her art unless she receives her ex-lover's approval.

Behind her, she locks the apartment door and makes her way along the dimly lit hallway, where someone has left a bag of take-out Chinese food by a neighbor's door. Downstairs in the lobby, she goes to unlock her mailbox, where—*surprise!*—more bills come spilling out. Rather than sift through them, though, she shoves them back inside. She's in no mood to deal with her financial straits. No, right now she's in desperate need of a little sisterly TLC. A night of gossiping and watching bad movies together. A hug from her nephew. A lick from Shelby's overly affectionate golden retriever. A milkshake. She tries Shelby again, but there's no answer.

Maybe I'll just go, she thinks. *What's Shelby going to do? Turn me away?* The thought occurs to her that perhaps her sisters could use some TLC, too. It's almost as if she can feel her mother's hand giving her a small shove in Hull's direction. *Family's everything, girls,* she was fond of saying. *Whatever you do, don't take each other for granted.*

Bree steps through the front door of the apartment complex, out into the crisp spring air. She breathes deeply, waiting for the oxygen to fill her lungs, and when the sun, greeting her for the first time in two days, dances across her upturned face, an inexplicably hopeful feeling washes over her. As if everything might be okay again. She practically skips to the studio.

9

SHELBY

Shelby is enjoying lunch with a small group of friends at Shipwreck'd out on Pemberton Point, not far from the high school and the soccer fields. The cool bite of the morning air has given way to a surprisingly pleasant afternoon, warm enough to comfortably sit outside on the deck, where cheerful yellow umbrellas dot blue tables.

Each month, this particular group of friends gathers for lunch at one of Hull's finest establishments to catch up on one another's lives—and all the local gossip. There's Julia, whom Shelby has known since moving to town twenty-some years ago when they waitressed together at Jake's Seafood. Julia is tall and skinny with straight black hair, high cheekbones, and an air about her that can best be described as intimidating if you don't know her. She also happens to be hilarious. Shelby and Julia are privy to each other's darkest secrets, although incredibly, Shelby has somehow managed to keep her relationship with Bo hidden from her friend. Incredibly, because Julia typically manages to extract Shelby's most shameful confidences, like the time when she and Ethan got caught having sex behind the grandstand during the Winter Fair by the town's master of ceremonies.

But Bo is *married*; Shelby can tell no one about them.

Then there's Meghan, petite, shoulder-length blonde hair, who owns a dog bakery shop in Hingham, but who was born in Hull and lives here now with her husband and young son. Shelby is fairly certain that Meghan possesses enough energy to power Hull's wind turbine for a month, if necessary. And finally, there's Georgie, another Realtor in town (a competitor!), who became Shelby's fast friend five years ago when they both got stiffed by the same buyer who made offers on their respective listings and then bowed out. Georgie is a few years older than the rest of the group, but she dyes her hair a deep blonde and gets her eyebrows tinted once a month in order to, as she puts it, "keep herself relevant."

Shelby loves these women almost as much as she loves her sisters, and some days, maybe even more. With them, there's no sibling rivalry, no drama whatsoever about who wore whose sweater or which child is the most loved.

"So how's the house on Q Street?" Georgie asks, sounding genuinely curious. She dips a fried clam into a tub of cocktail sauce and pops it in her mouth.

"Good," says Shelby. "At least I think so." Her fried haddock is piping hot, and she blows on it before taking a bite. "I did a run-through yesterday, and it looks in decent shape. It needs a few fixes before I list it. I'm hoping to get five hundred thousand, maybe six."

Georgie nods. "Interesting what those Alphabet street houses are going for these days. How many bedrooms?"

"Three bedrooms, one and a half baths. About fifteen hundred square feet. It's cute. Hardwood floors throughout. It'd make a nice starter home or a summer place."

Meghan shakes her head, disbelieving. "Who ever thought that a little cape in the Alphabets would one day fetch half a million dollars? It's incredible."

"Correction," Shelby adds. "I *hope* it will bring in that much. The open house is in a couple of weeks."

Georgie waves her hand in the air, her fingers glimmering with multiple silver rings, as if it's a foregone conclusion. "I'd put money on that place being gone within twenty-four hours of the open house." A speck of cocktail sauce hovers near the edge of her mouth, and Shelby reaches across the table to dab it with a napkin.

"Hold still a sec. You've got some sauce," she explains, wiping it away. "There, that's better."

"Thank you, honey." Georgie laughs. "What would I do without you guys to look after me?"

Shelby knows she's kidding, but she can't help but think her friend is onto something. These are the kinds of gestures that they'll be called upon to perform for each other as they age. Wipe away an errant crumb. Offer a much-needed tissue. Slip a broken tooth into the outside pocket of a purse for safekeeping until they can get to the dentist's office. It's bittersweet, both to know that she'll have friends to perform these small acts of kindness for her and to realize it's maybe not so far off in their future.

"Anyway, you've got yourself a deal," Shelby says now, agreeing to Georgie's bet. "Next lunch is on me if I sell Q Street within a day of the open house."

"I look forward to it." Georgie grins. "Hey, did you guys hear about Maeve Harding?"

"No, why?" Meg asks.

"I heard she broke her wrist in two different places."

"Ouch! How awful. Do you know how?"

Georgie's expression darkens. "Probably someone broke it for her."

"Georgie! You're terrible." But Shelby's laughing. There's no love lost for Maeve Harding at this table. A native of Hull, Maeve works in the town clerk's office, where she records every marriage and divorce, every birth and death—and makes a point of knowing everyone else's business. Shelby was briefly friends with her, until suddenly, she wasn't.

Because what she soon discovered, after a few girls' nights out, was that Maeve was the sort of woman who required forbearance. A bit of her could be intoxicating, a quick rush, like a thimbleful of tequila. Too much, and she left you feeling severely hungover. A couple of years ago, Shelby had also made the regrettable mistake of spotting Maeve a few thousand dollars. She claimed she needed the money for a new furnace, and if Shelby could help her out this once, she'd pay her back with interest. Shelby is still waiting.

"Seriously, do you know what happened?"

Georgie shrugs. "Who knows? Rumor has it that she tripped down her own stairs; guess she landed funny on her wrist. Her neighbor had to rush her to the emergency room. Because, you know, no one else would."

Meg rolls her eyes. "You're terrible, Georgie. I think Maeve is perfectly fine. I kind of feel sorry for her, actually. She used to be the life of the party. Now it seems like she hardly has any friends."

"I wonder why?" Georgie asks mockingly, then leans in and whispers, "I also heard she might have a little recreational drug problem."

"Oh, come on," Meg chides. "You're as bad as she is! Spreading rumors." Her focus shifts to Julia instead. "Hey, Jules, are you ever going to put down your phone so we can talk to you?"

Julia, who's been scrolling through images, looks up and places her cell next to her plate. "Sorry, I was just checking to see if I had any new messages."

"And?" Shelby asks. "Any bites? Any new Romeos out there asking you on a date?"

Across the table, Meg smirks because they all know precisely what Julia has been up to on her phone. Twice divorced, she's constantly on the prowl, scanning sites like Tinder or Match for possible dates. The rest of them find it gauche, but Julia tells them they're old-fashioned and remain single (except for Meg) for a reason.

Now she flips her long, dark hair over a shoulder and makes a *pfft* sound. "I wish. It's the slow time of the year, right before Memorial Day weekend when all the boys come out to play." She lowers her voice.

"Although I did have a fun date with an associate professor from MIT last week."

"And?" Georgie raises an eyebrow.

"Let's just say that not all smart men are geeks. Some are actually quite good in the bedroom, it turns out."

The women share a conspiratorial laugh before Julia gives a small nod toward the front of the restaurant, where customers queue up to place their lunch orders at the window. She leans in and whispers, "Speaking of good in the bedroom." Shelby glances over only to feel her stomach drop so swiftly that she's tempted to reach under the table to retrieve it. A flash of heat shoots up her neck.

"Not that I'd know, of course," says Julia slyly. "I've never been that lucky."

"Julia, stop it!" Meghan ducks her head, lowers her voice. "Dr. Bo is *married*," she hisses. "So hands off."

"Rumor has it that he's pretty hands *on*, actually." Julia grins.

There's another ripple of laughter around the table, and Shelby isn't sure if the heat that's rushing to her cheeks is turning them bright pink or dark crimson. Without thinking, she lifts a hand to touch her skin to see if maybe it has caught on fire. No one at this table knows about Bo. Nor can they. She will dive off the deck into the deep blue sea to make sure it remains that way. And even though she's trying her very best not to gaze in Bo's direction, it's impossible because he's here with Cindy (*his wife!*) and because they take a seat just two tables away.

Shelby can't believe it. Why on earth would he sit so close? Unless he hasn't spotted her yet? Her mind races, tunneling through every worst-case scenario, when Bo suddenly materializes at their table.

"Ladies, how are you? I couldn't resist coming over to say hello to some of my favorite clients." He's wearing khakis and a white button-down shirt, one extra button undone at the top. Aviator sunglasses pushed up on his head. He looks incredibly handsome. Shelby sits on her hands—*the very hands that were running across his chest last night!*—to prevent them from reaching out.

Cindy gives a friendly wave from their table about ten feet away, and Shelby waves back, despite herself. Cindy is wearing white capri pants, a black T-shirt, and a jean jacket. Shelby's dark-blue pantsuit suddenly feels matronly and much too formal for Shipwreck'd.

"Isn't that nice of you," says Georgie, the queen of politeness and never one to be easily undone by a man's charms. "We're doing fine, thank you. How about yourself?"

"Good, good. Great, actually," he says and gestures toward his table. "I'm out of the office enjoying lunch with my wife on a beautiful day, so I can't complain." He flashes his megawatt smile, those brilliant white teeth with razor-sharp incisors (no teeth-grinding for him) that have sent Shelby's stomach somersaulting untold times. But now they're being flashed to convey his sincerity, his absolute glee at having the chance to share a rare lunch with Cindy. All Shelby can think is what an adept liar he is. He has yet to meet her eyes.

"Everyone's doggos doing okay?" Bo's eyes cast around the table but avoid hers. Heads nod all around.

"Meghan, how's Doggie Delish doing? Business still good?"

"Yes," she says, a little too enthusiastically. "Our sales have gone up fifteen percent in the last three months."

"No kidding! That's terrific. I tell all my clients to go there, you know." He winks. "Soon enough, I might be asking you for a commission." Meghan grins good-naturedly, although Shelby already knows what her friend is thinking: *Like hell you will.*

If Shelby could melt into a puddle under the table and disappear, she would. It must be obvious that she's sleeping with Bo, and yet no one has turned to even acknowledge her in the conversation.

"Well, I don't want to keep you. You ladies enjoy your day."

"You too!" Julia calls out, not bothering to hide the flirtation in her voice.

They wait a few seconds until he's out of earshot. "Talk about Mr. McDreamy."

"Julia!" Meghan scolds again, but she's laughing. "He is pretty hot, don't you think, Shelby? All that dark hair, and those eyes . . ." Her voice drifts off.

For a second, Shelby panics that she's been found out, and that's why Meghan has singled her out. But her friends all stare at her, as if they're sincerely interested in her opinion. She struggles to tamp down her sprinting heart, shrugs, and says, "He's okay, I guess."

"Okay?" Julia exclaims. "Seriously? It doesn't get much better than that. Sorry, Meghan. I know *you're* happily married, but the rest of us? Not so much."

"I don't like the way he called us 'ladies,'" Georgie says now. "As if we're characters out of some Victorian novel."

Julia rolls her eyes. "Whatever. Hey, speaking of novels, have you guys read the latest by Wanda Morris? It's *so good*."

And just like that, the conversation rolls on, even though Shelby could swear she's been flattened by a wave. Bo only dared glance her way once, immediately before turning to leave their table. Shelby is dying to know what Julia meant when she said Bo was "hands on." Does he have a reputation as a philanderer? Is Shelby simply the next in line? But that's crazy! He already has a wife and a lover, namely *her*. She's trying to figure out a way to inquire discreetly, without pointing any arrows directly at herself.

Finally, she just blurts it out. "Hey, Jules, what did you mean when you said that Dr. Bo is 'hands on?'" It can't be helped. She *needs* to know.

Julia shrugs. "Oh, you know, only that he's been around the block a few times."

"Before he was married, though, right?" Meghan asks to clarify, and Shelby is so grateful that she could lean over and hug her.

"Oh, I'm sure he's a stand-up guy *now*," Julia amends. "I mean, we all trust him with our dogs, right, which is basically the equivalent of trusting him to be our health proxy or our gynecologist." The comment sparks another round of laughter, not least of all from Shelby herself.

Julia knows nothing, she thinks, flooding with relief. It's only conjecture and rumors, of which there are plenty already flying around their small peninsula. Still, she can't possibly stay here and enjoy the rest of her lunch; if she does, the floor will fall out beneath her or lightning will strike.

"Ladies," she says now for mock effect and pushes back her chair. "I'm really sorry, but I need to get going. I almost forgot: I'm meeting my sister and niece at three thirty."

"Oh, how's Kate doing? I love that girl," Georgie exclaims.

Shelby equivocates about exactly how much to reveal at the moment. Her friends adore Kate and vice versa. It doesn't feel right to betray her sister's confidence here, out in the open air at Shipwreck'd, especially before they even know if Trey has actually been cheating or not. "She's fine," she says. "They're staying up in Allerton."

"Oh, have they opened up the summer house already? That place is *divine.*" Georgie elongates the *dee* in divine.

"Sort of, I guess?" Shelby stands and fishes a twenty out of her wallet and slides it across the table. "I think Kate wanted to get a head start before the craziness of Memorial Day weekend descends."

"Good idea," Julia agrees. "Let us know when we should show up for the annual party." She winks. "I'll have to work it around my Figawi schedule, of course." At the mention of Figawi, a collective eye roll travels around the table. Julia is referring to the famous regatta in which hundreds of sailboats race from Hyannis Port to Nantucket over Memorial Day weekend. More important, those hundreds of sailboats are frequently captained by handsome, available men. Hence, Julia's annual commitment to Figawi.

"Oh, I bet you will," Shelby jokes. "I'll be sure to tell Kate you all say hello. See you later."

She turns on her heel and strides across the deck, away from her friends. Away from Bo Bannister and his darling wife. Without so much as a backward glance over her shoulder.

It almost kills her.

~

When she pulls into her driveway, though, it's not Kate's Land Rover that's parked in front of the house but Bree's blue Honda Civic.

What on earth? Shelby talked to Bree briefly last night, but she didn't intend for it to sound like a 911 call. What, exactly, she struggles to remember, did she say? Did she actually ask her sister to drive out to Hull?

Shelby parks and strides over to the Civic, but there's no one inside. Either Bree has gone for a walk along the beach or she's let herself inside with her spare key.

"Bree?" Shelby calls out when she opens the unlocked front door. "Is that you?"

"In here," her sister shouts from the kitchen.

Shelby hangs her purse on the mudroom hook and steers herself toward the kitchen. Her sister's head is stuck halfway in the freezer. "Just checking to see if you have any ice cream," she calls out. Tuukka, his tail wagging happily, has planted himself beside her.

"Oh, okay?" When Bree's head pops up above the freezer door, there are enormous purple bruises smudging both of her cheeks. Shelby's first thought is that she's been punched, maybe on the receiving end of a bar fight. It takes a nanosecond to register that it's bruising from her wisdom teeth. "Jesus, you look like hell."

"Good to see you, too." Bree straightens and lets the freezer door swing shut.

"Sorry." Shelby walks over and pulls her into a hug. "I wasn't expecting you, that's all. I thought you'd be curled up in bed for another week from the sound of you yesterday. Should you be driving if you're on painkillers?"

"Didn't need to take the last dose. Just some Advil." Bree positions herself behind the island, a carton of vanilla fudge swirl in front of her. She rips off the lid and begins scooping generous half-moons into a bowl. "I'm actually feeling a hundred times better than I was yesterday," she admits. "Even this morning. I called earlier to ask if it was okay if I came over. Guess you didn't get the message."

A light bulb blinks on in Shelby's head. Her phone buzzed during lunch, but when she saw it was Bree calling, she sent it straight to voicemail. She completely forgot. Bree must have been calling from the road to arrive here in such a short window of time.

"No worries. It's nice to have you here." And she means it. "I'm glad you're feeling a little better. The first couple of days are the worst, they say."

"So?" Bree demands. "Where's my favorite godson?"

"Track practice." Shelby grabs a clean glass from the dishwasher and fills it with cool water. "He probably won't be home till five at the earliest."

"Oh, right. Spring sports. How's the girlfriend?"

Shelby shrugs. "Good, I guess. I mean, he seems happier when she's around."

"I'll bet," Bree says. "Are they having sex yet?"

Shelby's hand practically ricochets off the countertop. "Bree, please! How on earth should I know? He tells me nothing. Besides, they've only been dating a few months."

Her sister's eyes roll up in her head. "You do realize that a few months is like a lifetime in teenage years, right? It's calculated in dog years or something."

"I have some idea, I think."

Bree makes little clicking noises with her tongue.

"What?"

"Oh, never mind. It's only that you're such a different person now that you're a *mom*. Sometimes I don't even recognize you."

"Yeah, well, you'll understand one day." Shelby gulps down the remainder of her water. "What you discover," she says, "is that you *really* don't want your kid repeating your same mistakes, you know?"

"Like getting drunk on peach schnapps and throwing up in the parking lot at graduation? Or climbing through your bedroom window late at night and breaking your ankle when you jump?"

"Noah's bedroom is directly above the garage. He won't have to jump," Shelby replies without missing a beat. "So that last one's not going to happen."

They share an easy laugh until Bree cries out, "Stop! Please! My cheeks still hurt. It's too soon to smile."

In the living room, Bree drops onto the couch, ice cream bowl in hand. "This is so nice," she says apropos of nothing. "And this couch is quite possibly the most comfortable couch I've ever been on. Is it new?" Her baby sister has always had a penchant for drama; it's probably the hundredth time Bree has sat on this exact same couch. But as if to better illustrate her point, she scooches farther down into the cushions.

"It's gotten a lot of use," Shelby says. But her mind is twirling— screaming, really—*That's where Bo and I made love last night! Is my bra still hidden under the pillow?* She's about to dash over and retrieve it before remembering that she yanked it out after he left and tossed it in the laundry.

"I mean, seriously," Bree continues, "this couch is like a bed."

Which is when it occurs to Shelby that her sister seems to be making herself awfully comfortable, maybe too comfortable. Is she planning on spending the night? A couple of nights? Because if it's more than a few nights, Bree's stay will seriously cut into Shelby's time with Bo. That's when she notices her sister's overstuffed Patagonia backpack, sitting on the floor next to her.

"So is that your way of telling me you're sleeping over?" The sooner she knows Bree's plans, the better. Once, when she was apartment-hunting in Somerville, Bree "crashed" with Shelby and Noah for three months. *Three months.* Shelby loves her sister, is genuinely happy to have her here, but Bree can be so, well, *needy.* And then, Shelby remembers: *Bree has a job!* She can't possibly stay for too long. Or does she? Shelby can't recall if she got fired from the coffee shop or not. Maybe she's confusing it with the shoe store.

"Not sure." Bree takes another bite of ice cream. "Guess that kind of depends on Kate. How's she doing?"

"A little better than yesterday, I think. She and Clara are coming over in"—Shelby checks her phone—"about twenty minutes. They're staying at the Allerton house right now."

"Oh?" Bree sits up straighter at this news. "I didn't realize she was out here with Clara. She must really be pissed. Guess I'm here in time for the intervention, then."

"Ha, very funny." Shelby slips off her work blazer, then her pumps, and folds herself into the oversize chair across the room. "I'm not sure intervention is the right word, but we definitely need to talk her down. I'm sure there's a reasonable explanation for why Trey was kissing a random woman on the streets of Boston."

"Undoubtedly." Bree waves her spoon in the air as if to underscore that she's 100 percent in agreement.

"What?" Shelby demands. "Trey adores Kate, and she adores him, which we're going to remind her of when she and Clara get here."

Bree laughs. "Sounds like a foolproof plan to me." She sets the empty bowl on the table.

"Oh, do you have a better idea?" Shelby goes to refill her water glass, annoyed. How is it that her baby sister—who doesn't even have a real job—can waltz into Shelby's home, make herself comfortable, and offer only sarcasm when it comes to rescuing Kate's marriage? *But, silly me,* Shelby thinks, waiting for her glass to fill. Bree's world revolves only around herself. Why would she expect anything else?

"For the record, I don't have a better idea," she says when Shelby returns. "I'm only saying, I'm not sure our sister will be so easily swayed. Katie can have a mean streak in her when she gets crossed. Remember when you told her you'd give her your allowance if she made your bed for a week and then you reneged on the deal?"

Shelby hasn't thought of this in ages. "You're right. But that was years ago when we were kids, and I deserved it when she dumped sand in my sheets for payback." (It took her days to brush all the sand out of her bed. Not once did it occur to her to throw the sheets in the washing machine.) Her phone buzzes on the table, and she quickly flips it over.

"And you don't think Trey deserves a little sand in his sheets for, I don't know"—Bree waves a hand in the air—"this? Whatever it is?"

"I honestly don't know what to think," Shelby says.

Which is when Bree wraps herself in the blanket on the couch and closes her eyes, as if readying for a nap. Tuukka, meanwhile, jumps up and rests his head on her legs.

Fine, you two go to sleep, Shelby thinks, but she can't tamp down the uneasy feeling that's suddenly descended, as if her house might not withstand the chaos that's about to hit.

More importantly, how long should she wait before replying to Bo's text, which skated across her phone moments ago?

I'm SO sorry about lunch. Didn't know you'd be at Shipwreck'd, too. What are the odds?!

A few more hours, she decides. Bo can definitely wait.

10

Robin

Memorial Day Weekend
Sunday, May 26

As much as Robin enjoys the pomp and celebration of Memorial Day weekend, she also privately dreads it. Nothing good ever happens on Memorial Day, the way it's supposed to. That she has such strong feelings about a holiday, yet no feelings whatsoever about the absence of a significant other in her life, concerns her older sister, Dana.

"It's the job," Dana likes to remind her, as she did when Robin was over for dinner last weekend. "How are you going to meet anyone when you're always working?"

"What do you mean?" Robin snapped. "I meet plenty of folks."

"Yeah, plenty of scumbags," Dana countered. "You need a nice guy who can protect you."

Robin made a puffing sound with her lips and dug into the slice of lemon meringue pie—her favorite—which her sister had baked especially for her. "When are you going to stop thinking I need someone to protect me? I *am* the police, remember?"

But Dana merely shrugged. "All the more reason to get a boyfriend. What if one of those crazies you put in jail gets out and comes after you?"

"You seriously need to find someone else to worry about. Don't we have enough brothers and sisters for you to pick on someone else?" she asked. And then little Jonah, Robin's two-year-old nephew, came running up, wailing because he'd caught his thumb on the bathroom door and thought he had a splinter.

The conversation, much to Robin's relief, came to an abrupt end.

She thinks back to the Memorial Day weekends of her childhood. The holiday always meant an extra day off from school, a parade with free candy, a gathering on the village green, cookouts with friends. If it was warm enough, swimming at Nantasket Beach with her siblings. When she was nine or ten and Paragon Park was still open, she and Dana, the two closest in age, would ride the Giant Coaster, screaming their heads off the entire way. They'd hop on the Bermuda Triangle, the Whip, the Indy 500 (all the rides, except for the carousel, were auctioned off when the park closed in 1984) and devour as much pizza and ice cream as their stomachs could hold. Later, when night fell, they'd camp out in the backyard and roast marshmallows, and sometimes—if there was enough money in the town's budget—watch the fireworks. To this day, she considers Memorial Day weekend, not the summer solstice or the Fourth of July, the official kickoff to summer.

Sometimes she likes to imagine how fabulous summers must have been when Hull was *the* vacation destination back in the early 1900s, when more than a million visitors would burst onto the town. When six steamboats crossed the harbor from Boston to Hull, dropping up to twenty thousand people a day, and trolley lines ran from Hingham and Cohasset. Thanks to George Dodge, a Boston native who made his money in the whalebone industry, Paragon Park, with its death-defying rides, opened in 1905, and the town quickly became known as "New England's Coney Island." Rumor had it that young Jack Kennedy summered here

(Rose Kennedy's father owned a house in the Point Allerton neighborhood), and that movie star Judy Garland and her son visited.

Those were Hull's glory days.

But now summer—and Memorial Day weekend, in particular—most often means drunk people behaving badly, usually foolishly. Being a police lieutenant has given Robin a new, unwelcome perspective on the holiday. Rather than enjoy the parades and the bands, all she can see is people peeing in public spaces, yelling obscenities, getting into nonsense fights. Generally well-meaning folks suddenly in need of direction.

She'll often find herself, late in the evening, herding revelers like stray cats along the Strip. Throughout the day, there's the pop-pop-pop of homemade fireworks shooting off, sending the number of concerned-neighbor calls about possible gunshots skyrocketing. It's a weekend when her radio is constantly buzzing and, when she's home, Hemingway barks nonstop.

Robin understands that alcohol can make people act in strange ways. But the irony of a day meant to honor American heroes that instead ends up showcasing people's bad behavior always surprises her. A day meant to celebrate national pride has somehow turned into a holiday where plenty of folks seem to forget what it means to be an American—respectful, honorable, kind. She's never had to fire her gun on the job (and for that, she's extremely grateful), but if she did, she suspects it would be on Memorial Day weekend, when out-of-towners descend, emotions run high, and mediocrity peaks.

Of course, she never expected she'd be searching for a missing person, or even perhaps a body, over the holiday weekend. News crews are beginning to assemble on the road above, which means that word has gotten out about the search and rescue. And that guy on board, who says his companion went missing? It turns out Robin knows him. Tommy radioed it in a few minutes ago.

"You're never gonna believe who's on the boat." He's not some random vacationer down for the long weekend but, in fact, as much a part of Hull as its oceanfront property or its carousel. Robin imagines him making the rounds at the parties last night. But how did he go from partying to passing out on his sailboat this morning? Are they dealing with a practical joker, a neighborly heckling that went south?

It's this perspective, she realizes, that the chief needs most from her right now. Because this case—whatever the outcome—is now very much a local one, steeped in Hull's history, including all its salty personalities and, yes, every one of its personal vendettas.

11

KATE

Earlier
Thursday Night, May 16

Kate sits at a high-rise table a few feet from the bar at the Parrot. Her spot offers an unobstructed view of the ocean through the floor-to-ceiling windows, which typically would be thrown open on a warm summer's day but are shut tight against the chill on this spring evening. The wind has picked up again, and whitecaps stretch out across the water like loopy cursive. She's glad she grabbed her knotty fisherman's sweater on the way out the door. Among all the restaurants and bars that line Nantasket Beach, the Parrot is her favorite. Before her sits a Tanqueray and tonic, sustenance to help calm her nerves. Normally, her drink of choice here would be a frozen rosé, but it's too cold for that tonight.

The restaurant has made a reasonable attempt at updating its decor by adding tin ceilings, a couple of wall-mounted televisions, and bare light bulbs that hang suspended above the bar in a Restoration-Hardware kind of way. Upstairs is another bar and banquet area, as well as a deck. The floors are imitation hardwood, easy for cleanup of sand and spills. Most of the waitresses here talk with hard-boiled Boston accents, dropping their *r*s whenever they ask, "How's your summah going?" It's part of the Parrot's peculiar charm. There's also just enough kitsch to remind customers that, despite any updates, the Parrot remains a seafaring bar at its core. Take, for instance, the buxom, bare-chested mermaid sculpture suspended from the ceiling at the front, whose breasts the odd sailor has been rumored to rub for good luck.

There are only a handful of customers here tonight, not atypical for a Thursday night in May, she supposes. A couple of old-timers nurse a bucket of beers at the counter; a few couples linger over food at tables. She wonders what their stories are. Often Kate has thought it would be nice if strangers walked around with dialogue balloons, filled with pithy descriptions, above their heads. Such as, *Going through a divorce.* Or, *Had a brutal argument with my teenage daughter this morning.* Or, *Up all night with a sick baby.* Not only would it make life more interesting but it would also encourage people to be kinder to one another.

She sips her cocktail, watches the door, checks her phone. Every time someone new walks in, her heart does a tiny flip. But it's not Trey. Not yet. Earlier, they agreed to meet at the Parrot instead of back at the house or at Shelby's. Neutral territory. Trey is driving out from Boston, ostensibly to convince her that he's not cheating. And Kate *so* wants to believe him. But she needs to see him in person before she can decide if her husband is being truthful.

Spending time with her sisters back at Shelby's earlier this afternoon helped settle her nerves somewhat. The last time they were all together was over the Easter holiday, more than a month ago, at Shelby's place in Wellesley. Shelby and Bree are as close as Clara will ever come to having another mom; in fact, sometimes Kate is convinced that Bree, in particular, would do a much better job of raising her daughter than she is. Her little sister possesses the kind of creative, carefree energy that mesmerizes young children. Around Bree, Clara instantly morphs into an adorable, loving child.

Her sisters assure Kate that it's the terrible threes and that the novelty of seeing her aunties mainly in the summertime works hugely in their favor. Naturally, Clara also adores her aunts because they spoil her nonstop—there's no need for her to throw a tantrum because she gets everything she could possibly want, and more. Just today, for instance, Shelby pulled out a brand-new LEGO set, which Clara played with for the next hour while Kate and her sisters talked in hushed voices over cups of tea.

"Sipping tea with you guys reminds me of Mom," Kate said wistfully. "I used to love her high teas when we were little. Pretending we were British and talking with funny accents."

"The cakes and cookies were the best part," Bree recalled.

"Agreed," said Shelby, setting out a plate of Milanos.

"I miss her," Kate admitted. "I wish she were here right now. She'd tell me what to do."

"Yeah, about that," Shelby said. "What's the word? Is Trey driving out tonight or not?"

"We're meeting at the Parrot at seven o'clock." Kate glanced up from her tea. "I was hoping you guys could maybe watch Clara?"

Shelby's face brightened instantly. "I was waiting for you to ask. I've got a new set of pj's for her." She paused. "And I'm glad Trey is headed here to straighten it all out. There has to be some explanation."

"Do you think he's in love with this other woman, whoever she is?" Bree asked innocently.

"What kind of question is that?" Shelby demanded.

"Sorry! I thought it was a fair question."

"Trey's not in love with some random person," Shelby said coolly. "He loves Kate."

Kate didn't mention *who* that particular person was because if her sisters found out it was Liz Macintosh, they might well have hunted her down themselves. (Liz once tried to persuade Trey to get back together with her *after* he'd already proposed to Kate, and for this, her family has never forgiven Liz.)

Now, Kate thinks, the moment of truth has arrived. She swipes at a rivulet of condensation trickling down her glass. All she's asking for is the truth. That shouldn't be so hard, should it?

When he steps through the door ten minutes late, Trey's hair is windblown, his cheeks pinked from the cold. She watches him scour the bar, not seeing her at first. He's wearing jeans, his brown leather jacket, and a dark-blue cotton sweater underneath. The thought strikes her for the thousandth time that her husband is handsome, objectively so. Meaning his entrance into the bar would most certainly grab her attention, even if they were strangers. She waits for his gaze to find her, and when it does, he shoots her a smile. *That smile!* Instant goose bumps.

"Hey, babe," he says and pulls her into a hug when he reaches the table. "I can't tell you how good it is to see you."

Instinctively, her body leans into his, but then stiffens. "Hey," she says, pulling away. "Thanks for coming."

"I missed you guys. Where's Clara-Beara?" He settles onto the stool across from Kate, his back to the windows. Even though children are welcome here, it didn't seem appropriate to bring their daughter so late, especially when Kate's hoping for a grown-up conversation.

"I left her at my sister's. Shelby and Bree are watching her."

"Bree's out here, too?"

"Yeah, she had her wisdom teeth pulled the other day. Remember? She's still recovering. Hoping for a little TLC from Shelby, I think."

"Oh, right." Their waitress appears, and Trey orders an IPA.

"So." He turns back to Kate. "You look good."

"Nice try," she says. "You've got some explaining to do. I'm still mad at you, you know." She hates that she can't give him the cold shoulder entirely, even though that's what she'd been coaching herself to do prior to his arrival. It's more of a lukewarm-shoulder greeting. Half a shoulder.

"Right." The waitress sets his beer in front of him, and he thanks her. "So," he begins again, waiting for their waitress to leave, and Kate braces herself for whatever's coming next. "I did some thinking on the drive over, and I want to say first off, that I'm really, *really* sorry for what I've put you through these past twenty-four hours." His voice trails off. "I can't imagine how pissed off you must have been—maybe still are?"

"I think it's fair to use the present tense," she confirms. "I'm waiting for you to look me in the eye and tell me that that kiss meant nothing."

He leans toward her, cups her face in his hands. The scent of his cologne, 1872 by Clive Christian, makes her oddly homesick. "I can honestly tell you, Kate Dowling, that it meant nothing. It was a random kiss. Nothing more. What else can I say? I'm an idiot."

"But why? Why would you even be tempted to do that? And with your old girlfriend?"

"Listen, I'm no more attracted to Liz than she is to me. We have our own families now. It was a little reunion. We haven't seen each other in years."

"I don't remember Liz looking like that."

"Like what?"

Kate shrugs. "I don't know. All that long, dark hair. Petite."

"Yeah, her hair is longer, I guess, but the rest of her is pretty much the same."

Kate can't decide if she should be comforted or distraught by this information. The past twenty-four hours have felt like one exhausting marathon. And her cocktail is doing precious little to help her organize her thoughts into tidy slots of *This is Right* and *This is Wrong*.

Mostly, she wants to be done with the whole debacle, to emerge on the other side of it relatively unscathed. She wants her husband back, the same man who rolled over and made love to her yesterday morning. Was it yesterday morning? It feels like last month, last year.

"So I'm being a paranoid wife, is that what you're saying?" A slight edge creeps into her voice. She hates being cast as the crazed, jealous woman when it's Trey who's gotten them into this mess in the first place. *It's not my fault,* she reminds herself.

His green eyes widen in surprise before he leans back, pulls his hand away. "To the contrary. I love that you still get jealous when you see me with someone else."

"That's a little weird, I think."

He grins. "Okay, you're probably right, but what I mean is that I think it's a sign of a healthy relationship, don't you? That we still care enough about each other to get jealous? If you didn't get upset, wouldn't that somehow be worse?"

"What would be best is if yesterday never happened at all." Trey flinches, and she lets the words sit between them a moment.

"You're right. I'm an idiot," he reiterates. "But you've got to trust me when I say it was only an innocent kiss between friends." His gaze meets hers, and she tries to decide if there's truth behind it, or deceit. It's hard to tell.

"So hypothetically," she continues, barreling down the jealousy gauntlet. "If you walked in here tonight and I was talking to some random, devastatingly handsome guy, you'd be jealous?"

Trey slaps the table, hard, with his open palm. Loud enough that a few customers at the adjacent table turn their heads. "Are you kidding me? Not only that, I'd want to punch him."

"Nice," she says, though she doesn't know what's nice about it, exactly. That her husband would stand up for her? Be jealous? Is capable of physical violence?

"What can I say?" She watches her husband straighten his back, sit up taller in his chair. "I love my wife. Of course I'd fight for you."

Inside, Kate wrestles with whether to forgive her husband in this instant or make him work harder for absolution. The thing is, she loves him, and he told her without blinking that the kiss meant nothing, blinking being the telltale sign of a liar, which she knows from watching a *60 Minutes* episode years ago. Does she believe him? She wavers for a second. So much hinges on her answer.

But *yes*. Yes, she does. He's her husband, so she's inclined to trust him—she understands this—but now that the memory of the actual kiss has grown a bit hazy in the past twenty-four hours, she supposes it's *possible* it was only a friendly goodbye kiss. It's her own memory that's being called into question now. She reminds herself that she was fighting traffic yesterday and had only minutes earlier tamed the wild beast who was her daughter in the back seat. What did she really see in those few short seconds before the light turned green? What *could* she see?

"And the fact that you guys were holding hands. How did you explain that again?"

"I don't think I did, actually." Trey shrugs. "It was part of the good-bye, you know, an It-was-good-to-see-you, Don't-be-a-stranger."

She bites her bottom lip, traces wet circles around her glass with her forefinger. "Well," she says, "I, for one, hope Liz Macintosh makes herself pretty damned scarce going forward."

Trey rakes his hand through his hair. "Yeah, I get that. I don't plan on seeing her again anytime soon."

"You'd better not."

"Agreed."

"And you swear you didn't sleep with her?" Kate blurts out. She must know. Then, for clarity's sake: "I mean recently, of course."

"Scouts' honor." His middle two fingers shoot up in a *V*.

Kate sighs, leans back in her chair, and sizes up her husband in one arguably defining moment. "I guess," she begins, choosing her words carefully, deliberately, "that I'm willing to put it behind us, if you are? I mean, it was only a kiss, right?"

"Right." Trey nods once, raises his bottle, and taps her glass. "To no more kissing," he says. Then adds, "With other people, that is." He flashes his most beguiling smile.

"And you swear never to engage in this kind of duplicitous, hurtful, outrageous . . ." She pauses, trying to think of other suitable adjectives.

"Egregious?" Trey supplies.

"Egregious, inappropriate, childish, inexcusable behavior again?"

"I promise."

~

Fifteen minutes later, they're back at the Allerton house, pulling their clothes off each other like two drunken teenagers. Kate wonders momentarily if the scattered boats on the water tonight can glimpse them through the upstairs window, where they've never bothered to hang curtains. She crosses the room and shuts off the light. Trey follows her and pulls her onto the bed, where he begins kissing her clavicle, her neck, her lips. Their foreplay, like wildfire, moves swiftly, a burst of pure flame. When they finally make love, Kate's entire body trembles from head to toe.

Afterward, her head rests on his chest as it rises and falls with each breath. If they could stay like this forever, she would. She listens to the wind whipping around the house, making the windows rattle in their panes, and waits for the sound of her husband's soft snoring.

After maybe five minutes, though, he moans and shifts her weight off his chest. "I should get going," he says apologetically.

Kate knows it's late, but how late? Past midnight? After texting Shelby that she and Trey were crashing at the Allerton house, she tossed her phone in her purse and forgot all about it. The digital clock on the bedstand is of no help; it flashes midnight from whenever the power last went out and she's yet to reset it.

"I need to be at work by seven tomorrow morning," he explains. "And I don't have any suits here."

"Don't go," she murmurs. "Get up early in the morning."

He kisses the top of her head. "You know I wish I could stay." Then, ever so slowly, he wiggles away from her and crawls out from under the covers. She watches while he tugs on his jeans and wrangles into his T-shirt and sweater. The moonlight through the window paints his body in a willowy shadow along the back wall.

"Are you guys coming home tomorrow?" he asks. "I mean, back to Wellesley?"

Kate flips over, wraps her arms around her pillow. "I'm not sure. We might stay a little longer. It's been so long since I've hung out with my sisters. And Clara's in heaven, of course."

"Of course." He walks over and bends down to lightly kiss her. His breath still smells of beer. "I'll talk to you tomorrow, and we can make a plan. Maybe I'll drive back out. Love you."

"Love you," she calls after him.

But then he pokes his head through the doorway again. "Hey, Katie?"

"Yeah?"

"Thanks for being so cool . . . you know, about the whole thing."

"Mm-hmm." She lifts her hand, waggles her fingers, then listens to his footsteps tromp down the stairs. *Cool?* she thinks. *How was I cool about "the whole thing"?* The word probably isn't one that she'd have chosen herself. Maybe *forgiving* or *tolerant* or *understanding.* "Cool" almost makes it sound as if she excused the fact that her husband flubbed the pizza order, returning home with pepperoni instead of cheese.

Then again, hasn't she always aspired to be the cool girlfriend, the chill wife, the one who doesn't freak out whenever Trey wants to spend a Sunday afternoon watching football with the guys or golfing all day? Something Trey told her when they were first dating comes back to her: her confidence, he said, was one of her most admirable traits.

"You can hang out with my buddies and not be intimidated by them. Whenever they give you a hard time, you give it right back to them."

"And they don't deserve it?" she countered.

"Sure they do. But that's what's so great about you. You don't let them rattle you. You know who you are. You're one cool customer, Kate Lancaster."

At the time, she was flattered. She didn't weather the rigorous competition at Brown, and later, at Bain & Company, to feel less than. All those late nights studying at the library paved the way to graduating valedictorian from Weymouth High and with highest honors at Brown. On the weekends, she often ended up besting the frat boys at beer pong, walking away with their hard-earned paychecks in her back pocket. Hanging out with the guys always felt natural, comfortable, even preferable. Kate had her sisters for girlfriends and wasn't interested in playing the popularity game with girls her age. But now she wonders if maybe, subconsciously, Trey was commending her on something else entirely. Maybe, early on, he sensed that Kate, unlike his previous girl-friends, would be more tolerant of his male antics. Maybe "confidence" was code for putting up with his bullshit without complaint.

Was that what made her cool?

She tells herself to stop. She's driving herself crazy. One bump in their marriage cannot, *will not* make her doubt their entire relationship. "You and Trey are solid," Shelby told her yesterday when they talked. "There's no way he's cheating on you." And Kate thought to herself, *That sounds right. Solid.* And perhaps a piece of her also smugly thought, *More solid than you and Ethan ever were.*

Kate groans and buries her head in the pillow. She's a terrible sister for thinking such thoughts and an even worse wife for assuming that Trey betrayed her. Maybe this staying-at-home gig isn't for her. Maybe, she thinks, getting back into the office is the only way for her to maintain her sanity. She'll raise the idea with Trey tomorrow, maybe even dust off her résumé. Too much time on her hands has led her to imagine the worst.

She flips over on her back, her mind racing, and tries counting to a hundred—*one, two, three, four.* Flips again so that her body half fills Trey's side. *Five, six, seven.* Usually right before she reaches one hundred, she's asleep. She stretches out her right leg, onto Trey's side, when something sharp, like a pin, pricks her calf. *Ouch!* She sits up and switches on the bedside lamp before digging under the sheets for the culprit. Almost immediately, her fingers land on it: another damn earring.

Held up to the light, it appears to be a small golden hoop with a diamond fleck in the middle. Except this earring isn't hers. It can't be. Kate is horribly allergic to gold; her ears would swell up like balloons if she wore these. Per doctor's orders, all her jewelry is sterling silver. She scrambles to locate the earring she found in the dark last night, the one that she assumed was hers and left on the bedside table, forgetting all about it. But it's still there, hiding behind the digital clock. When she holds it up next to the other hoop, it's obvious that they're a match.

But these aren't her earrings.

Someone else has been in her bed. In her sheets. The very sheets that she and Trey made love in moments ago. The four-hundred-thread-count linens from Garnet Hill, which are dotted with whimsical, happy blueberries. The sheets that Kate purchased specifically for the Hull house because blueberries always remind her of summertime. The sheets that she smoothed over the bed, tucking in the hospital corners, back in September, so that they'd have clean linens when they returned in May for Memorial Day weekend. Sheets that supposedly haven't been slept in since last night when she and Clara crashed here.

But the earrings.

Someone else has been sleeping in her bed. Little Bear's voice from Clara's book echoes in her head. *Someone's been sleeping in my bed!*

How did Kate get here?

12

BREE

Friday, May 17

When she called into work this morning, her manager, Debbie, was more than willing to give Bree a few extra days off next week. "Go ahead. You've earned it. Take another personal day or two. Don't you typically take the week after Memorial Day, anyway? Why not swap it with next week, instead?" Bree didn't remind her that she'd already used all her personal days this year, but she eagerly accepted the switch in her vacation time. It's slightly worrisome that her boss was so nonchalant about the whole thing, and Bree half thinks that she's already found her replacement, which is why she's letting her off so easily.

Nonetheless, it's an opportunity too good to pass up. A full week in Hull *before* Memorial Day with her sisters sounds like a godsend. Not that she's told Shelby or Noah her plans yet. After the look on her sister's face when she discovered Bree in her kitchen yesterday, Bree's simply grateful she was invited to sleep over in the guest room last night. She'll have to work her extended stay into a later conversation, preferably after Shelby has consumed a few glasses of wine.

By the time Bree pads downstairs in her slippers, it's ten thirty in the morning. Tuukka, his tail circling like a whirligig, bounds over to her.

"Whoa there, buddy. Good morning to you, too." Bree scratches between his ears, coaxes him down. "Wouldn't it be so much easier if humans had tails, too?" she muses aloud as she makes her way into the kitchen. The scent of coffee and something sweet, vanilla maybe, floods the air. "Three wags mean a person really likes you. One wag, not so much."

"I like that," Shelby says after commanding Tuukka to sit. "Especially in the dating world. Tail wags would clear up a lot of misunderstandings. Zero wags, and you can pretty much assume that they're not into you."

"Exactly."

From her counter stool, Clara shouts, "Auntie Bree! We made you pancakes for breakfast. They're soft so your tooths won't hurt when you eat them."

"That, my munchkin, is so thoughtful of you."

"Coffee?" Shelby asks.

"Yes, please. Clara-Beara, where's your cousin?"

"Still sleeping. Noah's a lazybones." She scrunches up her nose in judgment and goes back to coloring what appears to be a blue dinosaur with purple teeth.

"Well, he must have been really tired," Bree says, dropping onto the stool beside her. "It's tough work being a teenager, you know."

"Tell me about it." Shelby slides a mug of steaming coffee before her. On the side it says #1 Mom. "Milk, no sugar, right?"

"You've got it." After untold summers together, the sisters know each other's coffee preferences by heart. Hazelnut with extra milk for Bree. Hazelnut with two sugars and a dash of skim for Shelby. And dark roast for Kate, straight up, high-octane caffeine; there's no diluting Kate's coffee, just as there's no diluting Kate. Bree reaches for the carton on the counter and pours in a generous splash of milk.

"Noah's still growing. All his cells are multiplying," she continues to explain, although Clara appears to have lost interest. "He needs extra time to sleep so he can grow big and strong." Bree wonders momentarily if she's inadvertently fed her niece another stereotype—that is, that all boys must grow up strong. "I mean, not that he needs to be big and strong, but sleep is healthy. Especially when you're a teenager."

"But not when you're three," Clara pipes up gleefully. Bree and Shelby exchange smiles. She *has* been listening.

"Well, no, getting a lot of sleep is important when you're three, too," Bree says. "Your body is growing, so that's why it's important."

Clara ignores her, scribbles more blue crayon.

"Nice try." Shelby grins and slides an enormous pancake onto Bree's plate. "Someone was up at six thirty this morning." She stares intently at Bree. "Hey, your face is looking much better today."

"Very funny." Nonetheless, Bree reaches up to touch her cheeks gingerly with her fingers. "Yeah, it almost feels back to normal. I definitely slept like a baby, which was a switch from the other night." She grabs the syrup bottle and dribbles it across the pancake before stuffing a bite into her mouth. She's ravenous. "Wow, this is delish, Shel. Thank you."

"You're welcome."

Shelby says it like it's no big deal, but Bree is struck by how nice it is to have someone making her breakfast again. She'd almost forgotten. Aside from family gatherings on the holidays, no one has cooked for her since Hannah.

From the top of the staircase, there's a scuffling noise—Noah. Even though it's Friday, it's a teachers' "improvement day," so no school. Last night, Noah ducked in to say hello for a few minutes, but now, as he descends the stairs, Bree takes a hard look at her nephew. His hair is dark and curly—and long! Almost down to his shoulders, like a lot of boys' these days.

Bree watches them swagger into What's Brewing?, these teens with their mop tops, hair shooting out like sprigs or bangs sweeping so low she can barely make out their eyes—the quest to be seen and not seen simultaneously. She remembers that feeling like it was yesterday. Sometimes she *still* feels that way, especially when, on the odd occasion, a former classmate will wander into the coffee shop and seem surprised to find her behind the counter. *Oh, I thought you were in New York busy being an artist,* they'll say. Then they'll slide a generous tip into the jar, as if it's the least they can do to make up for all her wasted potential.

Noah is wearing gray sweatpants and a forest-green sweatshirt, DARTMOUTH stamped on the front. He looks like a college sophomore, not a junior in high school. He's easily six feet tall. "That's how it happens, though," Shelby said wistfully last night after the kids had gone to bed and the two of them were sharing a bottle of wine. "One day they're your little boy, and the next, they wake up and their feet have grown five inches and they smell to high heaven. If you ever have kids, Bree, you've gotta have a strong heart. Mom never told us that part—how hard it is to watch your own child turning into an adult."

"Noah!" Clara jumps off her stool and races over. First her arms, then her legs twine around his right leg, forming a human barnacle.

"Hiya, Clara-Beara." He crosses the kitchen as if he's got a peg-leg, his niece still clinging to him. "You know, it's going to be really hard to sit down and eat my breakfast with you holding on to me."

He makes as if he's about to tickle her, and Clara shoots off him and yelps, "No tickles!"

"Hey." He stops to admire her picture. "Nice dinosaur."

"It's a T. rex," Clara says, climbing back onto her stool. There's a tad of condescension in her voice, as if it's quite possible her cousin doesn't know what a T. rex is, but she's happy to help him out.

"Nice T. rex," he corrects himself, slides a grin Bree's way.

Bree and Shelby exchange glances. It's a rare event that they're witnessing here in the morning light, and they know it—this gangly monster-boy and his toddler cousin who appear to be equally enamored of each another. And a shot of some unidentifiable emotion— envy, regret, wistfulness?—shoots through Bree. What she'd give to be a teenager again! Minus the emotional angst, of course. Knowing that dinner would unfailingly appear on the table each night, that the electricity bill would be paid, that their home would be warm in the wintertime.

Now it's a constant game of Whack-a-Mole, deciding which bill to pay first, worrying whether there'll be enough money in her bank account to cover next month's rent and her art studio's rent. If she could, Bree would sleep in late every weekend, like this morning. In her dream world, she'd create art all day and not have to scramble to a job that she tolerates most days, and on others, truly hates.

It's no wonder that, when they were younger and wanted to be cruel, her sisters would tell her that she was adopted. And on more than one tearful occasion, Bree believed them. Because she was so, well, *different*. The boys Kate and Shelby crushed over didn't interest her. And while Kate strove to do everything to please their parents—and Shelby basically did everything to set them off—Bree was mainly indifferent. The motivation, the sheer ambition and sense of competition that propelled her sisters forward in life, was seemingly lacking from her genetic code. A part of her DNA chain gone missing, perhaps chopped off at birth.

And if she's being completely honest, her sisters have always seemed to harbor a kernel of resentment over her place in the family pecking order. As if Bree chose her birthday, insisted on being the youngest. She was spoiled, they complained. Bree got off easy, never had to do any chores because she was the baby. It wasn't fair, especially when she got to travel with their parents to Italy and Greece when Kate was in college and Shelby was already married. It didn't help that Bree was their dad's favorite.

Maybe it was because she shared his dark hair and blue eyes, unlike her sisters. Or maybe it was because, in Bree, her dad had sensed a kindred soul. While Kate and Shelby had to be dragged to church, Bree actually enjoyed it. The way her body folded into the wooden pew as if it belonged there. The crinkling sound of the Bible's pages when she turned to follow along with the morning's lesson. The pretty hymns and the way the organist could bang out any song her dad chose and then transition to the piano to accompany a guest violinist on Chopin's "Prelude in E Minor." She could almost feel her body levitating above the entire congregation, looking down.

Oftentimes, over brunch, her dad would seek out her opinion on the day's sermon. "Do you think it was fair that the father rewarded the prodigal son who squandered all his money?" he might ask. That he valued her opinion meant more to her than any stupid grade on a report card, any boy's interest. Her sisters would fidget at the table, eager to be excused. But not Bree. "My philosophical daughter," her dad would say with a catch of pride in his voice, if Bree offered a particularly thoughtful response.

Somedays, she thinks she can still feel the silent judgment radiating off her sisters. As if they're wondering when their baby sister will finally get her act together and land a "real" job teaching art or working in a museum. A sturdy career with health benefits and a 401(k). As if the art she's spent untold years creating, the filled sketchbooks and multiple prints (some already sold!), counts for nothing.

But rather than say this, Bree thinks, *What's the rush?*

All good things take time. It's not as if she's being lazy, and even if she were, slothfulness, in her opinion, gets a bad rap. It's a word meant to shame people when really it implies idleness, stillness, even patience. It doesn't make sense that it's ranked up there with the seven deadly sins. Cheating on a spouse or killing a man is supposedly the equivalent of enjoying a string of lazy Saturdays? Not to mention, Bree is gainfully employed—as a barista, yes, but still employed. And as an artist, her muse doesn't necessarily answer on command. Her sisters don't understand what it's like to be guided by a creative impulse, to live life intuitively rather than following a straight line, connecting one achievable dot to another.

Bree may not drive a Land Rover or own two houses like Kate, or live on the beach like Shelby, but that doesn't mean she's less successful. On the contrary, she tells herself that her life choices hew toward the soulful, the contemplative. That her parents would still be proud, *were* proud of her when they were alive. It might be a quieter, simpler life than that of her sisters, but it's still a rich one. And when her muffler falls off again or the credit card company calls, she'll remind herself it's okay. She's only thirty-six. There's no need to rush. They're not playing *The Amazing Race*, after all.

The vibration of Shelby's phone on the kitchen counter breaks Bree's reverie, making her suddenly aware of Kate's absence. Shelby glances at her cell before hitting a button and flipping it over.

"Hey, where's Kate?" Bree asks. "Still sleeping?"

"Mommy and Daddy slept at the Hull house last night," Clara informs her, apparently parroting what she's already been told. "We'll see Mommy later today."

"Ah." Bree locks eyes with Shelby and tries to gauge from her sister's expression how last night went for Kate. Did she and Trey make up? But Shelby only offers a shrug, which Bree takes to mean that she hasn't heard from Kate this morning either.

Even though Trey stands for most of what Bree generally disdains—ostentatious wealth, a smug air of confidence, and a career as a corporate lawyer (need she say more?), she hopes the two of them can work it out. Mainly for Clara's sake. Clara needs both her parents, and one of Trey's few admirable qualities, in Bree's humble opinion, is that he so clearly adores his daughter. Whenever they're at the beach house, he's joking around with Clara, tossing her up in the air, chasing her around in a game of hide-and-seek. It's impossible to watch them together and not be moved. If he and Kate divorce, it will wreck Clara. She's too young to understand why Daddy won't live in the same house anymore. Isn't it enough that Noah has endured the past few years without his dad around? It doesn't seem fair that her niece should have to go without, too.

"Well, that sounds like a plan," Bree says at last. "And what should we do, you think, until your mom gets here?"

"Lots of things." Clara twists her mouth into a thoughtful knot. "If it's warm enough, Auntie Shelby says we can play on the beach. Or we could play LEGOs. Or we could paint pictures on the deck. Or we could make slime!"

"All excellent ideas," Bree agrees, although above her niece's head she shakes her own and mouths the words, *No slime, No way,* to Shelby.

"Noah, do you want to play with us?" Clara asks, her voice shot through with so much hope that Bree can't imagine how her nephew could possibly refuse.

But he musses Clara's hair and says, "Maybe later, okay, buddy? I have to run some errands first."

"Really?" his mom asks, surprised. "And what might those be?"

Noah shrugs. "Stuff."

Shelby nods silently, as if she's heard it all before, but her fingertips press white against her coffee mug. "Okay, well it would be nice if you could hang out with us later on. I'm sure Clara would appreciate it."

"Can Lindsay come over?"

And there it is, the elephant in the kitchen. The real reason Noah is too busy to play with his cousin.

"I don't see why not," Shelby says agreeably. Her sister is being magnanimous, trying to keep the peace, and Bree watches Noah's expression brighten, as if he didn't think he'd get away with having his girlfriend over while his family visits. Suddenly, his day has improved exponentially, and his face cracks into a wide grin.

"What?" he asks when he catches Bree smiling.

"Oh, nothing." She shakes her head. "I'm looking forward to meeting Lindsay, that's all. I hope she's as great as your mom makes her out to be."

She watches Noah process this comment, parsing it for sarcasm, until he seems to settle on the fact that his girlfriend has been complimented. "Yeah, cool." He grabs his plate and stuffs it in the dishwasher, then whisks his keys off the rack above the kitchen desk. "I guess I'll catch you guys later, then," he says, heading for the front door, and they call out goodbye.

When the door slams shut behind him, Shelby slowly lifts her gaze from her coffee mug. "Welcome to the world of living with a teenager," she says with a weak smile.

"Aw, it's not so bad," Bree offers cheerfully. "At least he put his plate in the dishwasher. That's helpful."

"Yeah," Shelby concedes. "I guess I should focus on the little things."

13

SHELBY

All morning, Shelby's phone has been blowing up with texts from Bo. As much as she'd love to reply, she hasn't had a moment to herself. Bree is planted at the kitchen counter, and Clara clearly needs an adult to keep an eye on her. And even though her phone is set to vibrate, the caller name "health club" keeps popping up.

"My trainer," she explains, when she catches Bree eyeing it.

"Wow, maybe if I had a trainer who hounded me like that, I'd actually get in shape." Bree pauses a moment, then leans forward. "So," she asks softly, "no word from Kate?" Clara has positioned herself in front of the television on the other side of the room.

Shelby shakes her head and starts to load the remainder of the breakfast dishes into the dishwasher. "No. I was going to ask you the same. I've gotta think that their spending the night together is a good sign, though."

"I agree," her sister says. "Maybe that kiss really meant nothing. Because what kind of person does that? Cheat on his wife? And on Kate, of all people?"

"I don't know." Shelby sighs, even though she should be wearing a sign that reads WORLD'S BIGGEST HYPOCRITE around her neck. "For Kate's sake, though, I hope they figure it out." She waits until her sister heads upstairs to shower before sneaking into the study to return Bo's call.

"Hey, it's me," Shelby says quietly.

"Hi, me! I was beginning to think you were avoiding me after yesterday."

"Yesterday?"

"Yeah, at the restaurant. I'm really sorry about that. Cindy surprised me at work and insisted on going out to lunch. I had no idea we'd run into you at Shipwreck'd."

He's partially right—Shelby *is* annoyed and has been intentionally avoiding him since yesterday. All his apologetic texts have gone unanswered, aside from the first one, to which she texted back NBD a few hours later. *No big deal.* But, of course, it *was* a big deal. Seeing him with Cindy played on all her guilty consciences, and yes, there are multiple consciences battling with one another in her head. Guilt for betraying Noah; for betraying Cindy; for betraying Bo's girls. Nothing good can come of their relationship. And yet . . .

"Oh, right," she says as if the entire incident has slipped her mind. "That was awkward for sure, but no, my sister is staying with me, and I've been babysitting my three-year-old niece. I've been a little busy."

For whatever reason, it feels imperative that she remind him that she, too, has a full life, complete with the demands of family and a young niece. That it's not as if she sits around all day, waiting for him to be in touch. That she waits at his beck and call, like some pathetic mistress. Shelby Lancaster is a successful real estate agent, a mom, a sister, an aunt. Most definitely not someone to be toyed with.

"Oh, I knew Kate was in town, but I didn't realize you had everyone staying with you. Are you going into work today?"

Shelby strides over to the window and looks out on the dark-blue water. A few sailboats blithely bob offshore. "I hadn't planned on it. I'm taking the day off with my sisters in town. And Noah has the day off, too, although he just left, no doubt to hang out with Lindsay."

"Yeah, my girls are hanging out at home, too." A pause ensues, as if they both realize they've brought their other selves, their other lives, perhaps too deeply into this conversation. Shelby pictures Cindy curled up on the couch with the girls, bowls of popcorn in hand, watching reruns of *Gilmore Girls*. Which makes her jealous all over again. Not only does Cindy get to sleep next to Bo every night but she also has daughters who probably enjoy spending time with her on their day off. Who won't rush out of the house the first chance they get to be with their friends—or boyfriends. And suddenly, unjustifiably, a zing of loathing seizes Shelby. For a woman she barely knows. Because, in some twisted way, isn't Cindy the root of all her problems?

But for Cindy, what? What if Cindy were to magically disappear? Perhaps in a fluke boating accident?

Would Bo ask Shelby to marry him? It's possible, she thinks. *Why not?* But then she remembers he has yet to utter those three magical words: *I love you.* She tells herself it's out of loyalty to Cindy that he can't form those words until he's officially divorced. But they both know that's a few years off, at best. And once again, Shelby finds herself in the unenviable position of loving someone who is unattainable.

"I was thinking," Bo says, "of maybe cutting out of work early. My schedule is free after one o'clock. I had some cancellations." He clears his throat. "And my sailboat could use a good clean."

She inhales sharply. At the mention of his boat, it's clear that he's hoping she can join him. On more than a few Fridays, Bo's sailboat, a magnificent thirty-foot vessel, has provided a safe haven for their trysts. Belowdecks is a cabin, equipped with a pull-out bed and a small sink. Shelby eyes Clara in the living room, thinks of Bree showering upstairs. Could she swing it? Maybe, if Bree can be persuaded to babysit Clara until Kate returns. And suddenly, Bree's being here at the house, at this moment, seems more providential than irksome.

"I'll bet it could," she says. "Your sailboat, I mean."

Bo laughs on the other end. "Do you think you could drop by? I'll probably be there till six or so."

"Let me figure out what the plan is over here, and I'll get back to you."

Just then, Clara calls out from the living room. "Auntie Shelby, can you read to me?"

"Your niece?" Bo guesses.

"Yes, I have to go. I'll talk to you soon."

"You know where to find me," he says before clicking off.

"I'll be right there, honey," she calls out to Clara, but her phone is lighting up with another incoming call. *Kate.* "I'm going to take this call from your mommy first." She turns her back to the living room to better mute her conversation.

"Hey, how's it going?" Shelby's voice is upbeat, hopeful.

There's been only radio silence since Kate texted last night to say that she and Trey were headed back to their Allerton house for the night. Since then, Shelby's mind has been looping through the possibilities, mainly positive.

"That little shit," Kate declares without further ado.

"Oh!" Shelby gasps. It's not at all what she was expecting.

"He lied to me. And the worst part? I believed him! We went back to the house and fooled around . . . and then he left."

"Left?"

"He said he had to go into work early this morning and that all his suits were back home."

"Okay." Shelby's mind is leaping from one conclusion to another, giant lily pads stretching out across her mind. "That seems reasonable. What am I missing?"

"Yeah, reasonable, until I rolled over in bed, by *myself*, and got poked by an earring. A gold earring."

"Still not following, Katie. Help me out."

A long sigh follows and then a sound like a muffled sob. "I haven't worn gold jewelry since eighth grade when my ears got all red and itchy because of those dangly earrings Dawn Peterson gave me. Do you remember? You know you can only buy me sterling silver. I'm allergic to gold. *Trey* knows he can only give me sterling silver."

"Maybe the housekeeper's earring fell out when she was changing the sheets? Maybe—"

"We don't have a housekeeper," Kate snaps, as if it's the most ridiculous idea Shelby has ever suggested.

"Maybe Clara was playing with some of our jewelry. Both Bree and I wear gold. How do you know it wasn't ours? Or even Mom's? I think there's still some stuff in her jewelry box in the guest room. I think she had a pair of gold hoops."

"In my bed? That seems a little far-fetched, don't you think?" She pauses, but not long enough for Shelby to respond. "He looked me in the eye, Shel," Kate continues. "Looked me in the eye last night and swore to me that he wasn't having an affair."

"Then why not believe him? Take him at his word? It's like you're searching for something to be wrong."

As soon as she says it, Shelby wishes she could take it back, rein her words in like a skein of unruly yarn. "I'm sorry. I shouldn't have said that. You have every right to be suspicious. But, again, I'll say what we tell our kids: honesty is the best policy. Just *ask* him."

"Jesus, Shel. How much more evidence do I need? I saw him with another woman, and now I've found her earring *in our bed.* Why would I give him another chance to lie?"

"I don't know. I guess I'm not thinking clearly," Shelby hastens to add. "You should do whatever you think is best."

There's a sigh on Kate's end. "Listen, I really want to do some investigating of my own. Would it be okay if Clara hangs out with you guys a little longer? Until dinnertime, maybe?"

Shelby wants to say yes, wills herself to say it. How can she refuse her sister, who sounds as if she's on the verge of losing it?

But all she can think of is Bo, his shirt off, waxing the hull of his boat in the afternoon sun. Bo, whom she semi-promised she'd see later today. Bo, whom she hasn't been with for two days, which ordinarily wouldn't be that unusual, but given the run-in yesterday, feels as if it's been two excruciating months. Shelby needs to see him as soon as possible, to rake her fingers through his hair, feel his hands along her body. He's her vitamin D, her antidepressant. He gives her everything that Ethan never could in their last years together—affection, confidence, happiness. Without Bo, she doesn't know if she'll have the strength to help her sister through this.

Whatever "this" turns out to be.

"Um, yeah. Of course," she replies finally. "We'll figure it out. I might have to run into work for a few hours, but I'm sure Bree can handle it." It's amazing how easily the lie trips off her tongue.

"Thank you so much, sis. I owe you." And before Shelby can say another word, her sister hangs up.

$\sim$

When she pulls into the marina, a handful of cars fleck the parking lot: pickup trucks, a Prius, a couple of SUVs, an old Mercedes. Bo's bright-yellow Porsche convertible. She parks as far away as possible from the Porsche so as not to arouse suspicion. In the rearview mirror, Shelby checks herself one last time before getting out. Her head is covered in her floral Hermès scarf, and she's wearing freakishly large sunglasses, the ones Bo refers to as her "movie-star shades." She feels ridiculous wearing a long taupe raincoat and tall black Hunter boots on such a sunny day, but she can't risk being recognized. She even borrowed Bree's Honda Civic to further the disguise, and changed in the car.

No one can know that she's here.

Head bowed, she begins the trek across the parking lot, down to the metal gate (she has her own key), and lets herself in. She was initially surprised to learn that Bo docked his sailboat here; most Hullonians are members of the Yacht Club, where they keep their vessels. But Bo confided that he preferred the Sunset Bay Marina because he was less likely to bump into his clients here.

It's maybe twenty yards to Slip 18, but she might as well be walking a gauntlet. Her heart guns in her chest. A man spraying down a motorboat in Slip 3 glances up briefly, but she ducks her head before he can wave hello. It's later than she hoped—already ten minutes past three—but it was the best she could finagle. When she told Bree she was needed in the office for a few hours to smooth out a hiccup on a closing, her sister was more than happy to watch Clara.

Bo's boat, thirty feet of gleaming teak and cedar, glistens in the afternoon sun. There's no one on deck. Shelby's heart sinks when she imagines they've missed each other. But then she remembers his car in the parking lot; he must be around here somewhere. Right before she turns, the cabin door swings open.

"There you are! My mystery woman. I was beginning to think you'd stood me up." Late-afternoon stubble peppers his tanned jawline. A thatch of dark bangs falls across his eyes, and he swipes them away.

"I considered it. But you're kind of hard to stand up." He bounds up the stairs, takes her by the hand, and leads her aboard. She follows him down into the cabin.

"I'd have been very disappointed if you hadn't shown." The cabin door swings shut behind them, and Bo locks it. "My heart can only take so much, you know."

"Well, I'm here now." There's a regrettable brusqueness to her tone, but it can't be helped. She knows she shouldn't be here—and yet, she is. She unties her scarf, removes her sunglasses. It takes a moment for her eyes to adjust to the murkiness of the cabin. She's been on this boat probably a dozen times, but this is the first that she's ever really noticed the decor. Is it because they've always been too preoccupied with each other to notice?

Possibly. *No, probably.*

At the front, there's a galley kitchen, a stash of liquor bottles lining the wall. A bag of ice is propped up in the kitchen sink, two silver tumblers at the ready. A rag, a roll of paper towels, and a bottle of Windex sit in the porthole.

"So you *have* been cleaning." She nods toward the supplies. "I'm impressed." She sniffs the air, which smells of Windex and something else—maybe linseed oil?

"You should be. I've been polishing for two hours now. Just finished up the deck." Bo has never taken her out sailing; they seldom have that kind of leisurely time on their hands. Which is why, Shelby tells herself, she has yet to learn the difference between a jib and a spinnaker, the bow and the stern. Forgivable offenses, she thinks.

"Can I interest you in an afternoon libation?" He's standing behind the miniature bar, a crooked grin on his face.

"Yes, *please*. I'm having quite the day. How about a martini? Got any of those on board?"

"Coming up. No olives, though, sorry to say. Too early in the season."

"For picking or for eating?"

"For me to have a fully stocked cupboard."

"Ah." She drops onto the sofa and struggles to get comfortable. Liquor will help. "I suppose I'll survive."

She tugs off her boots and looks around. The cabin itself is no bigger than her kitchen, maybe ten by twenty feet, and when Bo steps up to grab a shaker from the top cupboard, he has to duck his head. The sofa sits adjacent to the kitchen. At the very end of the cabin is another couch, except this one is a futon, which has already been pulled out into a bed. A thin blue knit blanket appears to have been hastily thrown on top. Lining the walls are various mementos, including a half-empty tequila bottle, a crooked worm floating lazily at the bottom. There's a deck of playing cards, the game Go, a stack of *Sailing Today* magazines, and, somewhat inexplicably, a ukulele.

"Do you play?" she asks, her head cocked.

"The ukulele? Nah, but my girls like to fiddle around on it sometimes. We picked it up in Bermuda when the girls and I sailed down there a few years ago." Bo likes to joke that, in lieu of a Ferrari, the sailboat represents his midlife crisis. (She refrains from pointing out that he already owns a Porsche.) Cindy, she knows, doesn't care for sailing and has set foot on the boat exactly once. But his girls love it. They're taking sailing lessons this summer.

In the far corner, there's a safe built into the wall, and Shelby teases him. "You have a safe on your boat? I've never noticed it before. What's in it? Stacks of cash?"

He laughs. "Ha, I wish. That would help with the girls' college tuition one day, wouldn't it? No, it was there when I bought the boat. Guess it's handy if you have any valuables on board."

"And do you?"

He crosses over and hands her the martini. "Only you."

She smiles coyly and accepts the drink. "Well played." The martini tastes delicious, and soon, Bo's lips are grazing hers. He tastes like scotch, and her body lights up immediately, instinctively.

"I've been thinking about you all day."

"Really?" She pulls away. "Even though you have a wife to keep you company?" She can't help it if the words sting—they slip out. Yesterday's chance encounter has left her rattled.

A pained look crosses his face, and he leans back. "Ouch. I guess I deserved that. But yes, even if I have someone else to keep me company." His lack of the word "wife" does not escape her. "And she's not exactly good company," he adds. "At least, not for me."

Shelby silently coaches herself to stop harassing him. It's not Bo's fault that Cindy dragged him out to lunch. And if they want to keep up the charade, then it's necessary that he play along whenever Cindy asks him to do her bidding. She shakes her head, polishes off the rest of her drink. "I'm sorry. It's hard sometimes. Knowing that you're not all mine."

"I'm sorry, too," he says softly. "I wish it were otherwise." He sets her glass next to his on the bar, then stands and leads her to the bed, which is when she realizes that she's still wearing her raincoat. It's hardly a deterrent, though, because Bo easily unbuttons, then removes it. Next comes her T-shirt and jeans. From the bed, she watches him peel off his own shirt and khakis. Before she can say another word, he's tugging the blanket over their bodies and rolling toward her, his excitement pressing up against her. Hungrily, his lips begin to make their way across her body.

Somewhere around her elbow, though, her sister's insistent voice begins to call out in her head. *That little shit. He's cheating on me.* And she imagines Cindy, Bo's wife, uttering the exact same words. About Bo. Because Shelby is here in Bo's bed. That Cindy doesn't visit the boat often is irrelevant. What if, one day, she changes her mind and slides into this very bed and discovers one of *Shelby's* earrings? Or a ring? Or a random sock? Shelby will be at least partially responsible for Cindy's pain.

Which makes her as bad as Trey. Maybe even worse.

Because, despite her sister's suffering, Shelby is still here. On Bo's boat. In his bed. A mistress. When she should know better.

"No, wait. Stop." She pulls his hand away and pushes herself up into a sitting position, her arms cradling her bare knees.

"What? Do you hear something?" Bo casts a worried glance at the cabin door, even though it's locked.

"No." She shakes her head. "It's not that." Her body shivers as if it's fifty degrees in the cabin, not sixty-five. "I can't do this," she says. "Not here."

"But I thought you liked the boat?" He pushes up beside her so that their knees are touching, parallel. Short dark hairs that she's never noticed before sprout from his kneecaps like tiny weeds.

"I do. I did, I guess. It just feels risky—and not right, today."

It takes all her fortitude to climb out of bed—away from Bo—and get dressed. But she doesn't have a choice. She tells him she'll talk to him later but must go now.

Just then, his cell phone rings. He holds up a finger, gesturing for her to wait. "Hi, there," he says. "Can I call you back? I'm kind of in the middle of something." He pauses. "Um, no. Not right now. I think that would be a very bad idea. Okay, right, yes, I'll talk to you later."

"Everything okay?"

"Fine, just a crazy client." He stares at her, crestfallen. "Promise you'll call me later?"

"Yes, of course."

But as she makes her way to the car, the ridiculous scarf and sunglasses back in place, she keeps thinking about Kate's call this morning, how angry and hurt she sounded. And how Shelby is doing exactly the same thing to another innocent woman, another *mom*. All her guilt comes crashing down. No amount of reasoning can justify her actions.

But she's pretty sure she's in love.

What is she going to do?

14

KATE

Every ounce of goodwill Kate has been channeling toward her husband, every pound of trust, has been blasted to smithereens. She's never been more certain that he's lying to her. After discovering the other gold earring last night, she raced downstairs to flip open her laptop. Hands shaking, she willed herself to type in Liz Macintosh's name on Facebook, along with her Seattle location. The woman's profile photo—featuring two adorable girls, maybe six and eight, turning cartwheels on the beach—popped up instantly.

Kate scrolled down hurriedly, searching for a recent photo, until her finger paused on a picture taken at a holiday party last year. Dressed in a burgundy sheath, a small rope of pearls circling her neck, Liz stood beside a tall, attractive man with a buzz cut, presumably her husband. Her hair was styled in the pixie cut Kate remembered, her olive skin glowing. As she continued scrolling through the handful of profile shots, Kate grew even more convinced that the woman she'd spied with Trey a few days ago wasn't Liz. For one, Liz was taller than the mystery woman. And that hair . . . It was impossible that she could have grown it out so quickly. In her mind, Kate compared the image of the woman she'd spotted downtown to Liz's photo on the screen: they were two different people. Kate was sure of it.

But why would Trey lie? Wouldn't it have been easier to say it was some random person? Maybe a work acquaintance? Why weave Liz into his alibi when he knew Kate would get upset about an ex-girlfriend? She paced the kitchen, searching for an answer, a missing piece of a jigsaw puzzle she didn't particularly care to solve. Why not tell her it was a long-lost cousin, an old friend? By two in the morning, she gave up and crawled back into bed.

The answer didn't come to her until after speaking with her sister this morning. Trey would have no reason to lie about Liz—unless the real answer was obvious. Unless the woman he was kissing didn't actually return home to her family in Seattle as Liz would do—out of sight and out of mind—but was living right here in Boston, even, perhaps, working at his firm.

After she hung up with Shelby, Kate logged back on to the laptop and pulled up the company website for Murray and Sloane, her heart beating twice as fast. She hadn't checked the site in months because, well, why would she? The last time she'd visited the page was to confirm the correct spelling of Trey's boss's name, Stuart Murray (Stewart or Stuart?), when she'd wanted to send a proper thank-you note for an extravagant dinner at The Capital Grille, where Stuart and his lovely wife, Phoebe, treated them all to sirloins the size of Texas.

Kate took a deep breath, clicked on "Meet Our Team," and pawed through the masthead. There were Stuart and Jay, the founding partners, and a handful of other partners, mostly men, including Trey. She lingered a moment on Trey's photo, taken when he started at the firm, about ten years ago. Movie-star handsome—that's how her friends described him. A description that was hard to argue with. The toothy grin, the wavy hair, the deeply set green eyes. The man she fell in love with. There followed a few women partners, the notable power brokers of the city, and then a lengthy list of associates bookended by paralegals, office managers, human resources personnel, and the like. Kate skimmed the list so quickly the first time that she had to go back and begin again, searching for the face, the sweep of raven hair.

She remembered Trey's mentioning that the firm was making a concerted effort to recruit more women and people of color, and last year, he served on a hiring committee to help promote diversity. She continued flipping through, forcing herself to go slowly, until her finger came to rest on the photo of a young lawyer with straight black hair. She couldn't believe she'd missed her the first time. The woman looked younger on the computer screen, but the face was unmistakably hers. Attractive, pert nose, olive skin. "Sonja Britton, Of Counsel."

Her heart in her throat, Kate read the accompanying brief bio:

> Sonja Britton joins us with a joint JD and MBA from Harvard Law School and Harvard Business School. She received her undergraduate degree from the University of North Carolina at Chapel Hill. As counsel, she advises her corporate clients on all manner of insurance and tort cases, including personal injury and fraud. A native of Lexington, Massachusetts, Sonja enjoys hiking, running, and spending time with her Great Dane, Henry.

And screwing my husband, Kate thought uncharitably. She zoomed in and noticed the tiny gold hoops, flecked with a single diamond, gracing Sonja's delicate lobes. A hard, unforgiving knot formed in her chest.

She raced upstairs, ripped the sheets from their bed. Barreled down to the garage, where she stuffed the linens into the trash can. She didn't give a damn if the neighbors heard her cursing Trey's name. Too furious to cry, she ransacked the house in search of her pack of Lucky Strikes from last summer. At last she found them—tucked into one of her old hiding spots—the ceramic vase sitting atop the bookcase. With trembling fingers, she fished out a cigarette and smoked one, then another and another, ignoring the bitter taste of year-old nicotine while trying to figure out what to do next.

Now, with the afternoon sun pooling on the kitchen floor, she's beginning to see clearly what has been standing before her the entire time—her husband's infidelity. The host of reasons Trey supplied about why he couldn't make it home for untold dinners, for Clara's nightly tuck-ins. The various excuses about why he had to head into the office over the weekend. The "work trips" to Philadelphia for depositions and case review. "This case is huge, Kate," he told her. "If we can make it through this one, I'll be home by seven every night. I promise." Considered in this new light, his list of absences, which have piled up like an unwelcome stack of IOUs over the past several months, takes on new meaning.

Her husband hasn't been working late to better provide for his family, he's been whisking Sonja off to remote places—even to their Hull house!—to enjoy an affair of the heart.

Kate can feel the bile rising in her throat. Despite a few paltry hours of sleep, her anger is immense, her jealousy razor sharp. The tiny gold hoops are clutched in her hand like delicate miniature eggs, as if she could crush them. On the table sits an elongated ivory envelope.

Can she really do this? She's had more than a few hours to weigh her options.

It almost feels as if she's playing a role, stepping into someone else's skin. But she won't tolerate it, won't be lied to. *Who does he think she is?* Her husband seems to have forgotten that Kate used to be a senior consultant at Bain & Company before she agreed to stay home for "the sake of their child." Seems to have forgotten that she's in possession of *a brain*. On a Post-it note, she scrawls two deceptively simple questions in black ink: *Lose something? At the Hull house?* She sticks the earrings and Post-it note into the envelope, licks it, and seals it. On the front, she writes, *Trey Dowling, Esquire.*

The envelope slides easily enough into her purse. She throws on a baseball cap, grabs her keys. She knows exactly where she's headed. Into Boston. To Trey's building, where the lobby's white marble pillars rise up to greet the titans of the universe each day. Where she'll leave the envelope to be delivered to his office on the ninth floor, perhaps right after he's shared a laugh with Sonja at the copy machine. The only flaw in Kate's plan?

Not being able to see her husband's face when he opens it.

15

ROBIN

The rescue boats have been looping circles around the bay for the past three hours. Coast Guard vessels, fireboats, police boats, and, now, the state police. No sightings, thus far. Nor has anyone shown up at the medical center with symptoms of hypothermia. The man on board has been brought back to the station for questioning. Meanwhile, Hull's harbormaster, Tommy, has been checking in with Robin periodically from his boat, where he's helping to direct rescue teams to areas where a body might ride a current. Another officer has been dispatched to Bumpkin Island to conduct a comprehensive search along the shoreline. With each passing moment, hope of finding someone alive dims a little more.

About an hour ago, the Massachusetts Environmental Police marine unit, called in by the chief, arrived carrying their state-of-the-art sonar technology. Their presence here, Robin understands all too well, underscores the direness of the situation. Because if they're activating the sonar in the search, it most likely means they're looking for a body, not a living person. If there's someone down there, the side-scan sonar device can detect them more rapidly than divers swimming around aimlessly, combing miles of ocean for a speck of humanity. Robin understands vaguely how the sonar works, bouncing sound waves off the ocean floor to generate a rough image of the terrain on a computer screen. But the sonar can send back waves on any significant object, human or otherwise. It's easy to fan false hopes.

Originally, the rescue crews focused their search on a short radius from where the sailboat was first sighted. But since the boat owner doesn't appear to know where or when his companion fell—*rolled off? jumped? was pushed?*—overboard, the teams have had to cast a wider net. A body could have drifted farther out, into Hingham Bay, maybe even to the Gut by now. Hovering above the water, helicopters continue to *whoop-whoop* in circles.

It's evident from the way the Boston cops and state troopers speak in hushed tones that this particular search-and-rescue effort has taken a turn in the wrong direction. Robin has to refrain from marching over and shaking them to remind them that this is Hull, God's country, as she likes to call it. *Miracles happen here every day.* This is a community that looks out for each other. For centuries, Hullonians have weathered massive storms, devastating fires, and each time, the town has built itself up anew, a phoenix rising from the ashes.

Don't discount us just yet, she thinks.

Someone has kindly thought to bring in a tray of coffees for the officers, and Robin helps herself to one as she wanders the dock and stretches her legs. The morning chill has subsided, and the sun on her back feels good, as does the Styrofoam cup warming her hands. She's about to approach the young Boston cop for an update when a thunder of shouts breaks out on the right. "We've got something here!" a voice yells over the wavelength that everyone's radio is tuned to. There's a sudden burst of energy from the first responders waiting on shore; maybe they *will* be needed, after all. Robin steps out of the way as a few paramedics, armed with a stretcher and various medical equipment, hustle down to the edge of the dock.

Her chest feels as tight as a mussel in its shell. *We've got something here.* All of law enforcement huddles at the edge of the water while the news crews camped up above have fallen strangely quiet. *What? What do they have?*

It's the question that they've all been seeking the answer to.

16

BREE

Piles of LEGO bricks lie scattered across the worn Oriental rug in Shelby's living room. In the last hour and a half, Bree and Clara have built a small but impressive farmhouse flanked by an adjoining barn. There's a red tractor, flower boxes on the windows, a colorful vegetable garden. Next up, Clara directs, will be horses and cows, "and maybe a pony," because every farm needs animals.

Bree sweeps a pile of bricks toward her, does as she's told. Wonders how the heck she's supposed to make a cow out of LEGOs? But before she can begin, their play gets interrupted by the doorbell. Bree jumps to answer it, Tuukka chasing at her heels, and performs a cursory check of herself in the hallway mirror. Her face, much less swollen, looks more or less ready for public consumption, she decides. She grabs on to Tuukka's collar and opens the door.

On the front porch, a woman with short blonde hair and enormous brown eyes stares back at her. She seems surprised to see Bree.

"Oh, I'm sorry. I was looking for Shelby." The stranger glances around for a moment, as if to get her bearings. Encircling her right wrist is an enormous cast.

"I'm Shelby's sister, Bree. Shelby's gone into work. Can I help you?"

"Oh, Bree! Of course, it's you. Maeve Harding—remember me? Gosh, I haven't seen you in years. Guess you're all grown up now." Bree vaguely recalls the name but doesn't recognize her. She looks to be in her midforties or early fifties, and there's something about her that reminds Bree of a bird. Maybe it's the awkward cast that renders her so fragile or the fact that her head seems positively huge on top of her very skinny body.

Bree smiles, uncertain what to say. "Um, yeah, I guess so."

"Anyway, I'm really sorry to bother you. Of course she's at work! I'm such a dummy. I was on my lunch break, so I thought I'd stop by. To say hello. We haven't seen each other in so long."

"If it's urgent, you might try her at the office."

"Oh no, nothing urgent," Maeve says, peering over Bree's shoulder, as if to get a better glimpse into the house. "I'll catch up with her another time. Nice seeing you again, Bree. Take care." She turns to make her way down the stairs, gripping the railing with her good hand.

"I'll tell her you came by," Bree calls out.

"Thanks!"

When Bree shuts the door, Clara is standing behind her, wide-eyed. "Who was that?"

"Just a friend of Auntie Shelby's."

"Mommy says that you shouldn't open the door for strangers."

"And that's very good advice," Bree says, crouching down to her niece's level. "But that was Auntie Shelby's friend, so it was okay to answer the door. Plus, I'm an adult, and I'm not going to let anyone hurt you, right? You're safe with me." She says this, although inwardly she agrees that the whole encounter was odd. They head back into the living room, where Clara resumes building a fence.

Bree watches her niece, focused so intently on her project, and thinks, *How could Trey possibly cheat on this sweet child?* Because if that's, in fact, what he's done, then he's cheated on his entire family.

Before Shelby ran off for work, she shared that not all had gone well between Kate and Trey and that Kate won't be grabbing Clara until much later in the day. That after a reconciliation last night, something happened to make Kate suspect Trey of cheating all over again. Something about an earring? But it's unclear to Bree. She tries to imagine what her sister must be feeling right now—most likely a strange brew of outrage and disbelief. Bree had been about to text her, but then stopped. Better to hear the whole story from Kate before offering her condolences on a marriage that, Bree suspects, will eventually come crashing down, anyway.

It's no secret that Bree's relationship with her brother-in-law is distant, verging on chilly. Early on, she sensed that Trey was little more than a grown-up frat boy, accustomed to getting his own way. The condescension in his voice from the moment he learned she was an artist was evident. "That's cool," he said over dinner with the whole family on a balmy June evening in Boston's North End. "I've never really understood art. Especially the modern stuff that looks like finger painting. You don't do that kind of art, do you?" he asked.

And Bree responded coolly, "No, I don't *do* that kind," without going into further detail about lithography, the printing process made famous by artists like Toulouse-Lautrec, Diego Rivera, and M. C. Escher. About the joy she derives from drawing in greasy crayon on limestone, only to follow it with the involved, age-old process of inking the stone and transferring the original image to paper for a print. How to help him appreciate that the rosin, when applied, fills her studio with the fresh scent of pine, like a Christmas tree brought in from the cold. Or how the treatments of lithotine and asphaltum and water, all critical steps to ensuring that the ink adheres to the crayoned image (and not the negative space of the stone), is a ritual imbued with almost religious meaning for her. To make him understand the delight that surfaces whenever a new drawing appears on paper, only in reverse, after she runs it through the press.

No, it was impossible to explain the beauty of the process to a Neanderthal like Trey. No sense in describing how the hush of her artist's studio calms her mind and makes all her worries slip away. Trying to make him understand any part of her, in fact, seemed pointless.

But later that evening, when it became obvious to the entire family how completely enchanted he was with her sister, even Bree was willing to set aside her misgivings. A few months later, on the heels of a sunset proposal on Nantucket's Madaket Beach, Trey's position in the family as adopted son became official, as sparkling as the four-carat diamond ring he slid onto Kate's finger.

That he's apparently been engaged in extracurricular activities at work comes as a disappointment but not a surprise. Not to Bree, at least. She wonders if it comes as a surprise to Kate. Bree's always struck by those *Dateline* stories where the wife fails to notice the clues, like an incriminating trail of bread crumbs, pointing her straight to the husband's infidelity. The receipts for fancy dinners that didn't include her or the mini vacations without her. But Bree's willing to bet that most people see what they want to see, what they can *bear* to witness. When knowing the rest would flatten them, somehow ignoring it makes sense.

Tuukka plods over from the kitchen and makes a circle before flopping down in a splash of light beside Clara. The midafternoon sun cuts wide arcs across the room. Shelby's house is cozy in a lived-in kind of way. There are scuff marks running up the stairs, and the ghosts of fingerprints—some at Noah's height, others at Clara's—linger on doorframes. The floorboards in the den, warped from years of sea air, creak whenever anyone walks on them. And in the wintertime, the old radiators hiss to life in the upstairs bedrooms. But these oddities are all part of the house's charm. Bree much prefers it to the modern, open McMansions that most people seem drawn to these days. Those open floor plans make her nervous, make her feel as if someone is constantly watching her.

Her gaze skips along the wall, dotted with family photos of when the sisters were young, sun-kissed and grinning at the beach, their mom in her thirties, her dark hair pulled back in a ponytail. A natural beauty, everyone used to say. And of her dad, grinning over the barbecue, looking goofy with a cigar dangling from his mouth. The images make her chest tighten. *They should still be here,* Bree thinks. What she'd give to hear her dad say, "Attagirl!" one more time or to hear her mom's voice call out to her. A decade has passed since they left this world, but sometimes it feels like a week.

On the adjacent wall, there's a long, winding path of Noah photos, his chubby toddler face morphing into the angular adolescent face of this morning. It's both charming and a little weird, a kind of *This Is Your Life* display. She wonders if it embarrasses him when Lindsay comes over, or if she studies each picture and marvels at how adorable her boyfriend used to be, and still is.

Any pictures of Shelby and Ethan and Noah together as a family have long ago been taken down, but there's a framed photo of a young Noah and his dad out on the boat, which still sits on a shelf in Noah's bedroom. Noah's wearing a red windbreaker, smiling to reveal a gap where his front tooth used to be, and Ethan's hands rest on his shoulders. Ethan, a proud daddy, beams in the picture. Every time Bree walks past Noah's door, her eyes snag on it, and a little arrow pierces her heart. *The kid deserved better,* she thinks. *So much better.*

When her phone chimes with a text, she assumes it's Shelby writing to say she's on her way home. But when Bree rolls over to grab her cell, it's a response to a text that she sent out late last night in a rush of drunk-texting (after sharing a bottle of chardonnay with Shelby). There was no guarantee that she'd get a response, of course, when she told Audrey that she was back in town. Now that her friend's name is blinking on her phone, however, Bree realizes how much she's been hoping for a reply.

Great to hear from you! I'm hanging out at Toast, if you want to drop by and say hi. No pressure. Xoxo

Bree's heart performs a backflip. Audrey is at Toast *right now*. She hasn't seen her friend/ex-lover since last summer at Kate's Memorial Day party, back when Hannah was still Bree's girlfriend and throwing mental daggers anytime Audrey stepped over to say hello. But now that Hannah is living happily without her on the other side of the country, Bree thinks everything—and everyone—is fair game.

She glances at Clara and tries to perform the complicated calculus of making the logistics work: How to see Audrey while babysitting Clara? But then she simply asks, "Hey, Clara-Beara. Want to go get a treat? Maybe grab some hot chocolate at Toast?" It's still a chilly fifty-six degrees outside.

"Yes!" Clara exclaims and shoots straight up, almost knocking over the barn they've spent the entire morning building. "Can we go right now? Please?"

Bree laughs. Sometimes kids can be so frickin' easy. She doesn't know what Kate's complaining about all the time. "Absolutely. Let me grab the keys, and you find your jacket, okay?"

Will be there in fifteen minutes (I'm babysitting my niece), she texts. **See you soon.** Together, the two of them head outside, and Clara, zipped up in her tiny green jacket, reaches out to grab Bree's hand. It's a small gesture, automatic, but it nearly knocks Bree over. The unspoken ask for someone's help—and trusting that it will be forthcoming. *This,* she thinks, *is why people have kids.* They climb into Shelby's black Mercedes, where Clara's car seat is already strapped in. (Shelby suggested they trade cars for the day so they wouldn't have to mess with moving Clara's seat around.)

On the way to Toast, Bree winds past the middle school and over to the marina on A Street in order to placate Clara, who insists on seeing the boats first. The majority are settled back in the water now, their owners prepping for the gala that is Memorial Day weekend here. A few stragglers, wrapped up like ungainly sausages, remain on high stilts from the winter. Among the handful of cars and trucks parked in the lot, there's a blue Honda Civic that catches Bree's eye. The Civic, she knows, is an affordable, popular car for the midtwenties and thirties set. But the closer they get, the more she realizes it *is* her car. Her customized license plate, ARTAGIRL, stares back at her when she slows down. That's strange. Maybe Shelby had a closing on a boat? Maybe she's *shopping* for a boat? Bree shelves the thought in her brain for later. Because if Shelby has enough spare cash to buy a new boat, then she can most certainly afford to help Bree out of her financial predicament.

A few minutes later, she's pulling up directly in front of Toast and parking beside a lime-green VW camper. That's another charming quality about Hull: even during the off-season, there's an appealing counter-culture vibe about the place. She hops out to set Clara free, and again, her niece automatically reaches out for her hand. *Oh!*

Opening the front door to Toast releases the intoxicating scent of coffee mixed with cinnamon, and, as if on command, Bree's stomach grumbles while her eyes search the snug space. Quickly, her gaze lands on a corner table by the window. Audrey looks up from her notebook, sending her bangs falling across her eyes, waggles a few fingers in the air, and smiles. *Hello.*

And Bree and Clara, their fingers woven together as tightly as a child's dream catcher, walk over to say hello.

17

KATE

Kate is not a crier. To the contrary, she prides herself on being able to check her emotions—or, at the very least, put them on hold until she can process them in private, sometimes weeks, even years later. The phrase "Never let them see you cry" has marched across her mind during the occasional tense work meeting, and more recently, at her weekly mothers' playgroup. A get-together where it's all she can do not to shout at women whom she doesn't know particularly well, *But aren't you always tired? How do you keep it together? Aren't you bored of playing make-believe and slicing apples? Do you ever want to murder your husband for not helping out?*

Naturally, she's never uttered such thoughts aloud because the women in her group would think she's lost her mind. And at the moment, they are the one adult crowd upon whom the thin thread of her sanity depends.

But despite the old mantra of holding in her feelings, crying is exactly what Kate is doing right now. Big, fat, ugly tears roll down her face. Ever since returning from Trey's office, she's been laid out on the couch. Her body feels as if it's been tied to a spinning wheel so that she no longer knows which way is forward, which way is back. There should be a medical term for it, she thinks. *Whiplash-itis.* When a person ping-pongs between anger and despair, hope and fear, self-doubt and relief. The entire emotional gamut. She's been flattened—yet again.

Just when she'd convinced herself that she and Trey were fine, solid, he lied to her *again*. Just when she'd made her peace with a stray, meaningless kiss, she discovered it was anything but. Her mind keeps spinning scenarios where Sonja and Trey might have bumped into each other at the office. All the times in the break room, when they'd spy each other across the table or joke around by the Keurig machine. *What will it be today, Sonja? Tea? Hot chocolate? Your regular?* She imagines her husband flirting with this younger woman. Pictures his hand touching the small of her back, the exact same spot where it has rested on Kate's back countless times, to guide her out of a meeting. Maybe a midafternoon stroll past each other's offices, leaving token treats on the other's desk—red licorice, Starburst, a pack of gum. The very thought of it makes her skin burn.

Is it possible that others at the firm know? Over the years, Kate has attended enough work functions to count a handful of Trey's colleagues as friends. Wouldn't someone have felt compelled to alert her to the fact that her husband was messing around with another woman? Is it really so easy to avert their gaze and pretend nothing is happening? Kate's been witness to office romances before—as far as she recalls, they're pretty easy to spot.

She's tempted to call Roxanne Stafford, one of the younger attorneys who got her start at the firm around the same time as Trey. At a charity event for homeless people, she and Roxanne struck up a friendship, cemented by one too many Negronis and a shared dislike for the stodgier, misogynistic lawyers in attendance. A few weeks later, they went to see *Wicked* at Emerson Colonial Theatre and shared dinner at No. 9 Park. A graduate of Duke, Roxanne was southern to her core—and extremely funny. She was a welcome, convivial companion at firm events, where Trey often left Kate to go fraternize with "the boys."

"Why is it," Roxanne asked, sliding into an empty seat beside Kate at a fundraising dinner one night, "that everyone here is so uptight?" She leaned in closer and rested her hand on Kate's forearm, her thumb gliding up toward Kate's wrist. "Where I come from, people aren't afraid to kick back and have a little fun, you know what I mean?" Her heavy southern accent made every question charming, each verbal jab softer. She tossed a quick wink Kate's way, giving her wrist a flirtatious squeeze, and Kate thought, *Oh!*

Had she misunderstood her friend's intentions all along? The possibility had made her vaguely uncomfortable and, if it was true, strangely disappointed. Roxanne had become a good friend. Later that evening, they parted ways awkwardly—Roxanne whispering in her ear, *Call me, honey.* Kate hasn't seen or talked to her since. That was three months ago.

No, broaching the subject of her husband's affair with her old friend seems like a bad idea, one that could backfire into an even more difficult conversation.

She could try one of the partners—she's friendly enough with Stuart. But then again, it's not as if getting Trey fired is her goal. Or is it? *No!* Not when her financial well-being is directly entwined with her husband's. In exchange for Trey's financial support, Kate has stupidly forfeited her own annual salary, her own financial independence—all things she promised herself in college that she'd never do. Since she left Bain & Company, her orbit of friends and colleagues has shrunk dramatically, but at the moment, she can't recall ever feeling quite so isolated. If she extricates herself from her marriage, what, exactly, will be left? Kate could slap herself for signing a prenuptial agreement in the first place, where she agreed to waive any rights to Trey's inherited millions should they ever divorce. At the time, splitting up seemed unthinkable.

How will Kate manage alone?

Her cell phone pings. Again. Trey has been texting nonstop, which means he's received—and opened—the envelope. WTF? was his initial response, but she refuses to look at the lengthening string of texts on her phone. *What will his excuse be this time?* That he has no idea to whom the gold earrings belong? Or will he admit that there was another woman in their bed without actually confessing that it was the woman he was kissing downtown? Will he try to blame it on someone else? He's a clever man. Surely he'll come up with an equally clever lie.

But as much as she's hoping for a plausible explanation, it seems pretty apparent that there won't be one forthcoming. All the Hail Marys in her husband's playbook have been trotted out. It can't be a mere coincidence that Sonja Britton was wearing the exact same earrings in her photo on the firm's website. And even if the earrings don't, by some miracle, belong to her, it hardly matters. Now that Kate has identified the random woman as a colleague of Trey's, a woman whose *very existence* he tried to hide from her . . . well, why should she respond?

Loyalty. It's a trait that's etched into her being as deeply as her DNA. It's the underpinning to every relationship she's nurtured over a lifetime. Once a friend, always a friend. Once a spouse, always a spouse. When she and Trey professed their love for each other on a muggy August afternoon, surrounded by fragrant white lilies in Hull's Saint Nicholas United Methodist Church, they promised themselves to each other. Swore their love and loyalty till death do them part.

Or so she thought.

But now that Trey appears to have broken that trust, it would seem that her end of the bargain is up as well. Her vow shaken to the core.

Her mind rattles through possible next steps. Should she insist that Trey move out? Suggest a trial separation? Counseling? A divorce? It all sounds so ludicrous, incredible. That her entire world could come crumbling down so swiftly and easily. Can she even consider leaving him? A part of her wants to give him a second chance. Because as furious as she is, as much as she wants to rip him in two, she still loves him. *You don't stop loving someone overnight,* her dad explained once, when she'd asked why a high school friend's parents, who'd divorced, were still living together.

And there's the not-so-small matter of pride, the social standing that she and Trey have so carefully cultivated over the past several years. They're one of Boston's "it" couples, photographed about town. Regulars at charity events, where they get to rub elbows with local sports celebrities and newscasters. Ribbon cutters, along with the mayor, at grand openings about town. They're the envy of all their friends.

And now they'll be laughingstocks.

The phone starts ringing and she grabs her purse, digging for it. She's forgotten all about Shelby. What if Clara needs her? "Hello?" she answers in a slight panic.

"Jesus, Kate. You had me worried."

It's Trey. "Oh, I had *you* worried?" She wishes she could see his face, regrets answering. "I take it you got my care package then?"

"I did, and we have to talk. But not on the phone."

Kate can't believe he's still playing this cat-and-mouse game. "I know who she is, Trey," she hisses. *Enough with the charade.* "I found her on the company website. Sonja Britton."

Her comment is met with dead silence on the other end.

"Did you really think I wouldn't find out?" she cries. "That I'm a complete fool?" Her voice is rough and scratchy, and she hates that he can probably tell she's been crying.

"Katie, I'm sorry, but it's not what you think."

"*Mm-hmm.* I've heard that before. Honestly, Trey, how *could* you?" Her voice trembles, and she swallows hard, searching for any last crumbs of composure. "Clara and I will be staying at the Hull house through Memorial Day. After that, I'm not sure. I suggest you start looking for someplace else to live. Maybe you can shack up with your girlfriend." The cutting remark, surprisingly, flies off her tongue like a hatchet.

"Katie, you've got to at least give me a chance to explain."

"I thought that's what last night was for, but apparently I was mistaken."

He's quiet. "That was before you knew."

"Wait. Did you really just say that?" She leaps up from the couch, incredulous, and starts pacing the living room floor, her bare feet weaving up and down the wooden planks. "That's supposed to make me feel better? Don't you mean it was before you *lied* to me? Directly to my face?"

"Katie, please. Listen to me. I—"

"You know what, Trey? I'm done listening to you. You've had multiple chances to exonerate yourself, and instead, you've only made it a million times worse. Did you even consider our daughter while you were busy screwing another woman?"

Trey exhales deeply. "Kate, if only you knew how sorry I am. It wasn't supposed to happen like this . . ."

"Like how, Trey? Like me finding out?" When he doesn't reply, she gulps back tears. Because there it is: an admission of guilt. It's as near a confession as she's gotten, will probably ever get. She falls onto the couch, grabs a pillow, and hugs it to her chest.

"Jesus. How long, Trey?" Because that's what she really wants to know now that she *knows*. How long has her husband been making a fool of her? Of them? "Weeks? Months?" she yells. *"Years?"*

"No, no. Nothing like that. Just a few months, maybe? But it's over now. I broke things off with her. I swear."

Her stomach roils. "Just a few *months?*"

"Like I said, somewhere around there."

"Oh, that's rich. You're not even sure."

"It's complicated," he offers.

"Complicated." She spits out the word as if it's unpalatable. "Too bad you didn't think of that earlier."

"Not on the phone," Trey says quietly.

A laugh, like a cackle, escapes from somewhere deep inside her. "Because why? Is there a confidential reason why you're having an affair? Or do you need to keep it a secret from the client? Because wouldn't that be embarrassing, if your work has been compromised due to an unfortunate physical attraction!"

"Kate, I can't—"

"Yeah, don't bother. Because you know what? I don't want to know. To me, it all seems pretty straightforward. You cheated, and now you have to pay the consequences."

It's not worth delving into the longer litany of complaints she could access if she cared to dig deeper. The loneliness that she feels each night after she finally gets Clara to bed and pours herself a glass of wine. The constant wondering when her husband will walk through the front door. The emptiness and monotony of her days, how each one unspools like the next, day after day after day. That her anger, her jumping to conclusions, has served as an undercurrent to the enormous, murderous wave that's been building in her.

As much as Kate likes to pretend all is well, this is not the marriage she bargained for, not the partnership she was promised. If she's being honest with herself, she's been unhappy for a long time. At least three years, a thousand days. Trey's infidelity is merely the hurricane that has sent the wave hurtling toward shore.

"I wouldn't do that if I were you," he says now, a coolness creeping into his voice.

His tone sends a chill through her body. "Wait, is that a threat? Are you *threatening* me?"

"Of course not. It's only, think of Clara. What's best for her."

Kate's not falling for it. Not this time. "I'll tell you what's best for her. If her daddy hadn't cheated on her mommy in the first place. That's what's best for her. Can you rewind time?"

There's a sharp intake of breath on the other end, and Kate hesitates before saying more. What does she even want? A full-on admission and apology? A renunciation of any feelings for Sonja? A promise of sainthood? "We had something good, Trey, and you are *such* an ass to screw it up." She swallows hard. "And I really love you. Loved you. I don't even know which tense to use anymore."

"Present. You should use the present tense because that's how I feel. Nothing's changed, Katie. I still love you. So much. Clara, too."

She stares out the window at the sea, churning back and forth, as if it could steal away her disbelief, cleanse it like a stone and return her faith to her, shiny and new. Finally, she lifts the phone back to her ear. "That's where you're wrong, Trey," she says softly. "*Everything's* changed. You just don't realize it yet."

18

Shelby

Noah is driving her slightly crazy. Absolutely nothing she says is right. If she mentions that his jeans look a tad short, he'll tell her she's wrong. When he's in the passenger seat, he chides her for driving too slowly. When she reminds him that Friday is teacher-parent conferences and he has the day off, he'll tell her she's mistaken (even though, it turns out, she's correct). It's as if she's in a bad relationship with a guy who disregards and discredits whatever she says.

Except it's not her boyfriend; it's her son.

She's tried talking to Ethan about it, but whenever the topic comes up, he blows her off, saying Noah's just being a typical sixteen-year-old. "You know, he's only thinking about getting laid," he offered unhelpfully in one conversation.

Sometimes she wonders what the two of them do together on their rare father-son weekends, but Noah provides about as much information as his father: very little. "The weekend was fine," he'll say, tossing his overnight bag on the floor and showering before heading over to Lindsay's. "We went to Regina's in the North End," mentioning the popular pizzeria. Or, "Dad got last-minute tickets to the Celtics game." And now that Noah and Lindsay are dating, Noah's spending even less time with his dad. (They'd agreed that once Noah got his license, he could decide where he spent his weekends.)

Shelby tries not to worry, tells herself that it's typical adolescent behavior. But she misses the days when her little boy was sweet and innocent, when he once told a friend that he wasn't a virgin because he liked steak, mixing up the word with "vegan." Misses when she asked him to keep the house tidy because she'd cleaned it from "top to bottom," and Noah had asked in earnest, "But what about the sides?" Sometimes she wonders where her little boy went. Because he was here.

He was *just* here.

But then, adolescent Noah will disagree with her about whether the milk has soured or whether he made his bed this morning (when the evidence is clear he did *not*), and her heart will toughen again, just enough to let him out the front door, car keys clasped in his hand, the whole world waiting.

Maybe, she thinks, *that's precisely why sixteen-year-old boys are so insufferable. Otherwise, how else would their mothers let them go?* How else would she be okay with his spending the entire day with Lindsay when he said he'd be home to play with Clara later? It's five o'clock now, and he's nowhere to be found.

She shuts off the shower and steps out to grab a towel. Her phone, sitting by the sink, flashes with a voicemail message. Probably Noah calling to say he lost track of time and does she still want him home? Shelby's not in the mood to cut him any slack, though. Not today. He said he'd be here, and so he should be. It's as simple as that. She hits "Play," her anger mounting, and begins to towel off, her wet hair dripping down her body while she listens. But then she stops. It's not Noah.

The message is one that she's been dreading for months.

"Hey, Shel, checking in," says Georgie. "Listen, I ran into Maeve Harding at the market. You know how she is—a royal gossip. Anyway, she said that she was positive she saw you and Dr. Bo together outside of Mambo's last week, picking up food to go. I told her she was crazy, of course, that it couldn't have been you, but she kept insisting. I thought I should give you a heads-up, so you won't be blindsided or anything."

There's a pause. "You're not sleeping with him, right? Oh, shoot, gotta go. Bentley needs to go out."

Shelby thinks back to last Tuesday, when Bo called to say he was getting out of the house and could she meet him at Mambo's? He'd already put in a take-out order for coconut shrimp and lobster rangoon, her favorites. Minutes before she arrived, though, the skies opened up, and she stupidly threw the car into Park and hopped out to meet him coming through the restaurant doors, order in hand. Her rain parka hood was pulled up over her head. The chances of being recognized in the pouring rain—though she didn't give it much thought, to be honest—seemed slim. Running up to Bo that night was instinctive, and perhaps, she sees now, a grave mistake. They laughed at how soaked they were, the rain slicing sideways, and made a hasty plan to head to his boat. She jumped in her car and followed him to the marina.

But they were careless. Maeve Harding had spotted them.

Shelby tries to recall if they actually ran into Maeve, laid eyes on each other. But they'd seen no one in the downpour. Had Maeve been waiting in her car, a black BMW Z4, for her take-out order? There were a few other parked cars that night, their windshield wipers flicking back and forth, headlights cutting through the dark. It's possible, Shelby supposes, that Maeve sat behind the wheel of one. But Shelby and Bo only exchanged a quick, perfunctory kiss outside Mambo's—it could have been two friends saying hello. If Maeve Harding *did* spot them, so what? At most, she caught them bumping into each other, Shelby trailing behind Bo's car on the way out. Hardly a crime.

Her heart slows to a more regular beat. Maybe the news is not as devastating as it first seemed. *Maeve has nothing on us,* she tells herself.

But it's also not the full truth.

Because everyone in Hull knows that Maeve Harding has a reputation for gossip, that she thrives on the adrenaline rush it delivers, much like some people thrive on the caffeine blast of their cappuccinos. If she spotted them and is already cornering Shelby's friends about one chance encounter, then it's only the beginning. If she's not your friend, Maeve Harding can be a thousand times worse than a bloodhound tracking a scent.

Shelby reclaims her towel from the floor and winds it around her body. Georgie deserves a call back, especially if Shelby has any hope of stopping the rumor mill. But first she must talk to Bo, tell him what she should have told him on the boat earlier today: They can't keep doing this. It has to stop. Her sister has been on the unlucky end of Trey's indiscretion, and Shelby has witnessed firsthand the destruction it's wrought. It's not lost on her that she, like Trey's alleged lover, has been doing the exact same thing to Bo's wife. Cindy doesn't deserve this. No one does.

Shelby has been toting around a boulder of guilt. Big, hunkering, soul-crushing guilt. It's been her secret, and hers alone for the last eight months. And now it might be someone else's.

She hurries to locate a fresh set of clothes, wrestles into a pair of jeans and a light sweater, and grabs her phone. Thankfully, Bree is still out with Clara. She left a note saying they went to Toast for hot cocoa. Beyond the deck, the late-afternoon sun skates along the water, and Shelby drops into an Adirondack chair, her thumb hovering over the number. Telling Bo in person isn't an option—she'll only lose her nerve once she sees him. Best to keep the conversation short and to the point.

She hits the button.

When he picks up on the third ring, she takes a long, deep breath—and begins. "Hey you," she says. "I've been thinking."

19

BREE

One Week Later
Friday, May 24

The waves roll gently in and out, lapping at the shore. At first Bree assumes it's her sound machine and swats at the alarm clock to shut it off. But it's the real thing, the ocean beyond her window. It takes a moment to register that she's still in Shelby's guest room. A slant of early-morning sun cuts through the curtains, casting a lazy, elongated rectangle on the floor. Even with the windows closed, the ocean makes its presence known here. It's one of the myriad reasons why she loves staying at Shelby's. No cars honking. No buzzing traffic. No one yelling on the street or slamming doors in the hallway of her apartment complex. Only the rhythmic hum of the tides washing up on the beach.

A week has passed since she first showed up on her sister's doorstep, and if someone had told Bree how much her life would change in the seven short days since, she wouldn't have believed them. Not when she was lying in her bed in Somerville, nursing her mouth back to health, ignoring creditors' voicemail messages that continued to pile up like dirty socks on her answering machine. Since then, she's returned to her apartment only once, long enough to collect clothes for the remainder of her stay in Hull.

Late last night, after everyone else went to bed, Audrey snuck out of Bree's bedroom to head home—even though it's not as if Bree needs to keep her a secret. Especially since Audrey has more or less lived at Shelby's for the past week. But Bree's not quite ready to admit to her family—or perhaps to herself—how swiftly the relationship (if that's what she can call it) has progressed. That she's already invited Audrey into her bed, which, technically speaking, isn't even her bed. Bree understands that she's a guest here, and she treads that line carefully, not wanting to push past her welcome. Shelby is her sister and generous to the core—but even sisters can tire of each other.

That said, the thought of sending Audrey home last night after they snuggled on the couch to watch *Game of Thrones* was almost painful. It was much easier to lead her by the hand upstairs and climb into bed together, where they could give in to the heat that had been simmering between them all evening. Bree almost forgot how charged those first few days of dating could be! It was as if her very cells were vibrating, electrons zipping from one orbital to another. How every glance exchanged, every random touch, seemed to suggest so much more. When they finally made it upstairs, it was as if their bodies couldn't connect soon enough. Late into the night, Bree traced her lover's dips and curves, until reluctantly, Audrey pulled away to go home.

Before leaving, she asked, "So what's *really* up with you and Hannah? Did you two break up or are you just taking a break? I'm not exactly clear."

Bree was about to shrug off the question, to say that she was still processing it herself, but then stopped. Audrey stared back at her with such intensity, her dark-brown eyes flecked with gold, that she could only answer truthfully.

"I guess you could say that we broke up."

"You guess?"

"We did. Break up, I mean. Or more like, Hannah broke up with me. Broke my heart, actually, if you want to know."

Audrey gently traced the contour of Bree's cheek with her hand. "I'm sorry. You guys were together for a long time."

Bree nodded. "Yeah, well, she got the job offer of a lifetime. At the Getty Museum in LA. That's kind of hard to compete with, you know?"

"You didn't want to go?"

Did I? The question gave Bree pause for a moment. She never seriously contemplated moving, did she? It seemed impossible at the time, especially when Hannah so clearly, so effortlessly chose her career over Bree. Perhaps, somewhere deep inside, Bree already understood that moving to LA only meant postponing the inevitable heartbreak that came with dating Hannah.

It's funny, she thinks now, how life could surprise you. Just when Bree more or less convinced herself that a life without Hannah meant a life with no one, Audrey, like a lucky penny, has flipped that belief on its head. Audrey is affectionate, fun, guileless. With Hannah, life was endlessly complicated, a rope of twisted knots that Bree was constantly trying to untangle—or, at least, that's how she remembers it.

Though she couldn't have articulated it at the time, she's beginning to understand that her relationship with Hannah left her feeling perpetually "less than." A sense that she was less talented, less free with her emotions, less confident than Hannah. It's as if she can still hear Hannah in her ear, *tsk*ing her for being silly or not as quick-witted. With the benefit of time and distance, though, it seems possible, even probable, that Bree's infatuation with Hannah was exactly that—a mentee's fascination with her mentor. A relationship fueled by one person's power over another.

And Bree was oblivious to it all.

But with Audrey, everything feels comfortable, familiar. And although they hooked up a few summers ago, long enough to call each other "girlfriend" in passing, Bree doesn't remember experiencing the same heft of emotions for Audrey back then. When they mostly bumped into each other at the C Note or on the beach with a group of mutual friends. This summer, their relationship already feels different, substantial.

Even their six-year age difference seems insignificant; given Audrey's relative maturity and Bree's immaturity, the scales somehow even out. For Bree, Audrey is the equivalent of a brisk summer breeze blasting through the bedroom window, clearing out the wreckage of the last five months since Hannah's departure. Which makes the truth that Bree has been side-stepping all this time somewhat more palatable: Hannah isn't coming back.

At least, not for her.

And while ordinarily such a realization would render her useless, send her to bed for days, it hits Bree more like a sharp slap than a barreling punch. And when, for the first time in two weeks, her phone lit up with a text from Hannah yesterday, Bree didn't respond immediately. This is also a first. It's possible she's playing it coy, but she doesn't think so. Suddenly, it doesn't matter so much what Hannah is up to, whether she's as miserable as Bree, or whether she has any plans to return to Boston next month. The text itself was brief, maddeningly flirtatious: Hi, honey. What's new? Miss you!

Maybe Bree will craft a reply today. All's well! Hanging out in Hull with my sisters. Memorial Day weekend is finally here. There will be no invitation extended, no Wish you were here! Because truthfully, at the moment, Bree doesn't long for Hannah by her side.

This week, her sisters have tiptoed around Hannah's name, trying, Bree assumes, to give her some space. They don't want to press her about an old girlfriend when she and Audrey have been together all week. But she senses their glances, their questioning looks. *Does Hannah know about Audrey? Are things really over between you two?* These are the questions Bree imagines them asking if they were bold enough. That they assume she can care for only one person at a time, that her life's goal is to eventually find and wed "the One," also implies a certain worldview that Bree doesn't particularly care to call them on at the moment.

Because this week the focus has been on Kate and Trey's problems, shifting the spotlight off Bree. Admittedly, it feels good not to be the "problem sister" for once.

And something's off about Shelby, too. Shelby, who seemingly has infinite advice for Kate but has been oddly reserved about her own life. She's made herself scarce, spending most days at the office, returning home for dinner. Whenever her cell rings, she retreats to the den to take the call. Bree doesn't believe for one second, however, that it was Shelby's trainer who was texting her nonstop last week when her phone kept buzzing on the counter.

More like an impatient boyfriend.

But when Bree inquired if she was seeing anyone, Shelby quickly dismissed her. *Are you serious? When would I have time for a relationship? Right now, my life is about Noah and work. Besides, given my track record, I'm not sure I should ever get involved with a man again.*

How about a woman? Bree teased. *They're much easier to get along with, I find.*

Ha. Very funny.

If there *is* a man in her life, Shelby isn't telling. Maybe, like Bree, she's reluctant to bring up any good news about love when Kate is so clearly distressed.

Frankly, though, Bree is worried about both her sisters. Which is a change. Because for most of her life, it's been her sisters fretting over *her*. Growing up, Bree always seemed to be a source of confusion for them. *What are we going to do with her?* is what their furtive, puzzled looks seemed to say. As if maybe their parents had given them a baby elephant for a younger sibling instead of a playmate. But while it's true that Shelby and Kate have made financial successes for themselves, the rest of their lives, Bree is beginning to see, are kind of a mess.

Which makes it especially difficult to broach the subject of money with either one right now. Bree can't bring herself to confide in them, to tell them exactly how bad things have gotten. That she risks losing her art studio, which she and a handful of other artists depend on, because she's now three months delinquent on rent. Or that the landlord is threatening to throw her out. And since Kate generously agreed to be her cosigner on the lease two years ago, it's only a matter of time before the landlord calls Kate, demanding payment in full.

And Bree is afraid that if she asks Shelby for money, her oldest sister will take umbrage, pointing out that this is the kind of bs that "Bree always pulls." That Bree doesn't take responsibility for her own life. That Bree is constantly needing to be rescued by either Shelby or Kate. (And she won't be entirely wrong.) The week after Bree graduated from RISD, Shelby accused her of being a freeloader because Bree was still living with their parents. The accusation continues to sting. The last thing she wants is to confirm Shelby's suspicions, to prove her sisters right: that there's no place in the art world for her, at least no *paying* place in the art world.

"Everyone goes through rough times," her mother once told her, back when the popular middle school girls were teasing her about her Kmart jeans. "You'd be surprised, though. Somehow you get through it. It'll make you stronger eventually, even though it might not feel like it right now." *Yeah, or else harden me against the world forever,* Bree thought begrudgingly.

In the early-morning light, she makes a promise to herself: she will be present for her sisters this weekend, however and whenever they might need her. She will shelve her own problems for another day.

And honestly, if her own life is an unfixable mess, she might as well try to help with someone else's. This weekend, she'll act and think like a responsible adult, not like the freewheeling, creative spirit that she is. She'll trade in her metaphorical artist's cap for something more practical—perhaps a wool hat? She imagines her body stretching and transforming right there in bed—from the pixieish girl with long, dark hair into a powerful, no-nonsense executive dressed in high heels and a pencil skirt. Her sketch pad will morph into a clipboard so that she can keep everyone in line.

Whatever this weekend sends the Lancaster sisters' way, she'll handle it.

Because if she doesn't, who will?

20

SHELBY

The three sisters are sitting on Shelby's deck, cups of coffee cradled in hand, nubby blankets covering their legs to protect against the morning chill. Several yards away, Clara plays in the sand with Noah. Another Friday off from school will make this an extra-long Memorial Day weekend for him. Shelby is about to ask Bree what her plans are for the day, but her sister laughs when she gets a look at her.

"What's so funny? Do I look that terrible?"

"You do realize," Bree says, "that you have two pairs of glasses on top of your head, right?"

Shelby reaches up and touches first one, then a second pair of reading glasses. She shakes her head. "I'm losing it. It's hell getting old, Bree. Don't do it." But they're all laughing. It feels good to be spending time together again.

"Just please don't let me become one of those moms who wears sweaters announcing the seasons in big letters across their chests. *Fall, Summer.* You know what I'm talking about. You've seen them out in the world."

"You have my word. Absolutely no seasonal sweaters," Bree says, making a crisscross motion over her chest.

The silence rests easily between them for a few minutes before Kate turns and says, "So I've been thinking . . . and I think I need to leave Trey. Probably get a divorce."

"Whoa," says Bree. "There's a topic changer."

"Wait. When did you decide this?" Shelby can't quite believe what she's hearing, even though it's always been a possibility, she supposes.

"What other choice do I have? Bottom line: he cheated on me and lied about it. How can I ever trust him again?" Kate answers for herself, casting her gaze back out on the ocean. "I can't."

"Look, I know you're upset," Shelby begins, choosing her words carefully. "And you're hurting—and you have every right to be!" She pauses. "But why not take a little more time to think about it before making such a major life decision?"

"Because it's been a week!" Kate cries. "One week, exactly, and nothing has changed. Sonja is still working at the firm, even though Trey promised me she'd be gone by the end of the week." She meets her sisters' puzzled looks and stares down at her coffee. "I called the office, pretending I was a potential client and wanted to speak to her."

"Kate!" Bree's face rearranges itself in complete surprise. "What did you say when she got on the line?"

"Nothing. I hung up. I wanted to hear her voice, you know? Have a voice to match with the name and the face."

"And? What did she sound like?"

Kate shrugs. "Like she has her shit together."

"Figures." Bree flicks a stray muffin crumb off her chair's armrest. "They always do. The people you want to hate the most, I mean." She glances over at Shelby, as if uncertain about continuing, but soldiers on, anyway. "Personally, I disagree with you, Shelby. I think Kate *should* ditch Trey. He doesn't deserve her."

"You're positive that this has been ongoing? Not just, like, a few random hookups?" Shelby asks.

"Not that it should matter if it was once or a thousand times, but yes. Remember? When he more or less admitted to me that he's been seeing her for a few months, which I suspect means more like several months? This isn't a case of a few bad decisions. We're talking ongoing schmuckiness."

Did Shelby know this and forget? She's been so distracted with Bo. But yes, she guesses Trey did finally admit that he was in some kind of relationship after Kate found the woman's photo on the firm's website. *A few months.* Maybe Shelby has been trying to forget this detail; it's not even as long as she's been with Bo! "And the earrings? The ones you found in your bed?"

Kate snorts. "Incredibly, he maintains he knows nothing about them. Even though Sonja was wearing them in her profile photo on the firm's website."

Bree crinkles up her nose. *"Ewww."*

What a creep. Maybe Kate should *leave him,* Shelby thinks. *He doesn't deserve her.* But for some reason, she can't quite bring herself to admit it. "Okay, that's pretty bad. I'll give you that. But what's the harm in trying counseling? Seeing if you guys can work things out."

"Not going to happen." Kate shakes her head vigorously. "We're way past that."

"If I were him," Bree says quickly, "I'd be showing up on your doorstep every day, begging for mercy. Maybe he realizes his goose is cooked. I mean, what's the point of begging for forgiveness when your wife knows you cheated on her *and* lied about it? It's kind of a double whammy."

Kate shifts in her chair, pulls her knees up to her chin. "That's exactly right. Trust and loyalty are huge to me. I always said if someone cheated on me it was a deal-breaker. Now I've got a husband who has betrayed me. I can hardly believe I'm even talking about taking him back."

"Well, there's Clara now," Shelby offers quietly.

"Yes, I'm well aware of that," Kate snaps. "Thank you for the insight."

The truth is, if Shelby didn't feel complicit by association, she'd be on Bree's side, too. Kate has given Trey abundant chances to absolve himself, to make it right, and every time, he screws it up. It's as if he's *trying* to persuade Kate to divorce him.

Shelby should step back, recuse herself. She knows this. It's the most prudent course, particularly when she's hardly an unbiased party. She has weathered the storms of divorce and single motherhood; it's not easy, and frankly, she'd wish it on no one.

But there's more to it than that. The reason she cares so deeply about salvaging her sister's marriage is because, in her own mind, she keeps replaying what a split would mean for Bo and Cindy and their daughters. What if Cindy finds out about them and ends up divorcing Bo? It will all be Shelby's fault. And that's a guilt Shelby has zero interest in shouldering.

It's crazy, but if Kate and Trey can be persuaded to stay together, then Shelby's affair with Bo, assuming it's really over, might be forgivable in some parallel universe. If she can prevent her sister from divorcing, then maybe the gods can grant her mercy for sabotaging Bo's marriage for several months. The scales of karma will be righted once again.

"Clara will be fine," Bree pipes up. "She loves her mommy and, from the sound of it, she hardly sees Trey, anyway. He's at the office all the time. It won't be that different if you leave him. Clara can still see him on the weekends and over the summers, right, Shelby?"

Shelby shrugs noncommittally. "I guess so."

"Can I really do it, though? I'm not as strong as you, Shelby. I don't know if I'm cut out to be a single mom."

The comment prompts a dismissive grunt from Shelby. "No one's 'cut out' to be a single mom. You just do it, Kate." There's a tad of condescension in her voice, a veiled implication that Kate has had it easier than her sisters for a long time. Only now is she waking up to their version—to most people's version—of everyday life.

"I guess you're right," Kate concedes.

Bree, though, turns abruptly to Shelby, her voice laced with judgment. "Honestly, why do you care so much what Kate does? What does it matter to you if Kate gets a divorce?"

It's so sudden, so accusatory that Shelby nearly drops her mug. "Because she's our sister!" she exclaims, but she could swear her baby sister can see right through her, right down to her ugly, traitorous motives. As if, somehow, over the course of the week, Bree has stumbled onto her secret. "And Clara's our niece. And I love them both. I don't want them to get hurt."

"Well, it's too late for that," Kate says quietly. "Trey already took care of that himself."

21

KATE

What Kate hasn't admitted to her sisters is that as much as Trey's affair comes as a surprise, it also doesn't. It's almost as if she's been waiting for this particular avalanche to knock her off her feet for a very long time.

"I'm sorry," Shelby says now. "I'm on your side, really I am. It's just that I don't think I've ever seen you guys fight. Like ever. So divorce seems like a pretty radical step."

"Oh, we fight," Kate confirms, searching her mind for the details of their last big argument. "We definitely fight. Maybe not in public, but we fight." But do they fight *out loud*, she wonders? Or are their skirmishes more of the variety that takes place inside Kate's head, her secretly screaming at Trey while he sits in front of the television after work, not saying a word? Does Trey even know how unhappy she's been lately? Do her sisters?

Kate thinks back to when she went grocery shopping a few weeks ago. Clara hadn't slept well through the night, so they were both groggy and crotchety with each other. Grocery shopping was always a drag, but that Monday it was particularly bad. Most of the produce had yet to be restocked, and when she managed to locate some decent-looking oranges, the plastic bag she tore off the roll refused to open.

Normally, she'd lick a finger and be done with it, but she was reluctant to do so with all the recent viruses. So she struggled and struggled until she finally gave up and ripped the bag to shreds, tears rolling down her face. Clara, who'd been inconsolable moments earlier (Kate had yanked a box of Froot Loops from her hands), stopped whimpering and stared up at Kate, her eyes wide and imploring. In her sweetest voice, she asked, "Mommy, you okay? Why's Mommy sad?"

It was all Kate could do not to dash out of the store and leave the carriage behind with Clara in it. Was this who she was now? A mother who came undone after a fight with a plastic bag? Who dreamed of abandoning her child? No, she hasn't been completely happy. For how long, though? Kate's breakdown at the supermarket wasn't Clara's fault, of course, but somehow the two events—watching Clara and her failed marriage—are intertwined in her mind when she recalls her worst day in recent months.

Eventually, she pulled herself together and marched over to the frozen foods section, where she tossed a pint of mocha chip ice cream into the cart. Before they left the parking lot, she finished off half the pint while Clara giddily downed Froot Loops straight from the box. She never mentioned that day to Trey.

"Hello? Earth to Kate?" When she looks up, Bree is frowning at her.

Kate pushes a wisp of hair out of her face. A gentle breeze floats off the water, and rolling waves layer onto the shore, like tiers of a wedding cake. "Sorry, I was thinking," she begins. "Maybe Trey has no idea how unhappy I've been lately. Maybe this is all my fault."

"Whoa, there, Nelly." Shelby holds up two hands. "Nothing in this whole mess is your fault, and what do mean 'how unhappy you've been'?"

Kate can't blame her sisters for not noticing, not when she's held off confiding in them. Not when she's barely admitted to herself the pervasive sense of melancholy coloring her days, telling herself that she's fortunate to have the life that she does, that any other woman would give her right arm to be Trey Dowling's wife. Now she wonders: Has she been the proverbial frog in the pot, unaware of the water growing warmer and warmer around her before it starts to boil?

It occurs to her that possibly she's been fooling herself. That her marriage has not been one bright, dazzling monument to love and affection, but, in fact, a farce. And has been for quite some time. It's also possible that it's not her marriage that's getting her down so much as the fact that she barely recognizes herself anymore. This, accompanied by the fact that she can't remember ever feeling more exhausted. Tapped-out, tired-in-her-bones exhausted. Specifically, she is tired of tending to everyone else.

To Clara, for twelve- to fifteen-hour stretches a day. To Trey, whenever he decides to arrive home for dinner. To her sisters, who always seem so needy, especially Bree. Kate is sick to death of laundry and play-time and fixing dinner. Even though she knows that women everywhere are managing a similar slate of tasks, it doesn't assuage her exhaustion one bit. Kate is in the fortunate position where she could hire help, if she so chose, but it goes against every fiber of her being. Just once, she wishes her own mother could swoop in and pat her head as she used to do when Kate was little. "There, there," she'd say. "Don't worry. It will all be okay." And then with a snap of her fingers, everything in Kate's house, her life, would be magically whisked into order, like the dancing mice in *Cinderella*.

Maybe, she thinks, this is why more women get divorced in their midforties, once their children are old enough to take care of themselves. Maybe there comes a point in a woman's life when she's so fed up with taking care of everyone else—cleaning house, managing doctors' and dentists' appointments, grocery shopping, school drop-offs—while also trying to maintain her own sanity, that it's not worth it anymore. Maybe the reasons to leave begin to outweigh the reasons to stay. When the option of having your children for a week and then a week off (while your husband presumably takes them) becomes something that women fantasize about—and then, finally, act upon.

It's funny the way jealousy can creep up on a person, take her by the hand. When Kate thinks back to her days at the office, a twinge of longing corkscrews through her. It's not so much the job she misses but the knowledge that, in some small way, she was being productive, accomplishing a task. Now she finds herself envious of the Amazon delivery guy, the bank teller, the grocery store clerk, each one achieving a particular task within a finite window of time. Kate knows she's doing important, even critical, work—raising a child!—but some days it feels like the least productive, rewarding kind of work. There are no results to tabulate, no spreadsheets to share, no meetings to check off on her to-do list. No tangible sense of accomplishment where she can expect praise or a smiley-face sticker—or a paycheck.

Internally, she scolds herself: Is she really so small, so petty a person that she needs approbation from the outside world to feel worthy?

Well, maybe. A little bit, she thinks.

"I haven't been happy in a while," she says softly now. "I kept thinking, hoping things would get better. But they haven't. Obviously."

"Oh, Katydid." Bree sets her mug down. "I'm so sorry. I had no idea. Here I thought you were living the perfect life. You're my role model, you know."

"Yeah, me too," Shelby says. "Remember how girls used to tease you in middle school about being 'Miss Perfect?' Seriously, though, I had no idea things were so bad."

"Well, I didn't tell anyone." A nervous laugh escapes Kate. "That probably has something to do with it."

A silence falls over them, and Shelby is the first to speak again. "But I still have to ask: What's wrong with trying a separation first? See how it goes?"

Kate shakes her head angrily. Shelby isn't listening. "Um, because right now I'd like to kill him, and a separation seems much too kind after what he's done to me. To us."

Bree nods. "I agree."

Kate has been busily tearing her napkin into bits, and a mountain of shredded paper flutters on the armrest, as if readying to take flight. She gathers up the pieces and stuffs them into her empty coffee mug. "I can't forgive him for this. Not the affair, necessarily, but the lying, the mistrust. I don't have it in me. Even if it means Clara and I are destitute for the rest of our lives, so be it. I'll figure something out. I had a successful career before Clara."

"Right," Shelby says, but her doubt sneaks through.

"What, exactly, is it that you're worried about, Shelby?" Kate demands now, a tight fist forming in her chest. "Clara's well-being? Please don't forget: I'm doing all this for her." Because ultimately, isn't Clara the reason Kate *needs* to leave? To show her daughter the importance of self-worth, about respecting her own instincts, about never letting a man take advantage of her goodwill—or naivete, as it may be?

Shelby pushes up out of her chair and excuses herself—"Sorry, it's not my place to say, really"—and walks into the house.

Kate spins around to address Bree. "What was *that* about? It's like she's the one getting divorced. Do you think it's stirring up old memories for her?"

Bree shrugs. "More like new memories."

"Huh? What's that supposed to mean?"

"Oh, nothing." Bree slides her chair closer to Kate's so that they're kitty-corner. "For what it's worth, I think you're making the right call. Trey's a jerk, and you can do better. Much better."

"Thank you. Thank you for saying that." She wraps her arms around herself, and then Bree does the same, embracing her. Kate didn't realize how much she's been needing to hear those words. *You're making the right call.* "This is really hard," she finally says.

"I know. But you'll get through it. You're my amazing big sister, remember?"

The comment elicits a half smile from Kate. Maybe it's true that an older sibling can do no wrong in her baby sister's eyes. It's been years, though, since Kate has thought of herself in a positive light, probably not since her last promotion at Bain & Company. Probably because people rarely tell you that you're an amazing mom, a good person.

It's nice to be reminded.

22

ROBIN

Memorial Day Weekend
Sunday, May 26

There's a body, as certain as the morning sun that's been climbing the sky. Located about a mile from where the boat was first discovered. The search-and-rescue team radioed it in moments ago, officers' walkie-talkies buzzing to life all at once. Now everyone is strutting around the beach like a flock of worried hens, trapped on land while the action is happening out at sea. Helicopters continue to hover overhead. It's 11:46 a.m.

At the bottom of the bay, the MEP sonar indicated a large object tangled in a fishing net near a group of abandoned lobster pots. The ROV (remote operated vehicle) confirmed that it was a body and, by following the ROV's tether to the victim, divers were able to locate it. Robin's harbormaster tells her that efforts are underway to cut the body free. From initial reports, the victim does not appear to have been submerged for long; long enough, however, that no vital signs are evident.

Robin updates the chief with the latest details, even though she suspects his crew has already done the same. She inquires if there's more she should know about this particular rescue, gives him a chance to explain the early and ongoing presence of his crew, but he only responds, "Not at the moment." Over the course of the morning, he's gone from chatty to gruff, and she doesn't dare push her luck.

"Okay," she says then. "I'll keep you posted from my end."

Now that there's a body, an amplified hum of alarm worms its way through the crowd. The news crews that have been camping out on Cadish Avenue detect the fresh buzz; something major has happened, and they want in. A few hours ago, Robin issued a preliminary statement about the runaway boat and the ongoing activities, explaining the overhead presence of the helicopters. But now their search-and-rescue operation has switched to an official recovery effort. When the radio call comes in from the marine team, they get the final confirmation they need: the body, freed from the netting, is now aboard the Coast Guard rescue vessel. Despite attempts at resuscitation, the victim has been confirmed deceased. Identified as Caucasian, roughly one hundred and forty pounds, possibly mid to late forties.

But their victim is not a drunk guy out for a joyride or a middle-aged drinking buddy of the boat owner, as some might reasonably presume. To the contrary, the person they've all been searching for . . . is a woman. Robin has been concealing this fact from the reporters, even though the harbormaster informed her of the victim's sex earlier.

She didn't, however, have a name. Now, in yet another macabre twist, it appears that Robin knows the victim.

Her stomach feels funny, as if it might flip. She's not accustomed to dead bodies showing up in their bay, not that anyone around here is. And she's certainly not accustomed to people whom she *knows* turning up dead. Yesterday, everyone in the station was exclaiming over how pleasant it was to have a quiet Memorial Day weekend for once.

They should have known better; they jinxed themselves.

Now she remembers why she has come to dread this particular holiday stretch: there's no predicting what stupid things people might do after the winter thaw when everyone stumbles out into the sun like blinking zombies. Too much booze, too many cooped-up resentments. So many possibilities that could spark an otherwise preventable accident—or a deliberate act of violence.

Whatever happens, it almost always ends badly.

She really hates Memorial Day weekend.

23

BREE

The Party
Saturday, May 25

"Hear ye! Hear ye! All dogs will sleep until ten o'clock tomorrow morning, by order of the queen! That includes you, Tuukka."

Bree is pouring margarita mix into the blender on Saturday morning, while Tuukka sits at her feet. It's the pregame party, so to speak, before the actual Memorial Day. Bottles of tequila, triple sec, and lime juice are scattered across the kitchen counter, and she's pretty sure that there's some sticky salt already stuck in her hair. At five thirty this morning, Tuukka, her new best friend, surprised her by jumping into her bed, and she feels the need to school him on the importance of proper sleep for humans who don't have the option of napping all day.

"You know," Noah says, "ever since you've been hanging around, Tuukka doesn't bother me in the mornings. It's actually kind of nice. I can sleep in on the weekend."

Bree whips a slice of lime at her nephew, who manages to duck just in time. The dog scrambles up after it and swallows it, peel and all, before either of them can get there.

"Oops," she says with a defeated sigh. "Hopefully he won't puke that up later." Then, "Anyway, I guess it's nice to know I'm appreciated around here." She wipes her hands on her apron. "But if that dog wakes me up at five thirty tomorrow morning, so help me God, he'll be looking for a new home."

It's a bold statement, considering this is most definitely Tuukka's home and not hers, but Noah only lifts a questioning eyebrow. If Shelby were here, she might be inclined to remind Bree that her welcome is running out, that she is expected to report to What's Brewing? at nine o'clock sharp on Tuesday morning. And that, despite the fact that she's been holed up here for more than a week, this is not Bree's permanent home. She gets it. A lot has happened in the last several days.

That's an understatement. An *earthquake* has rumbled through their entire family, and by default, Shelby's house has become the command center. Bree can only imagine how eager her sister must be to have her house rid of them.

If Trey would only stop lying, Bree thinks maybe Kate could forgive him. But not until he was confronted with the name of the woman he was kissing did he start to fold. Even now, he's acting cagey, as if there's some larger reason that the universe has led him to stray. Why *should* her sister trust him when pretty much everything that comes out of his mouth is untrue? Trey Dowling is a cheat, a womanizer, a man incapable of keeping his hands to himself.

And Bree is done giving him the benefit of the doubt, even for Clara's sake. She hopes that he stays the hell away from Kate—from all of them—this weekend. They've weathered enough tsunamis for one summer already.

After a stretch of chilly days, it feels nice to be walking around in a T-shirt and shorts. Hull has been experiencing typical New England spring weather—freezing one day, balmy the next—but today is supposed to climb into the eighties, which will make for perfect party weather. Shelby has thrown open all the windows, and a soft breeze ruffles the curtains in the living room. At the moment, only Bree and

Noah (and Tuukka) are here, prepping for the party. Shelby has set off for the hardware store and then the grocery store to buy ice for the cooler and last-minute Popsicles. In the fridge are dozens of premade burgers and hot dogs awaiting grilling later today. Kate and Clara, still up at the house on Allerton Hill, should be over shortly to help.

It's a smaller group than usual this year—maybe fifteen or twenty friends, most of them Shelby's and Noah's—but Bree is simply pleased that the party is going forward. For a moment, it seemed it might not: Kate declared midweek that there would be no Memorial Day weekend celebration at her house this year. Shelby, in turn, jumped at the chance to steer the venue back to her place. *The way it used to be,* she said, a hint of nostalgia threading her voice.

"The ocean is right outside our back door. Guests can swim if it's warm enough. Noah can fire up the grill. The volleyball net is already set up. It'll be easy." Not that Bree required any convincing. "Maybe," Shelby added, "a party is exactly what we all need right now. I'm sure as heck not letting Trey Dowling rain on our Memorial Day parade."

Which means there will be no caterers dressed like penguins wandering around with hors d'oeuvres on silver trays, no hobnobbing of rich folk with whom Trey works, no fancy china or glassware. Only paper plates and cups, butter on a stick for greasing the corn, opened jars of relish and pickles, and scattered bags of potato chips on the picnic table. A stack of frayed, well-loved beach towels placed strategically on the deck stairs for anyone who cares to brave the water.

Bree never felt comfortable with the switch to Kate and Trey's house, anyway. Inevitably, midway through the party, she'd escape down to the beach with Hannah or Audrey or whoever was available to smoke some weed and poke fun at her sister's show-offy lifestyle. *Who even is my sister anymore?* she would demand. Kate had become unrecognizable to her, evidently more interested in befriending the very people they used to scoff at than hanging out with her own family.

But today all will be as it's supposed to be. The Lancaster summer party restored to its rightful home.

"So." Bree turns to Noah. "This is nice, right? You and me hanging out, preparty?"

"Yeah, it's awesome," he says with a sly grin. "Is this where you get to ask me all the questions my mom wants answers to?" He pours himself a bowl of Cheerios, a few leaping out of the bowl, and scoops them up with his hand. He tilts his head back and tosses them in.

"Wow, a little paranoid, are we?" But she laughs because they both know it's true. "Now that you bring it up, though, I suppose it can't hurt to share a few of your deepest, darkest secrets with your favorite aunt."

"Such as?" He's still in his pajama bottoms and a Red Sox T-shirt, bare feet. He douses the cereal in milk. "Whether Lindsay and I are having sex, you mean?" he asks around a mouthful of Cheerios.

Bree feels her eyes pop. "Again, not specifically what I was searching for, but *are* you?"

"What do you think?" From the way Noah's smirking at her, it's clear he's asking rhetorically.

"Probably?" she wagers aloud. "But if you are, your mom and I both hope that you're being safe. No one wants to be a grandma or a grand-aunt right now."

"Yeah, I know."

"And that you're being, you know, respectful to Lindsay."

Bree hits the blender button and the margarita concoction whirls around noisily, filling the awkward silence. When she shuts it off, she asks, "So is it serious? Do you love this girl or what?" Over the past several days, Bree has met Noah's girlfriend a handful of times, and each time Lindsay has struck her as nice, attractive, and confident beyond her years.

Noah appears to ponder the question seriously. "I don't know. I guess so? I definitely like her. A lot. I mean, how does anyone know what love is, really?"

"How very philosophical of you," Bree teases. "But you're right. I think it's more of a feeling than anything else."

"Like you and Hannah?" At the mention of Hannah, she stops pouring the margarita mix from the blender into the gallon ice-cream container that she's emptied for the express purpose of freezing the mix till the party starts.

"Maybe," she says cautiously.

"Or like you and Audrey?"

"Audrey and I are strictly friends," she corrects, although they both know it's stretching the truth. Because she and Audrey have been making out in the back of Audrey's VW camper and up in Bree's bedroom for the past week. That Noah is onto their shenanigans isn't surprising.

"Yeah, sure, whatever you say."

"Okay, maybe she's more than a friend, but we only reconnected last week. So I don't think that counts as true love."

"Definitely not." There's that smirk again.

"Hey, don't you have any chores to do before this party?" Bree asks, suddenly eager to be rid of him. "Or am I the one doing everything here?"

"Yeah, yeah. I'm going. Mom wants me to fix the table and cut the front lawn." He hops up, sticks his emptied bowl in the dishwasher.

"In your pajamas?" she calls out as Noah makes his way to the front door and slides on his sneakers.

"Haven't you heard? Pajamas are the new jeans these days."

Bree grins as he shuts the door behind him and pours a splash of margarita into her glass for sampling. It goes down smooth. It even *tastes* like summer. Satisfied, she snaps the top back on the margarita tub and slides it into the freezer. Wipes down the counter and restores the liquor bottles to their rightful place in the cabinet. Through the front window, she can see Noah's head bobbing up and down to a song on his AirPods. He's cutting the grass on the diagonal, which strikes her as infinitely harder than in straight lines, but it does make the lawn appear professionally manicured. Like most front lawns in Hull, Shelby's is modest, a mere postage stamp. Then again, when the ocean is your backyard, the front lawn hardly matters.

There are more chores on her sister's to-do list, such as hanging a star-spangled banner across the front porch and setting out folding tables. Covering them with the traditional red-and-white-checkered tablecloths. Near the deck door, Shelby has left a large metal bucket filled with a hodgepodge of sunblock products from previous summers that's in desperate need of tidying. Dozens of nearly empty tubes, squeezed into tight, toothpaste-like rolls, rusty aerosol cans, and gooey spray bottles.

Bree sighs. Organizing isn't her bailiwick, but she takes the pail out on the deck anyway and plants herself on the stairs. *If Shelby wants it done,* she thinks, *it shall be done.* It's the least Bree can do for being able to crash here all week. She tosses out the old mucky tubes, the nearly empty aerosols, and wipes down the bottles of lotion covered in greasy fingerprints. After maybe fifteen minutes, the bucket of sunblock looks presentable again, and she's on to her next chore.

When she scoots into the house, though, she sees Noah standing outside the living room window and talking to someone. Bree probably wouldn't recognize her were it not for the cast on her wrist. It's Maeve, the same woman who stopped by last Friday, looking for Shelby. Bree had forgotten to mention it until a couple of days later, and when Shelby heard, her face turned as pale as bone.

"Aren't you two friends?" Bree asked.

Shelby shook her head. "Not exactly. More like frenemies. What did she want?"

Bree shrugged. "She didn't say. It was kind of awkward, actually. She seemed lost, like maybe she was looking for someone else, too. Not just you."

"Huh." Shelby seemed to consider this. "I don't know."

And now here's Maeve again, apparently having a nice chat with Noah, who's nodding his head and smiling. Bree watches them from the living room while Maeve hands him a piece of paper. It looks like a flyer of some sort, and he takes it from her before she continues down the street.

When Noah saunters back in the house, Bree can't help herself. "Who was that you were talking to out there?"

"You mean Maeve? She lives a few blocks down. She's throwing a Memorial Day party, too, and wanted to invite us."

"Really?"

"Yeah, I think she kind of drives Mom nuts, although I'm not sure why. She's nice."

"Huh."

Bree files this under "Interesting Information" and makes a mental note to be sure Shelby sees the invite. Because as much as Shelby seems to dislike Maeve, the woman struck Bree as more strange than conniving. Maybe, Bree thinks, she's lonely and looking for a friend. Maybe she's misunderstood.

If so, Bree can relate.

24

SHELBY

Shelby should be at Nantasket Paint & Hardware, tracking down an extra set of lights to dangle across the front porch, but instead she's parked outside Breadbasket, ordering dog bones for Tuukka online. The kind with the bone marrow still intact. She'd meant to order them days ago, but now it's the morning of the party, and she's searching for the hourly delivery price on her phone. Turns out Tuukka's favorite bone is unavailable until the Tuesday after Memorial Day, which will do no good since the treat is meant to keep him entertained for the duration of the party. She can't help but notice that other customers who've purchased this particular bone have also bought multiple copies of *Braveheart*. At least, that's what the website tells her. This, in some weird way, makes sense to her.

Forget it, she tells herself. She'll stop at the butcher's and pick up a ham bone, even though Bo has warned her that real bones are terrible for dogs' teeth. Today will be the exception; she has bigger problems to tackle.

Such as that Kate hasn't spoken to her since yesterday, when Shelby encouraged her to consider counseling or a trial separation before filing for divorce. And at breakfast this morning, Bree kept shooting her hooded looks, as if Shelby's hypocrisy were obvious, a bright scarlet *A* embroidered on the lapel of her fuzzy white bathrobe. But how could Bree possibly know about her relationship with Bo? Has she spotted his texts on Shelby's phone? Or maybe Maeve Harding has somehow gotten word to her. Shelby sighs. Allowing Bree to stay at the house for this long has been a mistake.

She jumps out of the car and heads into Breadbasket. In the mercifully short coffee line, she spies Robin Shipman, an old friend. They used to share shifts at Jake's Seafood, but in recent years, Robin has risen through the ranks of the Hull police department. Shelby will always be indebted to her for handling a small incident with Noah quietly—he was caught spray-painting graffiti at Fort Revere Park a few years back. Robin was willing to look the other way, so long as Noah returned to clean up his mess.

"Long time no see, friend! How are you?" Shelby calls out, approaching her.

Robin pulls her into a hug, and Shelby is careful not to get too close to the gun that's hanging in her holster. "Hey, stranger! Good to see you. All's well with me. What's new with you? Any more houses sold?"

"Only the one over in Allerton Hill."

"Oh, right! The old Vendler house?"

Shelby nods.

"I heard about that one," Robin says. "Went for over two million?"

"It'll be in *South Shore Magazine* next month, so yes, I can confirm that."

Robin makes a whistling noise between her teeth. "Nice work. You sure have come a long way since Jake's."

"You and me both, sister," Shelby says, and they share an easy laugh.

When they both have their coffees in hand, Robin turns to Shelby and says, "We should get together sometime. Do you still do wine?"

Shelby rolls her eyes. "That's like asking a cat if it still meows."

Robin chuckles good-naturedly. "I'll call you next week then."

"Sounds good. You've got my number."

Back in the car, Shelby makes a loop through downtown, where red and white helium balloons festoon the bandstand in honor of Memorial Day weekend. Already the out-of-towners, here for a Saturday beach day, have begun their incursion. Traffic moves at a crawl, and everywhere Shelby's gaze falls, something reminds her of Bo. There's the section of beach where they first picnicked; there's the spot where she pulled up alongside his Porsche before heading into Boston for dinner; there's Mambo's. Maybe, she thinks, she should call him to suggest a quick coffee, if only to set the record straight, make sure he understands why she had to end it. It *was* rather sudden.

She guides the car into an empty spot and yanks the phone from the dashboard holder. Because as much as she's been trying to forget him, Shelby is going out of her mind.

It's been a week since she set foot on Bo's boat, since she felt his smooth skin against hers or smelled his aftershave, a mix of eucalyptus and sandalwood. And even though she told herself on the way home from the marina that it was the last time she'd see him—for Kate's sake, for Noah's sake, for her sanity's sake!—he's like a drug she can't go without. Her fix, her remedy, her therapy—all tied up into one. She's read about crystal meth, a drug so potent that each time a person shoots up, the body requires even more to achieve the same high as last time. Is Bo as powerful as a crystal meth craving, impossible to dismiss? Is there rehab for love, some special twelve-step program for her heart?

If so, she desperately needs it.

Because in Bo she's finally found someone who appreciates her, who doesn't expect her to take care of him but who wants to care *for her*. It's such a foreign concept, no wonder she's fallen so hard. Shelby almost forgot how nice it is to have someone looking out for her. That a relationship can be a two-way street.

Bo *gets* her. He understands her drive to be successful, even admires it. He worries that she works too hard and asks what he can do to help. He gives her the most wonderful foot massages and, on the rare occasions when he sleeps over, prepares decadent french toast topped with sliced bananas and cinnamon. Bo makes her feel special, wanted. Why should she have to give that up? When he's the one person in the world who brings her happiness?

Her fingers begin to type. Can I see you? Today? She stares at the screen, holding her breath. Will he get it, or has she been deleted from his contact list? Will he even respond? But the dots below her text appear almost immediately. I was starting to think I'd never hear from you again. Yes, please. Where and when? ASAP?

She hesitates before responding. Each new encounter with Bo means putting her job, her livelihood, her sisters' trust, and most important, Noah's trust, in jeopardy. If word ever got out, the world she's worked so hard to build after her divorce would blow up. *But let's be honest,* she tells herself, *if Maeve Harding has her suspicions, then for all intents and purposes, the word is out.*

Which was why Shelby put the kibosh on the relationship in the first place. Seeing Bo now will undo all the hard work of this week's withdrawal. Like an addict, she knows she shouldn't take another hit . . . but she can't help herself. The urge to see him outweighs every sensible argument in her head.

The devil always wins, she thinks.

She throws the car into gear and pulls out, heading toward Telegraph Hill, where they've agreed to meet at a secluded spot by the fort. Like the capable real estate agent that she is, Shelby itemizes the reasons why this meetup is justified. Such as: she has been a good sister—no, a *great* sister—to both Bree and Kate this past week, welcoming them into her home, helping out with Clara. Not once has she asked Bree to contribute to the grocery bill, to make dinner, or even to *pick up* dinner because Shelby, unlike her younger sister, has been working all week.

And even though Bree is here ostensibly to help (and grudgingly, Shelby admits she *has* been helpful with Clara), it seems like more of a personal vacation. As if Bree has checked into her very own sorority—welcome to *Alpha Pi Shelby!*—where she can sneak Audrey up to her bedroom at night (and, yes, Shelby has most definitely noticed) and pilfer snacks. It's Shelby who's been playing mother hen to her sisters all week, cooking meals, checking in, picking up the house, listening to their problems. All this while dealing with her own wrecked heart. Shelby has been the one to give and give, while no one else seems concerned with giving back.

And don't even get her started on Kate! At the beginning, she felt bad for her sister because Trey's infidelity came as such a shock. But as the week has worn on, Shelby's sympathies have started to wane. Yesterday, she wanted to shake Kate by the shoulders when she mentioned she talked to a lawyer. It's all Shelby can do to refrain from yelling, *Grow up! Get over it. You have a daughter to raise together!*

So what if Trey strayed? Before they married, he was the most sought-after bachelor in Boston; what did she expect? *Kate, my dear,* Shelby imagines herself saying. *You've lived a* very *charmed life. Only now are you experiencing what the rest of us have known all along: life isn't easy. Stop feeling sorry for yourself, and get on with it.*

There's also a small, uncharitable part of her that believes Kate got what she deserved. Perfect Kate, for whom all the pieces of her impeccable world have unfailingly aligned, locking effortlessly into place. In school. In college. In work. In marriage. That they've come crashing down is strangely, horribly gratifying. Shelby knows she's an awful person for thinking this, but there it is.

And her role as tolerant mom to Noah's disengaged teenager act should earn her a Golden Globes nomination, at the very least. How many times has she bit her tongue when he's talked back to her this week, knowing it will only spark further argument? How many times must she deliver folded laundry to his room, feed his dog, and be pleasant to Lindsay before she gets a single thank-you? Not an ounce of gratitude in her own house for all that she does. No, she's done playing Florence Nightingale.

The only person who appreciates her is Bo.

She deserves to see him! She deserves him.

These convincing arguments (and she's certain there are more) fuel her on toward Telegraph Hill. Her foot presses harder against the gas pedal; she's traveling slightly over the speed limit but not pull-your-car-over fast. She doesn't want to keep Bo waiting. In the rearview mirror, she checks herself and suddenly remembers that she's not wearing any makeup. But it doesn't matter! Bo likes her the way she is. Which is why it has proven intolerable to stay away. It's possible, she thinks, that when it comes to love, there's no such thing as right and wrong, black and white. Love is more of a silver hue, shiny and new.

Up ahead, the turn leading to Telegraph Hill comes into view. Shelby's heart vibrates in her chest as if it might burst through the windshield. A whole week without him. She's made it, but how silly to deny herself something—someone!—who makes her deliriously happy. Yes, she deserves this. If she's to survive the weekend, then there should be some excitement in it for her as well. It's only fair. She's almost to the turn, almost to Bo's warm embrace, when her phone buzzes in its holder. Noah's name flashes, prompting her to lift her foot off the accelerator.

Should she answer? Isn't he home with Bree?

She grips the steering wheel more tightly. *Bo or Noah? Noah or Bo? Damn it! Why do I always have to choose?* At the last second, she rotates the steering wheel in the opposite direction and executes a sharp U-turn, the car bumping up along the curb, wheels squealing. Her hands slam the steering wheel in frustration.

Because she knows what she has to do, what she's going to do. Because there *is* a black and white, even when it comes to love, maybe *especially* when it comes to love. She navigates the car back into the lane and heads toward town, toward the hardware store and the butcher and the farmers' market.

Toward the annual Lancaster Memorial Day weekend party.

Shelby makes herself hit the call button. "Hello? Noah, are you still there?" Maybe it's the bad acoustics in the car, but her voice sounds as if it's coming from a million miles away.

25

KATE

Even though she'd much prefer to avoid her big sister at the moment, the one who can't seem to support her decision to leave her cheating husband, Kate is packing her beach bag for the party. They have to go. For Clara's sake. For the family's sake. To sit out the annual Lancaster Memorial Day weekend party would be the equivalent of launching rocks at her sisters. They might as well get it over with.

As she's buckling Clara into her car seat, her daughter announces that she doesn't like her friend Adam anymore. The mention of Clara's buddy from playgroup surprises Kate; they haven't seen him in over a week. Why is Clara thinking about him now?

"He bited Abigail," Clara explains, as if reading her mind.

"Oh no! Poor Abigail." Kate climbs into the front seat of the Land Rover and wonders how long Clara has been carrying around this information, and if there's a reason why she's waited so long to tell. She tries to picture Adam, but there are too many "A" names, like Austin and Aiden, in her daughter's playgroup for Kate to conjure up any one particular face. "That wasn't very nice. Maybe he was having a bad day," she offers.

"He's mean."

"Well, maybe he was mean on that day," Kate tries again. "But that doesn't mean he's always mean."

"Mama," shouts Clara. "That's a lot of 'means'!"

"You're right." Kate grins at her clever daughter in the rearview mirror. "It is. But you know what I *mean*." Clara breaks into giggles.

Kate is about to launch into a bigger, pithier explanation of humanity. That everyone makes mistakes, that you can't deliver a summary judgment about a person based on one action (well, unless it's *really* bad, like murder). Then again, that's pretty much what she's done with Trey, isn't it? Cast a summary judgment. Still, she's pretty sure the exception rule applies here, too: *really bad*.

"You know what, honey?" she says instead. "That *was* mean. And you're allowed to change your mind about people." It's perhaps the best piece of advice she's given her daughter all week. Children are allowed to change their minds about people because they're still learning what constitutes kindness and what doesn't, who are true friends and who aren't. In her lifetime, Kate has changed her mind about people very rarely, but usually for the better. Trey's best buddy from college, for instance, was an irrepressible roving bachelor, but once he became a dad, he turned into a doting and devoted father. Conversely, a man she has loved deeply, trusted wholeheartedly, has become someone who, at least at the moment, inspires only disgust in her.

People change, Kate thinks, *and you're allowed to change your mind about them.* Maybe she needs to learn this again herself.

When they pull up to Shelby's house, a few cars—a metallic-blue Subaru, a white Jeep Cherokee, and Bree's Honda Civic—are already parked out front. The party officially kicks off at one, but they're early. It's only eleven. As soon as Kate releases Clara from her car seat, she races to the front door and bursts inside before Kate can stop her. By the time she makes it to the kitchen with the bags, her daughter is already informing Noah and Lindsay that she found a starfish on the beach yesterday but threw it back in the ocean because "starfishes can only live for a few minutes out of the water." Kate watches their eyes widen in appropriate wonder.

"Whoa," Noah says. "That's so cool that you know that."

"You're amazing," pronounces Lindsay. "How old are you again?"

"Three!"

In the fridge, Kate places the extra bottles of tonic that Bree requested and a pack of hard seltzers. Sets the extra bags of taco chips and potato chips on the counter. She's aware she has it easy this year, that Shelby has given her a gift by hosting the party at her house. And for that, Kate is grateful. "Hi, guys. Where's everyone else?"

"Mom's at the store," Noah says. "And Bree's out back, I think."

"Hi, Kate," Lindsay pipes up, offering a little wave from the couch. Over the past week, they've gotten to know each other, she and Lindsay, and Kate has decided that she likes Noah's girlfriend. But it still feels strange whenever she addresses Kate by her first name.

Kate smiles and pours herself a glass of Diet Coke. "You two want anything to drink?"

"All set. Thanks. As for you, Clara-Beara," Noah says, "are you going to come closer so I can take a bite out of you?"

Clara squeals and leaps into his arms. Kate uses it as an excuse to go look for Bree and lets herself out onto the deck.

"Hello?" she calls, but there's no sign of her sister. The folding tables are already set up, covered with red-and-white-checkered tablecloths, and topped by melamine platters awaiting chips and watermelon slices. The majority of prep work looks to be already done.

"Hey, Noah," Kate calls into the house. "Do you mind if I take a short walk down the beach and back?"

"Go ahead. We'll watch this kooky kid." There's another squeal from inside. Whenever Noah's around, Clara can be trusted to be compliant, a willing accomplice. Unlike with her own mother, when she has daily meltdowns. Yesterday, she refused to get dressed, wearing her pajamas to the beach. Even though Clara can't possibly understand the ways in which her world is unraveling, the sense that something is amiss, that Mommy hasn't been herself, must register somewhere on her toddler antennae.

Kate slides off her pink flip-flops and leaves them on the steps, then cuffs her jeans above her ankles. Her toes test the sand, but it's fine; it doesn't typically turn scorching hot until mid-June, anyway. She emits a small sigh, allowing herself to relax for a minute.

Whenever she and Trey hosted, the party always seemed to be searching for its equilibrium, as if they were trying too hard to put on an elaborate show. *Look at the view! Taste the appetizers! Aren't they marvelous? We're so glad you could join us!*

When all the family has ever needed was Shelby's deck, some drinks and burgers, access to the beach.

It occurs to Kate, and not for the first time, that maybe her exhaustion stems not so much from motherhood as the kind of lifestyle she's been trying to pull off in tandem: living in a country club world built on pretense and artifice more than genuine feeling. Having to look fabulous while feeling anything but. Bree, she knows, would point this out to her in a heartbeat ("Well, *duh*."), but it's the first time Kate allows that there might be some truth to those words.

She tells herself that her lifestyle is not so rarefied. She pumps her own gas, buys the organic apples and peaches only when they're on sale. She cleans her own house, watches her own kid. Highlights her hair every few months, instead of every six weeks like the moms at the club. She's been known to trim her own hair in the mirror.

But from the outside looking in, she understands that she lives a charmed life. And it makes sense to her now: why, at their annual barbecue, her sisters would head out early, as if they were uncomfortable among Trey's friends and the catering staff, who served beef tenderloin skewers and bespoke cocktails on silver trays. In an effort to make the party less stressful for everyone, Kate excised the parts that her family enjoyed the most—the grilling, the shucking of corn, the chance to zip into the ocean with Clara, no matter how freezing the water might be.

She wanders farther down the beach, toward a group of gulls who squawk and fly off when she approaches. Her anger over the past week has settled into something milder, more simmering than acute. An unfamiliar emotion. Disappointment, maybe? Sadness? Regret peppered by intermittent flares of rage? The question that keeps replaying in her mind, though, is one that she's yet to locate a satisfying answer to: *When did she and Trey begin to drift apart?* Was it Clara's arrival, when he was forced to share the spotlight, that caused him to first pull away?

But no, that sounds overly simplistic.

They were happy. A happy family of three. And yes, those midnight feedings during that first year left Kate wandering around like a zombie, but eventually they found their way. She even began to look forward to the late-night feedings, Clara snuggled in her arms while she stared up at her with those deep blue eyes. And Trey, if not always around, helped out, reading Clara board books in all the characters' voices. Watching him turn the pages, imitating Papa Bear's deep voice and Goldilocks's lilting tone, enraptured not only Clara but her.

They were good, she reminds herself. Until they weren't.

But when, exactly, was that?

There were moments, naturally, when Trey drove her crazy, but that was typical of any marriage, wasn't it? When she'd be telling him about her day as they drove into town for a fundraiser event, for instance, and he'd interrupt to ask for directions on her phone. That wasn't such a big deal—Trey is one of the few men she knows who's comfortable asking for directions—but then he'd forget about her story, never asking her to finish, as if he wasn't listening in the first place. And she'd spend the remainder of the ride fuming about how insensitive he was and how much her Spanx were digging into her stomach, her frustration mounting by the minute.

There were other warning signs. Of course there were. On the romantic side. The nights when she rolled away from him in bed, her body too exhausted to have anyone else pawing at it. Usually on the weekends, when Trey came to expect sex, as if it were his prize for working hard all week (*as if she hadn't!*). And she'd lie and tell him that she had her period. Trey could never keep track of her cycle, anyway.

Some days, she was too tired even to lie.

"Just pretend I have my period," she said one Saturday morning when Clara's bedroom monitor was blissfully silent and Kate was craving a few extra minutes of sleep.

"What does that even mean?" he asked.

"If you think I have my period, then you won't want sex."

"But to be clear: You don't have it?"

And there were times when his temper would flash with little provocation. The Wi-Fi would blink out at inconvenient moments, or the trash man would inadvertently skip their house, and Trey would kick the cans across the yard in frustration. He could grow short with her when he was dealing with a work email at home, delivering clipped, one-word answers when she'd already spent an entire day with a human being who provided one-word demands. *More. No! Mama. Up!* Whenever a piece of house equipment—such as the dishwasher or the garbage disposal—went on the fritz, he'd try to fix it by watching instructions on YouTube, only to fail and sometimes fling a wrench across the kitchen floor.

But these were normal enough reactions to life's annoyances, weren't they? He never once was violent toward her or Clara.

She thinks back to a long weekend, only the three of them, last year in Manhattan. It was a much-needed getaway (the firm settled a huge case that had gobbled up weeks of Trey's life), and he promised to spend a long weekend with "his girls." They booked a room at the Hotel Beacon on the Upper West Side for the first weekend in April. Kate hadn't been to the city since work, and it felt invigorating to be back. They spent the morning wandering the Museum of Natural History, pretending they could reach the whale's belly. Later, they downed cheeseburgers and milkshakes at the Shake Shack, and when Trey's old roommate Johnathan, who now lived in Tribeca, texted to see if he wanted to meet up for drinks, Kate amiably agreed. Ordinarily, it would have irritated her that Trey was abandoning them on their vacation weekend, but it was such a gorgeous spring day, not even Johnathan could ruin it.

A few blocks up, she and Clara practically skipped into the park, where the trees seemed to have switched on like fireworks overnight. The cherry blossoms were in full bloom, their pale-pink, feathery petals waving in the breeze. The dogwoods, heavy with white flowers, looked as if a snowfall had coated them just that morning. Kate marveled that such natural beauty could coexist alongside the noise and smog of the city.

They parked themselves on a bench and people-watched. Clara loved the dogs, especially; there was a friendly golden, a slightly aloof poodle, a few yippy Chihuahuas, and a sloppy Great Dane that paraded past them. Several yards away, a saxophonist played a bluesy melody, his case an open invitation to passersby to toss in a few spare coins.

Central Park in the springtime. It was the city at its best. A valentine to new beginnings, to hope and love.

When they left, Kate stopped to shoot a photograph, the fading tangerine light dappling the trees in tiny diamonds. It's still one of her favorites. But when she shared it with Trey on her phone later that night, he glanced at it and frowned. "What is it?" he asked, confused.

"Central Park, you goofball! Springtime in New York. Isn't it gorgeous?" And he shrugged. Actually shrugged! As if a photo without people or a historical landmark was hardly worth taking. As if there were no magic in the soft light playing on the trees, the park awash in color. She knew her photography skills were average at best, but to not register the beauty in the photo struck her as odd at best. And at worst, as cold and indifferent. Perhaps it was the first time that a small flare went up in her mind about how different they might actually be.

That was over a year ago.

26

BREE

So what if her sisters are barely speaking to each other? Bree can handle it. It's happened before. When Shelby and Ethan married, for instance, she and Kate were forced to wear bridesmaid dresses that made them look like giant canaries. Horrible yellow sheaths exploding with yards of tulle. Kate said she'd never forgive Shelby, but Bree just felt itchy all day. Later, she discovered big red welts—hives—covering her entire body. They got through it, though, as surely as they'll get through this weekend. Personally, Bree doesn't understand what the big deal is, why Shelby is so invested in Kate's staying with Trey. It seems like Kate deserves their support no matter what decision she makes.

For the last hour, Bree has been answering the door, welcoming guests into Shelby's home, while Shelby shuttles bowls of pasta salad, chips, and hamburger buns from the kitchen to the deck. Each time the door opens, Bree's heart seizes with the possibility that it might be Audrey. Inside, all the furniture has been pushed back against the walls to make room for mingling. But it's the back deck where the bulk of the party is happening: the grill is lit, Noah's tunes are blasting (old-school Hootie & the Blowfish), and a small crowd is beginning to gather.

"Keep an eye on those," Bree instructs her nephew, nodding toward two coolers at the edge of the deck, one labeled ADULT DRINKS and the other, NON-Adult Drinks. It's her code for saying that his friends better not make idiots of themselves by getting trashed today. She studies the horde of teens that has descended on the house in the last half hour. The boys are a strikingly athletic-looking bunch, while the girls are mostly skinny, dressed in belly-baring shirts and denim shorts, the inside pockets hanging out past the cuffs. The girls wear their hair long and straight and sip from Dunkin' Donuts iced-coffee cups, although the thought occurs to Bree that those cups might hold something other than coffee.

"You got it, boss." Noah grins, flips a burger. He's dressed in a Local 02045 T-shirt, swim trunks, and flip-flops. The epitome of casual cool. Overhead, the afternoon sun burns auspiciously in a powder-blue sky. The temperature, forecast to reach eighty-three degrees, is already nudging seventy-eight.

"You *guuuuys*." Bree spins around to see Georgie, Shelby's friend who arrived promptly at one and has been drinking ever since, walking toward them. "You guys," she repeats. "Thank you for ordering up this *gorgeous* weather. I mean, really, could you have picked a better day for a party?"

She's wearing movie-star sunglasses and a wraparound kimono decorated with enormous white and pink flowers. Her long, wavy hair, highlighted in caramel tones, brings to mind a slightly less-glamorous Jennifer Coolidge.

"We aim to please." Bree pulls up a chair for her. "Here, sit. I love your cover-up, or tunic, by the way. I never know what to call them."

"Thanks. It's never coming off, though. Not with all these young girls parading around in their itsy-bitsy bodies and their even itsier bikinis." Georgie gestures toward Noah's friends, as if they've all come out to ruin her fun. But before Bree can respond, Shelby's other girlfriends are pulling up chairs.

It's evident that Georgie plays queen bee to this particular hive.

"Jules!" Georgie exclaims. "You made it! With it being Figawi weekend and all, I thought we might not see you."

"Shh!" Julia cocks her head toward the end of the deck, where a tall, lean man dressed in khaki shorts and a blue polo is talking with a guy who introduced himself earlier as Meg's husband, Bill. Meg leans in and whisper-shouts, "That's Greg. Julia's professor friend. From MIT?"

Georgie's face brightens in sudden understanding. "Oh! You mean the guy you mentioned at lunch the other week? Everything's going well, then?"

"I guess you could say that," Julia confirms. "We're still in the getting-to-know-you phase."

"And how long does that last?" inquires Meg earnestly.

"Typically, a few hours," Julia replies, prompting a round of laughter.

When the doorbell out front rings, Bree excuses herself and yells, "Got it," as she crisscrosses the living room, just in case Shelby's scrambling to get there, too. But Shelby is nowhere to be found. Neither is Kate. When Bree opens the door, she takes a step back.

"Oh, hello," she says without thinking. For some reason, the striking man standing before her with a basket of—is it dog treats?—looks familiar. She's trying to place him when he steps forward.

"I'm sorry, do we know each other? I'm Bo Bannister, town vet. I'm here for Shelby." His gaze travels from Bree to the basket he's holding. "Or more like, Tuukka," he self-corrects with a half laugh.

Before Bree can respond, her sister materializes at her side.

"Oh! Hi there. I wasn't expecting you. What's up?" She's wearing a gauzy white maxi dress, and the faint line of her black one-piece bathing suit is visible underneath. There's an edge to her voice, a nervous warble. Something's off, though Bree can't say what. It feels as if all the oxygen has been sucked out of the air.

She watches while Dr. Bo's eyes unmistakably trace the length of her sister's body. "Hey, Shelby. Sorry to interrupt. I know you're having your big party today, but I couldn't help thinking about Tuukka's, er, situation."

"Situation?" Shelby's eyebrows knit in confusion.

"Yeah, you mentioned how he was having some, um, digestive issues, remember? And I thought these doggie treats for sensitive stomachs might help?" His sudden stammering is endearing. "No one wants a sick dog when they're throwing a party," he adds.

"Oh, right."

Bree can almost see the wheels spinning in Shelby's head, debating whether or not to invite him in. Is this the man her sister has been sneaking in conversations with? Who's been texting her nonstop?

"How thoughtful of you," she says finally and reaches for the basket. Is it Bree's imagination, or does Dr. Bo take a step back, as if he's not quite ready to part with Tuukka's treats?

Shelby shakes her head. "I'm sorry. I'm terrible at introductions. Bree, this is Dr. Bo, Tuukka's vet. Dr. Bo, this is my baby sister, Bree."

"Nice to meet you." He shifts the weight of the basket under his left arm, extends his right hand. His teeth are the pearly white of toothpaste ads. His chiseled jaw and chin dimple, the stuff of actors. He is, Bree must admit, incredibly handsome.

"Nice to meet you. I've heard a lot about you," he says, and Bree shakes his hand.

"I'm sure you're busy," Shelby says. "Thanks again for dropping these off."

Dr. Bo shuffles from foot to foot, so much so, that it seems Shelby might have to pry the basket from his hands. But then Tuukka arrives at the door, full of barks and tail-wagging. "There he is!" Dr. Bo crouches down to say hello, clearly relieved to have his own personal rescue dog. Tuukka makes a beeline for the basket.

"Do you want to come in?" Bree asks, prompting a sharp pinch on her arm from Shelby. She swivels to glare at her sister, who glowers back.

"Sure!" He straightens. "I can only stay for a few minutes, though."

Reluctantly, Shelby steps aside, making room for him to pass, and sets the basket on the hallway bench. "What was that all about?" Bree hisses as they follow him through the living room and out to the deck.

"I'll explain later," Shelby says sharply. "Just try not to do any more damage, okay?" She shoots Bree the evil eye, the one they used to give each other when they were kids, meaning there'll be payback.

For the next hour, Bree watches her sister and Bo together, how when Shelby offers him a soda from the cooler, he takes it from her, his hand lingering on her wrist. How she pulls her hand away suddenly. How he tries to make small talk with the teenagers and Shelby's friends, his gaze never straying long from her sister. How Shelby only deigns to look at him when his back is turned. It's both obvious and not obvious that there's a connection.

"Hey, you." It's Audrey, who has come up beside Bree now, squeezing her hand. She's wearing cutoff shorts and a fitted white tank top scattered with blue stars.

An instant ping of attraction shoots through Bree.

"Sorry I'm late. What did I miss?"

"You have no idea," Bree whispers and follows her to the beer cooler.

Later, when Dr. Bo finally moves to leave, Shelby hurries out behind him—and Bree follows.

"I missed you earlier. Where were you?" he asks her sister, but she hushes him as they head outside. From the living room window, Bree watches them walk to his car. And then he does the unthinkable: he grabs her sister's hands, glances around quickly—and kisses her. Bree takes a guilty step back, understanding that she's just witnessed something she shouldn't have.

Several minutes later, when her sister rejoins the party, Bree sidles up next to her. "So does your vet always make house calls?"

"No, not typically." Shelby helps herself to a burger, places it on a bun, and drizzles ketchup over it.

"I get the sense," Bree says, following her around the table, "that maybe there's more going on between the two of you than a doctor-patient relationship?"

"He's not my doctor," her sister snaps and takes a bite of her burger.

"You know what I mean. Shel. *He had a wedding ring on.*" Bree hadn't noticed the gold band until much later, when he was talking to Shelby's girlfriends. "He's married, right?"

"Why, yes, he is. You'd make a good little detective, wouldn't you?" She spins around to address her friends. "Anyone else care for another margarita?"

"Yes, please!" Georgie waves her glass in the air. Bree looks on, stunned, while her sister gathers up a handful of empty glasses and heads back into the house for refills, as if there's nothing more to discuss.

As if Bo Bannister is no big deal, only an unusually thoughtful vet.

But Bree understands that there's plenty left to discuss.

It's hard to fathom that, while they've been blasting Trey's infidelity all week, their sister has been off cavorting around with a man exactly like Trey. A *married* man. Bree's sure of it; this is the man who's been sending Shelby endless texts. The man who's been the focus of her attention, all times when she'd claimed it was work that was distracting her.

Shelby, it turns out, is a Janus, a two-faced god. And Kate, whether she knows it or not, has every right to want to murder her.

27

SHELBY

Shelby sits with Georgie along the deck's edge, closest to the water. An hour ago, Meghan and her husband left with their four-year-old son, Mason, who'd thrown up on the beach. "Too many chips and soda for this one," she explained, apologizing on their way out. Shelby's disappointed for Meg's sake, but she gets it. Kids come first. Just like Noah will always come first for her, and Clara for Kate.

Her frustration in the car this morning had been just that—irritation over not having seen Bo all week. But she understands that she hasn't exactly been fair to Kate, especially yesterday when she shamed her for thinking about divorcing Trey when Clara was involved. Didn't she file for divorce without a second thought once she realized that Ethan was more or less using her? She owes her sister an apology. Farther down the beach, Kate is kicking around a soccer ball with Clara. Her sister is a wonderful mom, but Shelby can't recall if she's ever told her that. She'll throw it in along with the apology.

Because she doesn't want to fight. She really doesn't. Especially when it comes to men. Like the man she showed to the door earlier. The man whose secret her sister, Bree, has inadvertently stumbled onto.

You can't show up here like this, unannounced! she whisper-yelled at Bo when he was leaving.

But when you weren't at the park, I was worried. I had to make sure you were okay.

I'm fine.

Then why didn't you show up?

Because it was a dumb idea. I shouldn't have called you. We have to stop. This is wrong on so many levels. And my sister, Kate—

What about Kate?

Her husband is having an affair.

Oh. I see.

We can't do this anymore. It isn't right.

Look, I'm leaving now, but this conversation isn't over, okay? It's to be continued.

And then he kissed her.

"How is it possible," Julia asks, interrupting Shelby's scrambled thoughts, "that every time I see Dr. Bo, he's even more handsome than the last?" She drops down into a chair beside her. Julia's long, dark hair is twisted into a messy bun, and she's wearing a pink bikini—mostly because she can get away with it and still look fantastic. A white gossamer sarong circles her hips.

"Settle down, Jules," Georgie admonishes. "Your new boyfriend is here, remember?"

"Who? Greg?" She waves a hand in the air if she's never heard of him. "Greg isn't in the boyfriend category yet. You have to earn that, if you know what I mean."

"I don't think I do, nor do I care to," replies Georgie.

Julia raises her shoulders in a *whatever* shrug, then shifts in her chair to better address Shelby. "So Dr. Bo certainly seems to be giving *you* the special treatment. Do tell: What's your secret?"

Shelby stares intently at her toes, painted cherry red, and wiggles them, feigning nonchalance. "I think he wanted to make sure Tuukka didn't puke all over the party. He's thoughtful that way."

"I'll say," Georgie says. "I didn't even realize Tuukka was sick." Shelby meets her friend's gaze, willing her not to mention the rumor that Maeve Harding has been spreading. "Seems like he might have a little crush on our Shelby."

Shelby rolls her eyes, but she can feel the heat rising to her cheeks. "Yeah, right. Washed-up mom with a sixteen-year-old kid. What every guy is looking for."

"You're not washed up!" Julia exclaims. "To the contrary, you're one hot mama. He'd be lucky to have you."

"Yeah, too bad he's married," Georgie pipes up. "Other than that, he'd be perfect for you."

Julia peers around to make sure no one else is within earshot, then leans in. "You know, I've heard that he's been spending a lot of time with someone other than Cindy these days." Shelby's heart comes to a full stop.

"You don't say." Georgie shifts uncomfortably in her seat.

"Yeah, I heard that he and Rachel Yearling, you know, the cute tennis instructor? Well, apparently, they were caught making out in the back of the Cohasset Tennis Club last week. Near the weight room. Like a couple of lovesick teenagers."

"What?" Disbelief mingled with nausea washes over Shelby. "That can't be true." Her eyes dart from Julia to Georgie and back again to Julia. "I mean, he's married. Who told you that?"

Julia shrugs. "I forget. I wouldn't be surprised if it's true, though. He's got quite the reputation as a philanderer. Who knows? Maybe he and Cindy have an open marriage." She stretches out her long legs, puts her feet up on the cooler.

The women sit in silence for a moment, contemplating this possibility until Julia murmurs, "Uh-oh."

Her gaze has wandered over to the volleyball game. "I guess I better check on Greg. He's having way too much fun playing volleyball with Noah's friends—and their cute girlfriends. Excuse me, ladies."

After she traipses far enough down the beach, Georgie spins around. "Shelby, what the hell is going on? Are you or aren't you fooling around with Bo Bannister?"

Shelby hesitates because she's still trying to make sense of what was revealed moments ago. But she might as well be trying to understand the nuances of the national debt. Bo fooling around with Rachel Yearling? Last week? How is that possible? Theoretically, she knows she broke things off over a week ago, but that seems insanely fast to start up a new relationship. Even for someone as charming as Bo. Especially for someone as *married* as Bo. And why would he show up at her door today if he's already cheating with someone else? Has he been cheating on Shelby the entire time?

It's not possible, is it, that she's merely one woman in a long chain of women whom Bo Bannister is sleeping with? *Can you be cheated on when you're the cheater?* It sounds like one of those tautological riddles from her college philosophy class, without a satisfying answer.

It's enormously tempting to spill everything to Georgie, right here and now. To unload her guilty conscience and admit that, yes, she and Bo had a relationship—quite a spectacular one, in fact—but that she ended it recently. That for months, she's felt terrible about it and has been dying to tell someone but had to keep it a secret for obvious reasons.

But Shelby feels blindsided, completely played. Here she thought she was special. *She's in love with Bo Bannister!* And maybe—she was hoping beyond hope—that he loved her, too. It's conceivable, she reasons now, that Julia has *no idea* what she's talking about. Admittedly, her friend has been wrong before.

Shelby wills her heart to unclench. She's no better than Maeve Harding if she starts jumping to conclusions. Best to go straight to the source than imagine all the possible iterations of her lover's affections. *Ex*-lover, she reminds herself.

No, betraying Bo to Georgie at the moment doesn't feel right, although given the copious amounts of alcohol her friend has had to drink, the details will probably escape her in the morning, anyway.

"Oh, Georgie," Shelby finally says. "I wish I could tell you. But if I did, I'd have to kill you."

28

KATE

Kate isn't entirely sure why Trey is here. Earlier in the week, they agreed he could take Clara *next* weekend. But it's the Saturday of the annual Lancaster party, and she made it very clear that he was not welcome today or anytime this weekend. The fact that he's shown up at six o'clock in the evening—unannounced and uninvited—can only be bad. Is he here to make a scene? Profess his undying love for her? Or is there a more sinister reason why her husband is standing on the edge of her sister's front lawn, hands in his pockets, staring forlornly at the porch?

"Look, I'm sorry about what I said earlier. You should do whatever you want with your marriage," Shelby offers now. "But you have to at least talk to him." They're standing off to the side of the living room window, trying to avoid being seen. "At least find out what he wants."

A heavy sigh escapes Kate. As much as she's still seething at Shelby, her sister is right about this. He's Clara's father, after all. It might be something important. "Keep an eye on Clara for me, will you? Julia has her out back."

"You got it."

Kate lets herself out, her posture ramrod straight despite the few beers she's consumed. Letting him witness how much his betrayal has broken her over the last week is something she won't allow.

As soon as he spots her, his shoulders relax. He's wearing blue shorts and a Chicago Bears T-shirt. "Katie," he calls out as he strides across the lawn. He goes as if to embrace her, but her body instinctively retreats a few steps back.

His eyes are rimmed with red, and his hair is rumpled, as if maybe he hasn't slept in a few days. He looks terrible. "What are you doing here, Trey?"

"You look amazing." She tilts her head. She *does* look amazing, she thinks. She's wearing the bikini Trey likes, the orange one with the ties on the side, and a crocheted cover-up. Over the week, the sun has given her skin a healthy glow. But she's not falling for it. "Sorry." He shakes his head, acknowledging the inappropriateness of the comment in the moment. "I'm here to talk."

"We've talked plenty. You get Clara next weekend. This is my weekend."

"Jeez, you make it sound like we're divorced."

"That's right." She waits for the gravity of her words to sink in, watches his face as he registers this information. "I talked to an attorney yesterday."

"No, Katie, please," he pleads. "You can't do that. Please, I'm begging you." His eyes scour the yard, panicky, like a wild animal. "Can we talk somewhere private?"

"What's wrong with right here? Everyone else is out back."

"Clara, too?"

"Yes?" She frowns, waiting to see why he's acting so paranoid.

"Can we at least sit down?" Kate is about to flop down right there on the grass but then thinks better of it. She motions for him to follow her to the side of the house, where two wrought iron chairs and a table sit on a cobblestone patio.

"What is it? What's going on? And why do you look like shit?" She settles into a chair.

Trey's eyes dart around the side yard, as if he's afraid someone else might be listening. As angry as she is, the thought crosses her mind that maybe her husband is having some kind of psychotic breakdown. Maybe his ill-advised affair with Sonja can all be blamed on a mental imbalance, a lack of dopamine or serotonin or one of those other important healthy brain hormones.

"I wanted to let you know that Sonja left the firm. She's gone."

"What do you mean, 'gone'?"

"I mean she handed in her resignation. She's already got another job lined up in LA."

"What about you two?"

"I already told you. Over. Done. She won't even talk to me."

"I'm sorry to hear that." Kate's sarcasm is so frosty, it could crack glass.

"Look. I deserve it. Whatever names you want to call me. If you want to punch me, be my guest." He thrusts his chest out as if to better brace himself for her fists.

Kate rolls her eyes.

"I don't blame you for hating me," he continues. "But the last week has been hell. You've got to give me a second chance, Katydid."

Her arms are crossed indignantly. "Why?"

"Why?" He frowns, as if the question baffles him.

"Why should I give you a second chance, even though technically, I've already given you a second chance. Back at the Parrot."

"Because I'm a good dad. Because we love each other. Because we took a vow. Because I'm your husband, and you're my wife."

"All excellent points," she says with obvious disdain, "until you get to the cheating part, which you forgot to mention. Where does *that* fit exactly?" A mild headache has been working its way across her brain all afternoon, and now it's taken up residence above her right eye, a small woodpecker hammering at her skull.

Slowly, he shakes his head. "It doesn't. I'm an asshole, I know. But I swear to you, I'll never do anything like this again. You have to understand, Katie . . . this case has been a living nightmare. I wasn't thinking clearly."

"Really?" She can feel the blood rushing to her face. "Seems like your penis was thinking pretty clearly."

He visibly recoils. "Whoa. Okay, I deserved that."

"Why weren't you thinking clearly, Trey?" Her voice rises. "Are you going to tell me that you have some kind of weird sex addiction and you couldn't help yourself?"

"No, of course not. Nothing like that."

She thrums her fingers on the table, waiting. She will not crack in his presence.

"It has to do with the case, actually."

"The case? Something that you're not permitted to tell me because of attorney-client privilege, I presume."

"Theoretically."

"Then why are you even mentioning it?" It's starting to feel as if Trey is only trying to inveigle her further. First, Sonja is leaving, and now his whole affair can be explained away because of a case?

"Because it might help you better understand what happened?" Even Trey sounds as if he's unconvinced. "I mean, Sonja and I were spending all this time together working on the case, and one thing led to another—"

"Oh, that's really rich. It was inevitable? Is that what you're saying?"

"If you can just give me a second to try and explain!" He rubs his eyes, then stares at her beseechingly.

"Be my guest."

"Okay." He lays his hands out flat on the table, as if preparing to make a presentation. "Look, I was a total dope for getting involved with her in the first place. I get it. But she came on to me a few times—and I understand that's not an excuse—but I thought you should know that I turned her down. And then, one night we were working late, and we had a few cocktails. And, well, I wasn't thinking straight."

"Clearly."

"Anyway, it wouldn't have happened again, except Sonja stumbled onto a memo that she wasn't supposed to see in the swing set case.

Something that could have been potentially bad for our client. Very bad."

"And?"

"And . . . it kind of got buried."

"What do you mean, 'got buried'?"

Trey shrugs. "It went away."

"Went away, how? Did you and Sonja destroy evidence together?" It hadn't occurred to Kate that blackmail might be behind her husband's affair, that he might be involved in *criminal* activity.

Trey hangs his head. "No, I told Sonja that I'd handle it, that I'd talk to Stuart."

"And?"

He glances around again, as if checking for hostile enemies hiding in the bushes. "You have to promise to tell no one."

"Whatever."

"No, I mean it, Katie. No one can know what I'm about to tell you."

"Okay, sure." She just wants this entire exchange to be over as quickly as possible. What can Trey possibly tell her that's worse than what he's already done?

"The memo was from the CEO of the company. He knew there was a faulty screw in the swing attachment. But instead of recalling all the old swing sets for a new part, he only ordered changes to the design of any new swings going forward."

It takes Kate a moment to assemble the pieces he's giving her in the correct order. Once she does, her stomach seizes in one enormous knot. "And the one that the little boy fell off, the one who brought the claim?" she asks softly, not wanting to hear the answer but already knowing it in her gut. "The boy who broke his back when the swing ripped off? That was one of the old swings?"

Trey bites his bottom lip, nods.

"Jesus, Trey!" She jumps up out of her chair. "You've been defending a criminal all this time? What happened? Did you guys settle?"

He shakes his head. "Not yet. I tried, I really did. I tried to do the right thing by showing Stuart the memo."

"How many more swings are out there?"

"I don't know. Dozens? Hundreds, maybe?"

"*Trey.* What did Stuart say?"

"He said it was unfortunate, but that he'd take care of it. That I shouldn't worry about it."

"And?"

"So I didn't. Worry about it, that is. But when Sonja saw the list of documents we were handing over for discovery, she noticed the memo was missing. She confronted me, and I promised her that I'd get to the bottom of it. But that she had to give me time. That it was a delicate matter, and the last thing either one of us wanted to do was piss off Stuart—or we could both lose our jobs. She agreed."

Trey pauses and rakes his fingers through his hair.

"That was about a month ago. I couldn't exactly break things off with her, you know? I had to keep her close so that she wouldn't turn on Stuart—or me. Even though I really wanted to end it. You've got to believe me."

"Uh-huh. That totally makes sense," Kate quips. "You had to keep seeing Sonja so that she wouldn't betray you or Stuart. I get it."

"Look, I know it sounds bad."

"No, Trey. It *is* bad."

"Katie, what was I supposed to do? If I ratted out Stuart, the entire firm would be finished. Stuart could go to jail and I could be disbarred. And then where would we be?"

"Where would *we* be?" Kate demands, stunned. "Undoubtedly in the same place."

She steps behind her chair. "I want you to leave."

"But I haven't seen Clara yet. Don't I even get to say hello?"

"I don't think so. Maybe another day."

She thinks back to when she and Trey talked, in broad strokes, about the swing set case months ago, when she first questioned the firm's motives. *How can you defend a company when a child was hurt on their product?* But Trey brushed her off, saying everyone deserves a fair trial and that the parents opted out of the pay-for-assembly option. The faulty swing was most likely due to the fact that the dad cut corners building it, lost a screw. Not the company's fault.

But it *was* the company's fault. And Trey and his boss failed to disclose it.

Disgusting, she thinks. There's something else that's bothering her, though. "I don't understand what's changed? You told me you broke off the affair with her. So does that mean you're going to share the memo with the plaintiff after all?"

Trey shakes his head. "What's changed is that Stuart offered Sonja a very generous severance package in exchange for signing a nondisclosure agreement. She should be financially set for a long time. He's the one who got her the job out in LA. If she talks, she'll lose everything."

"I thought you said she quit."

"Well, yeah, I guess she kind of had to."

"So basically, Stuart made the company's problem—and the firm's problem—go away in one fell swoop."

"I guess?"

"And just to be crystal clear," she forges on, even though she feels like she might be sick. "The worst thing to come out of this whole mess, in your opinion, would be your getting disbarred?" She can only marvel at this conclusion, uttered by a man whose very integrity she would have staked her life on two weeks ago.

"Yes?" It comes out as a question, although he must know it's the wrong answer.

"Oh, Trey," she says softly, tears welling in her eyes. "That poor boy. That poor family. How could you?"

29

SHELBY

Down on the beach, maybe twenty yards from the deck, a group of Noah's friends dance on the sand while Ed Sheeran plays on the portable speakers. Shelby's pretty sure that Noah and his buddies have snuck a few High Noons from the "Adult" cooler, but she's also confident that everyone's car keys are safely locked away in her bureau drawer upstairs (she demanded their keys as soon as they arrived).

The only way for someone to get home tonight is to walk.

Off to the right, Noah and Lindsay are sitting on a beach blanket with a few friends. Lindsay's legs are roped through Noah's. As much as Shelby likes Noah's girlfriend, she doesn't know that she'll ever get accustomed to seeing another woman kissing her son, snaking her arms around his neck. Shelby struggles to tamp down the urge to race over and peel first one arm, then the other, from around Noah's neck. She'd never do it, of course—but sometimes the impulse is almost unbearable. This is the same boy, after all, whose back she used to tickle with finger spiders.

So many of these kids she has watched grow up alongside Noah, from kindergarten to high school. In many ways, they're as familiar and precious to her as her own son, a part of the peculiar, extended family they've fashioned for themselves here in this sleepy town. Shelby has watched Noah's best friend, Logan, morph from a timid first grader into the vibrant soccer captain at the high school. There's Alex, the clown of the group, who famously won the hot-dog-eating contest in sixth grade—and infamously vomited afterward. Max, towheaded and perhaps the kindest of the bunch, was the first to help her carry in groceries from the car when the boys were in fourth grade. And Duncan, too handsome for his own good—startling blue eyes, blond hair, and a gorgeous smile—has been dating girls since third grade, when Claudia Jenkins informed him at the lunch table that he was her boyfriend.

The endless carpools to hockey rinks all across New England, the same group of boys in the back seat of her minivan, their fragrant hockey equipment stinking up the entire car. Over the years, she'd eavesdrop on their conversations, only to swap those stories with the other moms' tales. She remembers these boys when their hockey bags were twice as big as they were. She knows some, though certainly not all, of the stupid mistakes they've made over the years—the various detentions and demerits, the broken windows from a misguided baseball, hours logged in the penalty box, fractured bones, concussions, chagrined girlfriends, scary trips to the emergency room. These boys are not her boys, but deep down inside, they *feel* like her children. She loves each of them. And she suspects the other parents feel the same way about Noah.

She's tried explaining to Kate how it happens, how your child's friends' families become your friends, how you come to know which kid will eat only cheese pizza and which one is allergic to peanuts. Who has a sense of style, and who could care less. Who has a crush on a particular girl, and who's only interested in hockey, hockey, hockey. Which ones possess a modicum of common sense, and which ones desperately need some. Which ones have remained constant friends of Noah's, and which ones have faded out of his life for a year or two, only to come rushing back in. Small details, but over the years, they add up to a full picture, filling in the blank slates that were once the sweet, innocent faces of kindergarteners beaming at their parents from behind their desks on the first day of school.

It's enough to make her heart jump to her throat.

Down on the beach, the kids appear to be in the middle of a back-flip contest, boys versus girls. It's a stupid idea, especially since Shelby has zero desire to make a trip to the emergency room tonight. But she hesitates to intervene just yet. It would seem the girls—more than a few of whom are cheerleaders at Hull High—would have the upper hand. But it turns out the guys aren't terrible either. More than a few have mastered a running flip. Shelby watches while Noah races across the sand, plants his hands, and sends his legs soaring overhead only to land on his butt. "I'll give that a 6.0!" someone shouts, and the kids laugh good-naturedly.

The girls are declared the victors before everyone saunters back to the music, shooting each other high fives and collapsing on the sand. It's only then that Shelby notices that her friend Georgie is no longer by her side. Julia is down on the beach with Greg and the kids; Bree and Audrey headed off for a walk a while ago. And Kate, presumably, is still talking to Trey. It occurs to Shelby that in a few more years, after Noah leaves for college, this is conceivably what her life will look like—a woman sitting alone while everyone else is off doing their own thing. Aside from Tuukka, Shelby will be by herself. Without Bo. Without Noah.

The silence, she thinks, will be deafening. It's a sobering thought, one that makes her want to run into the ocean, dive under, and never come up for air.

"Auntie Shelby?" Clara, her striking blue eyes framed by frizzy dark curls, materializes at her side. "You want to color with me?"

Shelby takes a moment to gather herself and remembers she's supposed to be watching her niece. "I'd love to, honey." She scoots off the chair to join her on the deck floor, next to a box of crayons and a coloring book. "Which picture should we color?"

Clara hands her the book and points to two princesses twirling in their ballroom gowns. Since Noah was never into princesses, Shelby is terrible at remembering their names. She's not quite sure whom she's looking at.

"Pretty. Can you tell me their names?"

Clara frowns, as if her aunt's paltry knowledge of princesses is embarrassing, but then she says, "I'll give you a hint: they're sister princesses. Like you and Mommy and Auntie Bree."

"Are you sure about that?" she asks. "That there are princesses who are also sisters? Because that kind of sounds too good to be true."

"It's Elsa and Anna, silly!"

"Oh, right." How could Shelby forget? "I liked that movie. I liked Elsa and Anna."

"That's because they're sisters!" Clara explains again, as if it's obvious. Shelby wonders if her three-year-old niece might be onto something. What if the whole reason the movie appealed to Shelby in the first place was not because of its messages about self-acceptance and female empowerment but because it featured a pair of sisters who would do anything for each other?

Just then, her cell buzzes in her pocket. When she reaches for it, there's a text waiting. A week ago, it would have made her heart race. Tonight, though, there's a distinct tug of melancholy.

Can I see you later? Maybe after your party winds down? I'll be out on the boat. We should talk. xx

Honestly, Shelby thinks, *how many more times can I be expected to turn him away?*

30

BREE

When Bree and Audrey return from their walk, the party seems to have gone sideways. Which is to say, what was unfolding nicely enough an hour ago—the adults conversing politely, the teenagers playing volleyball—has taken a turn toward the wild. When Bree steps onto the deck, the ambience is far more frat party than family barbecue. All that's missing, she thinks, are the Jell-O shots. Easily a dozen more neighbors and friends have converged on Shelby's home, and a large group (Shelby included) is gathered around the picnic table for a game of quarters. Bree looks on while her sister bounces a coin across the table into a red Solo cup.

"Yes!" Shelby shouts and points to a stout man with thinning hair, dressed in a Hawaiian shirt and blue shorts. "Stan, your turn! Drink!"

Stan dutifully obeys, downing the beer in one gulp. A cheer goes up from the crowd while he fist-pumps the air. Evidently, Shelby has traded in her hostess hat for a party-girl tiara.

Meanwhile, Julia (apparently left in charge of Clara while Shelby mans the quarters table) is applying Neosporin and a Band-Aid to Clara's knee. "She skinned it coming up the stairs," she explains. Bree gives the offending boo-boo a kiss, then goes to fetch her niece a freeze pop from the cooler. Once Clara's cries subside, Bree hands her off to Audrey and heads into the house for more ice—and to find Kate.

But finding Kate proves easier than expected because she's standing in the front yard, with Trey. Bree's first instinct is to rush outside and intervene, like a referee, but then Trey spins around, aiming for his car. When his BMW thrums to life, Bree watches him back down the driveway, the tires squealing on the asphalt, before bombing down the road.

Slowly, Kate turns and wanders back into the house.

"Well, that went well." Her sister's longish blonde hair is pulled up in a tousled ponytail; her mascara is smeared at the corners. "Turns out my husband is an even bigger jerk than I thought."

"I'm sorry, Katydid. I had no idea he was coming to the party."

"Neither did I. He wasn't invited."

"Oh." Bree steps back, uncertain how to respond. Is Kate sad? Pissed off? Too drunk to care? "Well, that's just rude, then."

"I think he wanted to see Clara, but Shelby kept her out back, thank goodness. Trey's a mess." Bree doesn't mention that, at the moment, it's actually Audrey who's minding Clara, and Shelby's pretty much a wreck, too.

"What happened? Why was he here?"

She watches Kate pad over to the fridge and help herself to a hard seltzer. With a sad laugh, she says, "Where to begin? We rehashed a lot of the same old stuff—and some new stuff. My husband is an evil man. A no-do-gooder. But *shhhh*, I can't talk about it. It's a secret."

"I'll take your word for it." Bree has no idea what on earth her sister is referring to.

At that moment, the patio door slides open, and Shelby pops in. "There you two are!" She flings her arms wide open, sending her margarita sloshing over the rim of her cup. "C'mon. We're playing quarters." Then she turns on her heel and heads back outside.

"Whoa. Somebody better keep an eye on that one," warns Kate. "Is Shelby watching Clara or is it the other way around?"

"Good point. But don't worry; Audrey has her." Bree grabs the roll of paper towels from the counter and goes to wipe up the spill. "Maybe we should put Clara in charge of everyone tonight."

A feeble laugh escapes Kate, which gives Bree a flicker of hope. Because her sister has no idea about the secret Shelby has been keeping . . . and Bree has no idea how to tell her. They've spent the entire week hanging out at Shelby's house, and not once has she mentioned the very inconvenient fact that she, *like Trey*, is also a cheater, a liar by default. There's not a sliver of doubt in Bree's mind that Bo's the man her sister has been sneaking around with, who's been texting her nonstop. She saw them kissing!

One crisis at a time, Bree counsels herself.

And so, armed with a fresh bag of ice, she glides back out to the deck to refill the coolers. The quarters game has broken up, and, like individual galaxies born from the same cosmic soup, smaller, more intimate groups have spun off. Bree eavesdrops on a couple debating the merits of Tito's over Absolut. Another group chats about last year's Memorial Day party. (*Remember when Josie dared Phil to go skinny-dipping at Nantasket?* Laughter. *Oh man, I didn't think he was ever gonna find his pants!*) Then there's another guy, maybe in his late twenties, whom Bree has secretly labeled "random dude" because he's wandering around the party like a lost planet. There's a stoned vibe to him, and he keeps cranking up the volume on the speakers, which Bree then has to turn down.

She finds Audrey and Clara on the steps, playing rock, paper, scissors. The deck lights have come on in the descending darkness, and Kate swoops over to grab Clara for bedtime.

"Your sister certainly seems to be enjoying herself tonight," Audrey says when Bree flops down beside her. They both turn to look at Shelby, who, at the moment, is ducking under a broomstick for a game of limbo that's started up. For a moment, Bree flashes back to Shelby's senior year, when their parents vacationed on the Cape for a long weekend and Shelby threw a party for her friends. The house got completely trashed, and the next day was spent scrubbing vomit out of the carpet, sweeping up broken glass, and chasing Jimmy Chandler out of their parents' bed, where he passed out after one too many tequila shots. Bree was only eight at the time. She supposes they party a little more responsibly these days.

Although, then again, maybe not. Because Shelby is now dancing with Stan in the Hawaiian shirt and has wrapped a towel around his waist, as if preparing to slingshot him out into the night sky. Shelby's friend Julia has her tongue down her boyfriend's throat, a guy who looks to be maybe half her age. And in one of the lounge chairs, a semi-passed-out Georgie lies in a heap. Off to the side, Kate, who's returned from tucking Clara into bed, twirls drunkenly, colliding with the deck railing every so often.

It occurs to Bree that the sisterly thing to do—the *responsible* thing to do—would be to offer to watch Clara in the morning so that neither Kate nor Shelby will have to. Because it's possible that she's the least drunk Lancaster girl here tonight and—though this seems highly improbable—the most reliable one. She remembers her earlier promise to herself, to adult-up this weekend.

She's going to tell Kate not to worry about Clara, when on the other side of the house, the red-and-blue flash of police lights begins to dance in the sky, followed shortly by the sound of Shelby's doorbell ringing. Bree's first thought is to make a run for it, like they did in high school.

But, of course, that's the exact opposite of adulting-up. She exchanges glances with Audrey. "Guess somebody better get that."

Audrey's face cracks into a grin. "Looks like that somebody's going to be you."

31

ROBIN

When Robin pulls up to the Lancaster house, she makes a point of flashing the lights without running the sirens. There's no need to startle anyone unnecessarily. Besides, she and Shelby go way back, so much so that she knows Shelby's astrological sign: Cancer. It's also common knowledge that each year, every Saturday before Memorial Day, the Lancasters hold a bash that rivals no other. Their annual party sits squarely in its own league, in the same way that the University of Wisconsin-Madison (Robin's alma mater) isn't even included in the annual ranking of best party colleges in America. It simply surpasses all the rest; it would be like ranking a Mercedes among a bunch of Hondas. Pointless.

It also strikes Robin as one of those odd, cosmic coincidences that she bumped into Shelby at Breadbasket this morning, after having not seen her for two or three months. And now here she is, less than twelve hours later, knocking on Shelby's door due to a noise complaint. Memorial Day always brings its fair share of grumbling about illegal firecrackers, random drunks wandering into backyards, music being played too loud. Robin gets it: there are plenty of residents who live here for the solitude and quiet that Hull offers. Still, it wouldn't hurt a few of the complainers (always the same ones each year) to kick back and enjoy the holiday weekend themselves instead of speed-dialing the department every time they hear a noise.

Robin doesn't consider her job to be one of a bouncer, but that's essentially why she's here right now: to keep the peace, usher home any unruly guests, and convince Shelby to lower the music. Even on the front steps, she can clearly make out the laughter and animated chatter emanating from the backyard. Bob Seger's "Till It Shines" plays. Very old school and, Robin thinks with a wry smile, very Shelby. Across the street, two houses down, the curtains shift in the window ever so slightly—Mrs. Campbell (the "anonymous" caller), no doubt checking to make sure that Robin is doing her job.

When the door opens, Shelby's younger sister greets her with an alarmed expression. "Oh, hi, Officer. Everything okay?"

"Good evening. I realize it's still early, but we received a noise complaint from your neighbors. Any chance you can turn down the music, maybe move the party inside?" She feels like a complete killjoy, especially since it's only eight thirty. The majority of Hull's children haven't even crawled into bed yet.

"Oh, of course. Sorry, we'll turn it down right away." Behind the young woman's shoulder, Shelby's head pops up.

"Robin!"

"Hey, Shelby."

"Come in, come in. Can you join us for a beverage?"

"No, thanks. I'm on duty. Another time, maybe. I was just telling your sister that there've been a few complaints about the loud music from your backyard. Any chance you could tone it down a bit? Make me look good, like I'm doing my job for once?" she jokes.

Shelby waves a dismissive hand in the air. "Let me guess: Mrs. Campbell again? That old bat. I'm surprised she can hear anything at all!" Shelby hoots at her own joke and grabs on to her sister's shoulder for support. If it were another house, Robin might ask if she could come in, have a look around. Typically seeing an officer on the premises helps everyone to settle down right away. But it's Shelby. And it's not as if this house is party central all year. Only one day out of the year.

"Excuse me for one sec," the sister says. "Just going to turn down the music."

A few people are dancing in the living room, but most of the activity appears to be out back. Robin cranes her neck for a better view, but it's tough to see through the sliders. "Everything else okay?" she asks. "Everyone getting along?" The music fades by a significant number of decibels.

"Oh, yeah, yeah. Absolutely. No complaints here." Shelby's words are slurred, but Robin can't fault her for that. In fact, she kind of wishes she were on the other side of the door, spending time with friends, too. Enjoying Memorial Day weekend like a regular person. "Right, Bree?" Shelby says when her sister returns. "All's well here?"

"You bet."

Robin makes a mental note of the younger sister's name. *Bree*. She'd been thinking maybe Beth.

"Okay, then. I don't want to keep you. Just do me a favor and keep the noise level at a reasonable threshold."

"You got it, Lieutenant." Shelby gives her a mock salute. If it were anyone else, Robin might be tempted to haul her down to the station for contempt. But so much of her job involves reading a situation, reading people. There's no reason to escalate things here this evening. In a few short hours, Robin will likely have real problems to deal with, namely trying to steer all the drunkards home when the bars close and before the fights begin.

"Well, have a good night," she says before stepping away.

"Hey, Robin," Shelby calls out when she's almost to the cruiser. "Don't forget! You promised me wine next week."

Robin gives her a thumbs-up. "You got it." She starts the car, shuts off the light bar, and pulls out slowly, headed for the boardwalk to herd the proverbial stray cats of Memorial Day weekend.

32

BREE

After Robin's visit, Bree pilots herself to the ADULT DRINKS cooler for a beer. Their family has been throwing a Memorial Day party for years, and she can't recall the cops ever showing up on their doorstep. Her gaze wanders across the deck and out onto the beach, where the teenagers are dancing to Imagine Dragons. Is it really that much rowdier than in previous years? It doesn't feel like it.

She decides to blame it all on Random Dude. If he hadn't kept sneaking over to turn up the music, maybe the neighbors would have never called the police in the first place.

"Everything okay?" Audrey asks. She's still on the deck stairs, nursing a beer. The moonlight hits her face in such a way that she appears almost lit from within.

"You mean aside from a cop showing up at the front door? Yeah. Everything's great." Bree drops down next to her and cracks open her beer. "Fortunately, Shelby knows the cop. They're old pals."

"Ah. Well, I'm glad you're back. I was beginning to worry."

At that precise moment, a loud, shrill voice cuts through the crowd. "*Heeeellloooo*, everyone!" A new guest, clearly inebriated, has burst into the party, followed by a small entourage.

"Who's that?"

Bree turns and squints to better focus. The woman, maybe in her early fifties, wears a red sundress and, in a festive nod to the holiday, a red, white, and blue cowboy hat. Her short, blonde pixie cut reminds Bree of someone, but who? Then she spies the ungainly cast encircling the woman's wrist.

"Maeve!" A woman in red capris and a white sweater races over and slides her arm through Maeve's. "I thought you'd never get here! Come on! Everyone's dancing! You can still dance with that thing on, right?" she asks, gesturing to the cast, and Maeve nods.

A man with a beard, who may or may not be Maeve's date, heists a few beverages from the cooler and delivers them to Maeve and her friend.

"Don't look now," says Georgie, who's apparently risen from the dead, "but that's Maeve Harding, Hull's gossip queen. She knows your darkest secrets. Even the ones you didn't know you had."

"Yikes." Bree gets up to stand beside Georgie, and Audrey does the same.

"She's a clerk at town hall, so she knows everyone's business. Who's getting married, divorced, having a baby. Who died."

"I thought she looked familiar." Audrey drains the rest of her beer.

"What's she doing at our party?"

Georgie shrugs. "Your guess is as good as mine. Probably like half the people here, she invited herself. What's that saying about liquor paving the way to wherever your heart longs to go?"

"So she's a party crasher," Audrey says.

"Exactly."

Just then, Shelby comes up beside them and hisses, "What is *she* doing here?"

Georgie narrows her eyes. "You know that saying, 'You should make friends with your enemies'?"

"I thought it was, 'Keep your friends close and your enemies closer,'" Audrey supplies.

"Yeah, that's the one."

Shelby frowns. "I'm going to need another beer in that case. The fact that she's here must mean that her own party was a bust. She invited me, you know."

Bree shakes her head. "I don't get it. What's so awful about her?"

"Oh, nothing," her sister says. "Just that she still owes me money for a loan I gave her for a new furnace. Or, at least, that's what she said it was for. Although I'm beginning to wonder."

"Maybe she forgot?"

"Not a chance," quips Shelby.

"Well," Bree begins, "I'm not sure how much more this group can handle, anyway." The salty air suddenly feels clammy on her skin; exhaustion is beginning to pool in her body, right down to her toes. Most of these guests have been partying since one o'clock. "I was thinking maybe we'd have a last-drinks call and everyone could head off to the bars downtown?"

Georgie checks her watch, and someone puts "YMCA" on the speakers.

"At a quarter to nine?" she asks, incredulous. "No way. This crowd's just getting started!" She polishes off whatever she's drinking, hands Bree her empty cup, and elbows her way onto the dance floor, her arms lifted in a Y formation.

～

When Bree returns from checking on Clara (who's miraculously asleep), a noticeable hush has fallen over the party. At first, she assumes it's because everyone has finally cleared out, but when she reaches the sliding doors, she sees that Maeve Harding has pulled Shelby aside and is talking to her in A VERY LOUD VOICE.

"You've got to tell us how you snagged Dr. Bo," she says, poking Shelby's chest with her forefinger. Her words are slurry, like mud. "Because he's an almost impossible get." She makes a biting motion with her fingers and thumb, imitating a hand puppet snatching someone up.

"That's not to say he hasn't dated women *outside of Hull* before, but for him to go fishing so close to home, well, you must really be something." (It comes out sounding more like *somepin*.)

There's a palpable gasp among those standing within earshot.

"I don't know where you get your information, Maeve, but that's ridiculous," Shelby replies evenly. "You know as well as I do that Dr. Bo is married."

Maeve tilts her head, as if assessing Shelby with fresh eyes. "Yes, well, that's never mattered to him before." There's another gasp, and suddenly Random Dude is standing between Shelby and Maeve.

"Maeve, why don't you shut up?" There's a splotch of wet beer on his T-shirt. "You're drunk, and you don't know what you're talking about."

Maeve giggles, as if she thinks he might be silly or stupid, or both. "Oh, Jasper, you were always such a gullible little boy," she says dismissively. "Why don't you mind your own damn business."

"And why don't you?" Bree is surprised to find her own voice returning as she steps up beside Random Dude. Georgie, Julia, and Kate join her.

"Oh no, you don't," Maeve warns, as if they're purposely trying to distract her. Her eyes wobble in her head while she struggles to recall her point. "I have proof!" she finally declares. "I saw you guys, Shelby. At Mambo's, getting takeout last week. I saw you kissing him! Yeah, there was definitely something going on there. You and Dr. Bo are having an *affair*." She starts to tilt to one side, and the woman in red capris who first welcomed her races over.

"You know what, Maeve?" she says. "Why don't we get you home? I think we've all had enough to drink tonight."

"How. Dare. You." It's Shelby now who's taken a step forward, whose cheeks have blushed bright crimson, and whose hand is raised as if she might slap Maeve. "You ungrateful, bitchy woman. After all I've done for you, and you decide to ambush me in my own home? At my own party?" If the crowd was quiet before, it's absolutely stone silent now. Someone has switched off the music.

Maeve takes a woozy step forward, but even that small motion proves to be too much and she crashes to the floor with a loud *thunk*. Beneath their feet, the deck shakes.

Maeve begins to moan like a little girl. "Ouch, my fanny! There's gonna be a big, big bruise there."

Bree doesn't know whether to laugh or scream. Tuukka, who's been hiding in the house with his bone, races out and starts barking wildly. She restrains him by the collar.

The man who passed Maeve a beer upon arrival quickly crouches down beside her. "C'mon now, let's get you home, dearie." He hoists her up, grabbing her under the shoulders, with the help of Maeve's other friend.

"Really sorry about the interruption, Shelby," he says.

"Do you need some help, Jerry? Maybe a ride?" her sister inquires.

"Nah, thanks. We've got her. It's a short walk."

He tips his hat and says thanks again. A hush falls over the crowd while they watch Maeve being escorted out of the house by her friends.

"Well," Stan says, attempting to lighten the mood. "That was something else, wasn't it?" A wave of uneasy laughter and head-shaking ripples through the crowd. "You know, the other night, both Betsy here and I were at L Street Pizza, picking up takeout. I wonder if that means we're having an affair?" He hoots as if it's the funniest joke he's ever made, and while Bree appreciates the effort, she can't help but notice that Shelby's face has turned ashen.

"Hey, Shel?" She grabs her sister's arm, concerned she might faint. "Why don't we get you up to bed? Kate and I can handle the rest. The party's breaking up, anyway."

Shelby's gaze circles the deck, as if she's debating whether or not this is true. Slowly, she nods her head in agreement. "Well, folks," she announces. "Looks like the party's over. Time for everyone to go home or party somewhere else. Thanks for coming! Happy Memorial Day!"

The group begins to disperse, Shelby's friends say their goodbyes, and Bree attempts once more to coax her sister upstairs. But Shelby's not having it. *"Stooop,"* she scolds in a drunken voice. "I don't want to go to sleep. I want to take a walk and get some fresh air."

"Shel, you're in no condition to go for a walk by yourself. Come on, let's get you into bed." But her sister tugs her arm away.

"Where's Noah?"

"You don't have to worry about him," Bree reassures her. "He's still down on the beach with Lindsay. I'll see that he gets to bed eventually. Now come on."

She guides her sister up the stairs and helps her into bed, pulling the covers up to her chin, just as she does for Clara's tuck-ins. On the way out, Bree flips the light switch and clicks the door shut behind her, relieved to have that task completed.

~

Kate can tell that she's had a few too many, exceeded her capacity for gracefully holding her liquor. The initial tingling in her fingers and toes that accompanies her first few drinks has now settled into a leaden feeling. Her body must weigh three hundred pounds.

She recalls tucking Clara into bed and then dancing on the deck to Rihanna's "Diamonds." It had felt so good. No, correction: it had felt *fantastic*. The music flowed through her body, and for the first time in days, she felt free . . . and hopeful, like everything might actually be okay. She was leaving Trey; she was done with playing the understudy to her own life.

And yet now, as she stares at the text on her phone, the certainty and bravado that flooded her earlier drains away. She rests her hand against the kitchen wall to steady herself while she reads.

Hi, Sorry I took off like that. I needed some time to cool off and think. I'm still in Hull. Down at the marina. Thought I'd check on our boat while I'm around. Any chance I can persuade you to meet me here when the party's over?

The text came in at 9:05. It's now a quarter to ten. Kate hasn't thought about the boat all year. It's always been Trey's boy toy, his place to escape or go fishing with his buddies. But she vaguely recalls his making arrangements to get it back in the water in April. Apparently he's now sleeping there, too.

Of course I won't go, she thinks. *How stupid does he think I am?* She's not going to change her mind about them. It's over. If anything, Trey's latest revelation has cemented her conviction.

And yet. And yet, even though she knows she's not thinking clearly, there's a part of her that desperately wants to see him right now. She imagines how good it would feel to be in his arms, remembers how amazing their lovemaking was only a week ago. Would it be so terrible to spend one last night with her husband? On the boat?

She's in no condition to drive, and the marina seems much too far for walking. Getting an Uber is probably impossible tonight, so she decides that if she *can* find a ride, it will be the fates urging her to go. She pulls up the app on her phone, types in the destination, and waits.

Remarkably, a sedan pops up almost immediately. It can be at Shelby's place in five minutes. *It's a sign,* Kate thinks. She grabs her pocketbook and heads for the front door. Her sisters are nowhere to be found, but she'll text them later and ask them to keep an eye on Clara. Just in case she wakes.

Besides, if Kate found her sisters, she's pretty sure they would tell her not to go.

～

Shelby sits up in bed, suddenly panicked. She needs to get to the marina. *To see Bo.* It's a short distance, maybe half a mile, and easily walkable under normal circumstances. If she weren't so hammered, she'd make the trip by foot. But when she tries to call an Uber, there are none available. She decides she'll start walking, anyway, maybe catch a ride on the way there.

She slips a sweatshirt over her clothes and sneaks downstairs. The living room is empty, although the sound of Bree's and Audrey's voices drifts in from the deck. She tiptoes to the front door and shuts it gently behind her.

As she walks along, the jingle of laughter from the other parties on the street flecks the air. Shelby tells herself that she's making a good choice. Because if Maeve Harding can broadcast to the whole world that Shelby's having an affair with Bo Bannister—as she did tonight—then Shelby might as well reap the benefits.

A brief text goes out into the night: On my way. See you soon.

It's silly to hire a ride, she decides, when she can walk herself. The fresh air is helping to sober her up, anyway. Above her, the moon shines brilliantly, a luminous egg in the dark sky. *Waning gibbous,* she thinks. Ethan was always good at identifying the different lunar stages, and some of the names have stuck with her.

She decides to count her steps to keep her focused while she walks. *One, two, three.* She'll have to factor in an extra hundred or so for the steps already taken since leaving the house. *Four, five, six.* How many more before she reaches the marina? Maybe five hundred? A thousand? She has no idea.

While she walks, the crickets, who've struck up a raucous chorus, fail to register in her mind. Their chirping grows louder, but she continues to amble along, counting her steps. *One hundred and fifty-two. One hundred and fifty-four.* It's getting harder to keep track. Where did she leave off? She can't recall. Meanwhile, the crickets' voices rise and crescendo, as if in warning. As if they alone can sense the imminent danger and know what's about to befall their sleepy little town.

But no one in Hull is listening.

33

ROBIN

After the Party
Sunday, May 26

Yellow police tape cordons off a wide, triangular section of the marina parking lot, where officers and first responders are awaiting the delivery of the recovered body. The chief has given Robin the go-ahead to update local reporters camped out on-site. With a sour stomach, she climbs the slight embankment to where the news vans are parked and readies herself to make a statement. The smattering of journalists earlier this morning has grown into a pool of at least a dozen, all hungry for any crumb of information. It's tempting to make a joke about how it must be a slow news day with everyone gathered here, but she knows better.

A woman's life has been lost. In their harbor, off the coast of their idyllic seaside town.

She waits for the flash of cameras to subside and the crowd to quiet before reading the statement that the chief has vetted and given his permission to release.

"Thank you, everyone, for being here this morning." She pauses, waits for the crowd to settle before proceeding. "Unfortunately, I'm in the regrettable position of having to inform you that this morning's rescue mission has officially—and tragically—been deemed a recovery mission." There's an audible gasp among the journalists. "The details, as I'm able to share them with you at the moment, are as follows: At 7:37 this morning, we were informed of a rogue sailboat drifting in the harbor, allegedly unmanned. The Coast Guard was sent to investigate immediately. When they boarded the vessel, however, they discovered a single passenger on board, a forty-seven-year-old Caucasian male who was unresponsive. The individual was breathing, however, and paramedics were able to revive him from what appears to be an alcohol-induced incident. After being revived, the individual informed the Coast Guard that there had been another passenger on board. This led to an immediate search of the vessel and the surrounding area for a possible survivor.

"After approximately three hours and forty minutes of searching, our teams were able to locate a body using side-scan sonar, thanks to the Massachusetts Environmental Police. The body was found approximately a mile from the original location of the aforementioned boat." She pauses again, swallows. "The victim, when discovered, was caught in a fishing net, approximately eighteen feet below surface. As I speak, the victim's body is currently in the hands of the Coast Guard, who will be turning it over to the State Medical Examiner, as procedure dictates.

"We're currently in the process of notifying the family. Obviously, there are still a lot of questions about what happened. At the moment, I can tell you that we're investigating all possible angles and that this remains an active investigation. Hull Police and Fire Departments would like to especially thank the Boston Police Department, Mass. State Troopers, the Mass. State Dive team, and the Mass. Environmental Police, who brought their sonar technology to bear on today's search. Everyone played a critical role in this rescue and recovery mission. Are there any questions?"

"Over here!" shouts a young male in jeans and a blue windbreaker. "Do you have a name of the victim or the guy on the boat?"

"Once the victim's family has been notified, we'll provide you with a name. For the moment, we're not releasing the name of the gentleman."

"Any physical description of the victim?" someone else calls out from the back.

Robin hesitates. She doesn't want to reveal too much. "I can tell you that it's a Caucasian woman, anywhere from midthirties to fifties."

"That's a pretty big range," protests another journalist.

"Yeah, I realize that. But it's all you're going to get right now."

"Is this being considered a potential homicide?"

Robin has been expecting this question. "As I said earlier, it's an active investigation. That's all I can say at the moment."

The TV journalists buzz with more questions, but she shuts them down quickly. "Thanks; that's all for now, folks. We'll update you when we know more."

She turns her back and heads down the embankment, where her fellow officers are waiting.

"So how'd it go, Lieutenant?" they ask.

"About as well as can be expected," she says, "when there's a dead body involved."

～

The last thing Robin feels like doing right now is heading over to the Lancaster residence, especially since she paid the family a visit last night. It's twelve thirty on a Sunday afternoon, and the bright-blue sky above belies the news she's about to deliver.

But despite her reluctance to make this particular house call, she knows it's what she must do. Someone has died. There's a protocol to follow. On the west side of town, the rescue teams and helicopters have gone home, while their suspect has been brought into the station for questioning and his boat has been seized. And the more he's sobered up, the more intriguing his story has become.

She pulls up to the Lancaster driveway, scanning the yard for any signs of an altercation, but aside from a few stray plastic cups scattered across the grass, nothing appears to be amiss. She parks, climbs out of the squad car, and forces herself to approach the front door.

There are aspects of her job that she loves; there are others that make her want to hand in her badge. This particular house call falls into the latter category. She swallows hard before rapping on the door.

34

KATE

The last twenty-four hours feel like a movie that keeps replaying inside her head, but Kate can't seem to identify the plot points. She wakes up on the couch in Shelby's den with no idea how she got there. Trey visited the house yesterday—that much she knows—but the details of their talk remain murky. And then that obnoxious woman had crashed the party and accused Shelby of sleeping with someone. Who was it? *Oh, right. The cute veterinarian!* She'll have to get to the bottom of *that* this morning.

She pilots herself to the downstairs bathroom and locates a bottle of Tylenol in the medicine cabinet. Downs two caplets before going into the living room, where Clara and Bree are already up. Clara is watching TV and munching on cereal while Bree cradles a cup of coffee on the couch.

"God bless you," she tells her sister. "There's no way on this green earth that I could have woken up with Clara this morning." Her head throbs when she speaks. "How is it possible that you're even awake?" Gingerly, she lowers herself onto the couch. The world spins for a brief moment, then rights itself.

"Hi, Mommy," Clara says, not bothering to turn away from the TV.

"Good morning, honey."

Bree jumps up to pour her an extra cup of coffee. "Here. Drink this. It should help."

"Thank you so much." Kate takes it from her gratefully and glances around. "Where's Shelby?"

"Still sleeping, I think. Even though it's past noon. It was a pretty late night for everyone."

"You can say that again. And Audrey?"

"Went home last night."

"Quite the party," Kate says and sips.

"And then some." Neither one, it seems, is quite ready to rehash the events of the evening.

Kate debates whether to use this opportunity alone with her sister to ask about Audrey. It's possible Bree will take it the wrong way. But Kate's head hurts too much to self-censor right now. "So you and Audrey are getting pretty serious, huh?"

Bree's shoulders lift in a noncommittal way while she pretends to watch cartoons. "She's cute."

"No more Hannah, then? That's really over?" Kate always liked Hannah, thought of her as a good balancing influence on her baby sister. She assumed Hannah would eventually tire of the West Coast and come back to Bree.

"Sorry to disappoint you," Bree says, sipping her coffee, "but it wasn't the healthiest relationship."

"What do you mean?"

"She was more like a teacher or a mentor, I guess you'd say."

"Huh. I liked her. I thought Hannah might be, you know, the One."

"Hannah and I weren't really equals; she kind of took charge of the relationship."

"I guess I can see that," Kate demurs. "She was quite a bit older than you, wasn't she?"

"Ten years."

"Yeah, that counts as older, I'd say." She pauses, considers how best to proceed. "Well, Audrey seems nice. And very cute."

"Thanks. She is. I really like her."

Kate reaches out and rests a hand over Bree's. "Hey, I'm happy for you."

Her sister shoots her a smile. "Thanks. I appreciate it. By the way, where did you go last night?"

"Me?" Kate asks, slightly astonished. "I'm not sure." She tries to recall, but it's difficult to account for the hours between the time the party ended and when she woke up this morning.

And then a thought, like a sharp knife, cuts through her mind. *She was going to see Trey.* She even called an Uber! But she never made it to the marina. *Thank God.*

Because on her way out the door, a tiny voice had called out from the top of the stairs: *Mommy, where are you going?*

35

ROBIN

It takes a few minutes, but eventually the younger sister answers the door. She has long, dark hair and a small diamond piercing her nose. *Bree,* Robin reminds herself.

"Good afternoon," Robin begins.

"Oh, hello, Lieutenant." The look of surprise on her face is familiar. No one likes to see a cop standing on the other side of their door in the middle of the day. "Everything okay? Would you like to come in?"

"Yes, please." Robin takes a few steps into the entryway, then follows her into the kitchen. The other sister is sitting on the couch, and there's a young girl planted in front of the TV, who stares back at Robin with enormous blue eyes. Robin removes her hat. "I'm very sorry to bother you again," she begins, "but would it be okay if we sit down?"

She watches the sisters exchange worried glances and then drops into the chair where Bree gestures.

Robin thinks of the question her sister, a schoolteacher, asks her first graders whenever they tattle on someone: "But what happened right before Johnny (or whoever) hit you?" Because more often than not, the tattler did something earlier to incur Johnny's wrath. In a similar manner, Robin is here to inquire about what happened at Shelby's party last night that might have had any bearing on this morning's tragic events. Because their suspect, when asked to account for his whereabouts last night, mentioned Shelby's party.

"I can't imagine there have been any more noise complaints today?" Bree says.

"No, no. Nothing like that."

The blonde, the one who married the Boston millionaire, sits cross-legged on the couch.

"Noah home?" Robin inquires, glancing around.

"Still sleeping. Teenagers, you know?"

Robin nods, as if she can empathize. "That's just as well."

"Um, you've met my sister Kate, right?" Bree asks.

"I think so. Nice to see you again."

From her perch on the couch, Kate offers a small wave.

"Shelby's still asleep, too. At least, I assume so."

Robin raises an eyebrow. Her eyes sweep the living room, taking in its mildly disheveled state. Assorted bowls and cups lie scattered across the dining room table, and an oversize, stuffed trash bag sits in the corner. The air smells stale and, vaguely, like beer.

"Excuse the mess. We haven't done a proper cleanup yet," Bree apologizes, as if reading her mind.

"Oh, no worries." The state of Shelby's house is the least of Robin's concerns right now. There's a point to her visit, and she might as well get on with it.

"So," she begins, "I'll get straight to why I'm here. As you may have heard, a body was discovered in the bay this morning."

Bree gasps; Kate's hand flies to her mouth.

"How awful!" Bree exclaims. "No, we haven't heard anything. We slept in this morning, and the TV hasn't been on except for cartoons." She gestures toward the toddler.

"Do you know who it is?" asks Kate.

Robin hesitates. "Well, it appears that a woman went overboard on a boat out in the bay earlier this morning. It's possible that she fell or was pushed. Alcohol, possibly drugs, were likely involved. We're investigating all angles." She takes a deep breath and begins to say who the victim is when the front door swings open—and Shelby stumbles in, looking like hell.

"Shelby!" Bree cries out. "We thought you were asleep upstairs."

"Ha, I wish." Shelby limps over to the couch and kicks off her flip-flops. "What a night. I'm way too old to be sleeping on a park bench." She drops down, closes her eyes, then opens them again. "Hey, Robin. I thought I was hallucinating there for a minute. Is that really you?"

"I'm afraid so. I was just about to deliver some news to your sisters."

"What news?" She pushes herself up to a sitting position.

"As I was saying," Robin begins, then stops, glancing at the toddler. "Is it okay to talk here?"

Her mother nods. "Don't worry. She's completely absorbed in her show."

"This morning, rescue crews found a woman's body in the bay. It appears she went overboard at some point last night or early this morning. We're still trying to figure out how and why." Robin pauses. "Anyway, it turns out that the body belongs to someone who attended your party last night."

An eerie quiet settles over the room.

"The body, as it turns out, belongs to"—she pauses—"a woman named Maeve Harding."

Shelby inhales sharply and crosses herself. "Oh my God. We just saw her last night."

"Wait a minute," Kate says. "Just to be clear: we're talking about the woman with a cast on her wrist?"

"Right," confirms Bree. "She had *a lot* to drink."

"Any details you could provide would be extremely helpful." Robin scoots forward in her chair, notebook at the ready.

"It's weird, given the circumstances," Shelby begins quietly, as if the weight of Robin's words is beginning to sink in. "But she was a little out of control last night."

"I'll say." Bree nods in agreement.

"And I feel bad for saying it," continues Shelby, "but Maeve showed up uninvited. She had a lot to drink before she arrived, I think. She was being kind of rude, and the next thing we knew, she fell down on the deck."

"She could barely stand," Bree adds. "It was kind of embarrassing. Thankfully, that guy was here to help her home."

"What guy?" Robin asks.

"The one in the cowboy hat. What was his name again, Shelby? Roger something?"

"Jerry."

"Jerry Hammerly?" Robin inquires.

"Yeah, nice guy, Jerry." When Shelby says this, Robin nods because that's how he's known around town, as a nice guy. He's a mechanic at the local auto shop. This detail is also interesting because Jerry has been named a person of interest. Little pieces of the puzzle begin clicking into place. Jerry, Robin knows, is already at the station for questioning.

"And was Jerry equally drunk?" Robin asks.

Shelby shakes her head. "I don't think so. Do you, Bree?"

"No, he was definitely helping her up. He and that other woman in the red capris."

"Who was that?"

Shelby seems to consider this. "Oh, right. I forgot about her. What's her name? Oh, you know her, Robin. She lives in Hull. You guys probably went to high school together. Mindy something? Mandy, maybe?"

"Mandy Corrigan?"

"Yeah, that's it. She was helping Jerry get Maeve up after she fell on the deck. They were the ones who were going to take her home." Robin scribbles Mandy's name in her notebook.

"And did they?" she asks. "Take her home?"

Shelby shrugs. "I assume so? But it wasn't like we followed them. I'm pretty sure that's what Jerry intended to do, though." She stops, as if seized by a horrible thought. "Oh my gosh, you don't think Jerry had anything to do with this, do you?"

"Maybe she was being difficult." Kate jumps into the conversation. "She was hardly a saint when she was here. I can imagine her shrugging off that guy's help."

"What do you mean?" Robin pries. "How was she being difficult? Was there some kind of altercation at the party? Shelby, you said she was acting"—Robin checks her notes—"'kind of rude?'"

The sisters exchange looks. "What?" Robin presses. "We're trying to get to the bottom of this. Anything you tell me could be important."

"Basically," Shelby says softly, "she accused me of having an affair."

Robin straightens in her chair. "Really? With whom?" When Shelby hesitates, Robin adds, "You might as well tell me. I'm going to find out eventually, anyway."

"Bo Bannister."

Robin can feel her face register surprise. "And are you?" Part of her feels as if it's none of her business, but another part knows it's her job to ask. Stranger events have led to solving cases.

"I was. But I'm not anymore." The blonde, who appears as non-plussed as Robin by this comment, sucks in air.

"As of when?"

"Yesterday?"

Robin frowns, makes a mental note to talk with her friend more about it when they get together for a glass of wine later in the week.

"Is there any chance that Maeve was also dating Bo Bannister?"

Shelby's eyes widen, as if the thought hadn't occurred to her. "I don't think so. But I guess you never know."

"Was Bo at the party yesterday?"

"He was," Shelby admits. "But only for about an hour. And that was long before Maeve showed up."

"And where did he go from your house?"

"Back home, I assume," says Shelby.

"And what about Jerry and Maeve? Any relationship there?"

"Maybe?" Shelby guesses. "They arrived together."

Robin makes a note of this. "And did you sense any bad blood between the two of them? Was Jerry upset with Maeve for some reason last night?"

"Aside from being rip-roaring drunk, you mean?" Shelby asks. "I don't think so."

"Did Jerry make any mention of taking Maeve back to his boat? Or anyone else's boat, for that matter?"

"Not that I recall."

"Can anyone account for your three's whereabouts last night and this morning?"

The sisters glance at one another, seemingly taken aback by the question. "We can give you a list of the people at the party, if that helps," Shelby offers. "It pretty much broke up after Maeve and Jerry left. Kate and Bree were here all last night. Unfortunately, I passed out on a park bench. Didn't wake up until about half an hour ago."

"And why were you sleeping on a park bench, again?" Robin inquires.

"Yeah, I'd like to know the answer to that one, too," Bree says. "Last time I checked, you were in bed."

"Well." Shelby sighs. "At the time, I remember thinking that it was an excellent idea to head to the marina. Bo had texted me earlier that he was on his boat and wanted to talk."

"And did you? See Bo?"

Shelby shakes her head. "No, I never made it to the marina. I started walking, but then I spotted a bench about halfway there. I thought I'd rest for a few minutes." She laughs. "Guess it was more like several hours."

"Did anyone else see you last night?" Robin asks.

"I don't think so? Although a couple of kids woke me up. I couldn't tell you their names, though."

Robin flips her notebook shut. She has one last question. "Can any of you think of a reason why someone would want Maeve Harding dead?"

There's a beat of silence before Shelby answers. She's the local; if anyone had any hunches, it would be her. "Sorry, Robin. I have no idea. Couldn't it all have been a terrible accident?"

"That's what we're trying to figure out," Robin says. "And, frankly, that's what we're hoping." Because the alternative is too awful to contemplate.

36

SHELBY

After Robin leaves, Shelby wanders back into the living room. Her hands are trembling. "Well, that was unexpected."

"Ugh. The whole situation gives me the creeps." Bree wraps her arms around herself as if a sudden chill has crept into the room. "I mean, Maeve seemed a little crazy, but she didn't deserve to die."

"Definitely not," says Kate. "What do you think happened?"

Shelby slowly shakes her head. "I have no idea. Maybe she and Jerry never made it back to her house; maybe they stopped off for a nightcap on his boat?"

"But then how did they end up in the bay? Didn't the officer say that the boat was drifting out on the harbor?"

Shelby tries to think. "I can't remember. I think so? Either way, it's all very strange."

"I bet she was so drunk that she fell off, and then poor Jerry didn't know what to do. He probably panicked and now he's trying to cover his tracks, all for being a good Samaritan," Bree hypothesizes. "You know that saying, 'No good deed goes unpunished?' Well, this sounds like a classic case of that."

"But why would they go sailing in the middle of the night?" presses Shelby. "It makes no sense."

"Maybe they didn't. Maybe they slept on the boat and then went out early this morning. You know, to watch the sunrise or something."

"But then Maeve wouldn't have been drunk this morning, so that kind of ruins your whole theory about her falling off the boat."

"How do you know?" Bree insists. "They could have been downing mimosas this morning. Or they could have been up all night, drinking. Or maybe she slipped accidentally. Maybe a wave rocked the boat right when she was standing on the bow, and she lost her balance with that cast of hers. Or maybe that guy Jerry pushed her. How well do you know him?"

"Not that well, I guess," reflects Shelby. "But he's always willing to help whenever I bring my car in for an oil change. He doesn't strike me as the violent type, especially when he was the one person who tried to help Maeve when she was here."

"I agree," says Kate, as if they might actually be on their way to solving the case right here in Shelby's living room.

"I'm sure he has a perfectly plausible explanation that he's giving the cops right now." Shelby scoots her feet up under her legs. "I doubt there's any reason to think he's a suspect."

"Hey, maybe it wasn't even Jerry's boat," Bree interjects.

"Good point." But Shelby can't shake the feeling that they should do something. They were some of the last people to see Maeve before she died. Shouldn't they help? A knot of dread is slowly forming in her stomach. How many times had she wished Maeve dead? Well, maybe not dead exactly, but out of her life? Maeve had been spreading rumors about Shelby's relationship with Bo, and only days ago, Shelby had dreamed of confronting her. Maybe even retaliating by spreading a nasty rumor about Maeve.

She'd wished evil on the woman, and now she was gone. Possibly murdered.

"I have this awful feeling," she says quietly. "Like maybe somehow this is all our fault."

"What?" Kate demands. "What are you talking about? How can this be our fault? We weren't even there."

"I know, but we saw her. She was here, and she was really wasted. And we didn't offer to help—"

"Help? Why should we have helped her when she was yelling at you?" asks Bree.

Shelby bites her bottom lip. "Because she was trashed and we let her go. With Jerry. We didn't look after her ourselves."

Bree shakes her head. "Well, that's just crazy thinking, if you ask me."

At that moment, Noah wanders downstairs, still in his pajamas. His dark hair is mussed. He rubs his eyes, looks around. "What? Why does everyone look so weird?"

"Oh, never mind," says Bree.

"We might as well tell him," Shelby mumbles. "He's going to find out, anyway."

"Tell me what?"

She takes a deep breath. "Do you know who Maeve Harding is?"

"Maeve? Yeah, she lives a few blocks over. She was at the party last night, right? I think I saw her dancing when I ran up to grab a soda from the cooler." Thankfully, Noah and his friends had been down on the beach when Maeve began hurling accusations at Shelby.

"Yes, right. Well, her body turned up in the bay today."

Noah's eyes grow huge. "Whoa. Her body? Like her *dead* body?"

Shelby nods.

"Oh, man. That sucks. What happened?"

"No one really knows. They think maybe she fell off a boat."

Noah helps himself to coffee and drops onto the kitchen stool nearest Bree. "I'm not surprised, actually." He blows on the contents of his mug. "My buddies and I ran into her at the grocery store when we went out to get more ice around dinnertime. That woman was high as a kite."

37

KATE AND SHELBY

Kate's head is spinning. The facts relayed to her in the last half hour, as far as she can make sense of them, go like this:

- Shelby is having an affair with the sexy veterinarian. Or, at least, *was* having an affair with him.
- Maeve Harding, the same woman who came to their party last night and accused Shelby of having an affair, is dead.
- The cause of death is suspicious. Maybe she fell off a boat or was pushed sometime late last night or early this morning. Alcohol or drugs may have been involved.
- The boat may or may not have belonged to Jerry Hammerly.
- Kate is a terrible mother since she almost left her daughter behind at the house to go have sex with her shady husband.
- Trey was involved in something illegal at his firm. So was Stuart.

What she can't be sure of is, will Shelby somehow be implicated in Maeve's death? Because there were plenty of witnesses to their argument at the party. Does that give Shelby an alleged motive for murder? Kate knows what an insular town Hull can be, how loyalties can shift like quicksand when someone's loved one is being threatened. Shelby wouldn't harm a bug, but her alibi for last night seems shaky at best, even to Kate. *She snuck out of the house and slept on a park bench? Huh?* If Kate were the lieutenant, she'd be suspicious, too.

The three sisters huddle on the porch while Clara plays inside. "I'm sorry about Maeve—" Kate begins, but Shelby cuts her off.

"Yeah, I still can't quite believe it. She wasn't really my friend, though. More of an acquaintance. An annoying acquaintance at that." She wrings her hands together. "Sorry, I probably shouldn't speak ill of the dead."

"I wonder what happened. It all seems so surreal," says Bree.

"It's gotta be an accident, right?" Kate insists. "A slip and fall?"

Shelby sighs. "Probably, but who knows?"

"Does she have any family?"

"I think so?" Shelby weaves her hair into a braid. "I think her parents are still alive, but they retired somewhere else, someplace out west. No husband or kids, though."

"Or wife," Bree reminds them. "You know, there are queer people in this world, too."

"Sorry, you're right, of course."

Kate turns back to Shelby. "Okay, can we have a sidebar for one sec, because I need to get something straight."

"What?"

"Well, it was that little nugget of information that you passed along to the lieutenant. As in, you *were* dating the cute veterinarian. Are you still?"

"Yes, I was dating him. But, no, I'm not anymore. I broke it off with him about a week ago."

"But why?" Kate demands. "What am I missing here? He's gorgeous, he seems nice, he has a good job. What more do you need?"

Shelby shoots Bree a pained look.

"Oh, wait," Kate whispers. "Is he terrible in bed?"

Shelby laughs. "No, that was never a problem, I'm afraid. There were a few other issues, though."

"Such as?" Kate's dumbfounded. She truly doesn't understand.

"I'd tell you to sit down," Shelby begins, "but you already are."

~

Does Shelby dare answer her sister truthfully?

Earlier this morning, all she could think about was how much she wanted to crawl into her own bed—and for everyone to go home. How she craved having her house back to herself!

Someone at her office once quoted William Blake, saying, *You never know what is enough unless you know what is more than enough.* Well, Shelby's had more than enough. Her giving tree is fully picked, her well of goodwill utterly depleted. It's true that typically the family stays for the entire week following Memorial Day, but surely by now her sisters have figured out that her life is as big a mess as theirs, perhaps even more so.

The Memorial Day ship, so to speak, has sailed; it's time for everyone to go home.

But now Kate is demanding to know the real story, the truth.

And Kate is the one person Shelby *can't* tell. The one person who should be spared any further hardship, at least for a few weeks, a few months. When Kate asks, "Did I miss something?" it's all Shelby can do not to laugh manically.

Um, a little bit, she thinks.

Whether or not to fill in the blanks for her sister feels like one of those defining moments in life. Like when Tuukka bit off part of a bone he wasn't supposed to swallow and Shelby had mere seconds to decide whether she should reach into his germy mouth to grab it before he choked—or let it go. It's the kind of split-second decision armed with potentially dire consequences . . . or no consequences whatsoever. It could cut either way. She breathes in deeply.

"All right, I have something to tell you," she begins. "So about eight months ago—"

"Eight months! You've been seeing this guy for eight months, and you're only telling us *now*? I would've been parading him around town, if I were you," says Kate.

"It's complicated." Shelby can feel herself biting her lower lip. "It's complicated," she repeats. "Because he was married."

She watches Kate's jaw fall. "Oh, man. No, he wasn't."

"Yeah, and it's unfortunate." Her voice cracks. "Because I'm pretty sure I'm in love with him."

"*Okaaay,*" Kate says slowly, turning the idea over in her head. "But he's not married anymore, right?" She watches her sister trying to make sense of it all.

Shelby nods. "I'm afraid so."

A hushed silence falls over them. Bree clears her throat, says nothing.

"But he's in the middle of a divorce?" Kate presses on hopefully.

Shelby shakes her head.

"And when, exactly, did you find out he was married? Was that before or after you started seeing him?"

"Oh, Katie, how I wish I could tell you it was after. But I knew. I always knew—and I know it was wrong, but he told me he wasn't happily married. That he stayed in his marriage for his girls. That if he could leave, he would. I know that doesn't excuse it, but I thought it made it somehow less bad." They're pathetic excuses, even to her own ears.

"Wait, he has *kids?*" Disbelief marches across Kate's face.

"Older, much older than Clara. Like Noah's age. Fifteen or sixteen, I think."

"So, basically, you had an *affair* with a married man." Incredulity paints her voice.

Shelby nods, almost imperceptibly, before Kate jumps up. "What the hell, Shelby? How could you sit here all week, consoling me about Trey, when you were doing the exact same thing to another woman?"

"I don't know. I wanted to help you?"

"Help me?" Kate threads her hands through her hair. "Help me by destroying another woman's life? Another *family*? How does that help anyone? Please. Enlighten me." She spins around to confront Bree. "And *you*—you knew about this the whole time?"

"Not exactly," says Bree. "But I noticed his wedding band yesterday at the party, and then I caught him kissing Shelby before he left."

"You did?" both Shelby and Kate ask simultaneously.

Bree nods.

"Well, this is just terrific, isn't it?" Kate spits out the words. "Here I thought I'd come to a safe place, to be with my sisters, people I *trust*. Only to find out that you've both been keeping secrets from me. First Trey, and now you guys. There's no one left for me!"

"That's not true, Kate, and you know it," quips Shelby.

"Do I?" Kate demands. "Talk about the pot calling the kettle black. It used to be Mom's favorite expression, remember? It's funny; I never really understood it as a kid. But now I do. And I get why you were so eager for Trey and me to stay together all this time. You have a vested interest in our marriage working out. You don't want to believe that anything *you* might have done would cause someone else's marriage to unravel, do you? Well, guess what? You're wrong, Shelby. Actions have consequences. I hope you haven't destroyed another family."

Kate charges through the sliding doors and snatches up Clara from the floor, where she's coloring. "Come on, kiddo. We're going back to our house."

"But, Mommy, I want to stay *heeeere*."

"Thanks for a super party, Shelby," Kate calls out, grabbing her purse, Clara hoisted on her hip. "You really know how to throw 'em!"

When the front door slams, Shelby shoots Bree a withering look before heading inside, where she collapses on the couch and bursts into tears.

38

Kate, Bree, and Shelby

Kate can't recall ever feeling so betrayed except for, well, when she found out about Trey. And now her own sister! She tries to talk herself down, persuade herself that Shelby's falling in love with a married man has nothing to do with her own predicament. She should be glad that her sister found someone. It's not Shelby's fault that he was already married, is it?

But, yes. Yes, it is. Because *she knew*! The first time Shelby kissed the handsome veterinarian, her sister was fully aware that she was kissing another woman's husband. Kate's entire world, where right and wrong are easily discernible, has flipped upside down. The very things she once considered infallible—her parents, her marriage, her bond with her sisters—have been shaken to their core.

As soon as they get back to the Allerton house, she places Clara in her crib with a sippy cup of milk and a pile of Dr. Seuss books (they've yet to switch out the crib for a toddler bed).

"Mommy will be right back," she reassures her. "You stay here while I check on something." At least in her bedroom, Clara will be safe. Kate tromps downstairs and wanders out into the front yard, at a loss for what to do.

A few days ago, their gardener, Charles, who'd apparently been laid up with a broken foot all spring, had come out to perform emergency surgery on the yard. Now the pruned roses hang neatly from their trellises, and the meadow that was formerly her lawn has been trimmed to near golf-course perfection. Another week and the yellowed grass should be a lush blanket of green.

She wanders over to the garden bench and sits down. The scent of lilacs, her mother's favorite, is practically overwhelming. Kate tries to imagine what her mom would advise if she were here, sitting beside her. Undoubtedly, she'd be displeased that her daughters were fighting again. But she'd probably also tell Kate to quit being so judgmental. *It's not Shelby whom you're upset with, honey.*

And she'd be right.

Shelby is not the reason that Kate's marriage is unraveling.

Kate thinks back to that giddy time in her life when she and Trey first started dating. He checked all the husband boxes and more: he was dashing, smart, successful, and appeared to adore her. And perhaps he did adore her when they first fell in love. But somewhere in the past few years, the dynamics of their marriage have shifted. And adoration, Kate realizes, doesn't necessarily equate with love—or loyalty.

It's taken her forty years to grasp this simple, yet slippery, concept. For someone so gifted in school, it turns out she can be exceptionally stupid in life. She assumed that if she studied hard, worked hard, and acted from the heart, good things would come her way. But as facile as the realization may be, there are no givens, no guarantees in life.

Aside, perhaps, from the family you're given.

Ending her marriage might be the hardest thing she's ever done, but her mom's voice echoes in her head, as if encouraging her from above: *The hardest decisions in life are also the most worthy. That's why they're so difficult.*

Kate can do this.

She deserves a clean slate. She and Clara both do.

~

Bree regrets sending Audrey home last night after they picked up the worst of the trash from the party. At the time, it seemed like a good idea: both Shelby and Kate would surely be in rough shape this morning, and Audrey could wake up in her own bed while Bree was left to deal with any family theatrics. She didn't anticipate a cop showing up on their doorstep, however. Didn't foresee that one of their party guests would end up dead in the bay.

And now, despite her attempts to keep it a secret, it seems that creditors have discovered Bree's cell phone number, which can only mean that their patience is wearing thin, perhaps to the point of extinction. They've tracked her down—Mastercard, AmEx, two different collection agencies. Perhaps the most alarming message, though, is from her friend Sara at the studio.

> Hey, Bree. Hope you're doing okay. Haven't seen you around in a while. I'm texting cuz Robbie stopped by the studio yesterday and was threatening to turn off the electricity. Says we're behind on the rent by three months? Not sure what that's about. I know I'm all paid up but maybe some of the others owe you? Anyway, thought you should know. He seemed pretty pissed.

Bree has been expecting a text like this, but she hoped that by the end of the month, her money problems would be resolved. By way of a sweet cash infusion from one, or both, of her sisters. Even before she left for Hull, her art studio landlord was threatening eviction. His last message indicated that if he didn't receive payment in full by the first week in June, he'd be forced to terminate her lease. And now June is staring her straight in the face with an enormous, mocking grin.

Since Sara (and likely everyone else at the studio) knows they're in arrears, it's only a matter time before someone figures out that Bree has been siphoning the checks from her art studio friends into her own apartment fees. Of the two spaces, she can't afford to lose the one she calls home.

When she goes online to double-check her bank account, it's as she assumed: there's a negative balance where there needs to be thousands. And while Bree prides herself on knowing the exact moment to strike when it comes to asking her sisters for funds, not one of those moments has presented itself in the past week.

She's sunk, ruined. Doomed.

What little reputation she's built up as an artist will be overshadowed by the (true) rumor that she's not successful enough to pay her own bills.

Her only life buoy now is her sisters.

But Shelby is in her bedroom crying, and Kate has stolen away with Clara. Noah, Bree assumes, has gone off to meet up with Lindsay. If her parents were here, they'd be the first to tell their daughters to knock it off and stop feeling sorry for themselves. Her mother, in particular, wouldn't tolerate such bickering. Somewhere under THE RULES OF SUMMER is a mantra that Bree hasn't thought of in years: *No argument should last longer than ten minutes.* Originally meant for toddlers or teenage girls, but why not adult sisters, too?

She flops onto her bed and grabs her phone. Even though her mom isn't around to set the world right, Bree's willing to try. She reminds herself of her promise to look after her sisters for the duration of the weekend. Maybe there's a way to do that while also saving herself.

Her fingers tap out a hasty message to Kate: Hey. Can you come back? Please??? Shelby feels terrible. I feel terrible. We miss you already.

~

When Shelby wakes, there are voices coming from downstairs. She desperately hopes it's Kate and Clara who've returned. Maybe she can do a better job of explaining her relationship with Bo so that Kate won't hate her so much. As in, she's just another girl who's been deceived by a guy. Age-old story.

When she slinks downstairs, both of her sisters are reclining on the sofa in the living room. Clara is playing with Barbies in the den. Shelby steels herself for a barrage of criticism, but oddly enough, since Kate stomped out of the house maybe an hour ago, the conversation seems to have taken a turn. No one is talking about Shelby's affair, and Bree barely acknowledges her when she sinks into the easy chair across from them.

"But that's just it, Bree," Kate is saying. "You're responsible for *no one*. You don't have any kids or even a dog. Shelby and I have kids we have to look out for."

The idea that Kate is grouping herself with Shelby in any way right now is remarkable.

"Well," says Bree. "I'm responsible for myself, aren't I? I'm responsible for my art. When I'm watching Clara, aren't I responsible for her?"

"You know what I mean," Kate insists. "When are you going to settle down? Start a family?"

Bree's bewildered gaze travels to Shelby, then back to Kate. "I'm sorry, but did you really just say that? Because it doesn't seem like 'settling down,' i.e., getting married, has worked out so well for either you or Shelby."

There's a pause, and it occurs to Shelby that this may be the moment when Kate lurches across the couch to punch her sister. Instead, Bree continues, "Does the fact that I'm gay have anything to do with why I'm such a disappointment to you?"

Kate rolls her eyes. "Don't be ridiculous!"

"No, really," Bree soldiers on. "Just because I don't have all the things that *you* consider signs of success—a fancy job, a spouse, a child, a house—doesn't mean I concur with your definition of *success*."

Kate casts a sideways glance at Shelby before proceeding. "Did it ever occur to *you*," she says, "that maybe you're depressed?"

Bree's jaw drops. "Whoa. Another hit to left field. Where did that come from?"

"No, seriously. I mean, you're thirty-six years old with a college degree, and you still don't have a decent-paying job. How much longer are you going to play the artist card? Maybe you should talk to someone."

Shelby watches Bree's expression darken. This is *not* the direction she was expecting the conversation to take.

"I'm enjoying my life just fine," Bree says sharply. "But thank you so much for the judgment."

"Are you, though?" Kate's eyes narrow. "Are you really enjoying it?"

"Wow." Bree shakes her head, as if she can't quite believe this particular line of questioning. "Did it ever occur to you that not everyone needs two houses to be happy?"

"Oh, here we go again. Go ahead, play the Kate-only-cares-about-her-country-club card."

"And don't you?" Bree demands.

"No! But money has its benefits, you know. Do I need to remind you who cosigned the lease on your art studio?"

Bree picks at her cuticles. "Yeah, about that, I've been meaning to ask—"

"Oh no." Kate cuts her off, holding up a hand. "Don't even *think* of going there."

"Okay, I won't." Bree turns to Shelby. "Shelby, can I borrow a few thousand dollars from you to cover the rent on my art studio? I'm overdue for the past three months. I promise I'll pay you back."

There's a small gasp from Kate's corner. Shelby debates how best to respond. "Um, well, we can certainly talk about it." She pulls her legs up under her, crisscross-applesauce style. "How about later?"

"Sure, whatever." Bree dips her head, sending a curtain of hair across her face.

"You know," Kate remarks, "I came back over here to make peace, not to get attacked."

"Oh, I'm sorry. I thought *I* was the one being attacked." Bree lifts her head, meeting Kate's gaze. "You know what? I actually feel sorry for you. And not because Trey cheated on you. But because I don't even know who you *are* anymore. Since when do you care about being rich, about fitting in with the country club crowd?"

"Don't pull that holier-than-thou crap on me!" Kate shoots up from the couch as if she's about to march off but then reconsiders. "I'm curious, Bree: Have you ever been shy about asking me for money? And have I ever said no?" Kate waits a beat. "That's right. I've never said no because I've spent my entire life taking care of my baby sister. Don't you think it's time you took care of yourself for once?"

Tears well in Bree's eyes. Kate has struck an already-frayed nerve. "I'm so sorry," Bree says, "if my asking you to dip into your millions for a loan has inconvenienced you in any way. And let the record show, by the way, that I, for one, have *always* held a job."

"That's not what she's saying," Shelby tries, but it's too late. Bree leaps up from the couch and rushes out to the deck, her long, dark hair trailing behind her as she runs down to the beach.

"Jeez, Kate," Shelby says after a moment.

"So this is all my fault now?"

"No, but you know how sensitive Bree can be."

"Yeah, and I'm sick of it. Sick of always protecting her. I don't know why I thought coming back here was a good idea."

But Shelby doesn't wait to hear any more. Instead, she heads outside to chase after her baby sister.

~

A large bird's nest, probably knocked over by the wind, lies on the grass next to the deck. It's mostly still intact. Shelby will need to clean it up eventually . . . Or can she return it to its branch? She seems to recall some arcane fact about how humans should never touch a nest because a bird won't return if it carries a human scent. *Bo would know the answer,* she thinks. But on the heels of that thought comes, *I can't ask Bo anything anymore.*

Right now, she's too tired to move because she had to track Bree a mile down the beach before walking back with her. That's two more miles than she's accustomed to. On the positive side, though, she's managed to corral both her sisters back to the deck. And even if they haven't reached a truce, exactly, it seems that maybe they've arrived at some kind of détente.

Moments ago, she'd lost her cool with them both. "Stop it! Just stop, both of you. Okay? We're driving each other crazy, and my head hurts too much to be yelling." She dropped into a lounge chair and motioned for her sisters to do the same. "Sit."

"Look, it's been a tough week. Well, that's an understatement. It's been a shit show of a week. But none of us here is innocent. We all have our flaws, okay? I won't name them. But we also all have our strengths. I think maybe that's what we need to start focusing on."

"Such as?" Kate asked with a sly laugh. "What strengths?"

"Well, you, for one, are an amazing mom. And Bree's a gifted artist," Shelby supplied easily.

"That's so nice," Bree said, sounding genuinely touched. "And what about you?"

"Me? Perseverance. I keep on, no matter what. Weathering a divorce and then having to raise your son by yourself is no picnic, let me tell you."

"You win, Shel," Kate said snidely. "You always win."

"I'm not trying to *win* anything. I'm only pointing out the obvious. Besides, I'm the one who's always been jealous of you two."

"Jealous? Of *me?*" Bree cried. "But you have this great house and an amazing job. And Noah!"

"It's not a competition," Kate snapped. "Remember?"

"Maybe it doesn't feel that way when you're the one who's always winning." Out of the corner of her eye, Shelby thought she caught Bree nodding.

"And what's that supposed to mean?" Kate fired back.

"Oh, come on, Kate. Get real. You've had it easy. Look around." She gestured wildly. "Do you see anyone else supporting me and Noah? Other than yours truly? No."

"No one's contesting that you work hard."

"Maybe not, but from where I stand, you've always lived a charmed life. You've never had to worry about money. Not since you met Trey."

"I don't get it. Am I supposed to apologize for the fact that I've led a happy life up to this point? Is that what you want?" Kate's mouth hardened into an invisible line. "An apology? Is that what you both want from me?"

"Of course not. Don't be ridiculous." Shelby was striving mightily for equanimity. "But all week I've had to listen to you two complain about how difficult your lives are, when honestly, I don't think either of you has a clue how tough it's been for Noah and me. Not once did I ask you guys for money when I was going through the divorce. Noah and I managed. It wasn't always easy, but we did it."

"But *you* divorced Ethan," Kate countered. "It was your choice."

"Because he wasn't contributing to this family, financially or emotionally!"

"So now what? You're angry that we're here? Is that what's bothering you? You feel like we've taken advantage of your hospitality and your sisterly—what? Goodwill?" Kate challenged.

Shelby shook her head. That's not what she meant . . . or was it? Had Kate hit on it precisely, the irritation she felt at having to take care of everyone while no one was around to return the favor? Except for Bo?

But no one's coming. Not to help, at least. Not Bo, not Trey, not Hannah. It's just the three of them now.

No wonder they've been floundering.

"I'm sorry," Shelby says now. "Sorry for not telling you about Bo sooner. Sorry for letting myself get involved with him in the first place. It was a mistake." She pauses. "And I'm sorry for not being a better big sister. Sometimes I feel like I give and give but no one ever gives back, you know?"

Kate sighs. "I guess I've been too wrapped up in my own stuff to see that you were struggling. I'm sorry, too."

"Me three," Bree concurs, invoking the corny phrase they used to say as kids whenever the three of them agreed. "I'm sorry I haven't been there for you, Shel. I love you, you know. You too, Katie."

"Listen. I'm sorry about those awful things I said earlier. I didn't mean them. I guess I'm maybe a little jealous of your freedom, Bree."

"What's that poem about the center not holding?" Shelby muses aloud.

"Things fall apart; the center cannot hold," recites Kate. "It's Yeats, I think. 'The Second Coming.'"

"Figures you'd know," teases Bree.

"What?" Kate protests. "I studied in college. You can't fault me for that."

"Sure I can."

"Well, whoever wrote it," Shelby says, "it seems fitting." A breeze kicks up from the ocean, sending whitecaps skating across the water, and she tugs the wool blanket more tightly around herself.

"The question remains, though," Bree says in her mock philosopher's voice. "How do we get the center back?"

39

ROBIN

When Robin returns to the station, the air inside is humming with adrenaline. Boston police, state troopers, and her own team huddle in the main office area. She's hoping to finally get some answers, an explanation as to why the top brass has been involved from the get-go. What is it that they're not telling her? As far as Robin is concerned, she's been more than accommodating. Her entire station has been made available to them, yet they're offering her very little information. Once again, she feels as if she's standing outside an elite fraternity, peering in through the window on her tiptoes.

When she approaches the front desk to ask after Jerry Hammerly's whereabouts, a Boston lieutenant steps forward to inform her that Hammerly has been released until needed for further questioning. A pulse of anger courses through her. This remains an ongoing investigation in *her* precinct, and yet no one thought to consult her before letting a key witness go?

"That's a shame. Because I had some important questions for him. Next time check with me before you send a witness home, okay?" she barks.

It's not as if she's his superior, but she doesn't give a damn. If she gets written up, so what? It's her town, her precinct, her station. Her victim. She's probably one of the few people here who actually knows Jerry, has already earned his trust. And now they've set him free to do as he pleases? It's outrageous, especially since he was probably one of the last people to see Maeve.

The lieutenant shoots her a miffed look, then points to a metal gray door at the end of the hall. The interview room. "Looks like they've got bigger fish to fry now, anyhow."

"Okay if I go in?"

He shrugs. "Be my guest."

Robin uses her passkey to gain admittance to the observation room, which looks onto the interview room through one-way glass. She can see in, but the people on the other side can't see her. A few other cops have assembled here as well; they acknowledge her presence with a nod. On the other side of the glass, sitting at a rectangular table, are Chief Landry, a state trooper, and a DEA officer.

Across from the three of them is the owner of the runaway boat: Bo Bannister.

When the harbormaster called Robin earlier this morning to report who was on board, she was surprised to learn it wasn't an out-of-towner at all, but Hull's very own veterinarian.

Though she didn't divulge this information to the Lancaster sisters, Maeve Harding wasn't with Jerry Hammerly when she went missing. Allegedly, she was on Bo Bannister's sailboat.

It was Bo—not Jerry—who was going crazy with worry when he woke up and discovered Maeve gone. He was the one who described venturing out early in the morning, using only the motor, to catch the sunrise, but said that they'd both fallen asleep. Or more likely, passed out.

Which makes Robin think that maybe Bo *was* sleeping with Maeve Harding. And maybe Maeve discovered he was sleeping with Shelby at the same time? Which might have led to some kind of altercation on the boat. But the even bigger question for Robin at the moment is: What's the DEA doing here?

There's some muddled conversation on the chief's side of the table before he suddenly pushes back his chair and stands to leave. Bannister has yet to say a word since she's set foot in the observation room, but rather than stay to see what unfolds, she's already waiting on the other side of the conference room door when the chief steps out.

"Lieutenant," he says, letting the heavy metal door close behind him. "I've been wondering when I'd run into you. How's it going?"

"Hi, Chief. I should probably be asking you the same question. What brings you down here?" His presence makes her worry that he's had second thoughts, doesn't believe her team can handle an investigation of this caliber.

"Good question. I'm supposed to be at a parade with my granddaughter this afternoon, but"—he looks around as if he's surprised to find himself in Hull, let alone at the station—"here we are. Anyway, got a few minutes? I want to bring you up to speed."

"Always, for you." She leads him down the beige hallway to her office, the soles of their shoes making squeaking noises against the linoleum floor, and shuts the door behind them.

She settles into the chair behind her desk and waits for the chief to do the same. It's a bit awkward: Robin at her desk and the chief across from her when, really, it should be the other way around. When she realizes her mistake, she offers to switch sides, but he waves her off.

"So," Robin says. "What have you got? Because obviously there's something much bigger going on here than a slip and fall on a sailboat that ended tragically."

He pushes his glasses up on his closely shaved head and rubs his eyes. "How long have we known each other?" His glasses drop back down on his nose, his intense blue eyes staring at her.

Robin takes a moment to consider. "Probably ever since I moved up to detective, what? Seven years ago?"

"Yeah, it's been a while, that's for sure. Listen," he says. "Before we go any further, I want to say how sorry I am about Maeve Harding. I hoped we'd find her before it was too late."

"Yeah, me too. Thanks. She was certainly a fixture around here. Born and raised in Hull. Worked at the town clerk's office."

"That's what I've gathered. And how long has Bo Bannister been in town?"

"Since I can remember," she says. "Maybe twenty years? He's built himself quite a business as a veterinarian." She debates whether she should mention the rumors circulating about his various marital indiscretions but then thinks better of it. Best to let the chief fill her in first.

"That he has." He harrumphs in his chair. "As it turns out, he's not only running a successful veterinarian clinic, he's also been operating a nice little side gig."

This information makes Robin shift uncomfortably in her seat. She has no knowledge of a possible side gig, and her neck suddenly grows warm. *Is that why the DEA is here?* Half of her really doesn't care to know; the other half is eager to learn what's escaped her attention.

"Turns out he's been repurposing some of his animal drugs for a dealer in Boston."

Robin falls back in her seat.

"I only know this," the chief continues, "because we've been keeping an eye on a Boston dealer for months now, and we recently got intel that Bannister was one of his suppliers. Guess they go way back together, old college buddies. Supposedly, they were going to connect on a deal over Memorial Day weekend. But it didn't go quite as planned."

"A deal for animal drugs? I'm not sure I follow."

"Well, technically they're animal drugs, I guess," the chief says. "But the Boston dealer has been selling them to his very human clients."

"Oh, I see."

The chief shrugs. "I'm not very well versed in this stuff myself, which is why the DEA is running the show now. My understanding is that vets prescribe a lot of the same drugs we humans use—painkillers, sleeping pills, steroids. You name it, there seems to be a counterpoint in the animal world."

"So wait. You're telling me that you've known the whole time that we've been dealing with a drug trafficker while also searching for a dead body?" Robin, frankly, is stunned.

The chief lets go of a heavy sigh. "I'm afraid so. I'm sorry I couldn't fill you in on the details sooner."

"Yeah, and exactly why is that, again? Because it would have been nice to get a heads-up about what was happening in my own precinct." She doesn't care if she sounds irritated; that's exactly what she is.

He lifts a hand. "Now before you get upset with me, Lieutenant, let me tell you: I was instructed by the DEA to keep this close to my chest until we had Bannister in custody. There'd been some online discussion from our Boston guy about a deal going down on the water this weekend—tonight, in particular—and they didn't want anyone getting wind of it. They were afraid if the local forces knew, someone might tip off Bannister."

"Wait a sec." She stops him. "Might tip off Bannister? As in, there might be someone inside the department helping him out?"

The chief shrugs. "We couldn't be certain, but it was definitely a risk. The DEA wanted as few people as possible involved at the start, till we knew what we were dealing with. Whom we were dealing with."

It's not an apology exactly, but it does explain why everything is happening so fast—and why Robin feels like the last to find out.

"But how did you guys know about the loose sailboat this morning? Before we did?"

"Like I said, someone made a distress call to the Coast Guard on channel 16. But, truthfully? We've been listening for any radio chatter around Hull Bay. My guys have been in the area all weekend, both on water and land, ready to respond as needed. You may have spotted a few of my undercover detectives out on lobster boats earlier this morning. We had them positioned near the Gut, so they could keep an eye on any boats leaving or coming into the bay. Frankly, when we heard about the runaway boat, we thought maybe Bannister's luck had run out, that another dealer—maybe a Hull officer, even—had gotten to him first.

Heisted the drugs, dispensed with Bannister. We were worried our cover might have been blown."

"And you didn't think it was a good idea to tell me that there were drugs involved?"

The chief sighs, and Robin notices for the first time how tired he looks. "I take orders from someone, too, Lieutenant. Besides, I knew that our guys were about to board and secure the area."

She nods, trying to make sense of it all. "So what did you find? I assume you had a search warrant for Bannister's sailboat?"

The chief leans back and knits his fingers behind his head. "You bet we did. And once we got the boat back to shore, we discovered plenty of illegal goodies hiding in his safe. Tramadol, ketamine, some other stuff."

"Wow. And you're sure that Jerry Hammerly isn't involved in this somehow?"

"According to Jerry, he was doing his best to take Maeve home. She should have listened to him." The chief pauses for a moment, as if out of respect. "But according to him, she insisted that they go to Bannister's boat. She assured him that Bo had a little something that could 'help take the edge off.' Hammerly claims he didn't know she was referring to drugs. He also claims that he dropped her at the boat and left her with Bannister. That he never went down into the cabin, and that he most certainly never set sail with them."

"And you believe him?"

"We have your helpful harbormaster to confirm it. Says he saw Hammerly and Harding arrive together last night. Says they went out to Bannister's boat, but that Hammerly left alone, maybe five minutes later. My guys also confirmed this."

"But I didn't think Bannister was selling directly?"

The chief shrugs. "It sounds as if Maeve Harding might have had some information on him that he didn't want widely known. A few sources have told us that about a year ago, Ms. Harding and Mr. Bannister were in a relationship. I understand that he's married?"

Robin nods, thinking back to Shelby. "So Maeve Harding was blackmailing him, in other words."

"From preliminary conversations, that seems like a reasonable assumption. We'll see what Mr. Bannister has to say for himself, though."

"That might give him a motive. To make her disappear, I mean."

"Yeah, well, so far, he's not giving us much. But why wait a year to push her off a boat? If she was really threatening to reveal their affair, wouldn't he have shut her up a long time ago?"

"Maybe," Robin thinks aloud, "she wasn't desperate enough to threaten him until now. Maybe it was the drugs—she wanted them but couldn't pay for them—that made her do it."

"Could be. My money's on an accident, though. Whenever drugs or booze is involved, stupid stuff happens. She probably woke up and thought she'd go for a swim, not realizing how wasted she was. Anyway, at the moment, Bannister's buttoned up, waiting on his attorney. He already willingly provided his statement about Ms. Harding. Imagine his surprise when we told him we had a few more questions related to a search we performed of his boat."

She shakes her head. "The whole thing is just so sad. Has Maeve's family been told?"

The chief swipes at a dusting of lint on his blue trousers and nods. "We reached out to her parents; they've retired in Arizona. They're flying out to collect the body after the autopsy."

"And what about your Boston guy?"

"We'll have to catch him another day. No doubt he's already gotten word that his contact is in custody. Who knows, maybe Bannister will implicate him during questioning." He pauses, as if giving her time to let it all sink in. "Crazy stuff, huh? And here we thought nothing bad ever happened over in God's country." He winks at her, knows this is how Robin refers to Hull.

"Chief, one more question."

"Hit me."

"You said your guys had their eye on Bannister the entire time. How is it that no one saw what happened to Maeve Harding?"

The chief nods, as if he's been expecting this. "Good point. I wondered the same thing myself. My suspicion is that our victim went around the boat to where the cabin obstructed our guys' view. And then, under the cover of darkness, she either slipped or dove right in. It would be easy to miss, especially if my guys were focused on any boat coming into or leaving the bay."

"Why didn't you suspect Maeve as a go-between for your Boston dealer?"

"No offense, Lieutenant, but the guy we're dealing with here is hard core. He doesn't take any chances, not when so much money is at stake, at least. No, this was a deal he had every intention of handling himself. Till it went south, of course."

The chief stands, as does she. "I'll keep you updated as the day unfolds; we're waiting on Bannister's lawyer now."

"Thank you. I'd appreciate that."

Before going out the door, he spins around. "You should go home, Lieutenant. Get some rest. Take care of that dog of yours."

And that's when Robin remembers. She skipped lunch today, and it's Sunday. Her dog walker would have left at eleven this morning. Hemingway has been home alone for hours.

40

SHELBY AND KATE

Ever since the news broke on television a few hours ago, identifying the woman's body as Maeve, Shelby's phone has been blowing up with texts from last night's revelers. Did you hear? Can you believe it? What happened??! As if she'd have any better idea than they would about Maeve's whereabouts after she left the party. One message, in particular, though, troubled her the most. It was from Julia:

Oh, Shelby. You must have heard by now. So sad about Maeve. I know you're probably beating yourself up about it, but don't! This is NOT your fault. She was completely wasted when she got to the party. Whatever happened after she left is not on you. What happened to that Jerry guy anyway? Maybe he has some answers? Love you.

Julia is one of her best friends. If Julia immediately assumes that Shelby feels responsible in some way, then what must the rest of Hull think? The truth is, Shelby *does* feel responsible. If she hadn't been so furious with Maeve—if only she'd been able to wave off her accusation as no big deal since everyone *could see* that the woman was off her rocker—then maybe Maeve would still be alive today. Maybe she'd have danced until she passed out on a deck chair, and they would have tossed a warm blanket over her for the night. And when Shelby found her this morning, Maeve would have been as hungover as a sick dog, but *alive*. And Shelby would have brought her a warm cup of coffee so that they could make amends.

Or, at least, this is how she imagines it happening.

This is NOT your fault. She reads the words again.

What would have happened if Jerry and Maeve insisted on climbing into Jerry's car instead of walking home last night? Would Shelby have tried to stop them? *Without a doubt!* But how could anyone have guessed that the two of them would end up at the marina? It's not as if Shelby has psychic powers, and boarding a boat after leaving a party is most certainly not the equivalent of driving away drunk. The line of responsibility—or culpability—needs to be drawn somewhere, and Shelby tells herself that line was drawn as soon as Maeve exited through the front door on Jerry's arm.

This is not my fault, she repeats.

But then why does she feel sick to her stomach?

~

When Kate opens her eyes, she has no idea if it's still the afternoon or the middle of the night. Clara's small body, softly snoring, is curled up next to hers. Overhead, a fan whirls, blowing humid air across her skin. Then she remembers: they're at Shelby's house, in Shelby's bedroom. The sun is no longer pushing through the window blinds.

She climbs out of bed, careful not to disturb Clara, tiptoes into the bathroom to splash cool water on her face, and heads downstairs. It's awfully quiet, so quiet that it seems that maybe everyone has already turned in for the night. But in the den, she discovers Shelby planted in front of the TV. The wall clock tells her it's 7:20 p.m. She's been asleep for nearly three hours.

"Wow. I zonked out. You?" She slides in next to her sister on the couch.

"No, couldn't sleep. I'm glad you and Clara got to nap, though." She's not looking at Kate, however. Her gaze is focused on the local news, which is covering the day's breaking story—Maeve Harding. On the screen, there's a glamorous photo of Maeve, her head tilted back in laughter.

"She was pretty," Kate says.

"Yeah."

She reaches over to rub her sister's shoulder. "You doing all right?"

Shelby nods, almost imperceptibly. "The crazy part is," she says softly, "I didn't even like her, even though I know it's terrible to speak poorly of the dead. And she wasn't very nice last night. So I'm trying to wrap my head around that while still being sad that she's gone and that we're probably some of the last people who saw her. Other than Jerry."

"I'm sorry," Kate says, uncertain how best to respond. "Can I get you anything? Maybe a glass of water?"

"That would be nice. Yes. Please."

Kate gets up and bumps into Bree in the kitchen, who stretches her arms above her head. "Hey, there. Guess we were all in need of a nap."

"Yeah, I think—" But before Kate can say another word, Shelby starts shouting from the den.

"What the—" They hurry back in, where their sister is pointing at the TV.

On the screen, there's a photo of the handsome veterinarian. The newscaster rambles on, but all that registers for Kate is "unusually big news day in Hull" and "charged with possession to distribute class A drugs. Bags of tramadol and ketamine were found on Bannister's boat, the same boat from which a woman allegedly fell earlier today."

"You have *got* to be kidding," Bree shouts. "OMG. Shelby, did you have any idea?"

But Shelby, her face pale as sand, shakes her head and whispers, "No, not a clue." She turns to stare at her sisters. "And what the hell was Maeve Harding doing on Bo's boat?"

~

The photo is a recent one. Of a tanned Bo, smiling in a blue oxford button-down, staring back at the camera. He's sitting on a boulder that might even be at Gunrock Beach. She wonders if they got the picture from Cindy, and then immediately thinks, *Poor Cindy.* If Shelby is beyond stunned, then what must Cindy think? Bo's girls? Drugs? According to the news, massive amounts of opioids and tranquilizers were seized from his boat. *The very boat that she and Bo fooled around on!*

She thinks back to how, whenever Bo's phone buzzed, she was convinced that it was Cindy, calling to say that she needed him home or, worse, that she found out about them. But what if those buzzes weren't from Cindy but from his buyer?

Shelby suspected nothing, saw nothing. Eight months with one man, intimate enough to run her hands over his chest, and yet not sufficiently intimate to know his darkest secrets. Had he been protecting her by not telling her? Shelby would like to believe that's the case, but she knows it's giving Bo too much credit, their relationship too much heft.

It's as if she's been peering through the Phoroptor at the ophthalmologist, the lenses clicking back and forth while the doctor asks which is better—first or second? Her relationship with Bo has always been fuzzy and undefined, but with each new piece of information—he's a philanderer, he's a liar, he's a drug dealer!—it has click, click, clicked into place.

Until, at last, she's seeing him for who he really is.

She remembers thinking how Kate must have not been paying attention to her marriage if Trey strayed. Even as she was reassuring Kate that it wasn't her fault, internally there was a portion of Shelby that assumed her sister was somehow responsible for not being a "better" wife, for not knowing what her husband needed from their marriage.

Now she feels like a complete idiot. She regrets her hasty conclusions, her misjudgments—about her sister and, most especially, about Bo.

There's a knock at the door, and it slips through Shelby's mind that maybe she should sneak out the back. She *really* doesn't want to be called down to the station as a potential witness or, God forbid, a suspect. But when Bree runs to answer it, it's not Robin.

"Pizza delivery," Audrey announces when she steps into the entryway. "I thought you all might be in need of some sustenance. Oh, and I brought wine, too. Hair of the dog, you know."

"Bless you," says Shelby, noting how Bree's face brightens the moment she lays eyes on Audrey. "What a nice surprise. Come in, come in." She jumps up to grab the paper plates. Never before has she been so pleased to have Audrey in her home.

41

SHELBY

Memorial Day
Monday, May 27

Memorial Day breaks with weather suitably warm for shorts and a T-shirt, ideal for the parade and picnics on the village green. Apparently, in the wake of Maeve's death, there was talk of canceling the annual parade, but Hull's councilors decided that Maeve, town clerk that she was, would have wanted the Memorial Day tradition to continue. Aside from grabbing an ice-cream cone at Scoops later this afternoon, though, the Lancaster women are lying low for the day. They've had enough celebrating for a while.

Late last night, Kate knocked on Shelby's bedroom door. "I'm sorry I lost it when you told me about Bo," she said, poking her head in. "I guess I was having a hard time believing that my big sister would be involved with a married man when I'm going through my stuff with Trey."

"I get it." Shelby set her book aside, a biography of President Truman, and patted the comforter for her sister to come sit. "It was terrible timing. And I'm sorry, too. It was insensitive with a capital *I*. Not to mention wrong."

"I know every relationship has its own story, so I don't blame you," Kate continued. Skepticism must have skirted across Shelby's face, though, because she quickly added, "Really, I don't." Then admitted, "Maybe I wish you picked someone who wasn't already married, but love happens in strange ways."

"What Bo and I had wasn't love. Especially since it appears he was loving on a lot of different women at the same time. Maybe even Maeve."

"Yeah, well, I'm sorry about that. Sorry he turned out to be such a jerk. I guess we both fell in love with the wrong guy." She flashed a fleeting smile. "We have that in common."

Shelby flung herself back on the bed and stared up at the ceiling. "Why is it so hard? This love and marriage stuff? I mean, Mom and Dad were good at it. They had their fights, sure, but they always found their way back to each other. Married for thirty-nine years. Why can't we be so lucky?"

Kate shrugged. "I have no idea. I only know that Mom wouldn't have put up with the lies that we have."

The thought hadn't occurred to Shelby. "You're right."

"Once a liar, always a liar," Kate said softly. "It's why I have to leave Trey."

A beat passed before Shelby responded. "I know."

"You do?"

"Yeah, I get it." Shelby understood in a way that perhaps she hadn't earlier. There was such a thing as giving people a second chance, and then there was giving them multiple chances and still expecting a different result. Kate had given Trey myriad opportunities to make things right, and he blew it each time. In a similar fashion, Shelby tried to look the other way whenever there were hints about Bo's wandering eye, but that didn't stop it. Not to mention his drug involvement that she never saw coming.

Maybe it was crazy, but Maeve's death was beginning to make Shelby realize precisely how little control she—or anyone else, for that matter—had over the universe. (Why she assumed she had any in the first place will be a question for her hypothetical therapist in the future.) Maeve probably woke up excited about celebrating Memorial Day weekend, no idea that Saturday would be her last full day on earth. Two weeks ago, Shelby was imagining the clear, turquoise waters of Turks and Caicos, Bo swimming by her side, and now her ex-boyfriend was most likely headed to jail. It just showed that no one knew how things would turn out.

But that's life, Shelby thought. One minute you're dancing to "YMCA" with your friends, and the next minute a search-and-rescue team is looking for you. One minute you're enjoying bacon and eggs with your husband at your favorite diner, and the next, you're screaming for someone to call 911 because he's slumped over in his chair. Aside from the obvious, such as refraining from smoking and maintaining a healthy diet, no one had any say over when their time was up.

And, yet, somehow, even with this knowledge, people carried on. Maybe *because* of this knowledge, people carried on. Because if life could get screwed up so easily, why wouldn't you try to make the most of it? All anyone could really do, Shelby thought, was hope—and help. Hope for more good days ahead, while helping others do the same.

"Hey there," said Bree, who'd apparently been standing outside Shelby's room. "Sorry, I heard you guys talking. Am I interrupting?"

Shelby patted the bed. "Not at all. Come on in. We were just chatting."

"Not to change the subject or anything," Kate said as Bree joined them, "but now that you're both here, I've been wanting to share some news."

~

That was last night. Now the three of them watch while Clara tentatively wades into the ocean, clasping her cousin's hand. Noah, a boogie board tied to his wrist, tries to coax her farther out. This morning, he promised Clara that he'd teach her how to "surf," although what that means, exactly, remains to be seen.

"I wish Mom and Dad were here to watch the two of them together." Kate gazes out on the sparkling water. "They'd be so happy that their grandkids adore each other."

"I know. It's really sweet," Bree says. "Good parenting by you guys."

"And good aunting by you. Is it weird," Shelby asks, "that I miss their voices the most? I'd love to come home to find a voicemail from Mom, asking how my day was."

"Hmm . . . I know what you mean." Kate lets the silence hang comfortably between them. "Sometimes, though, I think I can still hear her."

"Me too," agrees Bree.

Clara lets out a squeal as soon as Noah drops her on the boogie board. They watch while she struggles to stand, but Noah encourages her onto her knees, where her sense of balance is more solid. Then he shows her how to use her hands to paddle.

He'll make a great dad someday, Shelby thinks.

And it strikes her that maybe when her son leaves for college, loneliness won't consume her after all. Maybe she won't be left staring at his empty bed, his shelves lined with dusty trophies, and wishing he were around just so she could remind him to put his plate in the dishwasher. She'll still have her work colleagues, her clients, and Georgie, Meg, and Julia. But it's not that knowledge that gives her a sense of peace. It's because in light of Kate's news last night, Shelby understands that the rest of her family will, soon enough, be only a short distance away.

"Mama, look!" Clara, who's now standing on the boogie board with Noah's help, shouts. "I'm surfing!"

Kate leaps to her feet, her sunglasses tumbling from her head onto the sand, and cries out, "You sure are, sweet girl! You've got this!"

And before she realizes it, Shelby's standing, too, applauding alongside her sisters. They're cheering like crazy—arms flapping, fists pumping—and for a brief instant, Noah sets Clara free on the board, her small body riding the waves triumphantly like Amphitrite.

42

BREE

On Monday evening, Bree packs her bags in the upstairs guest room. It's been almost two weeks, and unlike the dread she was expecting to feel, there's more of a vague sense of relief about heading back to Somerville. Tomorrow, she'll return to her apartment, where an avalanche of messages from creditors no doubt awaits. But she'll do so knowing that in her wallet is a check from Kate that will more than cover any outstanding debts. All as an advance against her salary as Clara's nanny, a position that Kate offered her last night. Because Kate is going back to work in a few short weeks; she'll need someone to watch Clara.

Personally, Bree can't imagine anything better than getting paid to be a glorified aunt. And she'll have her nights and weekends to focus on her art. Giving up her Cambridge art studio is a foregone conclusion, but with the money she'll save on rent alone by living with Kate and Clara in the Allerton house (Kate insisted), she should be able to build a small nest egg for a studio in Hull one day. This afternoon, she gave notice at What's Brewing?, an announcement that didn't seem to faze her boss in the least. She even wished Bree good luck on her next endeavor.

It's funny, but moving to Hull to be closer to her sisters—especially now that Kate will be here, too—instinctively feels like the right decision;

in fact, Bree can't believe it's taken her so long. All this time, she's been trying to prove herself—her worth as an artist; her ability to make it on her own—while practically killing herself in the process. But to what end? Because she's been fooling no one, most especially not her sisters.

Perhaps, it seems, only herself.

In fact, in retrospect, she's been fooling herself about a lot in life. When Hannah texted earlier today, wishing "Bree and fam" a very happy Memorial Day, Bree began to type back, but then stopped, deleting her words. Because what were she and Hannah doing other than prolonging the pain of their not-so-recent breakup?

And so, she began again. Thanks. Same to you. Think you should know that I'm seeing someone new. And we should probably stop texting each other, at least for a while. She'd waited for the dots to appear underneath, wondering how Hannah would respond, until finally three words appeared: Good for you.

Recently, a long-forgotten, unfamiliar sensation has crept up on Bree: excitement. Because suddenly, she wants *so much*. She wants her family nearby and the ocean a short walk away from her front door. She wants the chance to focus on her art without worrying about next month's rent, which is what nannying will allow her to do.

Perhaps most importantly, she wants love and passion in her life again. Not the inequitable kind she and Hannah shared, nor the heady rush of a one-night stand after clubbing with friends, but a more sustainable brand of love. Who knows if she and Audrey will stay together for a month or a year, but the fact that Bree can open herself up again to the *possibility* of love is what she's been searching for all this time.

She just didn't realize it.

She lugs her bags downstairs and deposits them in the mudroom. Tomorrow morning, she'll strip the sheets off the bed, but tonight, she's going out to the C Note to celebrate her new job and toast new beginnings. When she hears the familiar rattle of Audrey's VW bus pulling into the driveway, she calls out goodbye to her sisters, who're settled in the living room, playing UNO with Clara and Noah. They know that she's headed out tonight—whom she's with and where she'll be.

And for Bree, that knowledge is almost as comforting as understanding that when she returns, it won't be to an empty, echoey apartment. But instead to a house full of noise and chaos and the people she loves most in the world. And, that, she realizes, is the way that she's always wanted it to be.

43

KATE

Two Weeks Later
Monday, June 10

"Yes, over there in the right-hand corner, please." Kate directs two movers, big, burly men, through the entryway and into the living room. They're in the middle of hefting her mother's china cabinet across the floor, the one that has been in Wellesley and is now coming home to Hull, where she and Clara—and Bree—will be staying indefinitely. Trey never liked the ancient mahogany cabinet with its glass-paned doors and lion's paw feet, but it's a family keepsake, not to mention a useful piece of furniture. There were only a few other items she wanted moved from the Wellesley house, such as their clothing, her favorite books, Clara's bedroom set. Everything else could stay; most of the furniture was better suited to Wellesley, anyway.

Considering litigation is his vocation, Trey has been surprisingly gracious when it comes to discussing the division of personal assets. For the moment, he's still living at the Wellesley residence. If he decides to sell, they've agreed to split the proceeds. Kate understands this is only a verbal agreement and that negotiations have a way of unraveling the closer the actual divorce proceedings get. That's what happened to her friend Bernie, whose husband agreed that she could keep their million-dollar mansion, only to renege and say that he wanted it for himself and his new girlfriend. But a combination of guilt and knowing that he has millions more to pull from (thanks to his family inheritance) has probably helped pave the way for Trey's amenability. Kate has been bracing herself for a custody battle, but even she is willing to be reasonable on that front, so long as it's no less than joint custody. No matter how lousy a husband Trey might be, he's a good, steady father.

Later today, Bree will be moving in her belongings. She assures Kate that there's no need to hire a moving van, that the new tenant bought the majority of her furniture and that everything else will fit into her car. On the second floor, adjacent to Clara's room, the guest room has already been prepared, awaiting Bree's arrival. There are fresh linens on the bed, a new comforter, and a vase of freshly cut peonies on the bedside table. In the corner of the room sits the slanted artist's table, which Kate specially ordered for her sister.

Honestly, she's a little nervous about having her baby sister under the same roof again. There's so much history, so much that has gone unsaid. But she knows that her parents would be pleased to have their daughters back together again. It will take some getting used to, this new family unit of theirs, but Kate is confident they'll figure it out. She steps back into the house, having sent the movers away and collected the mail from outside.

"Mommy, I made a picture for Auntie Bree. Do you think she'll like it?"

"Oh, can I see?"

Clara holds up a drawing of two people, one small with dark curls, the other tall with long, brown hair. They're standing next to the ocean, holding hands, their crayoned faces beaming back bright smiles. "She's going to love it, squirt," Kate says and posts it on the fridge.

"Why don't you help yourself to a snack?" she suggests, pointing Clara to the pantry, where there's now a shelf of semi-healthy treats within easy reach for a three-year-old. In her mission to make her daughter more self-sufficient, Kate is hoping to free up her own brain cells for other tasks, such as starting back to work at Bain & Company in a few short weeks. Much to her relief, her old boss has agreed to rehire her.

Across the kitchen table lie the assorted magazines and bills from today's mail. As she sifts through them, a long envelope addressed in familiar handwriting falls out. Does Trey owe her a check that she's forgotten about? But when she rips it open, there's a handwritten letter inside.

> Dear Katie,
>
> I'm writing to let you know that, as of yesterday, I'm no longer with Murray and Sloane. I've resigned, and the information we discussed in confidence has been turned over to the State Bar. Although I regret how I initially handled the information, I did have the fore-sight to make a copy of the memo mentioned. That copy is with the State Bar now, and the matter is in their hands to deal with as they see fit.
>
> I suspect that, in your mind, this is an instance of "too little, too late." But I thought you deserved to know that I did the right thing. Why is it that it always takes me a little longer than you to figure out what the "right thing" is?
>
> As sad as I am to see us going our separate ways, I'll always be Clara's proud daddy. I love that kid more than life itself. But I think you already knew that.
>
> Sorry for messing everything up so badly.
>
> Much love,
>
> Trey

Kate is not a crier. She reminds herself of this when she finishes reading Trey's letter, but it's no use. The letter sounds like the old Trey, the one she fell in love with, the daddy whom Clara adores. Where has he been this past year? When she's needed him more than ever?

Clara skips into the kitchen, a granola bar in each hand, then stops abruptly. "Are those happy tears, Mama?" she asks, eyeing her warily.

Kate half smiles, swipes at her eyes. Recently, they discussed the difference between happy tears and sad tears, and the concept fascinated Clara. "Yes, I think so," she says. "I was just reading a letter from Daddy."

And at the mention of her father, Clara hangs her head, offering up her beautiful crown of curls. "I miss Daddy," she murmurs.

"I know you do, honey." Kate pulls her into a hug and thinks, *Here we go.* How many more times will her daughter utter these precise words? Hundreds? Thousands? Probably more times than she can count, and each time, it will surely cut Kate's heart a little deeper. "But you're going to see him tomorrow, remember?"

"I am?" Clara's eyes light up, and the excitement in her voice is enough to make Kate doubt every decision she's made in the last few weeks. "When? Morning time or nighttime?"

Kate gets up, stuffs the letter back in its envelope. "Morning time. Daddy's driving out to pick you up and then you get to sleep over at the Wellesley house tomorrow night." She crosses to the stove to warm the teakettle.

"Are you coming, too, Mommy?"

Another arrow to her heart. "Not this time. It's going to be a special Daddy and Clara day."

"Oh." Her daughter's lips twist into a thoughtful bow while she considers this. "Okay." And then she darts into the living room to resume playing with her dolls, as if they've just been discussing whether to have tuna or ham sandwiches for lunch.

Ever so slowly, Kate's lungs expand again.

So there's still some of the good old Trey left in her husband. Soon to be *ex*-husband, she reminds herself. The teakettle whistles, and she pours the bubbling water into her mug. She doesn't know if she'll ever be able to forgive him. For the lies and the cheating. But at least this letter, his resignation, is a step in the right direction.

There will always be a part of her that misses Trey, wishes he were around. His booming voice, his bear hugs, his antics with Clara. The way he used to make her collapse in belly laughs. This sharing of their child will take some getting used to, but once the joint custody arrangements are agreed upon, their lives should fall into some semblance of normal. At least, this is what she tells herself.

When she goes to sip her tea, the sound of Bree's Honda Civic pulling into the driveway sends Clara racing to the front door. Kate gets up to follow her.

"You're here!" Clara exclaims, throwing the door open.

"Of course I'm here," Bree says, climbing out of the car and holding her arms wide for her niece to jump into. "Did you think I wouldn't come, silly?"

Kate steps out into the summer light to join them, these two people whom she would do anything for—slay dragons, sleep on a bed of tacks. "Oh, we knew you'd come," she says, smiling.

"That's right," says Bree. "We're family, remember?"

44

ROBIN

When the autopsy report comes in, the chief calls Robin to alert her that it's on the way. Her computer cursor hovers over the document attached to his email while she debates whether or not to click on it. Like any cop worth her salt, she wants answers. But there's a small part of her that worries about what she might discover in its pages.

Because if it's drugs that ultimately killed Maeve, Robin will feel partially responsible. She's the one who's charged with keeping the citizens of Hull safe. And in a manner of speaking, she failed to keep Maeve safe.

On this humid June morning, the station has more or less returned to normal, the buzz of the investigation a couple of weeks ago gone. The Boston police and the DEA have cleared out, as have the news crews. The general mayhem of Memorial Day weekend has practically been forgotten as Hullonians begin transitioning into summer proper.

Robin's calendar is mostly filled with requests for paperwork, a summary of the arrest finally made for the break-ins in the Alphabet section of town. She was surprised to learn from a fellow officer that her instincts about the case were wrong. It wasn't a group of kids robbing houses but, instead, two grown-up men in search of cash. Brent, her junior officer, stumbled onto them as they were sneaking out a side door, a flat-screen TV and laptop in hand, the cords still dangling from the back. Currently, they're awaiting their day in court, as is Bo Bannister.

The cursor blinks, and Robin sips her iced coffee, debating. Finally, she clicks on the document and waits for it to fill the screen. Her eyes quickly scan the boxes, her heart racing. There's a lot of identifying information, and then she spies the box she's looking for:

CAUSE OF DEATH: Drowning/boating fatality. Accident. Froth and sediment discovered in airways. Collapsed lungs. No sign of foul play.

The toxicology report lists alcohol and the pain reliever tramadol in Maeve's system, but not at levels high enough to have caused death. The tramadol could have come from Bannister or Harding's own doctor, for that matter, for her broken wrist.

Robin will share the basics of the report with Shelby because she deserves to know—and they've yet to meet for that glass of wine. Not that the autopsy report will clarify why Maeve was on Bo's boat that fateful night. Yet it seems likely that she went in search of drugs. Further investigation has led Robin to believe that not only did Maeve have a drug problem, she also had a previous relationship with Bo Bannister, as suspected.

Abundant scenarios have played out in Robin's mind over the past few weeks. Maybe Maeve woke up confused on the boat and dove into the dark water herself; maybe she lost her balance and slipped. Or maybe Maeve did threaten to tell Bo's wife about his affairs, and he shoved her in anger, never intending for her to fall overboard. Robin will be interested to learn what he has to say at trial, if anything.

For the moment, though, she's learning to live with uncertainty. That doesn't mean she likes it, but sometimes it's part of the job.

When her cell rings, the chief's name pops up.

"So I assume you've read the report?" he asks.

"Yeah."

"Looks like it was a drowning after all. An unfortunate accident. She probably slipped off the boat."

"I'm sure that's what Bannister's attorney will argue."

"Come on. You really still think the guy's a murderer?"

"Guess we'll never know, will we, Chief? Whatever happened, it's Bannister's word against a dead woman's."

"I hear you. But don't forget . . ."

"Yeah?"

"Don't forget he's being charged with possession to distribute class A drugs. He's going to be spending plenty of time behind bars as it is."

"Right. Not sure that's going to make the Harding family feel any better, though."

"Understood. But you know as well as I do that this job comes with a lot of gray areas. As long as we catch the bad guys, Robin, we're ahead."

It's the first time he's addressed her by her real name, and she appreciates the more personal approach. "You're right. Thanks for the reminder, Chief."

"You're welcome. And you know what else? Feel free to call me by my first name for a change. After all this time, seems like we can dispense with the formalities, don't you think?"

"Sure, Chief."

"Do you even know what my first name is?"

She smiles into the phone. "Um . . . Eric, maybe?"

"You do know!" He sounds genuinely pleased. "Listen, not to change the subject, but how about you and me grabbing dinner one of these nights? Talk about something other than bad guys and dead people. What do you say?"

It takes her a moment to process his question. Is Chief asking her out as a colleague whom he wants to get to know better—or is he asking her out on a date? Doesn't he have grandchildren? He must be at least a decade older than she is.

But then she hears her sister's voice in her head. *You mean to tell me you turned down the one guy I've actually heard you speak highly of? What could it hurt? He's a cop! It's not like he's going to murder you.*

The question churns in her mind. "You still there?" he asks.

"Yeah, sorry. I was thinking." There's a stack of quarters on her desk that she keeps for the vending machine in the lobby. Some days it's the best she can manage for lunch—a stale Snickers bar, a bag of trail mix, and a Coke. She takes a quarter now and rests it between her thumb and forefinger. *Heads* she'll say yes. *Tails* she'll say no.

She flips it. *Tails.*

"You know," she begins, "that's really nice of you, but—" She stops, her sister's voice ringing in her ears. "I mean, sure, that sounds good. Let me know what day works best for you."

"Terrific," he exclaims. "I'll get back to you soon."

When she hangs up, Sheila pokes her head in the office. "Hey, we've got a possible break-in over at the high school. Want to come along?"

Robin pushes up from behind her desk. "You bet," she says, glad to have her colleague and friend back in the office. Her cell buzzes again, and she holds up a finger, indicating this might take a second. But it's not the chief calling. Rather, it's a text from the local animal shelter, where Maeve Harding's schnauzer, Archie, has been staying. When Robin got wind of the fact that Maeve's dog needed a new owner, it felt as if the universe was extending an invitation directly to her. Robin may not have been able to save Maeve, but perhaps her pup can at least make a home with Robin and Hemingway.

She'll see if Hemingway agrees when they pick up Archie after work today.

"Coming, Lieutenant?" Sheila asks, sticking her head in for a second time.

"Yeah, sorry about that. I'm on my way." Robin snatches the quarter off her desk, rubs her thumb across its cool metal, and slides it into her pocket before heading out the door.

You never know, she thinks, *when your luck might change.*

Acknowledgments

The writing process never seems to get any easier. Thank goodness I've had countless helpers along the way. My thanks to agents Annelise Robey and Meg Ruley for their enthusiasm and expertise as they steered this book into the right hands. To Erin Adair-Hodges, my gratitude for your guidance and for understanding the heart of this novel as soon as you signed it. To Selena James, thank you for ushering the manuscript through its final stages with equal parts skill and brio. To Ronit Wagman, you pushed me to make this story as strong as it could be, and I'm indebted to you for your editorial acumen as well as your polite nudges to update my characters' cocktail choices. (Who else would send me links to the trendiest libations?) Thanks as well to the entire team at Lake Union Publishing, who've been instrumental in launching this new book out into the world: Rachael Clark, Kyra Wojdyla, Angela Elson, and Adrienne Krogh. Special thanks to cover designer Shasti O'Leary-Soudant.

Thank you to my friends who kept me laughing and offered support whenever I went looking for it, especially lifelong pals Lora Levin, Lisa Goldman, Barbara Berlin, and Katherine Ozment. To Lori Galvin, adviser and dear friend, thanks for everything. Thanks also to my local besties, Trina Ruggiero and Sarah Wood, and my Jack 'n' Jill gang: Jennifer Lofgren, Nancy Conte, and AnnMarie Ford. A special shout-out to Jen Lofgren and her father, John Hansen, for the insider intel on the town of Hull. Both answered my many questions, and Jen was one of my first readers. I couldn't have captured Hull's spirit or history without you. To Officer Ken Wood, much appreciation for answering my myriad questions and explaining how an emergency water rescue might go down. Any mistakes in the book are my own.

And to those in the writing community and beyond—authors, bloggers, social media enthusiasts, readers, and booksellers—thank you for helping to get the word out about the books you love. I say that as an author and as a reader. There's nothing quite like someone's pressing a book into your hands with the words: "Read this."

To my brother, Pete, thanks as ever for the excellent car tips.

And to my family—Mike, Nick, Michael Jr., and Katherine—without you, there would be no books. Thank you for the love, the stories, and the support.

About the Author

Photo © Claudia Starkey

Wendy Francis is a former book editor and the author of six novels, including *Summertime Guests*, *The Summer of Good Intentions*, and *Three Good Things*. Her writing has also appeared in *Good Housekeeping*, the *Washington Post*, and NPR's *Cognoscenti*, among others. She lives outside Boston with her husband and fifteen-year-old son. For more information, visit www.wendyfrancisauthor.wordpress.com.